Unto
These
Hills

Emily Sue Harvey

T0168132

THE
STORY PLANT

The Story Plant
The Aronica-Miller Publishing Project, LLC
P.O. Box 4331
Stamford, CT 06907

Print ISBN-13: 978-1-61188-025-0
E-book ISBN: 978-1-61188-026-7

Visit our website at www.thestoryplant.com

First Story Plant Printing: November 2011

Printed in The United States of America

Dedication

To all my Tucapau mill hill "family," those still living and those who have gone on. And to all mill hill folks in surrounding mill villages of the south and indeed, those up north, who lived and shared together that unique culture of yesteryear that is depicted in my story. It was a special bonding we experienced on those cozy, hilly terrains, in near identical dwellings and echelon, where family extended beyond the four walls and encompassed an entire village. Where villagers, having lived and experienced such ties, never forgot. Those roots will forever remain a part of us.

And to Leland, my love, who brought me back to my little village, to my roots. Who understands and shares my homage unto these marvelous hills.

IN MEMORY OF

Fitzhugh Powers, our village policeman who protected and affected our lives all through the years. He was a surrogate daddy to all of us, tough when he had to be but careful to season it all with love and wisdom.

Abb Willingham, whose café, Abb's Corner, gave us refuge, nourishment, and entertainment. He was a cheerful, good man whose listening ear and broad smile was always available.

Myrtle Payne and Gladys Kyle, my surrogate mothers, who inspired and nurtured through hard times. Miss you both.

Acknowledgments

Unto These Hills is fiction. However, the story is set on Tucapau Hill, the South Carolina mill hill where I grew up. In later years, to my sorrow, it was renamed Startex. Most of us still use Tucapau and Startex interchangeably. The characters are purely imaginary but to mill hill folks, they will feel uncommonly familiar

During the story's creation, through recall and research, I chronicled the decline of my snug, hilly fortress. The emotions here are pure and heartfelt and linger with me 'til this very day.

Muses for my story include Charlene Toney O'Blenis, whose input, transparency and generosity provided infinite dimension to Sunny's character. Retired teachers, Laura Odom and Othello Ballenger afforded their impact on Sunny's early, wise choices.

Other muses include Eleanor Payne Mitchem, Gail Bridges Gibson, Erlene Johnson Frady, Geneva Payne McGraw, Glenda Quinn Ward, Patsy Miller Roach, Marlene Blackwell Brown, Elaine Turner Leonard, Nancy Smith Oliver, Patsy Belcher Vaughn, and Betty Pruitt Walker, close mill hill days girlfriends, as well as others from adjoining textile mill villages of Lyman, Jackson and Fairmont. You all know who you are.

And special thanks to Lou Aronica and Peter Miller, my agent, publishers, mentors, and friends, who guide me over the rocky shoals of a very uncertain business. Thanks for your belief in me and all that I do. Words cannot express how much that means to me.

Prologue

From my upstairs window, the distant view of familiar hills and river swims before me. _Home. My safe place._ But today the vision fails to bolster me. Sweat gathers over my forehead in great beads. Nausea churns my insides and my icy fingers drop the simple four-line poem I've been reading, one I wrote — how long ago?

A lifetime. Was life ever that simple?

Panic spasms through me.

I've got to decide. Time's running out. Which will it be?

He wants an answer today. _What about my dream?_

What dream, Sunny? Face it. It's gone.

But what if —

It won't happen. Grab this lifeline, girl! Are you nuts? Slowly, I pick up the paper from the floor and I wonder _where were you, God, when I needed you?_

But then, you haven't been doing me any favors lately.

Tears blur the words of my girlhood ode:

UNTO THESE HILLS
Red clay dirt heaped round and high
dips low then rises again to the sky...
Hills they're called. To me they're HOME
From them, my shelter, I will never roam.

By Sunny Acklin, age 14

And I remember another day — before innocence died.

Part One

"Who can find a virtuous wife? For her price is far above rubies."
Proverbs 31:10

The late forties to the seventies

Chapter One
Four Years Earlier

That dawn remains, all these years later, etched in golden solar rays in my memory as *the happiest morning of my life*. It was in my fifteenth year. I arose early, dressed for the May Pole dance, and quietly stole from our two-story Maple Street dwelling planted amongst hundreds of Tucapau — South Carolina's mill hill houses — all predominantly identical except for varying roof line pitches and story levels.

I spied Daniel across the street, tall, whipcord thin and magnificent as he slung the swing blade, shearing grass as easily as scattering dandelion tufts. A white cotton T-shirt rode his broad shoulders like a second skin. As always, the sight of his midnight dark head, bent to task, so intense, almost heated, stirred my senses.

He hadn't yet seen me and, for once, I didn't call out to him but slipped around the house to the alley and rushed on, zig-zagging a detour, intent on seeking out my *harbor*, my stronghold, so to speak: a knoll overlooking my domain.

I wanted to privately bask in pure joy.

Water lapped against land as I cut through Ash Street and neared the dam. I took a deep breath and pushed back the fearful awesomeness of the Middle Tyger River. I watched the sun break the horizon and happiness burst and splintered through me as I clasped my hands to my bosom in exultation.

Nothing of the splendid sunrise whispered of portent.

Forgotten in those precise daylight moments were Ruthie Bonds' screams, that carried, two years earlier, over these waters that, nightly, transformed into murky black depths. Now, those same depths that nearly claimed her life rippled and reflected sun rays like tossed sequins, seductive…bewitching.

Forgotten today was that Ruthie bore a child within six short months, one called *bastard*, a beautiful little girl who, wagging tongues had it, was sired by Harly Kale, her rescuer on that fateful night. Harly was my friend Gladys' sorry, no-good husband.

Forgotten for the moment was that, after that, Ruth's stigmata and self-imposed exile terrorized me as much as those nighttime black waters.

Today, none of this rippled my peace. I D-*double-dog* dared it to as I forded the river by way of an ancient steel bridge, spanned a narrow road, then climbed precipitous concrete steps to the site that offered a panoramic view of my homeland.

Reverently, I ascended a steep hill where once the old schoolhouse perched. No longer. At its summit, my lids lowered and I inhaled the fecund vegetation-mud aroma that rode the breeze.

The wind was soft and gentle, ruffling my shorn hominy-white hair, the sun warm on my olive-complected skin, and my near-translucent blue eyes drank in the beloved sight.

Hope oozed through me like an endorphin overdose, one akin (I would much later discover) to orgasm. Today was a new beginning. I believed that as only a fifteen- year-old heart could.

I gazed out over the hills that birthed and nurtured me, to the river that winds lazily to the dam where, harnessed, water becomes the captured power of over a hundred horses. A furious sight when unleashed upon the rocky shoals below, a beautiful portrait when integrated into the womb of these hilly shores.

Today the orchestrated enchantment of bliss and water rushing over stony, undulating riverbed made music in my ears, music that set my feet to dancing and my heart a'soaring with the white clouds above me. The melody called out to me, lifted me above the fears that struggled to trickle through my euphoria.

Even as I danced, they were there, hovering like a daggum sulking thundercloud. I split in two: One smiling and dancing. The other hidden and vigilant.

Thoughts simmered, bloated, and then blasted out to the four winds. *Please God. Let Mama and Daddy love each other…keep us together.*

I flung the dark thoughts aside

My white dress flowed in the wind as I twirled and spun and leaped, lifting my face to the sky, excited about the *here and now*, the May Pole dance and for the sense of *family* that grappled for a secure place inside me. *Mama and Daddy will be there.*

So will Daniel, who just moved in across the street, and who makes me feel more alive than I've ever felt before.

And then, he was there with me in spirit, head thrown back in laughter, dancing with me in his loose, boneless way and I felt happier than I'd ever felt in my life, knowing he heard what I heard and felt what I felt. It didn't matter that I couldn't see him.

I felt him.

My feet skipped and twirled me back down the stone steps, across the old bridge, where foaming river rode the rocks below, kicking up the wind to cool my warmed cheeks.

The happy notes detoured me up the alley behind the hotel, away from the men who sat on her rock wall corner, opposite the mill, waiting for the seven-thirty a.m .whistle to signal shift change. My celebration was not for them to see.

From maple and walnut trees birds harmonized with the music flooding my soul.

Main Street was just coming alive on this early May morning hour when I meandered from the alley, across the lush hotel lawn, and my feet connected with the big concrete sidewalk. From the old hotel where Mama served as a maid in her cute little black uniform with its frilly white apron and cap, Daisy the cook, taking a moment's break from the hot kitchen, waved to me from the long front porch with its endless rocking chairs.

"Mornin' Sunny!" she called, caramel-complected face a'beamin'. *"You shore look purdy!"*

I turned back and waved and, tamping down my crazy dancing feet, moved on past the village Doctor's Office, which anybody and everybody on the hill frequented for anything from a hangnail to pneumonia. The visits had been more frequent hereabouts since Dr. Brock, the new, handsome young doctor had come to practice, taking up residence in the hotel. He looked a bit like Tim Holt or Alan Ladd.

"Hey, Sunny," Mr. Mason called. He was proprietor of the Company Store, which insured that all villagers had food, even if on credit. I waved at Mr. Mason as he swept around the front doors.

And I exulted that all these entities were bonding forces, ones that declared each living, breathing resident thereabout as my *family.* On second thought, I will have to clarify here that almost all mill hill residents seemed like family. *Almost.* There were a rare *few I* didn't claim. But I'll get to them later.

The old movie house came into view, my favorite place of all, whose Saturday afternoon matinees turned the silver screen to magic with Roy Rogers and Dale Evans, Tim Holt, Lash LaRue, Humphrey Bogart and hosts of other actors.

"Sunny!" called a deep male voice. I twirled toward the sound, heart a thumpin' like a bass drum as I realized he'd been following me from the riverbank.

He'd been watching me from afar — had seen me dancing. I grinned even wider. *I was glad he saw my joy!* Oh it was so *good* to be alive and *loved* and to have both my biological and village family rally for this morning's celebration.

"Daniel! Hey." I felt myself flush, warm with pleasure as he joined me on my trek, slowing my feet down even more, At sixteen, he neared six-foot tall. And because he walked beside me I felt luminous and beautiful. His male splendor smote me like an invisible explosion that left every atom reeling

His family moved in across the street from us a few short months back. It's kinda complicated, the Stone family. The family carries three different surnames: Stone, Hicks, and Daniel's last name is Collins. Doretha's stepfather, Ol' Tom Stone, a former policeman from up North, married Doretha's mama after moving South. Walter Stone, an older son, lived with them.

Daniel Collins was a foster-child, came to live with them when he was nine, right after the Stones married. The

16

entire family loved Daniel. Except Ol' Tom. To him, Daniel simply represented free labor and he took pure evil advantage of a good boy. But that's another story entirely.

In short months, this family became central to my life.

"Wait up!" called Doretha as she rushed to catch up with Daniel and me. Slightly winded, she joined us on our walk to the celebration and as we locked arms I was reminded of the trio dancing their way to the Land of Oz.

I would, later that day, ironically reflect upon that moment's sheer magic, wishing fervently to recall it.

"Sunny," came Doretha's whispery little voice, "you look sooo pur-dy."

And I smiled and leaned to give her a quick peck on her cheek.

Doretha Hicks, Daniel's foster-sister, blew into our lives — mine and my buddy Emaline's — like a fragrant spring breeze, bringing to us a new, perpetual state of delight. Doretha's childlike charm and ancient insight fascinated Emaline and me. In her presence we were somehow *more*. She had the indefinable ability to augment us beyond what we thought we could ever be.

She was my sister Francine's age, sixteen. There, likeness ceased. Doretha — pronounced *Dor-EE'-tha* — was as unsophisticated as Francine was worldly. She was as plain, upon initial encounter, as Francine was stunning. She was small and reed thin, with her desolate youth shining from her eyes.

I adored her.

Soon, the village park came into view. First family member I spotted was my animated older sister Francine, in saucy pimento shorts and white gypsy blouse tied at the waist. Late April sun had already deepened her naturally olive-toned skin to bronze. A new guy, Tack Turner, sniffed around her, keeping at bay the rest of the male pack.

I disliked him on sight.

Next, I saw my best friend, Emaline. Pecan brown hair slicked back from her heart-shaped face, nape-tied by a white ribbon, coordinating with her billowy white dress that matched my own, both home-sewn by Renie, her sweet mama who today was all a'glow with pride in both of 'her girls', as she referred to me and Emaline.

Shorter and rounder than me, Emaline was, then and now, beautiful from the inside out. Though shorter by two inches than me, and brunette, at a distance and in her full, fluid white dress she could almost be my twin and we laughed as we rushed to hug, grasping hands and stepping back to examine each other from head to toe. Eight other teen girls, identically attired as we, meandered about the May Pole, gingerly testing the elaborate long blue ribbons for tethering strength as they slowly orchestrated the up-coming choreography.

Emaline's mama stood nearby. Usually pleasingly fluffy, Renie, recently suffering from mysterious headaches, had melted down till she scarcely resembled herself. But when she lifted her heart-shaped face and looked at me, her generous smile was pure Renie.

"*Hey, darlin',*" she crooned. It was her way of loving me. Her affection splashed over and soaked into me. Her validation was profound. Tears stung my eyes and nose. She always affected me that way.

How I *loved* my village family.

Then I saw them: *Mama and Daddy.* World War II had interrupted Mama and Daddy's limping, bloodied marriage. This sunny May week reunited them when Daddy, look-ing more like Mama's movie idol, Tyrone Power, than ever, reappeared on our mill hill scene, shining like a new silver dollar in his army uniform.

The war was over and his Peacetime Occupation stint in Japan had finally, five years later, ended. The fifties era had already surfaced. Dark wavy hair and eyes the color of our mahogany shift robe, flirted from beneath Daddy's snappy cap and had Mama clinging to him like a morning glory vine.

A true miracle it was, this devotion-interval, given my mama's lusty appetite for anything wearing jockey shorts. Or any other style, even butt-naked, truth be known.

I was so happy that they appeared so in love, I didn't even mind that they'd immediately thrust us four siblings into Nana's stringent care, then disappeared to the near-by Cotton Club to dance and drink the homecoming night away. I hoped that now Daddy was back, Mama would stop embarrassing me with her brazen ways.

Today, they looked as cozy as Bogart and Bergman in *Casablanca.*

I smell lemon-drops! The realization stretched my lips from ear to ear. I always whiffed them when happy. And right at that instant I could have reached up and touched the sky.

I waved to my parents. Blew them kisses, which they returned a'beamin' all over themselves.

Please God. Let it last.

~~~~~

The Duncan High School Band, festive in navy blue, gold braided uniforms, struck up *Country Garden* and for the next five minutes we mill hill girls brushed up as close to *Camelot* as we ever again would. The performance ended with perfectly concerted pirouettes and we preened as the gathering of village-family, a goodly count of about fifty, applauded.

"Sunny, you were sooo good!" little sister, Sheila squealed as she and younger brother Timmy tackled me with bear hugs.

Then I felt his touch on my arm before I gazed up into those bottomless turquoise eyes that hid myriad emotions. But for me, they glimmered of deep caring. "Sunny, you looked like an angel out there. I love to watch you dance." His voice rumbled smoothly — like no other timber I'd ever heard. Rich yet soft. Reminded me of Clark Gable's. "And I love your smile," he added.

He bent quickly, squeezed my upper arm and kissed the top of my head. I felt it all the way out my toes. He whispered, "gotta run. Ol' Tom'll miss me." His grin was rakish, lop-sided, and decidedly *defiant.* "But it was worth it."

I watched him rush off, strong legs eating up the sidewalk as he loped with stallion agility down Main Street.

Then other arms wrapped me. As laughter and warmth engulfed me, I inhaled two distinctive fragrances that, for my entire life span, would plop me right back to that particular time and place: *Old Spice After Shave* and *Blue Waltz perfume.*

"C'mon, Sunshine," Mama gurgled with laughter, calling me by the full name she'd given me at birth, insisting I was her 'sunshine girl.' "We Acklins are a'gonna celebrate today. School's out and there's fun to be had!"

My heart soared because nobody, but *nobody* did *fun* like my mama.

~~~~~

We went back by the house where we dressed for comfort, except for Mama, who remained dressed-up all the way to her spike heels and Francine, who couldn't actually strip down any more and not get arrested.

I traded my white dress for a modest buttercup-yellow sundress, whose handkerchief type straps tied over each shoulder.

Nana, Mama's mother, eyed us speculatively. She pulled Mama into the kitchen as Daddy whistled and sang and cut up with Sheila and Timmy on the porch. I could hear her whispering to Mama and edged close enough to hear.

"Ruby, behave yourself, now, y'hear?"

Laughter. "Now, Mama. Don't be such a fussy-butt. What in heavens' name do you think I'm a'gonna do? Strip naked and do *the Huckle-Buck*?" More bubbly laughter.

Nana reached up to touch Mama's cheek and said gently, "Just mind what I say, honey. Ever'thing'sa'goin' right for you now. You just count your blessin's and —"

"Aww, Mama," my mother grabbed Nana in a big ol' bear hug and kissed her soundly on the wrinkled cheek, "You *worry* too much."

Ageless, white-haired Nana, a grass-widow, lived near us in her brother Charlie's single-level village dwelling, several doors from our two-story mill hill house. But she was always on baby-sitting and housekeeping call.

As usual, today the only colorful thing in her apparel was her home-sewn floral apron. Black lace-up shoes and cotton stockings emerged below her nondescript dress. Her snowy hair, now in a sedate bun on her nape, could transform into witchy disarray when loosed at night, especially when she yanked Sheila from sleep and castigated her for bed-wetting.

Still, all these years later, those long nights flash before me, with Nana in her flapping flannel gown, long white hair flying loose, leaning over Sheila's bed in the wee dark hours, looking chillingly witchy.

"*You done soaked this bed*, you lazy heifer! Too durned *no-account* to get up and walk to the bathroom is what you are." And I see Sheila's eyes, sleep-dazed, confused, and humiliated. I now cringe that I said nothing in her defense, even when Nana's anger strongly peppered her language.

But I cannot go back and relive one day.

To her credit, Nana laundered the urine-soaked sheets and kept a rubber cover over the mattress to protect it. The daily toil must have been backbreaking for a woman her age. Now, past the age she was at that time, in retrospect, I recognize the effort she spent keeping two households up and running; Uncle Charlie's and ours'.

Nana, despite her horror of Mama's ways, indulged her green-eyed, utterly outrageous 'baby', Ruby, whom God, for whatever His reasons, blessed with a beautiful face and perfect curves that could cause a traffic pile-up.

I understood. Nana couldn't *help* but adore Mama — despite her visceral condemnation of Mama's whoring. Neither could I resist her. Neither could my handsome daddy, whose driving force had been, as far back as I could remember, to placate Mama's incessant quest for thrills and anything zany.

Yet, despite all his efforts, on that lovely May day, during our exuberant family outing, failure smacked him broadside.

~~~~~

We ate an early lunch at Abb's Corner, the village café hangout located downstairs from the Movie House. Outside steps took us down to the lowest level of the Community Center. *Divorce Me COD* spilled from the jukebox as we piled into a large booth and Daddy splurged to buy hamburgers, fries and tall frosty milk shakes for the lot of us, including sixteen-year-old Francine, who usually by-passed family things.

I hated the divorce song. Soon Frank Sinatra soothed the airwaves with *Night and Day* and I relaxed and counted my blessings that we were *together.*

I caught glimpses of conjecture on my sister's cynical face and I *knew.* She, too, hoped Mama would for once in her screwed-up life be good, and think of us rather than *herself.* I frowned at her, discouraging her dark skepticism.

Afterward, at Mama's request, Daddy parked the car on the curb near the post office, as close to the Company Store as he could get. Mama hopped out, then stuck her head in the back window, where we huddled, her offspring, beguiling us with *Blue Waltz* fragrance and her incandescent smile.

Her white silk, clingy shoulder-padded blouse, tucked into fashionable pearl-gray, loose-legged slacks, cupped what Francine had informed me were *lush* breasts — much like her own, she smugly added, which had drawn my dismayed gaze downward to my own comparatively small assets, ones that resembled two once-over-lightly fried eggs.

"Can we go, Mama?" whined Sheila.

"*Nonono.*" Laughter, rich as hot fudge, gurgled from her as she reached over to tweak the little freckled nose. "Doncha know I'm gonna get ya'll each a *surprise*? Even Daddy gets one," she said in her throaty way, rolling her vibrant greens at Daddy. I was just beginning to realize what everybody meant by 'Ruby's bedroom eyes', when her lids lowered like a silk curtain, exposing only a sliver of sea mist glimmer.

"Now ya'll be good for Daddy, y'hear? I'll be a little while." Her voice oozed slow and thick as honey. She wrinkled her perfect nose. "Promise?"

"Promise," chirruped everybody except Francine, who considered such compliance unbearably soppy.

Nobody, but *nobody* could stir my butterflies like Mama. Fact was, with her infectious, teasing laughter and melodious voice, she had the power to sweep us all from calamity to ecstasy in seconds flat. And despite her equally quicksilver explosive fights with Daddy, and her loose ways, in that lovely sun-filled moment I adored her.

After all, my brain desperately let fly, this is a new beginning.

At the Company Store entrance, Mama turned and blew us a big ol' kiss, gazing at us for a long, long moment before disappearing through the double glass doors.

I'm gonna get y'all each a surprise! Even Daddy gets one. I recall , in that heartbeat of time, I thought how Mama, despite her faults, possessed, when she *had* anything, a generous, giving spirit, fairly shoveling it all out to others.

We kids and Daddy waited patiently in our old 1947 mud-brown Ford, lustily singing *I'm Looking Over A Four-leaf Clover* while Mama shopped. Honeysuckle breezes wafted in through lowered car windows. We tried harmony with *Don't Sit Under the Apple Tree*, but, what with Daddy's tone-deafness, ended up sounding like a Chinese laundry quartet. Francine and I laughed till we cried while Daddy remained oblivious.

Then Francine, who utterly idolized Hank Williams, did her nasal rendition of *Your Cheatin' Heart*, as earnest and reverent as I'd ever seen her.

I didn't take undue notice of Mama's lengthy absence till Francine cranked up *Hey, Good Looking*, and Daddy's brow furrowed when he hiked up his wrist to peer at his watch. Sensing the change in him, Francine fell silent, a phenomenon within itself because Francine's focus usually opaqued anything beyond her immediate whim. Daddy kept checking the time, his brow corrugating deeper by the moment.

My stomach butterflies ceased their flapping, pushed aside by the dread that oozed inside me and settled like cold concrete.

Francine shot me a *"here we go again"* look, rolled her tiger-tawny eyes, almost the exact shade of her hair, folded her slender arms, and shifted to stare stone-faced — yet appraisingly — out the back window at the men perched like sentry hawks on the rock wall curb facing Tucapau Cotton Mill. While disparaging Mama's whimsical nature, Francine was blind to her own like-quirks, remaining blissfully unencumbered by any big-sister responsibility.

That was left entirely to me. Timmy, at eleven, a small, dark carbon of Daddy, already harbored cynicism in his whiskey golden gaze, one much too somber and vigilant. I had my work cut out just keeping our heads above dank, murky waters that threatened to obliterate our family unit.

"I'll be back in a minute," Daddy sprang from the car and dashed into the store, his movements jerky and desperate.

"Where's Mama?" asked my little nine-year-old sister, Sheila. The picture of Mama, Sheila was perfection with big jade eyes and elegant oval features framed softly by russet and wheat streaked hair. She would someday, I suspected, be the family beauty.

"She's inside the store," I said, a bit more cheerfully than I felt. A vague premonition froze the smile that struggled to reach my lips. Instead, I patted her plump little fingers that laced loosely in her lap, their wiggly dance belying her calm demeanor.

Her resignation smote me. Then shot terror through me. I blinked and surreptitiously breathed deeply to allay anxiety, like Nana, in her stoical monotone, always instructed me. I groped for an inside button to turn off my roiling emotions. Finding none, I simply rode the bucking tumult.

Moments later, Daddy reappeared alone, pale as burnt out ashes. His hands trembled as he climbed into the front seat and gripped the steering wheel, anchoring himself as he stared off at some obscured horror, a stunned expression erasing all but ghostly laughter crinkles from his handsome features.

Long tense moments passed. Packed together like little sardines in the car's back seat, neither of us four kids spoke. Were afraid to. Being accustomed to disappointment didn't exactly inspire us to reach out and seize it.

I garnered courage. "Where's Mama?" My voice rasped, quivered.

Daddy's head swiveled and our gazes collided. The pain in his caused my breath to hitch. "Is she coming?" I ventured tremulously, weak from the inquiry's effort.

Slowly, his head moved from side to side. "No, honey. She's not coming."

Tears sprang to my eyes, of hurt, of anger. Of myriad, unnameable emotions. "Why?" I didn't want to know.

"Because," his knuckles whitened on the steering wheel. "She's gone."

"Where did she go?" Hysteria shimmied my voice up to shrill.

Francine huffed in disgust, tossed her thick tousled wheat mane back against the seat, and melted into its crease. Sheila didn't move an eyelash. She sat frozen, her fingers dancing…dancing.

Timmy's big Cocker Spaniel eyes, focused on me, drew my notice — his dark lashes were as thick as any girl's — and as I gazed into them, I saw a plea glimmering in the golden depths. *Make it all right, Sunny*, they whimpered.

I gulped at the enormity of his need. Thought I'd drown in it.

Daddy took a deep, ragged breath then slowly blew it out and, as he did so, his lean torso slumped and his forehead connected with the steering wheel. "Only way out was the back exit."

Hope seized me. "But maybe — maybe she *was* inside and you just didn't see her. Maybe she was —"

Beside me, Francine's snort of dismay failed to dash my burst of optimism.

But when Daddy's dark mahogany head lifted, pity spilled from his eyes, snuffing hope as a fire hydrant's flush would a candle-flicker. "Mr. Mason saw her duck out the back door, Sunny. She got into a car there."

"Why am I not surprised?" muttered Francine and viciously crossed long bronze legs protruding saucily from flaming shorts.

Because, the thought flitted through my reeling brain, *it takes one to know one* and was instantly ashamed of the disdain I felt for my own flesh-and-blood sister.

"What's wrong?" Sheila's green eyes gazed up at me with a trust that hit me like a sledgehammer. It scared the daylights out of me. Then, amazingly, calmed me. It made me able to smile at her, to pretend everything was okay. To toss Timmy a feeble wink of encouragement.

And in some fuzzy corner of my psyche my role snapped into place. I would be the kids' caretaker. On some level I knew.

When Daddy cranked the Ford — an act that declared Mama *gone* — the mundaneness of the revving engine struck me as surreal.

And I knew. Deep, deep inside, I *knew.* Don't know how or why. But I knew.

Mama was not coming back.

~~~~~

Three things blasted a mill hill woman's good name to smidgens; sexual immorality, neglecting one's kids, and a filthy house, in that order. Though Nana's vigilance spared Mama from the latter, her own folly cost her the entire substance of respectability.

The horror of it all traumatized me in ways I'd never before experienced.

Men began leering at me, a thing that sent me scurrying home to soak for hours in our old rust-stained bathtub, trying to wash away the *shame* Mama had foisted upon me.

"Ruby Acklin's name is worse than mud; it's *slime*," I murmured days later to a sympathetic Doretha as I swirled my straw in watery Coke at Abb's Corner, where she, Daniel, and Emaline commiserated with me on the turn of events. From the jukebox, Jimmy Wakely empathized with *One Has my Name (the Other Has my Heart).* "People don't blame you for her mess, Sunny," insisted Emaline, sweet optimistic Emaline, her green eyes sad as a Bassett's.

I snorted. "Not only has she done across-the-board adultery, this time she's run off with the village doctor, who is," I rolled my eyes, "ten years younger'n her. And to think, I used to think he looked like Tim Holt." I shook my head in disbelief, scowled and blinked back tears. "Now he's got horns and fangs that drip blood." I gazed at my buddy through tears. *"Our blood."*

I sighed heavily. "I'll bet Doctor Worley don't appreciate her tomfoolery forcing 'im from retirement."

Across the café I spotted teenaged Buck Edmonds, paying for his order and as he turned to leave he blatantly caught my eye and winked. Sneaky-like. So as not to draw Daniel's attention. Then he nearly collided with Fitzhugh Powers, our village policeman, and his face composed into angelic repose. In blue uniform, Fitzhugh was formidable, a force to be reckoned with by mischief-makers. Underneath, he was every villager's daddy.

Uggh! I hated Buck Edmonds. His interest crawled over my skin like a passel of loosed snakes. I shivered.

"Hey, ya'll." Fizhugh waved to us, sending me an especially sympathetic look as he slid his tight, toned form onto a red/chrome swivel stool at the counter for his daily coffee and chat with Abb, his buddy and our other father figure who always had time to hear our problems.

We waved back and Daniel leaned impulsively and kissed my cheek, encouraging my angry venting.

"Then — then she ran out on 'er kids," I added. "Tallied up in mill hill math, Emaline, Mama's worth is a big fat *zero*. And I see how the men're looking at me."

"Who?" Daniel was instantly alert, like a jungle beast sniffing danger.

Uh oh. Back pedal. "Nobody in particular. Just — oh, I don't know. Maybe I'm just imagining it."

But I knew I wasn't. I just didn't want Daniel going and getting in trouble over something I couldn't even prove if I wanted to. Besides, I didn't want to draw attention to myself. Fair or not, some folks would think I'd done something to attract the men. Everybody in the village didn't consider *me* as *family*, either.

Daniel, sitting next to me on the inside, settled against the wall. He grew quiet and still as death. Yet, I felt this subterranean wildness churning through him, sizzling, one peculiar to him, one that stands out till this day in my memory. And I knew not to say something to send him tumbling over the edge.

"Poor Sunny," Doretha murmured, oozing with sympathy and her own brand of otherworldliness that she wore like a rare deep South fragrance. Emaline looked at her in wonder, awed.

A waif-like creature, a mill hill, *poor* version of Audrey Hepburn, Doretha effortlessly exuded power. She gave me one of her long, assessing looks. Seemed she could read things nobody else could — *see* things. "You think her whorin's gonna drag you down, too, don't you? Like — 'cause you're *her's*, folks'll think you're like'er."

I nodded. "The stinking feeling just *clings*, y'know?" I lolled against the red leather booth backrest. "Look — I know it don' make sense to *feel* somebody else's shame. But a mama's not just *somebody else*. She's the person who *spawned* you, who knows the feel of your skin and your smell — I can't wash it away." Tears puddled along my lower lids and I sat up straight and swiped them away. I swallowed a couple of times before speaking again. "I'm *not like her.*"

Daniel grunted assent and shifted sharply, his anger palpable. I knew it took giant effort for him not to bellow with frustration and rage.

" 'Course you're not." Emaline grasped my hand across the table and squeezed, blinking back tears.

"Daggum right!" I nodded, gazing at her. "I — I thought when Daddy came home from the war, things would change. I once thought the divorce thing was like a square block of wood being hammered into a round hole. Divorce on the mill hill just — wasn't done. And now," I splayed my fingers at the ceiling, "My *own Mama and Daddy* are *getting divorced.*" Anger surged through me. "I hope Mama's satisfied!"

"She can't help it. That's just who she is," Doretha said, coming around to sit beside me as I scooted over against Daniel to make room. She wrapped an arm around my skinny shoulders. "But she stole your childhood away from you, Sunny," she said quietly, in her gentle, assured way. "She oughtta be ashamed of that, if nothin' else."

I looked at her in amazement. How could she know? But she did. That was the magic that was Doretha. "Remember you once't told me you smell lemon-drops when you're real happy?" She looked at me with the saddest eyes.

I nodded, wiping a tear from my cheek, and heard Emaline snuffle.

"Well, you don' smell 'em now, do you?"

I felt Daniel's strong fingers come up under my upper arm and squeeze and I gazed up into his solemn face. "No," I said hoarsely, "I don't smell 'em anymore."

His hand slid down my arm till his big, callused fingers clasped mine. "You will," he murmured fiercely, nostrils a'flare. "I promise you, Sunny. Someday, you will."

~~~~~

We Acklins each dealt with Mama's unsavoriness in our own way. Daddy escaped up north to job-hunt, leaving us in Nana's care.

Francine barricaded herself in our upstairs room, pulled hidden Camel cigarettes from beneath her mattress, threw open the window and inhaled like the smoke was water and her guts were on fire. Her nightly vanishing-out-the-window act increased.

I'd begun hearing asides about Francine, too, more lewd ones, but I'd pushed them away. They always made my insides squirm like a hooked-worm, even as I lifted my chin in defiance. I would *not* be like Mama. Or Francine.

Timmy and Sheila became my appendages, echoing my own erratic emotions during those first months. The Sunny they'd known before Mama's abandonment had gone away inside herself. I'd always played with Sheila and Timmy, as into *play-like* as they were. Waif-like skinny, I'd have passed for a twelve-year-old any day of the week.

"It's your eyes that give you away," Doretha told me one night as we sat around on the Acklin couch next to the white plastic Philco table radio, listening to Our Miss Brooks. "They're the eyes of an old woman," she insisted in her insightful way.

"*Yuck,*" groaned Francine as she polished her fingernails.

Aunt Tina, Mama's sister with whom she shared a mutual love-hate association, stuck her head in the front door, "Alvin wanted to stay here while I go to the company store for a few things," she shrilled, announcing her son's indolent entrance to join us. They lived down Maple Street, four doors away.

Alvin is the most un-animated person I've ever known. Compared to his Mama, he's dead. *Rigor mortis* stage. This evening, he shrugged and exchanged a half-hearted, gauntlet-tossing gaze with Francine. Then he plopped, bored, down onto the sofa, whistling through his teeth as Francine dismissed him with a mere toss of thick, tawny mane.

I noticed, however, that one thing did hook his attention. Doretha.

Doretha never missed a beat extracting me from Francine's talons.

"Never you mind, Francine," Doretha gently scolded, "Sunny feels things deeper'n most folk." Being her kind self, Doretha didn't add *'deeper'n you.* "I don't mean she *looks* old. It's just — her eyes show her hurts."

"Mama used to sing and dance for us," Sheila piped in, desperate to change the sad subject and, I suspected, to gain the spotlight. I was hoping that her flair for fabrication to get attention wouldn't burgeon with the turn of events.

"Yeh." Longing rode Timmy's soft voice. "She was good, too."

Emaline smiled and sighed. "She was sooo pretty in her white and black hotel maid's uniform and apron. And that little triangle hat that tied like a nurse's to her head. Shoot, she coulda been Betty Grable or Alice Faye singing and tap dancing across that big ol' silver screen."

"*Shhh!*" Francine snapped. "I can't hear." She pretended inordinate interest in Arnold Stang's dialogue with Our Miss Brooks.

Alvin stared baldly at her, scrutinizing her audacity.

Ignoring her, Sheila gushed. "When she saw us watchin' 'er, she'd grab Grandpa Dexter's old cane from the closet. He'd left it when he run off with that girl younger'n Mama." Oh, how Sheila loved to repeat gossip and purse those little lips importantly. That *always* drew attention. " Mama'd sing

Pennies From Heaven, making pennies fall through the air and land at our feet. Wouldn't she, Sunny?"

I could still hear throaty belly-laughter erupt from Mama as she watched us scuttle about on our knees to scoop up the money and pocket it.

That was the blinding-fun side of her wildness.

"Yep," I smiled at Sheila, "Mama *was* enchanting."

"You sure use purdy words," Doretha said thoughtfully, impressed. Because of her limited education, she thought I had the smartest brain wedged between two ears.

"*Enchanting?*" I laughed out loud and shrugged. "She *was* enchanting."

Plain and simple, despite her careening excesses and self-absorption, we missed Mama's magic.

"Huh," Francine disparaged while examining her wet fire-red nails, blatantly refusing to reverence our nostalgia. "She wudn't around long enough to make too much of a splash. Always gone somewhere or 'nuther, 'doin' her own thing. Everything was about *her*. Always *her*."

But then, Francine wasn't inclined to enchantment. Except of her own making. And I thought how Francine had, to a tee, just described her own self.

~~~~~

More religion. That's what I needed.

December sunlight warmed our faces and shoulders while an arctic breeze chilled our other parts as Daniel and I strolled, hand-in-hand, to the village outskirts. The hilly terrain was as much a part of me as the air I breathed. It undulated under and around me, securing me like a fortress. How I loved those gently sloping hills, whose paved avenues led to everything of joy and sustenance. To family and friends.

Today they led to church.

I'd finally talked Daniel into going with me to the little village Pentecostal Church, where I found respite from the hellish hopelessness that plagued me day and night. As I look back, I think it was my desperation, on that particular occasion, that overrode his aversion to anything remotely emotional.

Inside the church, Daniel and I sat with Gladys Kale, our friend and neighbor, at whose nearby house we frequently hung out. That is, when her sorry, no-good husband, Harly wasn't home. I learned that descriptive term from Gladys and, with reference to Harly, used it without fail: *sorry, no-good husband.*

Today, Daniel was a mite uncomfortable but I didn't feel guilty a'tall that I'd finagled him into coming by telling him I needed him to go with me to church, that I needed something strong to keep me a'going, what with Mama's shenanigans and all.

I knew what buttons to push in Daniel. He hated what both our mamas represented. So here he was, as uncomfortable as a long-tailed cat on the hotel porch with its endless creakin' rocking chairs. I looked around. Emaline, my pal, was not there. She'd apparently decided to attend Tucapau Methodist Church with her mama, daddy, and grandparents.

My disappointment evaporated when the music cranked up and exploded, filling that little tabernacle till the walls seemed to expand and throb in time. Today's service was especially lively, everything spiritual my daily, dark existence denied.

Daniel did okay until later, when an altar call issued forth.

"Come to *Je-sus!*" Pastor trumpeted like a bull elephant. "*To-daaay!*"

When folks started spilling down the aisle a'weeping and travailing and collapsing into heaps of agonized repentance at the rail, my heart tripped into a syncopated song of ecstasy. I clasped my hands to my flat bosom and just grinned and grinned. That Daniel stood beside me rigid as an oak, and that his hands clamped onto the back of the pew turned his knuckles whiter'n new snow did not disturb my bliss.

He grew more and more jittery as the pastor's penetrating gaze swept the congregation for guilt-stricken countenances. Daniel's poker face gained him a temporary reprieve.

Having weeks earlier done the long aisle walk, I now gaped at the spectacle around that altar, grinning, *enraptured* by all the hullabaloo, with its backslapping and admonitions to '*hang on*' and '*let go.*'.

When Daniel grabbed hold of my elbow and steered me outside quicker'n you could say 'scat' I didn't worry. I just smiled and smiled as his brow furrowed and he propelled us down that village street faster'n two startled bobcats.

I knew.

Daniel would one day give in. And we'd have the best daggum marriage on the face of this *earth!*

~~~~~

One April night, we walked to our favorite retreat, the village park. The lush setting was deserted except for the two of us.

"Daniel," I can't believe it." I was beside myself with joy. "You hit Ol' Tom!"

I settled beside him on the bench. "Yeh. I let 'im have it right between the eyes." He didn't look proud. That wasn't Daniel. Just at peace that he'd finally, after all those years, settled it with the old man.

"What did Walter say about you hittin' his daddy?"

"Said I shoulda done it a long time ago. 'Course I've just now got enough size on me to give 'im back as good as he gives."

I laughed with delight. Walter, Daniel's twenty-something foster brother, was okay.

"Huh. He won't be bothering *you* anymore, I'll bet."

Daniel draped his arm around my shoulders as we snuggled together on the wooden bench, one of several that marked the expanse of grassy knoll punctuated by fir, maple, and oak trees.

I knew of the beatings Ol' man Stone gave Daniel. Doretha had whispered of them to me. It broke my heart. Daniel never spoke of them, defiantly ignored them. Tonight, he broke that trend when he said, "I'd a'run away from that sorry trash before now, but I can't leave you, Sunny."

"So you just did what you had to do," I said, grinning. Then I sobered. "Too bad you couldn't trust him to treat you fairly. You deserve respect, Daniel."

"I lost trust in *adults* long ago," he said softly, almost to himself.

"I haven't completely given up on 'em," I assured Daniel. Somehow it seemed important that one of us believe in humanity's good. "I don't exactly *not* trust. I just no longer live in a world where adults make everything all right. Y'know?"

Trust had begun to morph away from absolute.

Daniel gazed at me with pain-glazed eyes. Then he slowly shook his dark head. "You've got somethin' in you

I don't have, Sunny. After what we saw your mama —" He stopped, squeezed his eyes shut and held out a hand in appeasement, then ran fingers through his thick hair. "I'm sorry, honey. I shouldn't've said that."

But my tears already shimmered, blinding me as I remembered that night....

"Mama — where you goin'?" I squinted up at her from my folding-seat in the dimness of the movie house. Beside me, Daniel squeezed my hand, sensing my apprehension.

"I'll be back in a minute, Sweetie." The drift of *Blue Waltz* did little to reassure me as Mama disappeared up the aisle. Fifteen minutes later, Daniel and I searched the lobby. Something deep, deep inside insisted I could save Mama from herself. Somehow, Daniel understood.

"She went outside. Said she wud'n feelin' well," said Lib, the ticket girl, cynicism and pity spilling from her big ol' curious eyes. Outside, Mama's rich, lusty laughter sliced through June's thick, humid evening air. My younger siblings were at home after a long afternoon matinee. Daniel and I came with Mama tonight, at her request. I still wondered why the rare invitation.

"Wait," Daniel touched my arm to stay me. Then he swiftly moved ahead to the parked car across the street, from whence spiraled Mama's bawdy, animal noises. I followed him, knowing he wanted to protect me. But it was my mess, not his. Mama and Toy Narson didn't even see us when we peered through the car's half-open window.

"C'mon," Daniel's harsh whisper wasn't soon enough. His fingers gripped my arm as he tugged me away and I knew his anger in part was because he'd failed to shield me. Worse still, I knew his rage was at my mama and her stud of the moment, a married man who this very moment rode her in that back seat like a rutting dog.

"My God," he rasped, looking absolutely ill. "Don't she realize how loud she is?" The shame of it was too much to bear and I tore off running down the street, tears streaming my face. When riled, I could, in my youth, run like a greyhound and Daniel didn't catch up till I was nearly home, by now gasping and retching and sobbing intermittently.

"I'm sorry, Sunny," he whispered as he steered then settled me on our back stoop. "I shouldn't'a said that." He turned me into his arms and comforted me with soothing, crooning words. "Don't let 'er get to you. She's not you. Let it go."

"Now I know why she a-asked me to go with her to-night," I hiccuped, snuffling. "S-she just wanted to get around Nana. Nana's been fussin' at 'er this week sayin' 'don't see how you can roll over on your back for every Tom, Dick, and Harry'. She just used us, Daniel. And I thought she really wanted to s-spend time —" My sobs recommenced stronger than ever.

This time, Daniel turned me on the step and embraced me to his chest, his voice husky with feeling. "Don't you dare give up, Sunny. These next four years'll pass fast and then we'll be married and nobody'll hurt you again. Her shame ain't your shame. Y'hear? It's-not-yours."

"It's e-easy for you to say. Your mama don't live right here, whoring right under everybody's nose and —"

"She used to bring men in our house, Sunny. Think that don't do things to you? So I understand how you feel." His lips brushed my cheek and lips, soft as a butterfly a'lightin'. "We'll get through this together, y'hear? Together."

Daniel always calmed me with that magic word: *together.*

Chapter Two

Daddy only came back to visit after that. He wanted to take us up North with him when he found a pipe-fitters job. I always protested. I couldn't bear to think of leaving the mill hill. And I didn't want to leave Daniel. Or Emaline. Or Doretha. Or Gladys.

The list was endless. I simply wanted to stay here with my entire village family and the flowing, familiar terrain.

And strangely, I didn't want to leave Nana, who was the closest biologically I had to a real mama.

Daddy's next visit proved bittersweet, like persimmons on the cusp of ripeness yet leaving the mouth puffy and cheated. We all were overjoyed to see him. He looked tired yet content to be with us that first day or two.

Then, gradually, the contentment oozed out, and he appeared, to me, to be merely going through the motions of living. The substance of him seemed sucked away by Mama, leaving only a shell of the handsome, once hearty man. A restless energy possessed him at times and he would pace like a caged lion, peering unseeing out the windows, barely lighting to share meals with us.

Then, in a heartbeat, he'd curl up on the couch and pass out, sleeping like one drugged. I'd slide off his shoes and cover him with a blanket, so as not to disturb him when his dozing slid into earnest snores. Several nights, that's how he slept, an exhausted heap, mouth agape, as though poised for the next horrific venture.

One evening, fired by an agitated surge, he piled us kids in the old car he still drove and parked in front of the village hotel. Daniel even managed to sneak off with us. Francine raised her eyebrows at me, as puzzled as I over Daddy's obsessive need to light there. Soon, Francine, Sheila, Timmy, Daniel, and I ate leftover biscuits and fried ham in the deserted dining room. Daisy, the cook, served them from the big wood stove's warmer.

With Sheila's small hand clasped in mine, I feasted my curiosity about Mama's workplace — where she'd served as maid — that daily awed me as I made my way past the formidable white, two-story structure wrapped with a colossal front porch and ivy-bedecked, screened-in side veranda, whose endless oak rocking chairs seemed always occupied.

Daddy, in the meantime, huddled in a far corner with Mama's friend and former co-worker, Leona, for a whispery, fervent heart-to-heart. Francine and I looked at each other again. Her's was a knowing smirk, like *only reason Daddy came home was to milk Leona for information about Mama.*

I felt heartsick myself that we weren't enough motivation for Daddy to get past his and Mama's sick tragedy.

Later that night, back at the house, as Daniel and I sat on the front door step, overhearing phrases from Daddy's and Nana's private powwow, I heard *"what she said in that note"* and *"...no use in the kids a'knowin'..."* So, there'd been a note left with Leona.

"What don't they want us to know?" I muttered fiercely wiping tears from my cheeks. "I used to never cry. Now, seems like that's all I do. It's just —"

"I can't believe he's doing this," Daniel muttered through clenched teeth, squeezing my shoulder with his strong arm. "He's running off, leaving you — just like she did."

"He's *lost* without her. Can't you see that?" Pity for Daddy swamped me. "Mama was his *life*."

"No. I don't see, " Daniel snarled and as his gaze met mine I nearly cried out at the venom in his eyes, the likes of nothing I'd ever before glimpsed. "I don't see how Robert can desert ya'll, too. And I don't see how he could still love a woman so — so *trashy* Where's his pride?"

"Daniel!"

He blinked and withdrew his arm from around me. He propped elbows on knees, hung his head and studied his dangling hands for long tense moments. "I'm sorry," he murmured. "I shouldn't a'said that. Pride's not what it's all about."

"No, you shouldn't've, Daniel. I know what she is but she's still my Mama." His words smarted, even in the face of what she'd done. "At the same time, I know you've got your own devils to fight." I reached out to rub his shoulder and he turned and pulled me into his arms.

"Sunny, that's why I love you so much," he murmured against my hair. "You're so understanding. So clean and pure. So *not* like Ruby and Mona." He kissed me then, a gentle meeting of lips, an almost worshipful act. "Don't ever change, Sunny. I couldn't bear it."

I looked deep into his eyes and saw something I'd not seen there before.

Fear.

"Why, Daniel Collins, you're afraid." I put my arms around him and squeezed. "Don't you know that you'll be the only man in my life. Ever?"

"Promise?" He pulled back to look me in the eye, as serious as I'd ever seen him.

I crossed my heart. "I promise or I hope to die."

~~~~~

So far, I hadn't succeeded in getting Daniel back in church after that first time. He remained spooked, not only from feeling 'hunted' but, I figured, by the exuberance of it all.

I understood.

Too much emotion threatened Daniel, like liquor does an alcoholic. Should Daniel crack the door, all his feelings he'd so carefully packed and stomped down, could erupt like a volcano. Despite his tightly harnessed control, Daniel could, I strongly suspected, in an eye's blink, be blasted to smithereens by those feelings.

So, I didn't, at that time, push him to go to church. Nana wasn't too keen on me going to such a 'noisy, peculiar' church. But oh, how I *loved* the wild liveliness of it and the joy I felt when I stepped through those doors.

Thing was, at that precise heartbeat, I needed a miracle. The trauma of abandonment had left me depleted in many ways. A sense of aloneness riddled me daily. I used to never feel that way. Seemed the day Mama left was a defining time in my life, one that remained like a raw, open wound.

I'd heard Gladys Kale pray over lots of stuff and, soon, her current problem would resolve itself. All except for Harly, her womanizing, drunkard, no-good, sorry excuse of a husband.

So I began to quietly slip out late afternoons into an unoccupied house on our block, nailed a picture of Jesus to the wall and spent hours there meditating, reading the

Bible, and just plain enjoying my newfound tranquility. I even took a little battery radio Mama had left behind and played soothing music by Dick Haymes, Frank Sinatra or the Guy Lombardo Orchestra. I'd never felt so liberated. So *all together*. The torture of abandonment eased.

Nana found out.

"She's *crazy*," she'd muttered to my siblings, fully convinced of it. I resented Nana's attempt to undermine my siblings' respect for me, though they didn't seem to give her accusations weight.

Only other relative who even remotely respected the Almighty was Daddy's Methodist preacher cousin, Wayne Acklin.

Nana's scorn was bad enough and then, one evening , while on my skinny knees at the empty house, in the throes of worship, I sensed a dark presence enter my private inner sanctum. When my eyes sprang open, there, before me, squatted my worst horror: *Buck Edmonds*, hunkered down, eye-level with me.

Shock sucked the life from me and I plopped flat on my fanny, mouth open, eyes wide.

His mud-colored gaze raked me while his scruffy hand reached out slow-like, as if to stroke my breast. He represented to me in that moment the Devil-Serpent. His full lower lip hung slack like some idiot's.

My sprightliness caught ol' Buck off guard as I shot to my feet and hightailed it out the back door. He recovered quick enough to trail me as far as the back stoop, laughing like some demented beast from a Bela Lugosi horror film.

"I ain't gon' hurt you, Sunny. C'mon back. Let's have some fun," he called as I spanned the alley in record time and hit our steps running. *"Hey! You'd like it."*

Slothful Betty Edmonds, Buck's mama, had ruined her good name with a filthy house. That, I could excuse. But raising a scumbag like Buck was unforgivable. He was one school grade ahead of me but lots older.

The big joke all over the hill was that the only way to get Buck out of the schoolhouse was to dynamite it. Shoot, I could even overlook his stupidity if he'd *stay-the-heck-away from me!* Just hearing his name made my skin crawl.

I didn't dare tell Daniel. I could just hear him fussing. *"Whatta'you mean, bein' in that empty house all by yourself? And it turnin' night. Are you nuts, Sunny?"* Then he'd beat the crap out of Buck and be in deep dung with Fitzhugh, our village policeman.

So I'd abandoned my private meditations. I still went to church and prayed to the Almighty but toned down any outward displays of spirituality for fear of dire consequences.

I'd had a gut-full of 'em.

~~~~~

Gladys' house smelled of vanilla. I loved going to her house on Fridays, when she got revenge on Harly, her sorry, no-good husband, by loading up a heap of groceries at the Company Store and charging them to his account.

Fridays were Banana Pudding Day.

Daniel and I made regular visits there for heaping helpings of her delicious specialty. My younger siblings paired off to play outdoors with her two close-in-age kids, Vince and Sissy, and our time together was fun.

Gladys was then and remains till this day that rare breed who can, in an eye's blink, change from a serious, elegant woman to a playful child. She looked a lot like actress Ali MacGraw in her younger day. Her kindness is not negotiable. It's God-given, static, real, and never-ending. She was mine and Emaline's spiritual role model.

Daniel loved her, too. "Hey, Sunny," she'd embrace me in welcome, "if I was a few years younger, and single, I'd give you some competition for this feller." Then she'd hug Daniel like a mama and say, "C'mon in, good-looking."

Then we'd move on to stupid, silly stuff: Daniel: "Knock, knock." Me:"Who's there?" Daniel: "Who wants to know?" Me: "I do." Daniel: "Well, who are you?"

"Who wants to know?"

"I do."

And on and on it'd go till Gladys would erupt, "If ya'll don't *shut up* I'm gonna take a broom to your hind-ends!"

"I can run faster'n you," Daniel would counter.

"Now, you don't know that for sure, do you? I used to be the fastest runner at Tucapau Grammar School."

"Nah," Daniel insisted. "You won't ever catch me. Or Sunny either, for that matter."

Gladys' eyes took on a twinkle. "Then you won't get no Banana Pudding."

"Hey," I laughed, "That's *always* the last word."

Then there were the times, on pretty days, when we'd go out into the back yard while Gladys hung her laundry on the line and she'd say, "Cut us a cartwheel, Sunny."

And I would, thrilled to see both her's and Daniel's mouths spread into grins and their eyes shine. My acrobatic agility was a huge source of pride for them.

Other times, she'd have her newly bought, company store TV on American Bandstand and Daniel and I would dance. How she loved to watch us. Daniel's the best natural dancer I've ever seen. His movements are smooth as silk yet vigorous.

One day, Gladys' took me aside, a rare, worried look on her face. "Sunny —"

"What?" I said.

"Sunny —" She hesitated, then came to a decision. "Don't ever come into my house when I'm not here. I mean — if Harly's here, and I'm not, don't come in. I wouldn't trust him."

She was as solemn as I'd ever seen her. I nodded. "Remember Ruthie Bonds?" Gladys said kindly. "I feel sorry for that girl and her little one. I don't blame her for nothin'. It was all Harly's fault. I know he done what he did to her and —" She looked at me like a mama. "Just mind what I say. Don't ever let yourself get caught alone with him."

I nodded, a knot of fear in my stomach as I remembered Ruthie's near suicide in the big river. And her shame. And I promised myself to heed Gladys' advice.

~~~~~

I sighed and wiped the plate clean. "I know Daddy loves being with us so I can't understand why he doesn't come back to live with us. Anyway, it's not fair to leave us four kids with you, Nana." I shoved back a frisson of apprehension that he might come back for us.

"I ain't complained, have I?" she said in her understated way but I knew she was thinking about it by the way her lips tightened. She couldn't be happy, saddled with Mama and Daddy's four kids. Not at her age. *Why, Daddy?* None of it made sense.

But then, logic was beginning to reshape before me.

I don't know why, but later on that particular November Saturday night, after spending the afternoon with Daniel at the village movie matinee, I broke down and began to weep while listening to the Grand Old Opry. I suspect it was Mama's favorite songs that set me off. *Faded Love* and *Divorce Me C.O.D* socked me especially hard. All it took was a glimpse of that picture of her on the mantle for the dam to burst.

Looking back, I figure it had to do with the fact that I'd started my period that morning and felt headachy and melancholy. Daniel, sympathetic to my plight, had left earlier in the evening. Cousin Alvin, Aunt Tina's teenaged brat, was visiting at the time. If you could call being planted in a chair for hours at a time 'visiting.' Didn't matter. If the President himself had been sitting there, the result would've been the same.

Mama and Aunt Tina had always been competitive. Hated each other. And here I came along, near albino, the spittin' image of Aunt Tina. God does have a sense of humor.

Tonight, all that paled in comparison to what I was feeling.

"What's the matter with you?" Nana snapped, uncomfortable with such an outburst of emotion. Such goings-on simply weren't done, to her way of thinking. Too much emotion was shameful.

Sheila's eyes puddled, too, but for me, I suspect, rather than for Mama. Timmy scooted closer, plastering himself to my side, but kept his misty eyes downcast, picking at the loose hem of his cotton shirt. Francine, for once, said nothing. Just watched me, baldly curious.

Alvin, too, watched me. Moments later, he was gone.

The more Nana scolded me — for scolded me she did, such was her exasperation and helplessness — the more my grief swelled and split and distended again. For some reason, Nana didn't go get her mammoth switch she kept on the closet shelf for emergencies like this.

"I m-miss Mama!" I finally hiccuped only to burst into fresh wails.

"Can't understand *why*," Francine snorted angrily, springing from the couch and stalking to the front door, where she pivoted to face me. "Hey! Ol' Ruby just hopped in Doc Brock's car and rode off into the sunset." She laughed, a brittle, harsh eruption. "Had to do it with somebody *famous*. Had to do it *big*. Does that *surprise me*? *Nah*. Can't see why you're actin' like somebody's up and *died*."

"That's enough, young lady." Nana appeared in the kitchen doorway. Her staid, faded sky-blue gaze homed in on Francine, raking her half-clothed frame with displeasure. " Don't you *ever* talk about 'er that way. I don't like what she done, neither. But she's still your mama and I won't have you speaking ill of 'er. Y'hear?"

Francine tipped back her head to view Nana through narrowed eyes. "Yeh, Nana, I hear," she drawled. "You speak ill of her every day. So does everybody else who knows 'er. And you expect *us* to keep quiet about her runnin' off and leavin' us? *Huh*. "

Nana looked like she wanted to slap Francine but her voice was low. "She's still your mama."

Francine's eyes slitted and she took a step forward. "*I* know it. And *you* know it. But does *she*? Huh? Tell me that."

With that final shot, she aimed like a bullet for the front door.

I figured she would slip under the house, which sat high upon the hilly terrain, where she kept an extra pack of Camels — supplied by Tack Turner, the snobby, son-of-a-boss-man rat — and would curl up on the dirt and suck nicotine till her eyes emptied and she grew still as death.

"Francine!" The door's loud *slam* swallowed Nana's reprimand as Francine disappeared down the front steps.

Nana snapped off the radio and went into the kitchen, leaving me doubled up, squalling like a three-month-old, with only my little brother and sister to weather the emotional mayhem with me.

Nana's presence, in the kitchen doorway, swam in my peripheral vision but by now I knew that, though she loved Mama, she'd not be my ally. Mama was God-only-knew where, leaving Nana with a gaggle of grandkids to raise.

That *unwanted* feeling lay like a comatose elephant upon me tonight.

I struggled to sit up straight, tried to focus my red, swollen eyes. I snuffled, an automatic hiccuppy sound.

"Are you through?" Nana hissed, stuffing her handkerchief into her apron pocket. "Never seen such goings-on in all my life. Y'should be over all that by now."

"B-but, Nana — I *miss* her so." I wanted desperately to make her understand but tears suddenly puddled again and the fact that it enraged Nana did nothing to ward off the torrential downpour that had Sheila and Timmy both wailing.

Aunt Tina burst through the front door, Alvin trailing behind. And I knew he'd ran like a greyhound to sic his mama on me. What irony, I thought fuzzily, that he *could* manage to move faster'n a turtle.

"Are you going to *shut up that snivelin'?*" Aunt Tina's voice hurt my ears. Her tall, lanky form was all angles and strength as she reached for me. Then she was hauling me to my feet, her long-taloned fingers gripping my blouse with such force I felt two buttons pop.

"Do you know what happens to folks who pitch conniption fits and make little kids cry? Huh?" She was nose to nose with me, her pale eyes blazing like blow torches in the night.

I didn't answer, couldn't. I was weeping afresh. In that moment I hated my nonstop tears over which I had no control. That infuriated her more. "Well, I'll tell you what happens to such trouble makers," she hissed. "They get throwed in the river. C'mon Talley," she motioned to her pug-faced husband, who hovered in the doorway. "Help me and we'll take her down to the river and make a believer outta her."

…They get throwed in the river….

Pure *panic* seized me because, at that time, I feared those icy, dark, *bottomless* waters more than anything in the world. At night. I couldn't forget Ruthie Bond's near fatal experience.

Tonight, it was that — the terror — that drew a noose around the wails, snuffing them like sand on embers. I simply froze with fear.

"That's more like it." Aunt Tina loosed me, squared her shoulders, and took her brood and left.

When the door slammed behind them, Timmy and Sheila let out fresh howls.

"That's it," Nana snarled and herded the two up the stairs and off to bed. I heard their wailing slowly subside.

Within minutes, Daniel knocked at the front door and I was on the porch, in his arms. He quietly led me to the swing suspended from porch's ceiling. And I cast Francine a grateful, howbeit teary look as she sashayed past us into the house, casting me a blatant *you owe me one* expression over her shoulder.

"Well whaddaya know?" I said hoarsely. "Francine brought you to my *rescue?*"

But Daniel didn't laugh. He watched me intently, care oozing from him like warm honey. By now, I was so numb I thought I'd never again feel anything beyond the great chasm of screaming emptiness inside me. But his caring unleashed yet more of my belated grief to spill forth in a healing gush.

With Daniel's strong arm squeezing me, the knot in my chest looped tighter. Suddenly, new pain lanced me. And Mama's specter rose before me in living technicolor, the winsome, loving side of her. *"Oh Mama — didn't I do enough?"* Words spilled from me like a discharged slot machine. *" I tried by helping with Sheila and Timmy and not whining when you were gone most every night —"* I pressed my hands to my mouth to stem the sob that heaved and swirled and thrashed about in my chest.

"Sunny…" Daniel leaned to peer into my face. "Please — *don't*. It wasn't *anything you did or didn't do.*"

"D-Daniel…I feel so alone," I whispered, closing my eyes and sagging.

"Hey," Daniel's finger guided my chin until I looked him squarely in the eyes. *"I'm* here. I'll always be here. And I want you to know how proud I am of you. You're good and strong and wonderful. Pure goodness is what you are."

"Ahh, Daniel," I whispered. I reached up to touch his cheek. "You've been here, too, just where I am. You understand."

He slowly nodded.

"C'mon," he pulled me to my feet, "let's walk." I dashed inside and grabbed my coat from the little coat closet and we headed out.

We short-cut through the alley and set out up North Main toward the village outskirts. Street lights polished the sidewalks and dwellings a golden cast.

After long minutes of silence, Daniel spoke without preamble. "I hate Ruby for what she's done to you, just like I hate Mona," he said matter-of-factly, with little apparent emotion on his angular, hawk -like face. Daniel tightly banked his feelings. I suspect that's how he survived all he did.

"Don't hate 'em, Daniel," I pleaded hoarsely, not even fully understanding why. " I certainly don't like my own mama, but I don't *hate* 'er. Truth is, I don't know exactly what I feel for her anymore. But *hate* is such an intense word."

"Yeh," he drawled and thrust callused hands deeply into his jacket pockets as we walked to the village park, our oasis whose carpet of grass in coming months would alter from winter buff to summer emerald.

"We've got two real prize *Mama mias,*" he drawled, then snorted. "At least you know who your daddy is. I never will." He looked at me, his lips a thin line, his eyes cold. "'Cause *Mona* don't. Now, ain't that just dandy?" His voice dripped sarcasm. He laughed then. Not a pretty sound, Daniel's riled laughter. More like a bark that erupted from deep in his gut while his mouth curled in scorn.

I watched him exhale chilly vapor into donuts, pulling my own nearly outgrown, thin coat more tightly around me. "You hardly ever mention your mama. Why?"

He shrugged and his features emptied. "I don't really think about Mona much. Y'know?"

"Do you still love her at all?"

Another shrug, more elaborate. A decisive, "No. She killed that when she tossed me to the foster care system — after promising me she'd never do it again. Mostly, I'm mad at 'er. Can't count on 'er." He looked at me then, his magnificent turquoise eyes aglitter with pain. "Y'know?"

I nodded. "Oh, yeh I do. To survive, one does what one has to do to gouge out that ol' throbbin' stinger. Anger's easier to handle than hurt." Yes, I understood. Daniel and I resonated together with like-wounds.

"Y'know what?" he said, abruptly changing direction.

"What?"

He pulled me to my feet and swept his hand out in a wide arc. "Some day, which is not so far off now, you'll have your house, right here in the middle of this land." He paused and swallowed hard and I thought I saw mist in his eyes. " It'll be awesome. And we'll live happily ever after."

I laughed, then snuffled. "Oh, Daniel. You're something else."

He slung his arm around me as we began to make our way home. "I am, ain't I?"

I poked him playfully in the ribs and we laughed uproariously as our feet connected with sidewalk.

I shook my head. "What?" he asked quietly.

"I've been such a whine-y tonight. Nana would love to switch me good for being such a coward. Bad as I need your courage, Daniel, I can't get used to leaning too hard on *anybody.*" I hooked my arm around his waist. "You've got your own burdens to carry. You don't need mine, too."

I made another decision in that moment. "I've shed my last tears over Mama."

"Good," Daniel said quietly and squeezed my shoulder.

That was a promise I kept for many, many years to come.

~~~~~

Doretha was not what Emaline and I could ever label "pretty."

Yet we would forevermore agree she was the loveliest person we knew. Countering Francine's cynicism was Doretha's guilelessness. At times, our friend's deep-set, hazel gaze seemed eons old, reflecting an elusive, inexpressible sadness.

The fact that she'd already dropped out of school seemed not at all strange to us. In some mystifying way, she seemed above ordinary schooling.

She'd steadfastly declared her surname *Hicks*. "I don't *ever* want to be called Stone." Her estimation of ol' Tom was right down there with everyone else's. "I don't remember my own Daddy. He died when I was three."

Today, Doretha used her mama's best china dessert plates to serve the chocolate offering we bore. Bertha Stone, her mother, welcomed us warmly, belying her formidable appearance. Bigger in stature than her daughter, her only biological child, Bertha, or *Berthie*, the mill hill pronunciation, was a handsome woman with a long swan neck and porcelain skin that needed no cold cream.

She was as assertive and driven as Doretha was timorous and hesitant. I discovered Berthie to be as diligent and organized in housekeeping as an ant colony while Doretha day-dreamed and went about life as though she lived in a cave of disposables.

Yet underlying all that I sensed a mutual, deep love.

"Here," Doretha addressed me in her soft little voice, "let me pour you some tea. Or would you rather have cold milk?" She relished the hostess role. I had to remind myself that we weren't playing house.

"Tea."

Daniel strolled in, eyes so hungry to sight me one would never know he'd seen me only an hour ago over at Emaline's. "Hey!" He plopped down across from me and turned on his slow smile that started deep in his eyes like a tiny ember and grew until it filled his ocean-green, beautiful irises. And in that heartbeat, *déjà vu* submerged me in memories from six months earlier….

That day, as Emaline and I visited, bearing cookies for the occasion, Doretha dashed out of the kitchen and moments later returned with a tall, lanky boy in tow and announced proudly, "This is Daniel."

First thing I noticed about Daniel was his piercing turquoise eyes, the shade of which I'd never before seen, like sea-tide overlaid with translucent blue. Coupled with his midnight black hair, they stunned me.

Emaline seemed not affected, however, because she never missed a beat. "Hey, Daniel. Nice t' meet you."

He nodded, flushing ever so slightly as he lifted his strong, cleft chin in boldness. Defiance, maybe, but of what, I couldn't fathom. If his aim was to impress, he sure as heck succeeded. There was about him an almost savage elegance. A subterranean wildness simmered behind his unrefined composure.

Sort of like a young Sir Laurence Olivier, as Heathcliffe in Wuthering Heights.

Then, his attention slid to me. Our gazes locked.

Something profound clicked inside me when I gazed into his proud countenance because beneath it I glimpsed an incredible vulnerability. "Hey, Daniel," I said softly.

"This is Sunny," said Doretha, as though showing off a treasure. "Ain't that a purdy name? Come on and sit down. We're having some chocolate chip cookies the girls brought over. And they baked 'em themselves." She nibbled a bite and closed her eyes ecstatically. "Mmmm. They're so go-o-o-d. Ain't that sweet of 'em?"

Brave-hearted Renie, Emaline's mama, had turned us loose in her kitchen. Emaline and I had trashed the kitchen doing the doughy clumps, then painstakingly cleaned it up as they baked into slightly scorched but edible cookies. All this in order to dazzle Doretha, just to hear her oohs and ahhs. She never let us down.

"Yeh," Daniel muttered, nodding, his turquoise eyes holding mine, even as he moved across from me and took a seat. His threadbare cotton shirt and jeans were clean and pressed. His well-shaped hands were scruffy and callused, the short nails slightly stained underneath. I could tell he'd tried to clean them. His fingers curled under, as though hiding from my probing gaze. I quickly averted my eyes and continued to nibble.

"Where did you live before you moved here?" Emaline asked him just before she bit into a cookie.

"Gastonia."

Doretha and Daniel spoke simultaneously, then Doretha gave her little tittering laugh. "Daniel come to live with us four years ago."

"Oh." Emaline blinked twice, waiting for more information, and when none came forth, she shrugged and took a sip of iced tea. She was and is the most down-to-earth, unassuming person I know.

"I'm what's called a foster child," Daniel drawled as though amused, pinching off a chunk of cookie and mashing it between his fingers. Then he looked directly at me, his eyes aglitter. "What that really means is I'm nobody's kid. I just hang my hat where I land."

It took my breath, his quiet vehemence that, in some odd way, challenged me. Only later, after Mama's abandonment, did I even begin to understand.

"Why Daniel," Doretha scolded good-naturedly, "you're my brother now. I ain't never had a brother before."

He looked at her then. "There's Walter," he said matter-of-factly. Daniel's logic was bald at that time, completely unadorned.

Doretha nibbled her wafer for long moments, gazing at her tea glass as though analyzing the outside moisture trickle. Then, without looking up, she shook her head. "Walter don't count."

It would be years before I compared brunette Doretha to Audrey Hepburn, with her near-emaciation and vulnerability propped up by an elusive dignity. Her breathy little voice was a cross between Jackie Kennedy's and Marilyn Monroe's. More like Jackie's, I think, because there wasn't a Monroe-sexy inclination in her entire framework.

"Who's Walter?" asked Emaline. I was too busy studying Daniel to add to the conversation, which was unusual since I usually had opinions on any and every topic under the sun.

Without forethought, Doretha said, "He's Tom's boy," then, by way of explanation, added, "Tom's married to my mama."

Doretha's refusal to label Tom 'stepfather' later spawned curious nuances to entertain Emaline's and my imaginations. On the lighter side, her Walter-rebuffs provided much comical relief through those years.

"Daniel!" roared a man's voice from outside. "Git out here. You ain't through."

"That's Tom," Doretha whispered solemnly then slid Daniel a contrite look. "I'm sorry, Daniel. I didn't mean to get you in trouble."

"S'okay." Daniel stood so abruptly I jumped. "Nice meetin' y'all," he said tersely and quickly disappeared through the kitchen door.

Doretha smiled, a sad old-woman smile. "Daniel's a good boy. He don't want nobody to know he — that he's treated like he is." She dabbed at her mouth with the white linen napkin, her eyes downcast. "He tries hard to keep bad things from happening; don't want to hurt nobody."

"What things?" asked Emaline before I had a chance.

Doretha looked at us for long moments, her gaze far-away and infinitely sad. "You'll find out."

~~~~~

I did in those following days. Tom Stone had lots of bones to pick, using Daniel's carcass. His was a near silent rage that I observed while visiting the Stone's residence, one that roiled and pulsated beneath empty eyes and ham-like hands whose thick fingers — I vividly envisioned — could roll into a fist in an eye's blink. I shuddered to think what that fist could do to Daniel's thin flesh and bone frame.

Doretha intimated the beatings, her bottomless eyes welling as she told, in her whispery, breathy little voice, of Tom's cruelties to the helpless boy.

"Daniel just stands there a'starin' straight ahead. He won't cry. Just grinds his teeth and clenches his fists. Mama hates it. She tries to do what she can but she's afraid to make Tom mad enough to turn on her." She slowly shook her head. "Daniel tries hard not to get nobody else involved. Acts like Tom's fists and words don't hurt. He's that way — good-hearted."

"What about Walter?" I'd referred to her stepbrother, who set many a girls' hearts aflutter with his golden-blonde good looks. He'd graduated high school the year before they moved to the mill hill, giving him the distinction of being 'older,' a thing that enraptured many females. Not me. Once having glimpsed Daniel, my heart filled up with him.

Doretha took her own good time to answer. "Walter's not here much. But — to give credit where credit's due, I have to say that when he is, he takes up for Daniel."

This she seemed to admit grudgingly, again puzzling me with her gentle complexities. And nuances. She shrugged. "Trouble is, Tom's smart enough to pick on Daniel when nobody ain't around to take up for 'im." She shook her head sadly. "Least ways, nobody who's *big* enough to stand up to 'im."

"Mama didn't know about that side of Tom till after they'd been married awhile. Shoot, when they was dating, he treated me like a princess. That lasted till they got home from the notary's house." She snickered delicately then whispered, "A preacher had better sense than to marry 'em."

More and more, I sought out Daniel, whose chin always lifted eloquently from whatever task engaged him to warmly greet me, whose voice conveyed no terror, who gave no indication of inhumane afflictions.

Now, four years later, he'd courageously emancipated himself.

Chapter Three

During the fifties, mill hill life hit its zenith. That Saturday, Main Street bustled when kids from three to twenty-three spilled on to her from every avenue. The weekly pilgrimage to the afternoon movie matinee took our parade down Main Street, past folks sitting on porches, some calling out greetings to us.

With Daniel beside me, and my siblings hooked up with buddies, it was a carefree, ebullient time, when being villagers was our magical, shimmering common bond. For an afternoon, at least, the enchanted silver screen melted us into sterling camaraderie where toleration for even stinkos like Buck Edmonds abounded.

Today, Tack Turner, an older twenty-something, accompanied Francine, who now mysteriously had money for whatever appetite flared, whether cigarettes, movies, lipstick, or candy bars. It shamed me to know that Tack furnished her funds. Francine, however, had no such qualms; did, in fact, feel entitled.

Tack, tall and crane-thin, sprouted a shock of walnut-hued hair, abundant except on top. His regular features were too cynical and brooding to be called handsome but his attitude took up the slack. Tack, whose ego knew no bounds, felt that we, the Acklins, were infinitely beneath him in station — with the exception of Francine, of course, whom he regarded as a cross between Sadie Thompson and Cleopatra.

"Get lost, kid," I heard him grouse at Timmy, who'd made the mistake of teasingly asking Tack for popcorn money.

My hackles rose. "Timmy, *don't.*" I scowled my disapproval at him. He knew not to beg that jerk for anything. Timmy suppressed a grin and I realized he was simply aggravating Tack for amusement. Daniel fell in beside me, flanked by Walter, his foster-brother.

"Hey!" Walter playfully cuffed Daniel's shoulder. "How does something as ugly as you rate such a *cute lil' thang?*" Walter flashed his quick, white grin at me and I thought *he's a blonde James Dean.* I smiled back. I liked the eternal-kid Walter, especially the fact that he'd stood up for Daniel through the years.

"Lucky," replied Daniel, sliding his arm possessively around my waist. "Just plain lucky." He winked at me.

Walter sidled up to Doretha, who walked ahead with Emaline and pointedly ignored her stepbrother, her usual reaction to him. Walter swooped and kissed Doretha's cheek, did a Daffy-Duck *whoop* as she disgustedly swiped it away, then scuttled ahead to flirt outrageously with other bobby-soxers. Timmy and Sheila strolled ahead of me, chattering away with Emaline's sister, Polly, and the Kale kids.

Pure contentment surged through me when the big brick movie house loomed into view. Like a long, happy Chinese-parade paper-dragon, we wound up wide cement, brick-trimmed steps to the ticket window, where we filed past to pay fifteen-cents apiece to enjoy a long afternoon of silver screen magic. That warm April day, sultry, pouty-lipped Jane Russell and sensuous Marilyn Monroe filled an

entire poster beside the window. Bold block letters spelled
GENTLEMEN PREFER BLONDES.

During the lull, while Daniel and I waited in line to pay,
he took my hand and lifted it to his lips, unconcerned about
onlookers. I grinned at him and was rewarded with that
slow, warm smile that revealed perfect white teeth, snowy
against his olive complexion. I had to look up to him. At
seventeen, he already towered over six-feet and what with
hacking tall weeds and grass with that old swing blade so
much, he was quite muscular.

He turned my hand in his, admiring my tapered fingers,
a thing that fascinated him. Then, on his thumb, I saw a
bleeding blister.

"Does it hurt?" I asked, alarmed, instinctively cupping
the finger.

He gazed down at the watery sore that looked ready to
ooze blood. "Naw." Up came the chin and the turquoise gaze
blazed into mine. "Not a bit."

I swallowed back a lump and forced a smile, knowing
when to shut up. I quickly air-kissed the finger, then slowly
released his hand. "Yeh, well, it's our turn to pay."

"I'll pay yours," Daniel offered as he always did.

"No, thank you." I refused as I always did, eaten alive
with proving I didn't take handouts like Francine.

Daniel sat with me in the darkened theater, whose enchanted screen-images painted us like moonlight. We held
hands in those innocent days, an occasional innocuous kiss
being our limit. Maybe because we were rarely alone or
that we found endless fascination with life's everyday little
things to share, we didn't wade into sexual temptation.

That was mere months away.

Tom Stone, despite his meanness, had begun paying
Daniel a fair wage for his work. Maybe it was his warped

view of trade-out. Or perhaps it was Daniel's emancipation that drew an ounce of respect . Whatever, it spared Daniel the indignity of destitution.

And so Daniel always bought a large popcorn to share with me. When Sheila and Timmy, settled into folding seats behind us, hooked their chins over his shoulder and whined for some, Daniel magnanimously passed the bag to them.

And when, within minutes, the bag returned empty, Daniel merely threw back his head, laughed, and went to buy more. I'd learned long ago that Daniel enjoyed sharing his meager resources, a fact that made something inside me soar like a sun-washed butterfly.

Forevermore, the smell and flavor of buttery popcorn would remind me of Daniel's generous sweetness.

~~~~~

Another year passed. Daddy's letters waned to perhaps one every other month., sometimes less. He took odd jobs until he could land a pipe-fitters position. The money eventually stopped.

Food grew scarce. One good thing did evolve during that difficult period: I began to relax, hoping that I wouldn't be forced to move away from the mill hill after all.

Another thing I noticed: since I'd put thoughts of Mama aside, I'd begun to feel tiny bursts of joy again. Not as acutely as I once had, but they did, to some degree, return.

~~~~~

In those twilight years of village life, poverty was not a word clearly defined. It was only when our food supply ran short, after our parents left, that it began to emerge at all. The mill hill was, in material senses, an equalizer.

Nana's monthly welfare check amounted to forty-five dollars and didn't go far with four extra mouths to feed.

So, to help feed and clothe the family, I began to take in sewing. Nana had an old peddle-type machine in the back bedroom and, in my high school home ec classes, I quickly learned to convert cloth and thread into fashionable outfits. Most of my clients bought extra cloth for me to make outfits for the girls in the family.

"I'm gonna take the maid's job at the hotel," Francine announced one day as we sat at the kitchen table eating navy beans and cornbread. "I'm tired of not havin' decent food. Too, Aunt Tina might have to move in with us to qualify us for this housing. The grace period's about over. And I know neither of us wants that."

I saw Nana's shoulders droop as she stood at the stove, back to us. I knew our complaining about a sparse diet hurt her. She was doing the best she could.

"Francine," I pleaded with my headstrong sister, "please don't drop out of school. After this year, you only have one more year and you'll be done. You need your education."

"For what?" drawled Francine, who, I realized, had already made up her mind. Her idea of planning for the future consisted of deciding what to wear to the Cotton Club dance that night. She refused Tack's constant marriage proposals.

So she took the hotel maid position.

Seeing her in a uniform like Mama's was like a sad *déjà vu*. The job fit my sister as snugly as the outfit. So many circling male admirers exhilarated Francine. Tack Turner sulked and pouted. Francine ignored him.

Francine and I joined forces to raise up our little family a notch above destitution. Now, she and I independently clad ourselves. And while I salvaged leftover material scraps to fashion garments for Sheila, Francine fitted Timmy with jeans, shirts, and shoes for both kids at the Company Store. With teamwork, we at least didn't go hungry and looked decent. Being a member of the prestigious Beta Club in school gave my morale a boost. It also insured my college scholarship. Daniel managed to get on the honor roll as well. We studied together whenever possible.

Mrs. Odom, my Home Economics teacher at the new James F. Byrnes High School, was a lovely, elegant lady whose posture suggested aristocracy. She became another of my role models. I practiced before a mirror until I had it perfected.

I didn't realize it then, but I'd begun to reinvent myself.

~~~~~

Every mill hill resident at least had a chance at a decent dwelling since village houses consisted of three architectural designs, varying only in roof line pitches and story levels. The head — or other occupants — of each dwelling worked in the cotton mill or an auxiliary such as the hotel, ice house, or numerous other positions. Rental fees were nominal.

The Company Store erased most notions of a caste system by providing villagers with a perpetual credit-line for groceries, clothing, and other essentials. Nobody went hungry. Or ragged.

Would you believe, we *still* had our *haves* and *have-nots*?

That soap was available didn't mean everybody utilized it. Dirty houses and unkempt kids still mottled the hilly avenues. Deprivation was not the source. Slothfulness was. Some folks could move into a meticulously clean dwelling and, within days, reduce it to skid row rubble. Others, inclined to cleanliness, could take that same skid row house and, within days, restore its sparkling demeanor.

Likewise, sleazy Buck Edmonds could don a snow-white, Palm Beach suit and, within an hour, look as though he'd slept a week in it while Daniel could wear the simplest of jeans and shirts and look as fresh and crisp as the dawn.

Privation didn't bother Gladys Kale at all. She didn't see Harly's paycheck anyway. But she did have access to the Company Store. She was Emaline's and my religious connection, my spiritual role model. We continued to traipse to Gladys' little Pentecostal church every chance we got and, if we had a problem, we'd pray. But I was convinced it was Gladys' fervent prayers that eradicated life's glitches in no time flat.

~~~~~

Daniel's emancipation rose another notch when he landed a job. He now spent afternoons driving the Company ice truck, helping Bill Melton, Emaline's grandpa, with ice deliveries.

"If we save every penny," he spoke quietly as we lolled on my back porch steps, "we'll have enough for the first year's tuition at Clemson College. Maybe more."

"I've just *gotta* get a job." I bit my lip before revealing my cards, ones dealt by Francine. "And, y'know — Francine says a maid's position is opening at the hotel. Leona's due date is only four weeks away. They'll be hurting for help." I held my breath.

I'll swear I felt antennas sprout in all directions from Daniel. He froze for long moments before speaking. Then, "I don't know. So many men are in and out of there, Sunny. I'd hate —"

I was ready. "Don't you trust me? I mean — you're tromping through women's houses most every afternoon, delivering ice. I have to trust *you*, don't I?"

He mulled it over for a long moment. I knew I had his number. The furrow between his brows smoothed. "Yeh. You do." He took my hand, looked at it, squeezing gently. "I s'pose that to turn our lives in another direction, we gotta do some things different. Things we don't exactly *want* to do."

I flexed like a contented cat. "Ahh, Daniel. I can hardly wait to become a teacher. Next to the clergy, it's the most noble profession on earth. What an opportunity to make a difference in lives."

That made him chuckle. "That's so true, darlin'. You already make a big difference in mine." He gave me a peck on the lips and then grew serious. "Between now and when I graduate this June, I should be able to save enough for both semesters."

"It's almost here — your venturing out. And I'll be right behind you next June. Then we'll be married and live happily forever and ever."

Daniel grinned from ear to ear, the picture of contentment. "Not to dispute your prediction, darlin' but we'll be busy tackling college degrees following the wedding, holding down jobs at the same time. Not exactly Utopia."

"We can do it," I insisted, not in the least worried.

"No doubt about it."

"Mama's scandal now seems almost unreal." I didn't realize I'd spoken aloud until Daniel spoke.

"We're going to make a new life, Sunny. All that will be gone."

Daniel's emotional control and common sense continued to astound me. With him, I felt safe.

~~~~~

"Sheila?" I called tersely, upset by the chaotic scene I'd just witnessed.

I felt her at my elbow and turned. Her face cupped up, with eyes huge and anxious. "Are — are you mad at me?" she whispered tremulously. "I'm sorry I lied about Francine driving Tack's car on Sundays."

"Yeh. I am mad, Sheila." I nodded firmly, all the time my heart turning to mush at the fear I saw in the green depths. "You shouldn't lie." I took a deep breath, then let it out slowly, closing my eyes for a long moment.

"I'm *sorry*," she whispered, more fervently.

I opened my eyes then took her hand and steered her to our lumpy sofa. "Sit down, Sheila. I need to talk to you."

She seated herself next to me, clasped her small hands in her lap, and gazed expectantly at me, as though I could turn the world right side up again.

"Sheila...what's wrong? Why are you doing these things? Lying on Francine. And Timmy. You got him a whipping for lying that he'd taken money from Nana's purse. And me — just now, I could've been beaten, too." Francine had bolted from the house before Nana could wield the switch but that was beside the point.

I kept my voice kind. I couldn't bear to add to her list of hurts. Tears pooled along her lower lids as she continued to gaze at me. They burgeoned, then slipped over and ran trails down her usually rosy cheeks, now paled from trauma.

"*Why*, Sheila? Why are you so desperate for attention? Is anything wrong? Anything you want to talk to me about?"

She swallowed hard, then nodded.

"What? Tell me."

Sheila's gaze dropped to stare at her fingers, now doing their dance in her lap. She snuffled. "Uncle Charlie…" she began, then stopped, the fingers moving faster, faster.

"Uncle Charlie *what?*" I asked, dread slithering like a copperhead through me. Nana usually took Sheila with her to Uncle Charlie's while she cleaned and cooked for him.

"He," her gaze lifted and linked with mine. She whispered, "He *touches me.*"

My gut knotted. *Oh God.* "Where does Uncle Charlie touch you?" I asked quietly, dreading her reply as I would an atomic blast.

Her gaze slid downward again. "You know," she whispered, "down *there*. Between my legs. He pulled me in his bed while Nanny was hanging out laundry."

"Oh, Sheila," I groaned. Oh God, ohGodohGod. Mama and Daddy, where are you?

"Was that the only time?" *Please God*. I gathered her in my arms.

"No. He's done it lots of times and he told me I better not tell anybody or he'd throw me in the river," she spoke against my chest, clutching me to her, and, in her embrace, I heard her cry for help. "I *hate it*, Sunny. Please make 'im stop." She burst into turbulent tears. I realized my cheeks, too, were wet.

"Well, he won't do it again," I said and snuffled.

With God's help, I meant to keep that promise.

~~~~~

"She's lying!" Uncle Charlie insisted.

I'd shared Sheila's accusations with an extremely skeptical Nana, who'd immediately marched us into the cold December temperatures and over to her brother's house to confront him. She'd awakened him and now, mid-afternoon, he sat on the side of his bed in rumpled pajamas, bleary-eyed and indignant.

"Why'd you wanna go and tell somethin' like that, Sheila? Huh?" He scratched his near bald head, his lined face a marquee of sorrow and disappointment. "Hadn't I always been good to you? And saying I threatened to throw you in the river, of all things?"

He rolled his head back, closed his eyes, and expelled a huff of woeful air.

Sheila, at my elbow, shrank even farther behind me, trembling. Nana scowled at her now. "She's been lying 'bout lots of things," Nana punctuated his denial with substantiation.

My head swam with uncertainty. Uncle Charlie was so convincing…. Sheila *had* been dreaming up lots of things in that little head of hers. She'd heard Aunt Tina's threats to throw me in the river that night — could that have given her the idea? Her fabrications had been rampant and indiscriminate. She'd hurt each of us, her siblings, with her unquenchable obsession for attention. Now, Uncle Charlie stood before her pointing finger. Was he, too, a victim?

"I'd hide, too, if I was you. You li'l liar. I'd better never hear another word of this *trash*. Y'hear?" Nana glowered at Sheila's outline protruding from behind me. "Get her outta here, Sunny, 'fore I cut loose on 'er."

My heart turned icy as I grabbed my little sister and ushered her out the door and across the frozen back yard. Whether liar or victim — I had no way of knowing for certain — Sheila was my sibling.

What if she *was* telling the truth? I was perhaps the only one willing to give her the benefit of a doubt. 'Course, I knew I could count on Daniel.

I also knew it was left up to me to protect her.

~~~~~

"Hey." Daniel's strong hands gently steadied me. Concern painted his features. "What's goin' on?"

I burrowed my face into his chest, breathing comfort and calm from him. Sheila and I had collided with him in the alley as we rushed home

I quietly relayed the story to him, there with my cheek pressed to his down-filled bomber jacket, inhaling his male scent mingled with soap and wintry air, feeling his muscles tauten as rage built in him. When I'd finished, I lifted my head to gauge his reaction. His eyes blazed like simmering coals, so dilated were his pupils, and, in a voice whispery furious, he asked, "Would you like for me to go beat the hell out of 'im? Cause that's what he's full of. "

"*Nonono* — see, Nana doesn't *believe* Sheila. It would only make things worse."

"But —"

"*Heavens, no!* Look, Daniel — look, I have to live with Nana."

He deliberately reined in his temper and took a deep, steadying breath, looking at the sky as if he wanted to pummel it. Of all people, Daniel understood my helplessness at not being able to fight back.

"Hey, sugar, " his finger captured Sheila's wobbly chin, "let me know if he ever lays his filthy hands on you again. Y'hear?"

Sheila nodded, her features pathetically grateful. Daniel gazed into my eyes. "See you later, doll." He gave me that slow grin of his and planted a quick, solid kiss on my lips, leaving behind his signature of strength and goodness and unconditional love as he loped off toward home.

Home. Entering my own front door, I wanted to pull in her warm walls to embrace me, to shield me and my siblings from all the harshness out there in the world. A world that propelled my little sister to fabricate and embellish, that blasted Francine from one adrenaline rush to another, that altered Timmy's demeanor to that of an old man who carried on his small shoulders the weight of generations.

A world in which men's lusting eyes raked my flesh, that turned me into my mother, that made me squirm with shame and an overwhelming urge to run away and hide forever.

The warped little Christmas tree Francine, Timmy, Sheila, Daniel and I had found in the woods, chopped down, and decorated with Mama's box of ornaments, drew my gaze and I found myself calming before its simple rustic beauty and symbolism. I inhaled its pungent pine fragrance. Yuletide visions from years gone by, ones mingled with both joy and pain, assailed me. I opened my eyes. *I've got to start celebrating the good rather than grieving the lost.*

I would see Daddy briefly when he came bearing us gifts. I would cling to that.

I hugged Sheila to me, willing comfort to spill from these walls. Fortification. *Please God, help us.* I felt a warm touch. Just that. And the room suddenly felt...

Like home again. I sagged with relief.

Daddy would come soon. For now, that was enough.

Chapter Four

While Tack Turner's worship of Francine was earthy and sensual, Daniel's esteem for me held almost a holy hush. His restraint, so binding of his emotions, carried over into our courtship enticements.

Nana liked Daniel. She trusted him and that made me happy. He earned her trust, actually, because Nana had this sixth-sense about innocence and integrity. Like Gladys, she seemed to *know*.

"It's up t'the girl to say no," Nana steadfastly contended. Not that she ever provided me a birds-and-bees education. *Shoot no*. Her only concession to such talk was disdain for any female "hot tail" who "rolled over on her back."

Such was my view of sex. So, I was extra careful to shut down those appalling urges. And if Nana's opinion of females was less than charitable, her contempt for the male of the species was merciless.

"A man don't think with the head on his shoulders but the one in his pants," she disparaged when on the subject of Grandpa Dexter.

And each time, I'd think it's true: Hell hath no fury like a woman scorned.

~~~~~

Walter occasionally loaned Daniel his car for short evening outings. Our secluded dates laid plowed-ground for temptation. We'd drive to the Super Grill on Highway 290, and park in the copse of trees behind the concession bar, a cement-block structure shaped like a giant milk shake.

For a long, long time, Daniel and I both practiced restraint when alone.

Then, in my seventeenth year, something happened that shook my faith in myself.

One night, parked in our favorite dark spot behind the Super Grill, Daniel kissed me more passionately than usual. My skin tingled as he moved his hand up my back , then around to cup my chin as his lips softly plundered mine. When the kiss deepened and our tongues tangled, my senses went crazy. Desire exploded in me like a raging bonfire

As usual, Daniel kept tight rein on his urges. I was shocked as mine loped ahead, embarrassing, *condemning* me as I squirmed beneath him, arching myself at him like a she dog in heat, my breath coming in short spurts, punctuated by keening animal noises as my hands clutched at his hips, pulling him in to me with the force of a bulldozer. That burning inside me took over.

I was no longer me.

"Sunny," he rasped, slowly disentangling, wriggling loose, gazing into my face with tortured eyes, his breathing as labored as mine. *"Sunny."* And I realized I still moaned and strained toward him.

"We *can't*, honey." His hands, gentle yet firm, stayed me. How he garnered the strength to stop, I'll never know because even now, years later, I'm convinced he wanted me as desperately as I wanted him.

I scrambled upright, scooted to my corner, and covered my face to hide my frustration and shame. Nana hadn't told me a girl could get carried away. I *frightened* myself in that moment. *How could I act so disgracefully?*

Is this how Mama feels? Ohgodohgod.

His arms came around me and his lips kissed my temples, my cheeks, then the palm of my hand that he turned ever so gently to his own cheek. "I love you so, Sunny." His words were a hoarse whisper.

"I know. I'm so sorry, Daniel." I shrugged elaborately, still buzzing from shock and self-contempt and passion. "Maybe I *am* like Mama. Maybe —"

"*No.*" Daniel's voice turned harsh as his fingers covered my lips. "You are *not* like your mama. Or mine. You're my sweet Sunny — good through and through." He took my face tenderly between his big, gentle hands and turned it up to his. "Sunny, it means so much to me — you, *us* being the first with each other and all — getting a fresh clean start in marriage." His lips touched mine, as soft as baby's breath. Then his eyes darkened. "It's too important for us to let a moment's craziness drag us down to the level of our no-account mothers."

The fierce note in his voice caused my breath to hitch. "You don't think I'm —"

He pulled me to him, almost roughly, turning my face into the hollow of his neck. "I think you're the sweetest, *purest* girl in the world. That's why I love you so."

I closed my eyes, inhaled his wonderful Aqua Velva fragrance, relaxed and felt my world turn right side up again.

Nearly thirty years would pass before I figured out that my estrogen had, that night, simply caught up with me.

~~~~~

The next day, I lit out across the village on foot to deliver a dress I'd sewn for Thelma Bond. She was Ruthie's mama and grandma to little Sally, the village's illegitimate child. As I set out the sky suddenly grew overcast.

Uh oh. Huge April showers in the making. I'd crossed the river bridge when a clap of thunder parted the skies and rain began pelting me. I figured I was as near Thelma's as I was to home so I commenced running, holding my small handbag over my head in a ridiculously vain attempt to ward off some of the deluge. I clutched the plastic garment bag under my arm, hoping Thelma's new dress wouldn't get soaked.

The blast of a horn halted and swiveled me about to squint curiously as the village ice truck rumbled up alongside me, tires screeching to a halt. "*Daniel!*" I quickly opened the door and scrambled up into the passenger seat, dripping wet, rolled up jeans and blouse plastered to me.

"Gosh! I'm glad —" My words died. "Mr. Melton — I thought you were Daniel."

"Daniel's working in the ice house part of the afternoon. Where you headed in this downpour?" He pulled away from the curb and up the road running parallel to the river.

"Uh, Thelma Bond's house. I appreciate the ride, Mr. Melton."

"You're welcome, Sunny. I hope you don't mind me making a couple of ice drop-offs along the way."

"Not at all." I relaxed, glad Mr. Melton had come along. I didn't know him all that well, except to occasionally see him at Emaline's house. But I liked him and found him easy to talk to. It was raining so hard I couldn't see out the windshield during the stop at the Cantrell's house. I tugged at my soaked blouse, hoping it didn't show too much. Though not nearly as lush as Francine's, they weren't flat anymore.

I thought of how lucky Emaline was to have a nice grandpa. At that moment, I'd have given almost anything for a caring grandfather.

"Sorry," he muttered as he hopped back in the driver's seat, rain sliding off his yellow slicker. He was white-haired, like Nana, but I could tell he'd once been a nice-looking man, with his lanky build and pleasant smile. His hands, I noticed, showed his years with their heavy veins and age spots. I thought how old age is unfair.

"One more stop before Ruth's house."

I stared at him a moment, wondering at his alluding to it being *Ruth's* house. Then I shrugged and asked about his wife. He and his wife attended Tucapau Baptist Church quite regularly, according to Emaline. I didn't notice that we'd turned off the road into the secluded wooded stretch of river shore until we suddenly rocked to a stop.

"Wh-what's wrong?" I asked, peering through the rain, freezing at the sight of the rushing river, now muddied from the fresh downpour. My breath hitched painfully and I felt as though I were sinking in its murky depths. Something felt terribly wrong.

"Mr. Melton —"

In the next heartbeat, his hands were all over me, groping, probing, squeezing. I froze for several heartbeats, in shock. *Emaline's grandpa! Ohgodohgodohgod!*

I heard an endless, blood-curdling scream. *"Sto-o-op!"* From nightmare murkiness, I recognized it as my voice. I cut loose clawing and scratching and shoving him away with all my might. I was bawling, crying my heart out and plastering myself to the corner farthest from him. *"Please, stop!"* I sobbed, holding my hands out as a shield, "How *could* you? Emaline a-adores you! She thinks you're the b-best grandpa in the whole world!" *How wrong she is. Poor Emaline.*

At Emaline's name, the old man froze for a long moment, then slumped back against the door. "You're just so — *enticing*, Sunny. Your laugh and your smile make a man feel—." He frowned, then blinked as if dispelling a mist. " I suppose a girl *can* make up her mind to be nice, against all odds —" he said hoarsely, *incredulously*, swiping his weathered hand across dazed eyes.

I snuffled and glared at him. "Why did you think I wasn't?" I'd never given him any reason to think otherwise.

Or had I? Apprehension paralyzed me for that long moment before he spoke.

"What with you bein' friends with Ruth Bond and all. And your sister. And your Mama …." He shook his head and looked unseeing out into the rain, grasping the steering wheel so hard his body trembled.

Anger turned everything red in that moment. It shot out my fingers, my toes, and flared out my mouth and nose."*I'm…not…my…maa-maaaaa!*" I shrieked until my breath ran out, then burst into fresh sobs. "*I-I'm not!*" My fists clenched as my head moved from side to side. "*I'm not,*" I finished in a hoarse whisper, snuffling like a year-old.

He reached out to pat me but withdrew his hand when I shrank away. " Don't, Sunny," he said quietly, cranked the truck and drove to the Bond dwelling. There, I wrenched open the door and jumped out.

"Sunny?"

I turned to look at him, on the verge of retching to hear my name spill from his disgusting mouth. "You ain't gonna tell Emaline, are you?" His voice quavered with desperation and I saw his hands tremble. I didn't feel sympathy for him. Only repulsion.

I felt faint and fluttery, icy with outrage and principle.

"No." My reply was flat. "You see — I couldn't stand to see her hurt."

I slammed the door and didn't look back as the truck swiftly rumbled away.

~~~~~

Miraculously, the new dress wasn't wet. My hands still trembled as I placed it on the kitchen table while Ruthie Bond poured us coffee. I'd whiffed the inimitable aroma of rich coffee upon entering the sparkling clean Bond house.

The linoleum rug gleamed and smelled of Johnson's Wax. In the living room, little Sally sat on the floor, playing with empty thread spools I'd just given her. Using Sheila's half-used-up water paint set Daddy had given her for Christmas, I'd shaded them different colors.

Ruth reminded me of Eva Marie Saint, the leading lady in the new movie, "On the Waterfront." Sandy-colored, shoulder-length hair curled under in a neat pageboy. Her face, nearly devoid of makeup, transformed when she smiled shyly from one demure and unassuming to one warm and approachable. She was slight in stature, and her walk was graceful and purposeful.

If Ruth had noticed my shaken, tearful appearance when I arrived, she hadn't let on. Of course, with it raining buckets and me drenched I don't suppose tear-streaks were that evident. Her mama was off visiting relatives across the village this afternoon.

Ruth set steaming cups on the glass-topped coffee table and motioned me to sit on the sofa facing her. Her obvious loneliness pulled at my heart. Despite her notoriety, she was known as being tight-lipped about herself. So when she began to talk up a blue streak I was touched.

"Sally's already talkin' like a five-year-old," she stated with obvious pride. The three-year-old, playing near my feet, looked up at me and I saw the crystal blue of Harly Kale's eyes, yet these were innocent and sweet. I smiled at her and was rewarded by a full, dimpled grin and a red spool she held up to share with me.

"Thank you," I said, taking it from her chubby fingers, my eyes inexplicably moist.

"You welcome," she said clearly. Startled, I began to laugh.

"She really is bright," I said. "You're blessed." The expectancy of someday having Daniel's child lay nestled inside me.

Ruth looked thoughtful before answering. "At one time, I didn't think so."

How thoughtless of me to bring it up. "You don't have to talk about —"

"No," Ruth shook her head, "I want to. I've kept it in too long as it is. And I know you won't talk. Most folks round here do. You see," she dropped her voice to a whisper so Sally wouldn't hear, "Harly raped me."

I gasped. "Ruth —"

She nodded solemnly. "It was when I went visiting my Uncle Clarence. Him and Harly are drinking buddies, y'know? Well, Uncle Clarence had gone somewhere and left Harly there to sleep off a drunk. I happened in and —"

"My Lord, Ruth. Why didn't you tell somebody?"

"I thought at first if I didn't say anything, nobody would ever know. And by the time I realized — you know, I was already —" she was trying not to distract Sally from her play. "Harly was all apologies and all. Uncle Clarence knew.

He'd come in just as I was crawling from the bed and tore through the house looking for his shotgun. Harly begged Uncle Clarence not to shoot 'im. Bein' his buddy and all, Uncle Clarence didn't have the heart to follow through." She sighed and fidgeted with a piece of stray thread. "Harly *was* drunk and didn't really know what —"

"Hogwash! He *did* so know what he was doing. Folks should have been told that he — well, that he violated you. At least that way you wouldn't —"

"That way," Ruth lowered her voice again, "my daughter would know she was a product of darkness…well, you know. I just couldn't do that to 'er, Sunny."

"Still…you shouldn't have to carry such a stigma of something over which you had no control."

"Well," Ruth shook her head sadly, resigned, "the harm was done. I thought the world had ended." She lowered her voice again, "To make matters worse, Uncle Charlie runs his mouth when he's drinking. Let it out that Harly was the one who —" She shrugged. "You and ever'body on the hill knows what I did…the river and all." She dropped her head, shamed.

'What did you do, Mama?" piped Sally, whose astute, curious blue eyes remained trained on her hands stacking the spools.

Ruth looked startled, then laughed. "You lil' bugger. All ears."

Despite the morbid topic, I, too, burst into laughter,

I scooped the girl into my arms and gooched her good, pitching her into spasms of giggles.

"Who plays?" I gestured toward an old upright piano in the living room corner.

"Me," Ruth said, blushing slightly. "Grandma Bond taught me some and the rest, I learnt myself." Amazing.

She'd had to drop out of school at fifteen, when she got pregnant. "It give me somethin' to do the past four years b'sides just sittin' and twiddling my thumbs and trying to avoid people staring at me and whisperin'an' all."

"I'm sorry, Ruth, that you had to go through all that. It's not fair." I sighed and looked down into Sally's upturned face. She was trying to read our angst. "And don't ask me what's not fair, Miss Sally," I gooched her again, garnering more rolling belly laughs.

"Play something for me," I gushed, thrilled at this other dimension of Ruth, glad there was more to her than gossip speculated. "Please?" I shifted Sally into a comfortable slouch across my lap as Ruth hesitantly settled herself on the scarred mahogany bench.

For the next twenty minutes Ruth Bond's fingers flew over those ivories making tunes I'd heard on the radio; *Dancing in the Dark*, *Sunny Side of the Street*, *Pennies from Heaven* — misting my eyes with memories of Mama singing. Then she swung into Boogie Woogie as easily as Esther Williams diving off a high dive board. *In the Mood* had me on my feet dancing with Sally in my arms, shrieking with glee. The last song Ruth played was a mellow rendition of Red Foley's *Peace in the Valley*, which, again, had my eyes teary. With her, for some reason, probably because of her own openness, I didn't mind *feeling*.

"Thank you, Ruth," I hugged her profusely when she arose from the aged, dignified instrument. "You need to do something with your talent. You read music?"

"Jus' a little. I know the key a song's wrote in and the notes and all but — I can listen to a tune and play it better'n trying to read it, if that makes sense." She blushed to her sandy roots, camouflaging, for a moment, her scattering of light freckles.

"That's — incredible." I was impressed beyond measure. "Thanks again, y'hear? I don't want this to be the last concert you play for me."

This time, when I hugged her, she hugged back and I sensed Ruth had had as much fun entertaining as I'd had listening. Lo and behold, for a time, she'd made me forget the horrible episode with Emaline's grandpa.

Her mama returned shortly, gave me my share of material and paid me a handsome tip to boot. Ruth and I exchanged warm good-byes.

And, sadly, I knew that socializing like this today was a rare thing for her. I felt a strange sense that I was abandoning her in her exile.

~~~~~

Outside, the rain had stopped and the earth smelled washed-clean. Sunlight filtered through dispersing clouds, warming me as I walked home. I felt better, having talked to Ruth. She didn't seem as tragic up close. Yet I knew many wouldn't agree with me. And that beautiful little girl. It was *unconscionable* that folks held her accountable for Harly's evil.

The ice truck rumbled onto Maple Street as I turned the corner there. I picked up my stride, head down. When the tires screeched to a halt, my pulse skipped into a frantic cadence as I prepared to turn tail and make a dash for home.

"Hey, gorgeous!" Daniel called, hooking his elbow over the window ledge. I took a deep steadying breath and walked over to the truck.

"Sunny?" His smile dissolved. "You look like you seen a ghost. Anything wrong?"

I opened my mouth to spill my guts about Bill Melton groping me and making me feel like trash...but the words wouldn't come. Daniel would — well, he'd go ape. And Emaline — I couldn't destroy her belief in her grandpa. She would surely find out and be devastated. It would end our friendship.

It hurt to learn that I no longer trusted unconditional love.

"No. Nothing's wrong. Just a long afternoon."

Some things are more important than spilling your guts.

~~~~~

The crisis came on suddenly, with the velocity of two planets ramming each other and exploding. Emaline crashed through my door, sobbing that her mama, Renie, had taken 'bad off' and was in the hospital. The three of us, Daniel, Emaline, and I immediately dashed off to Gladys' house for consolation and prayer.

Gladys' aura of peace and tranquility sang out to me in those moments it took to span our back yard, the dirt alley, their back lawn and screened-in porch. There is, I'm convinced, a mystical, inexplicable sense of family between villagers.

"Gladys!" I called out.

She appeared in the kitchen doorway, dark eyes keenly assessing our tear-stained features. Her face instantly gentled. "My, this is bad, ain't it?" She pulled us inside, taking us each by the arm and into her embrace. Over our shoulder, she gently told Daniel, "Pull out a chair for the girls, handsome boy."

"M-Mama's bad off," Emaline sobbed. "In Spartanburg General. A blood clot...only a fifty-fifty chance...." More sobs.

For twenty minutes Emaline poured out her heart, her fears, and her hopes. Gladys sat silently, listening as no one else I know listens. With her heart and soul. No distractions of self-serving thoughts. One-hundred-ten percent *there*.

When Emaline finished, her tears abated, her emotions spent for a spell, only then did Gladys lean forward, elbows on kitchen table, to reach and take our hands in hers. She commenced praying, not the hollering, desperate demands I've heard from some but with a calm serenity seasoned with unwavering faith. Mostly, she asked God to take care of Emaline and Polly. And their daddy. She did ask Him to be with the doctors at the hospital and comfort Renie with His presence. I kept waiting on her to ask God to *heal* Renie. "Amen," she said. *Maybe she just forgot,* I thought.

Anyway, Emaline and I both hung onto God's hem during the next thirty-six hours.

But despite all our prayers, Renie died that night.

~~~~~

After they brought Renie's pitiful little wasted body home for the wake, I never left Emaline's side. In true mill hill spirit, folks descended to care for the bereaved family and friends. There, death is as much a part of existence as life. In an inexplicable way, nurturing absorbed a bit of tragedy's sting.

Daniel saw to our every need, hovering in the sweetest, non-intrusive way. Neighbors came and went with food and consoling words. Nana, to whom words did not easily come, came bearing a chocolate cake, a truly sacrificial love offering. The cost would set her back nearly a week. Relatives ascended in waves, reaching out to Jack and the girls but it was me upon whom Emaline leaned in those dark hours. Gladys wafted in and out with soft words and hugs and a huge Banana Pudding.

Strange, she hadn't seemed really shocked at Renie's passing. How had she known? She was one of a handful of people I've met in life with that extra sense of *knowing*. I don't believe it is presumption. Not in Gladys' case, anyway. It goes deeper and I completely respect its veracity.

Walter came by, handsome and quite comforting. Doretha appeared, alone, and offered her soft-spoken solace. Even Francine and Tack dropped by for a short spell. I silently thanked the good Lord because there were few things Francine truly reverenced. Timmy stayed close by during those hours, quietly, unobtrusively, but I felt his presence. Daniel included him in his protective circle. Sheila hung closely with Polly. I was proud of her.

Daniel, well, he was a tower of strength for us all, defiantly sticking close those days, to the point of neglecting his duties at the Stone residence. Yeh, he still had them *plus* his ice house job. I admired his courage, praying he wouldn't face too much verbal retribution. Though Tom didn't physically abuse him anymore, according to Doretha, "He's still got a filthy mouth."

"Isn't she beautiful?" I murmured, gazing at Renie, who, in death, looked like a sleeping movie star in her silk baby-blue gown.

Emaline wept softly beside me. Our arms entwined each other's waists. Daniel and Doretha had gone home moments earlier. "Tonight's special," Emaline whispered. "Our last time with her."

We burst into tears at the finality of it. We spent that entire night bunked down on the couch near the casket, gazing at the sweet profile framed with lustrous brown hair and I thought how ironic that hair lived on after flesh died.

~~~~~

The Pentecostal church was packed out for the funeral. I sat with the family, with Daniel next to me. The pastor related how he'd visited Renie at the hospital and prayed the sinner's prayer with her during a lucid moment.

Emaline and I had burst into grateful tears at this news and Gladys, sitting in the pew behind us, reached up to gently squeeze our shoulders. Daniel's fingers intertwined with and squeezed mine.

We filed out to the song I Won't Have to Cross Jordan Alone.

That's when I saw him. *Daddy.*

He stood in the church parking lot, where everybody dispersed to their cars to drive to the nearby cemetery for Renie's burial.

I rushed to him, Emaline attached to one elbow, Daniel to the other. "Daddy!" We were in each other's arms. "You made it in time for the funeral." I stepped back and looked up into his saddened face. "Who — how did you find out about Renie?"

"I didn't — not till I got to Nana's. She told me and I rushed on over." Nana had opted not to come. Too sad, she said.

I stared at Daddy, fear gathering in my gut. "Then — why did you...."

"I came to get you kids. I got a job." He smiled softly at me. "We're going to Chicago."

~~~~~

The next afternoon, I stuck my head in the Kale's back door and called out. "Gladys? You home?" My voice was scratchy from crying and pleading with Daddy to leave me behind. He'd refused, saying it wasn't fair to Nana, that we were his responsibility, not hers. *Funny,* I thought resentfully, *he hasn't worried about that for all this time.*

I wanted to bid Gladys a private goodbye. Too, I wanted her to pray for a miracle, that somehow I could stay. Today, what with Renie's death and all, and us leaving for Chicago, Nana seemed overly protective. Daddy was at the garage getting his old Ford serviced for the long drive up North. Nana had wanted all of us to accompany her to Uncle Charlie's. Francine had pulled me aside and threatened to strangle me if I didn't insist on staying home, so she could. I'd discreetly warned Sheila to stick to Nana's side, away from Uncle Charlie.

Soon as Nana disappeared down the street, Francine did her disappearing act. To the hotel, I suspected, to say goodbye to Daisy and Leona, Mama's old buddy. Too, it wasn't in Francine to miss this last chance to flirt with the men boarders who congregated in big porch rockers or in the lobby with its chintz settees and easy chairs. Her maid duties — on this, her last day — had ended at three-thirty so this was free, fun time. I'd gone with her on other days. Today, I'd rather be with Gladys.

"Gladys!" I called again, taking a few steps into her kitchen, closing the door behind me. "Where are you?"

"Boo!" Harly appeared around the doorway so quickly that I jumped. "Come on in, purdy girl." His blue eyes sparkled with mischief. "Pure meanness," was Gladys' spin on his devilish black patent-leather hair and near colorless blue-gray eyes that showcased black, black irises.

"Oh, ahh…" I backed up till my spine touched the back door, "I-is Gladys home?" I already knew the answer. How *stupid* of me. My fingers groped behind me for the door knob.

"No." Grin firmly in place, he spanned the distance in a breath, standing nearly toe to toe with me. A chill rippled over me as I gazed into a purely wicked countenance, one that, years later, I compared to the malevolent Henry Fonda character in the movie, *Once Upon A Time in the West.*

"But *I'm* here," he said, his hairy long arms slithering around me. The odors of his sweat, greasy hair tonic, and liquor hit me so strongly I nearly gagged. Terror seized me. I could see tiny opaque specks in his irises and the pores on his oily nose.

"Harly raped me." Ruth's words echoed and beat about in my brain.

Reaction set in. "Let me go," I screeched, twisting away to wrench open the door.

Hands snared me. "Where y' goin' in such a hurry? Huh? You're purdy like your mama, girl. And so *soft.* Why ain't you friendly like her? Huh? " His voice slithered over me like slime let loose, taunting, laughing, his hands snaring, pulling, pulling me against him. I retched as he groped my breasts — then ducked quickly, sliding through the door like a snake startled from its nest.

I lickety-split across the back yard and shot through the alley to our house, his wild, wicked laughter trailing me like smoke from a bonfire.

"You're purdy as your mama, little girl…."

Shame crashed over me in tidal waves.

And with it, anger. At Mama's wantonness. At Harly's depravity. I slammed through our front door, raced up the stairs, and threw myself across the bed and squalled out my horror and grief. That horrible man actually compared me to Mama.

He thought I was like Mama. Oh God, oh God.

I'm not like Mama. I'm not, I'm not, I'm not!

~~~~~

Gladys had warned me. I didn't tell Daniel about Harly, certain my own stupidity had caused the whole mess. I should have knocked and not entered Gladys' door before knowing she was there. Too, I didn't want Daniel involved because Gladys was still my friend and any kind of obnoxious confrontation between Daniel and Harly would affect that relationship. Gladys didn't need any more hurt over that crazy man.

Anyway, the looming specter of Chicago quickly pushed the ugly thing into the black hole in which it belonged. I don't know who was most distraught; Daniel, Emaline, or me.

"What am I gonna *do*, Sunny?" Emaline howled, tears trailing down her pale cheeks as she helped me pack my meager wardrobe, one that'd dwindled greatly with Mama's absence, in spite of my seamstress efforts. I'd had a growing spurt and many of my hemlines couldn't be let out to accommodate an extra inch and a half of height. I passed them on to Emaline, who, at five-feet-three inches was now two inches shorter than me.

"All our mamas are gone," Emaline said sadly, stuffing my mated socks into a corner of my small, scarred suitcase.

"Only thing," Daniel drawled, not unkindly, "your mama didn't have a choice. Ours did."

Daniel sprawled on Timmy's bed, his hooded eyes stalking me. He'd ignored Tom Taylor's wrathful tirades several times in the last two days to be near me. In private, sitting on my back door stoop, he'd oscillated between silent brooding and hawkish vigilance. Seemed he didn't miss a single move I made nor a single comment.

"Whatta you mean, you might not ever come back?" he asked that evening, after the packing was done and Emaline had gone home. We sat on the back door stoop, bundled in sweaters and exhaling November vapor into the night. Daniel held my hand, his index gently examining each finger, his voice low and dead.

"It was just a statement — you know, like I'll die if I don't ever get to come back."

His thick lashes lifted then, revealing turquoise irises lackluster with sadness. "Your Nana'll be here. Surely you'll come visit her."

"I guess. I mean — I know we will. Just don't know *when.*" I sighed and squeezed his hand, wanting to console him yet angry that life was being so *mean.* "Daniel, you know how much I hate to leave. Everything that means anything to me is *here.* This here mill hill just wraps around me like a big ol' blanket, makin' me warm and — safe. Chicago's like — *Mars.* Leavin' here's like — *dying.*"

He half arose and reached to slide his hand into his jean's pocket, then pulled out a little rolled up paper bag. "I want to give you something." He extracted a small box and handed it to me, resettling beside me. I slowly opened it, my vision suddenly blurred with tears. In it was a ring, the diamond was miniscule but it was an *engagement ring, by golly.*

His face was as grave as I'd ever seen it. "Someday," he said quietly, slipping it on my finger, "I'll buy you one you deserve."

"Oh, Daniel," I sputtered, misting up, laughing richly, "I-it's *beautiful.*" Anything from Daniel was beautiful. "It's only for a year or two. Somehow, we'll be married when I finish school. I'll move back and we'll both go to Clemson College, as planned."

"Why don't you stay with Nana?" he asked, not even trying to conceal the desperation in his eyes, those wonderful, *brave* eyes.

I sighed painfully. "I asked Nana and she said, 'your place is with your Daddy now, Sunny.'" It had hurt me dreadfully, her rejection. But I understood her need to disentangle from so much responsibility. "Didn't leave any room for argument." His broad shoulders seemed to slump even more.

I hugged him. "I need to leave something for you to remember me by."

He gazed at me for a long moment, his green eyes aglimmer with emotion. "I don't need anything. I have you," he laid a callused hand over his chest, " right here."

I swallowed back tears, trying to be strong for him. "We'll write, Daniel. Regular."

He nodded, slowly, his eyes roaming my features as though photographing each detail. "I'm counting on that, Sunny."

~~~~~

It hit me like a bolt of lightning the next morning as we Acklins packed the car and prepared to depart: *I'm leaving home.* And *Renie's dead.* I caved in. Not *Renie. Sweet, sweet Renie with kind eyes and soft words.*

It was like losing Mama all over except Renie cared. Turning Emaline and me loose in her kitchen to bake and mess up…letting me help Emaline with chores for matinee movie money…huggin' and lovin' on me. She was more mother than my own. Shock coursed through me at the realization. I sank down on the bottom front doorstep as Daddy and my siblings passed with mismatched, scarred luggage, head on knees, and gave way, my grief blending with the cacophony of leave taking sounds.

Then, I felt strong hands tugging at me, pulling me upward. I lifted my head and peered into Daniel's pain-glazed eyes. He pulled me to him. Another tug on my blouse. It was Emaline. Daniel opened his arms wide to pull Emaline into our circle of love. Then closed them around us both . Emaline moaned,

"What am I gonna do, Sunny?" Emaline moaned. " My mama's gone. And now you —"

I had no answer. The three of us stood there, arms wrapped around each other. It was too, too much to bear.

~~~~~

"Shut up that *whining*, Sheila," Daddy roared from the front seat of our old rust-brown Ford as we crossed the North Carolina State line. Yep, Daddy still drove that old car. He was a good mechanic and somehow kept it a'running. We'd been on the road three hours already and at one-thirty everybody grated on each other's nerves.

"I-I don't w-want to leave Polly," Sheila wailed, echoing what I felt inside.

"You already *have, beetle-brain*," Francine rasped from the back seat corner, rousing from her nap to glare bleary-eyed at Sheila. "Case you hadn't *noticed.*"

Of all of us, Francine alone was excited about moving to Chicago. She'd dropped her job like a red-hot poker and was packed before you could say 'boo,' totally insensible to Tack Turner's devastation. Timmy was — well, Timmy was okay as long as I was okay. So I tried to act nonchalant once on the road while my insides twisted and roiled at life's cruelty.

Lordy, Emaline and I had cried buckets and pleaded with Daddy to leave me behind to stay with her but he refused. In the end, we'd embraced and vowed to write twice a week. How my heart bled for my best friend in her grief. My grief, too. I already missed Renie dreadfully. At least, together, Emaline and I had each bolstered the other. Separated, the sorrow was much keener.

Nana had been peculiarly affectionate at our leave-taking, not hugging but making us promise, "Now, ya'll take care of each other. Y'hear?"

Seeing what appeared to be tears in her eyes, as we pulled off with our bags and old suitcases stuffed in every nook and cranny, did little to reassure me about this change of worlds.

Daniel hadn't come to see me off. We'd decided to say goodbye last night. He'd gently kissed me on the lips and held me for a long, long time. And I knew.

Daniel didn't want anybody to see him cry.

I'd looked back as we drove away and glimpsed him at his upstairs bedroom window. Our gazes locked in that heartbeat and my fingers instinctively moved to cup my ringed finger. I'd insisted on giving him a lock of my hair. He'd solemnly put it in his wallet, taped to the back of my picture. Seeing my gesture from his window, his lips had curved, ever so slowly into a bittersweet smile…. My throat knotted at the memory.

Daddy said very little during all this time on the road, except to issue reprimands to Sheila. He seemed to have lots on his mind. I suspected it had to do with the fact that seeing us again reminded him more of Mama. But then, seeing him did us the same way.

Sheila's whimpering and crankiness revved up again half way across North Carolina. Suddenly, the car screeched to a stop, barely swerving to a curb and out of the path of traffic.

Francine, limp with slumber, flew from her seat into the floor, as did Timmy. I sat in the front beside Daddy, so I collided with the dashboard, barely escaping injury when my palms quickly cushioned the impact.

Daddy pivoted about sharply and reached over the seat to haul Sheila from where she'd been thrown against the back of the passenger seat to where their noses nearly met. "Shut the *hell* up," he ordered in a voice I barely recognized as his. "I've put up with your sniveling long enough."

His glare dissolved Sheila's grief into a hysterical hiccup. Snuffling and gulping back her sobs, she peered glassy-eyed at him and I realized in that moment what moving had cost her. Dear *God*, she had so little.

Daddy seemed geared to continue ranting but instead released her, threw up his hands and turned away, muttering as he cranked the engine, "Why the hell am I fighting to keep you?" Then, he muttered through clenched teeth, "You're not even *mine.*"

I couldn't bring myself to turn and look at Sheila, who shrank into the backseat corner. The viciousness of it was too much to handle.

If Daddy realized the impact of his words on Sheila or the rest of us, he didn't let on.

I remember thinking Mama's reduced his existence to one not only lacking direction, but wisdom as well.

Years later, before her death, Nana would reveal the irony of that statement. Mama's goodbye note had revealed her bitterness that Daddy, on their first night together upon his homecoming from the war, had betrayed his promise to never again mention Ruby's unfaithfulness, one that resulted in Sheila's conception.

Of course, Mama was good at rationalization. That she already carried on a hot, steamy affair with the doctor was beside the point. That she lied through her teeth every day of her life meant nothing, as did her abandoning Sheila to Daddy's care, knowing she was not his. What did matter, in her self-absorbed mind, was that Daddy broke a promise.

Hah!

And so, nobody repeated those hateful words. We seemed to accept that if we ignored them, they would go away.

"…you're not even mine."

Chapter Five

Oil. The fragrance of Chicago.

Everything was strange, from the color of dirt, what little I saw, to the smell of the atmosphere.

Riding through downtown Chicago, I had my first experience with claustrophobia, certain I was going to die of suffocation. Tall buildings blocked out the sky. I had to look straight up to see blue and the air tasted like petroleum.

On Thanksgiving Day, we moved in with Aunt Dottie. Thus began my year in purgatory, one that passed in a blur. The apartment building, held up by flanking twin apartment structures, faced a mental asylum whose spear-tipped black fence bore portent of my odyssey there…the smell of baked turkey assailing us as we hauled beat-up suitcases up the stairs…both Daddy's sisters, dark and exotic as plump Spanish flamenco dancers, working as cocktail waitresses at the same lounge, The Top Hat, Daddy's new drop-by-after-work hangout…Daddy's absence freeing Francine and Cousin Brandy to streets, men, and deadly cigarette indulgence…. Aunt Dottie's giving token resistance to the girls' cigarette habit but since she herself emptied two packs a day, her objections were sounding brass…Daddy's seeming unawareness of Francine's shenanigans….

Looking back, I suspect he'd simply given up on her. I figure that decision saved him a lot of frustration and heartache. I know Tack Turner sent her money because she never missed a lick buying cigarettes.

I vaguely remember the wonderful smells of that Thanksgiving — Aunt Dottie had knocked herself out with holiday preparations. Daddy's other sister, Elsie, and brother-in-law, Glenn, were there as well and they all talked and laughed about old times and how great it was being together again. My grief was such that I cannot recall a word they spoke. Yet amid it all, one memory remains till this day as clear as the peal of a church bell.

I could hardly wait till that first Thanksgiving dinner ended and I could politely excuse myself. I rushed to the large bedroom I shared with Francine, cousin Brandy, and Sheila. Timmy, cousin Eddie, and Daddy shared another room. Only Aunt Dottie had her own private space

I had two letters to write. One to Emaline. Dear, poor Emaline, whose anguish I could feel hundreds of miles away.

And Daniel. My fingers touched the ring. I knew how he'd worked and scrimped to buy it. That it represented our future together struck a deep, resonant chord in me. His beautiful callused hand, pressed to his heart and his husky, fervent, "I've got you — right here" rang and swelled in my soul like the *Alleluia Chorus.* I began to write.

"My dear Daniel, how I miss you!"

~~~~~

The following months' happenings run together in my head. As happens when one is miserable, I repressed much of it. Now, decades later, I recall it mostly in strobe-like

snatches...teachers' Yankee-dialect, at first like a foreign language...our drawled dialect even more baffling to
them...self-absorbed Francine back to high school, in new-
kid-on-the-block Paradise, ignoring Tack's letters till she
needed money...boys' eyes drinking her in...Timmy and
Cousin Eddie, both pretty tame sorts, bunking, riding bikes,
and playing checkers together while Sheila's new friend,
Lindi, who lived across the hall, included her in many of
her family activities, a wonderful, uplifting time for my little
sis.

Each letter from Daniel tugged my heart toward home.

~~~~~

Daddy met Rosalee Sanchez at the Top Hat. Things
quickly grew serious. For a Yankee girl, Rosalee was pretty
likeable. Only in her mid-twenties, she was short, bosomy,
and round. Not fat. Just fluffy. Nothing like as pretty as
Mama but then, not many could hold a candle to Mama's
good looks.

Yet — with exotic Spanish coloring and even features,
Rosalee wasn't bad looking. I took to her right away, seeing as how she drove back the sadness in Daddy's whiskey
brown eyes.

And I knew that, eventually, she would become his wife.
Two years later, my prophecy came to pass.

Francine didn't like her. But then, Francine didn't especially commit to liking anybody or anything. Except fun
and outlandish characters. Especially those with money.
Like Tack, whose daddy was a "boss man," as cotton mill
supervisors were called, and who were regarded as a type
of royalty. His clout earned Tack one of the higher paying
mill positions. So his gifts to Francine kept a'comin'.

~~~~~

Holidays came and went. Memories of Mama surfaced but I brutally shoved them away. I put on a good face. Inside, I was wretched. Being away from Daniel and Emaline and familiar sights and smells made me nearly crazy. I asked Daddy to take us to visit Nana but he said he couldn't afford it. I wanted to feel Daniel's arms around me so badly I often hid in my room and bawled.

Nana wrote occasionally, short terse messages entailing cursory bits of village news like Mama's playmate, Toy Narson, dying in a car wreck and Shirley Cox giving birth to twin girls. Out of wedlock. *At least little Sally's not alone anymore.* Yet, I knew they would wear the stigma for years to come. I thanked God it wasn't me.

Emaline wrote long detailed letters of both hope and despair as her grief ebbed and gushed through those long wintry months. Springtime saw a different flavor emerge from the pages of Hallmark stationery, (the Company Store's very best brand). A strawberry flavor. She began dating a boy named John Davidson and soon, rather than grief, I sensed romance in bloom. I was happy for her.

Daniel's letters came regularly. My heart did a funny little leap each time I saw the envelope addressed to me with his scrawly handwriting.

~~~~~

To divert my angst that following year, I focused on the North/South cultural differences into which I was thrust. Southern girls considered soft-spokenness right up there with lace on panties. Northern females valued volume.

And while a few Dixie chicks — like Mama — drank, most were discreet, considering anything otherwise unladylike. Northern women freely and openly imbibed. Raucous hen parties occurred weekly in homes, highlighted with drinking and hair-tinting, a process of foamy mixtures applied with toothbrushes.

I learned the proof and age of each bottle of liquor in Aunt Dottie's well-stocked pantry. Games. Those and school activities helped ease my homesickness.

During recess, I joined in a popular game called Rooster Fight. Beside tame southern competition, this one was quite aggressive. The rules were to draw a circle, in which two opponents balanced on one foot. Each draped their arms around themselves, like in a straight jacket. The idea was to bump each other out of the circle. Being competitive and agile, I couldn't resist the challenge. I won most every time. It made up, in a tiny way, for my deprivation of Daniel and Emaline.

It also vented my anger at being uprooted.

~~~~~

When Francine began coughing more than usual, we all attributed it to her heavy smoking. But when blood showed up in her spit, a big alarm went off.

Turned out Francine had tuberculosis.

She was quickly quarantined in Aunt Elsie's apartment, since there were no children there and she could have her own quarters. We weren't allowed to visit her at all, except for Daddy and Aunt Dottie, which compounded my depression. Tack Turner made three trips to Chicago in the coming months to see Francine, defying doctor's orders to visit her room. And Francine, being so lonely and all, was uncommonly grateful.

Looking back, I do believe Francine's greatest tribulation during that long health-bout was the aloneness, preceded only by the denial of cigarettes. She'd handled Nana's switchings much more gracefully than the nearly yearlong, smoke-free lock-up.

I finished my junior year in high school. Daniel sent pictures of himself in cap and gown, that big ol' grin of his stretching from ear to ear, warming me right down to my toes and drawing tears to my eyes. I hated so much missing his graduation. Finding a solitary moment in my room, I had a good old-fashioned crying spell. I felt deprived of Gladys' prayers more than ever in that moment.

I wrote him a poem for his graduation gift, following a solitary walk in a nearby park:

EARLY MORNING WONDER
Each lovely joy encountered today
Each sweet sound heard along the way
Down the trail to sense the sight
Back again 'neath gray sky bright.

Strange to me once again
Common 'cause its always been
To see, to sense, to hold, to know
You are everywhere I go.

You really are heart of my heart
You really are a living part
Of what I am and am to be.
I am no longer I-but I am we.

How I love you
I do not know
It is just good
To love you so.

Sunny

I was on my own. I prayed as I hadn't in years.

Lord, please get me home. Someway. I don't care how. I'm so unhappy here. If you do, I'll be ever so grateful. Amen.

~~~~~

Our father rarely mentioned Mama anymore. Looking back, I think we all methodically drove thoughts of her away, slowly but surely extinguishing her beauty from our lives, reprogramming ourselves to laugh and sing without her inspiration, denying that much of the luster and brilliance was gone.

That I could tune out hurts was a remarkable revelation to me, one that, more and more, I tapped into.

~~~~~

It happened so quickly, I still marvel. Aunt Elsie's friend, Bethany, a nurse who'd so faithfully helped out with Francine's care, suddenly moved to California. Panicked, Daddy sent Nana a telegram to come help out with Francine, knowing how alien such an uprooting gesture would be to her. Such was his desperation.

Courageously, Nana rode a bus, alone, to Chicago.

Nana lasted exactly two weeks.

"I'm a'going home. I don't like this big city life," she announced flatly to Daddy. Then coming to a decision, she squared her shoulders and declared, "and I'm taking the kids with me. I can nurse Francine there better'n I can here." Actually, the doctor had upgraded Francine's condition somewhat so that we could briefly visit her now. But she was on bed rest to regain her strength.

That was that. No sooner was it said than we were packed and Daddy was driving us to South Carolina. I couldn't believe it. Even without Gladys' backup, it was done.

My prayer was answered. *I was going home!*

Chapter Six

When we crossed the river bridge, my heart sang merrily at familiar landmarks. The village hummed with life as folks bustled about, jackets and sweaters trussing and warming, headed for the Company Store or to work, or simply hanging out, legs dangling from rock walls that lined Main Street. The occupied hotel rockers moved rhythmically and lazily under a warming afternoon sun. Some of the faces were new, some not. Many waved cheerfully at us as our old Ford ambled toward Maple Street

Sheila was antsy to see Polly, and Timmy, though sad to leave his cousin in Chicago, was just as eager to see Vince Kale, his pal.

Me — I nearly swooned just to be back. Butterflies flapped as I anticipated seeing Daniel. And Emaline. Only a brief, sorrowful instant jolted me when my brain processed Renie among those I'd come back to. Having been away had spared me the day to day readjustment to that loss. Now, it hit me head on.

We'd just arrived and were climbing stiffly from the car when Emaline came bounding across the yard and tackled me. We boo-hooed and hugged and carried on forever before helping tote all the baggage in. Then, we escaped to the back door stoop. We laughed at the tear-sodden mess we were.

"Lordy, Emaline, I never thought this red-dirt, hilly land could look so beautiful. And even with Lyman Plant's stinky dye let loose in the water at times, it smells better'n Chicago." We laughed uproariously

"Is Darrel Ploughman still calling you up saying, 'I gotta go flush the commode. Tucapau needs the water'?" I asked. Darrel lived in Lyman Mill village, which was up-river — as the crow flies — about three miles from Tucapau Mill. Lyman released their dye refuse into the river, sending it downstream. The stench, at its worst, was akin to rotten eggs.

"No, thank the good Lord. Not since I've been dating John." She balefully rolled her eyes. "I never could understand that joke's logic since it's *their* garbage that stinks up our water." Actually, the pong came sporadically, only after a dumping.

Fact was, Fairmont Mill village, downriver from Tucapau, got the worst of the stench since the chemicals, by the time it reached them, were *really* rotten.

"S'all in fun," I said, feeling magnanimous, even affectionate toward our neighboring classmates, experiencing an overwhelming appreciation of my own turf.

"Sorry I've not written as often lately." Emaline cut her watery eyes at me and cringed comically, as though expecting me to hit her.

"Well," I hiked my red nose up in the air, "you *ought* to be, you hussy."

We giggled outrageously until we ran out of steam, then just sat there in our sweaters — South Carolina's March climate being much milder than Chicago's — and simply basked in the old familiar solidarity. "So," I crossed my arms and ankles and plastered my back to the doorjamb, "tell me all about him."

Emaline, cheeks magenta with emotions, gushed, "we've been dating for six months now. Oh, and Daddy's got a girl-friend." She sighed and watched my reaction. It didn't seem right, somehow, replacing Renie but Emaline seemed not upset at the idea.

"Do you like her? Who is she?" My insides flailed about in protest.

"Mmm. Yeh. She's nice. Name's Doris. She and Daddy met in the mill. Lordy!" She wrinkled her nose cutely. "Every female on the hill's been matchmaking."

My insides began to settle down, seeing as how Emaline wasn't opposed to the idea of her daddy with another woman. I'd just have to adjust, in time.

Footsteps crunched around the corner of the house. My heart leaped as he approached us, hands shoved in jack-et pockets, tall and splendid in a new maturity. The face seemed more chiseled somehow, more angular. And had he always been that tall and *masculine?* A thrill shot through me.

"Hey, Sunny," he said as softly as a butterfly lighting.

"Lord have mercy, *Daniel,*" I whispered, feeling my eyes go wide. Then misty. I couldn't help but show my astonish-ment at how he'd changed. Didn't care that he saw.

"Oh." Emaline jumped to her feet, blushing furiously. "Ahhh — I'll be running along now and give you two time to…." She shrugged and disappeared in an eye's blink.

He stood there for long moments, those turquoise eyes probing deep, deep inside me, drawing feelings I'd never before felt. I realized I was holding my breath and let it out on a rush. I patted the step beside me, not trusting my limbs to hold me up and take me to him.

Wordlessly, he spanned the space and lowered himself beside me, his long legs easily stretching across three steps, with room to spare. His solidness, settled against me, felt so good and his fragrance, spicy and mannish, made my head spin. "You've grown a little," I teased breathlessly, scrooching up my shoulders, something wonderful flailing about inside me.

He grinned then, that slow lingering smile that engulfed and warmed me. And I felt Heaven burst over me. "Yeh. I guess I have." His gaze held mine, the blue-green shimmering like a thousand sun rays tossed over Silver Lake. "And you're even prettier."

I felt my cheeks warm but still couldn't tear my gaze from his. "So are you." The words slipped out and we both laughed then. "Good grief," I groaned. "You are anything but *pretty.*" Then I grabbed my hot cheeks. "That's not what I mean, Daniel. You are —"

Suddenly, his hands covered mine and tilted my face up. His lips touched mine with such reverence I heard my breath suck in on a hiss. Then his arms slipped around me and pulled me gently to him. His face fit into the hollow of my shoulder, where I felt his warm breath against my neck.

"Ahh, Sunny," the words rode out on a groan, "I've missed you so."

I ran my fingers along his shoulder and up to cup his head to me. "I missed you, too, Daniel. So, so much." The sweetness of that moment lingers till this very day, triggered unfailingly by a mere whiff of Aqua Velva.

~~~~~

Nana invited Daniel to eat dinner with us, a fancy feast by her standards: fried chicken, mashed potatoes, yams, string beans cooked in ham drippings, and my grandmother's buttermilk biscuits.

Aunt Tina had undoubtedly helped Nana out with buying the food, it being a homecoming and all, because Uncle Charlie had died suddenly in the past year of a stroke, leaving Nana without the paltry amount she earned for doing his cooking and cleaning.

That I'd not grieved his passing reaped me no guilt. Rather, I felt relief. I wouldn't have to worry about Sheila being around him. Nana had mixed her meager furniture with ours in our vacated residence and Aunt Tina made special arrangements with Mr. Montgomery to pay Nana's rent.

In the past year, Aunt Tina's husband, short squat, ugly Talley Seay, left her for another woman. Devastated, Aunt Tina had resumed Nana's rent after she and her spoiled son, Alvin, moved into our house with Nana.

Just one big happy family, I thought, acknowledging I felt a tad sarcastic. Still — it was good to be home, inside familiar walls with family and kin.

And to feel the mill hill wrap me in safety.

I was disappointed to see that pieces of Mama's furniture had been doled out to relatives. "It's all we could do," insisted Aunt Tina, non-apologetically. "After all, ya'll wud'n here. Didn't even know if you was ever comin' back, to tell the truth."

Dad blame it! Daniel and I coulda used that furniture after we marry. I held my tongue, determined not to allow her to steal my joy.

She shrugged, then continued filing her long red nails. "Ya'll can have your same upstairs room back. Alvin'll take the room next to it and Mama'll share my room with me. Francine will have the other room to herself while she's still ailin'."

Great. Timmy will be crammed in with two near grown sisters while Alvin lounges in a big ol' room all by himself.

But, like the rest of us, Timmy didn't complain. He was just happy to be home.

Even Francine seemed contented to heal in familiar surroundings.

Me? I felt only a brush of guilt at counting my lucky stars — at the expense of Francine's illness.

Didn't matter that Aunt Tina invaded our space and we had to put up with Alvin. What mattered was that we were back on the mill hill. A sweetness hummed inside me that sang of family and friends and roots.

I was home.

~~~~~

In those first days back home, Daniel was there nearly every waking moment, his unreadable gaze following me, his ear inclined to my every word. He touched me little but I knew when he wanted to. Oh yes, I could feel his need.

To everyone else, Daniel was invincible, a strong rock upon which to lean, I could tell by the way Nana now deferred to him. He'd won her respect. Not a small accomplishment. I alone knew the innermost Daniel, the young boy who'd been beaten and downtrodden, who'd stood strong and tall still. Who'd hidden his pain from everyone but me.

I saw past his patina of toughness. Daniel needed me.

Just as I needed him.

~~~~~

Doretha, Walter, and Daniel threw a homecoming party for us the second night back. It was a simple, thrown-together, last-minute thing. When domestically-challenged Doretha chickened out, Berthie baked a four-layer chocolate cake. Sandwiches, chips, dips, and cookies completed the refreshments.

Still exhausted from the long ride, bedridden Francine's morale did its lowest plunge ever. "Don't see why I can't go," she pouted but fatigue thinned her voice to a near whisper.

She was still on bed rest, though no longer considered contagious. Sheila and Timmy were excited to be co-guests of honor with me. Sheila, now thirteen, wore an outfit of mine, filling out the blue clingy sweater much better than I ever could. She had the lushness Francine boasted of, with steadily lengthening legs that rivaled Francine's. I laughed at times to hear Francine's disparagement of our little sis.

Sheila was, after all, the family beauty with her breathtaking, ethereal combination of perfect features, olive complexion, green, long-lashed, bedroom eyes so like Mama's they caused mouths to drop open. Jealousy ate Francine alive.

"Why's *she going* tonight?" she snarled from her bed. "She's still a kid."

"So is Timmy. Doesn't matter, Francine," I shushed her. "Doretha made it clear we all are guests of honor."

"'Cept me." Francine's anger slid right through the fatigue. "I *hate* this pissy ol' TB. This stupid bed. No fun. No cigarettes. No *nothin'!* I'd be better off dead."

I struggled to keep from smiling. I'd heard it all before. It no longer drew sympathy. I finally talked her into loaning us her record player and all-the-latest-hits record collection. All gifts from Tack.

"I'll bring you a big plate of refreshments and tell you all about it," I bartered.

She still sulked, cutting her eyes accusingly at me. "Everything? You won't leave nothin' out, will you?"

"Promise. Anyway, Tack's coming to keep you company." I ignored her eyes' dramatic roll, as in 'so what?' I didn't like Tack but I had to hand it to him in his devotion to Francine. Her earlier gratefulness to him now lay in tarnished ruins.

The party was wonderful. Emaline and John, Daniel and I danced every dance together, except one, when Walter cut in and we monkey shined to *Mister Sandman.*

"Hey," he stage-whispered over the music, "when you get tired of ol' ugly over there, I'll be next in line. Okay?"

Humor glimmered in his blue, blue eyes, now half-mooned over a silly grin. "Yeh, Walter. Sure." I joked back, "I'll remember that." The Chordettes loosed Mister Sandman and the dance ended.

"Thanks, Sunshine," Walter winked and flashed me that quick smile of his before handing me back over to Daniel, who'd pulled a passable dance out of inexperienced Sheila. Afterward, she beamed, whispering to me, "Did you see me dance, Sunny? Huh?"

"Yeh," I grinned back. "A regular ol' Betty Grable."

Doretha flirted a little with Aunt Tina's son, Alvin. His response was so *flat* she soon moved on to tease Timmy, who blushed and let her coax him into dancing to *Sh-Boom,* an awkward but fun venture for both. Alvin's bland gaze followed Doretha, who was not usually the flirty, partying, dancing type. Tonight, she stretched herself. All to honor us, the Acklins.

The McGuire Sisters' *Sincerely,* Daniel's and my song, had everybody on their feet in the crowded room. I giggled as Walter tried to pull Doretha in his arms and she swatted him soundly, then succinctly put the distance of the room between them. He winked at me and seized Sheila for a spin, delighting her to no end.

We'd pushed back all the chairs and sofa to make dance space and Daniel's arms felt wonderful and snug and *right*. Our cheeks melded and his breath rustled my temple hair. Anticipation threaded its way through me like a warm fizzly spring. Soon we'd be married and experience the fullness of love.

"Mama!" Doretha shrieked, that in itself phenomenal, since she normally barely spoke above a whisper. Daniel and I sprang apart, startled as our gazes followed hers to the kitchen doorway, where Berthie stood, blinking in confusion. It took a moment to register.

She wore only a loose-fitting brassiere from which she spilled like mounds of soft rounded, kneaded dough, and a half-slip that revealed her nakedness underneath. Even her feet were bare. The sight, so at odds with the strong, dignified Berthie I'd come to know, smote me profoundly.

Doretha rushed and herded her away. "Now, Mama, you know…" Her voice faded as they climbed the stairs to Berthie's bedroom.

My heart grieved. The Berthie I knew was not behind those eyes.

Walter looked a mite flushed as he hurried to cover the awkward moment. "Berthie, she — ahhh, she's growing a bit forgetful at times." His brow furrowed. "I wonder where Dad is?" He seemed irritated that his father hadn't prevented the scene. Then suddenly, his quick, James Dean-crooked grin appeared. "Hey, let's get back to partying."

We did. But the evening had lost its magic.

~~~~~

"Let's walk." Daniel's fingers intertwined with mine and, in comfortable silence, we strolled up Main Street, past the movie house and the mill executive's residences, which were roomier and nicer than ours. We passed the big Turner house, where Tack lived. The past week back home had been like a dream.

Tonight, it seemed I had a new set of eyes. Everything looked new and bigger than life somehow. It was as though I'd never been to our favorite place before. Park Pointe marked the village outskirts, the beautiful, triangular oasis laid with lush carpet grass, now in winter a soft buff, where benches beneath stately oaks and dogwoods beckoned and welcomed one to stop and rest. Wordlessly, Daniel and I sank onto one nestled up to a lone, huge white oak.

The park, painstakingly groomed and preserved by Tucapau Mill's maintenance crew, hosted an array of occasions, from textile awards, civic and church group meetings, to the Boys Scouts, and picnics. Adjoining it was the village baseball field.

"It's beautiful, Daniel," I said, gazing about me. "Remember what you once told me? I like to pretend this is ours, this spot, with a lovely cottage right there in the middle, underneath those giant oaks."

Daniel's fingers laced with mine and I loved the way his callused palm stroked my tender one. It stirred something deep inside me, dormant until recent days. "Someday, you'll have it," he said softly, remembering his earlier promise.

"Su-ure," I murmured, sighed, then slid him a smile that came from that deep, deep spot inside me reserved just for him. "But I appreciate the thought. I'm becoming more a realist every day I live. These village folks would never agree to turning this lovely park it into a residential site. Why, the

Boy Scouts would *scalp us!*" I laughed, gesturing toward the log Scout Hut on the north corner of the site.

Daniel didn't laugh. "All things change." His gaze locked with mine. "All things. Someday," he said solemnly, "your house will set right here."

I think it was then, in that moment, with his eyes ablaze with a tender, fierce protectiveness, that I began to think of him as Daniel, my Lion-Man.

~~~~~

I couldn't bring myself to tell Gladys about Harly's coming on to me that day over a year earlier. Living in Chicago, I'd not had to deal with it. Now, things were different.

She'd warned me and, somehow, I felt inexplicably guilty for what happened that day when she was away. I didn't want her to know of my stupidity but superceding that was my reluctance to hurt her. So I avoided her.

I met Doris, Jack Melton's fiancée. She wasn't Renie but — she was nice. There would, I realized, never be another Renie — her uniqueness could never be plagiarized.

I first noticed trinkets showing up in Sheila's pocketbook during my senior year at James F. Byrnes High, which accommodated not only Tucapau but Lyman, Jackson, and Fairmont mill hills as well. When I asked her one day where she'd gotten the money to buy lipstick and mascara, she gave me a smile I'd seen on her face before. With a thudding heart, I recognized it from bygone days, when she'd flirted with everybody, charming them with her cuteness.

"Where does she get money?" I asked Francine, who still rested frequently through the day. Her schooling was over. The initiative would never again arise. I'd gone to work at the hotel. Pressed to keep up with my studies, I took the afternoon shift. Daniel and I scrimped and put back like squirrels preparing for winter. Our wedding was only three months away. While I was in Chicago, Daniel had continued to save, managing to lay aside a pretty good nest egg for our future. He gave it to me to start a joint savings account in the bank.

"She's got a little thing going with the boys, Sunny," Francine said, propped up on pillows, hands-on-hips, as in *don't you know anything?*

"Oh, no, Francine." I dropped into a kitchen chair I'd shuttled into the room

"'Fraid so, Sunny." Francine's voice softened. We'd grown closer in recent months. Maturity can do marvelous things for sibling relationships. "That's why I don't want any kids."

I narrowed my gaze at her. "You don't mean that."

She raised an eyebrow over eyes too cynical, too hard. "Oh but I do. I don't wanna take a chance on lettin' kids down like Mama did us. I got too much o' her in me, Sunny. You know that."

I couldn't argue with that. But still. "You've got a lot of time to change your mind."

"Don't hold your breath." She winked at me, taking my breath with a mannerism so *Mama.*

~~~~~

The fragrance of baking cornbread set my mouth to watering.

"You still gonna have your reception here, darlin'?" Daisy asked, holding out a fresh, hot buttered corn muffin to me. I took it and bit into it, taking a minute to get my breath between maid duties. I sat down in a hotel dining room chair and slid off my white maid's shoes for a moment, wiggling my toes to shed fatigue.

"Mmm. You make the best cornbread in the South, Daisy." I licked melted butter off my fingers. "Yes. I'm still planning on having my wedding reception here."

"An' the weddin' at the Meth'dist Church?"

I nodded. I was also sewing my own wedding gown. I'd worked on it for months, using the heavy-duty machine in the hotel's little upstairs mending room. I took the money for pattern and cloth from the bank account. Daniel's idea.

After leaving Chicago, I'd begun attending services at the Tucapau Methodist Church where my daddy's cousin, Wayne Acklin, now pastored. Emaline, true friend that she was, attended there, too. One reason being her boyfriend, John Davidson, now attended Asbury Seminary and would eventually pastor in the Methodist Church.

Anyway, I couldn't go back to the Pentecostal church because of Gladys, whom I still avoided. She was too, too intuitive not to sense something if I was around her long.

"My cousin pastors there," I told Daisy. "I want you to help me plan the food."

"I be glad to help out. My labor being free o'charge, darlin'. That'll be my weddin' present to you and that honey o'your'n."

"Aww, Daisy," my eyes misted, "you don't have to —"

"It done. So hesh up." She slid me that mischievous grin of hers and enfolded me in her long golden arms for a huge hug.

~~~~~

My shift from Pentecostalism to Methodism was akin to an abrupt grind-down gearshift from race car-high to mountain-climbing low. I missed the freedom and exuberance of the Pentecostal brethren. Most of all, I missed the toe-tapping lively music that kept even the fussiest of babies enraptured.

Today, with song leader Ernie North laid-up with the flu, Pastor Wayne filled in badly. I'd always known my daddy's musical pitch wasn't the best and now I knew it was genetic. Even Daniel, who usually took little note of such, raised his brows at me during the hymn *It Is Well With My Soul*, indicating it *wasn't*. Cousin Wayne's voice crossed a wolf's bay at the moon with an octogenarian's audible yawn.

His wife, Lula, seemed unaffected by the racket and sang along like she was surrounded by the Byrnes High Glee Club. I decided then and there to take some hot potato soup to Ernie and pray especially hard for his recovery.

Pastor Wayne's four kids — ages four to ten — lined the front pew like stair steps. Matthew, Mark, Luke and Rachel. All four heads sprouted thick amber-toned hair with degrees of natural curl, ranging from Matthews's Afro to Rachel's lustrous waist-length waves. The curly tops bobbed to and fro, up and down constantly during the service. Not hugely, just more like busy insects on the perimeter of a picnic.

Some of the members shot irritated looks their way but Lula seemed as impervious to that as she was to her husband's tone-deafness. She sat planted like a stalwart bookend next to little Rachel while ten-year-old Matthew bookended the other side of eight-year-old Luke. Mark, the middle child seemed, characteristically, the best behaved of the bunch. Remembering some of my psychology, I wondered if it was birth order that determined it or if he'd simply inherited his mother's placid genes. Which led me to ponder again spoiled Cousin Alvin's impassiveness — if genetic, it had leap-frogged over Aunt Tina and Uncle Talley.

Daniel watched the kids for amusement, his eyes smiling and I knew he thought of our own children, yet unbirthed. He took my hand and squeezed, sliding me a look that confirmed my suspicion. Joy floated through me like warm bubbles that, when full, burst, flooding me with happiness and contentment.

Emaline and John sat with us. I was glad our two guys liked each other. Had they not, ours would have been a hard row to plow, Emaline's and mine. Halfway through preaching, Emaline leaned to whisper in my ear.

"Cornelia is moving to Cowpens next week. Needs to move closer to help her sick mama."

My eyes rounded in shock. Cornelia, our capable pianist, leaving? I surreptitiously looked around. To my knowledge, nobody else there could read a note of music. Oh, how I wished I could.

Pastor Wayne caught me in the church vestibule after the service ended. "Say Sunny, do you by chance know anybody who plays piano well enough to take Cornelia's place?" My throat constricted at his resemblance to Daddy. How I missed him.

"Yes, I do," I said without hesitation. "Ruth Bond. She lives on the other side of the river on Pine Street. Number ten."

Wayne's frown eased. He patted my arm. "Thanks, Sunny."

~~~~~

"Are you *crazy?*" shrieked Aunt Tina, glaring at me across the supper table as though I were a simpering idiot. "Ruth Bond can't play *in church.*"

"And why not?" I shot back, ignoring the fact that I had to share these walls with this woman until I married. "She's really good. You ought to hear her —"

"I don't care if she plays like *Eddie Duchin,* she's not fit to play in church."

"That's not fair, Aunt Tina." I sensed Nana stirring restlessly in her chair at the other end of the table — Aunt Tina occupied the head, with Alvin at her elbow. "Ruth is a good mother and —"

"She ain't married." Aunt Tina's flat reply blasted my temper right out the top of my head.

"Neither are you." The words bypassed my brain and shot right out my mouth.

The hissed intake of her breath could have been heard over at the Taylors. "How *dare you!*" Then she totally shocked me by bursting into tears and fleeing the kitchen. The *slam* of her bedroom door reverberated throughout the house.

Silence around the kitchen table hummed and sizzled after her abrupt departure. Sheila's eyes riveted to her plate. Tim's danced with hurt and anger — at Aunt Tina. Timmy, always my champion.

"You shouldn't oughta said that to'er," Nana scolded. "You need to go apologize."

I gazed at her, stunned. "For *what?*"

"You know she's touchy about Talley leavin' 'er for that girl."

I stared at Nana for long moments. "All the more reason she should have more compassion. She shouldn't've said what she said about Ruth Bond, Nana."

Aunt Tina burst back into the kitchen. "You compared me to that-that *whore?* I can't *believe it.*" She stared at me as though I'd grown fangs

"Don't call Ruth that," I said through tight lips.

"That's what she *is,* Sunny," Aunt Tina fairly hissed, hands planted on hips. "If it looks like a dog and barks like a dog —"

"I don't have to listen to this." I stood and strode from the room.

"You come back here!" Aunt Tina screamed as I slammed through the front door and headed blindly down the steps and across the street to Doretha's. "That's *fine!*" shrieked Aunt Tina to my rigid, retreating back. *"Don't come back! Don't ever come back. Y'hear? Never!"*

"What's the matter, Sunny?" Doretha took me in her arms as soon as I burst through her door with tears streaming down my face. "C'mon in my room," she said in her soft way that always comforted me.

I glimpsed Berthie, brow wrinkled as she gazed at me from the kitchen table, where she sipped coffee. Most of her moments were lucid. This being one of them. I read concern on her face. Tom Taylor sat across from Berthie, elbows on table, huge hands clasping coffee cup, never raising his head to acknowledge us. I suppose my emotional state made him uncomfortable. I didn't care.

"Hey, Sunny," Daniel called, a smile already forming as he spotted us from the kitchen, where, at the sink, he ran cool tap water into a glass. His smile dissolved instantly. "Hey, what's wrong?" The glass plunked into the sink, water forgotten as he rushed to my side. His big hand cupped my chin and surveyed my features. I despised the fact that my lips continued to wobble.

"C'mon," Doretha gently tugged me through the door to her room and firmly closed it behind Daniel. "Sit down, ya'll," she gestured toward her bed as she took a straight wicker-seated kitchen chair and lowered herself onto it. "What's wrong, Sunny?" she softly queried. She folded one scrawny denimed leg beneath her.

It all poured out — Aunt Tina's ugly outburst, my defense of Ruth, and the horrible replies. When I finished, out of breath and trembling, the two of them remained silent for long moments. Doretha broke the silence. "You really do *love*, don't you, Sunny? I mean — you *really* love ever'body, dontcha? You ain't puttin' on, are you?"

I snuffled and peered at her through bleary eyes. "No," I croaked, mildly surprised at the question. "I'm not putting on. Why would I?"

"'Cause most people here in Tucapau wouldn't own up to likin' Ruth Bond." She gazed quietly at me, her heart in her gray eyes. "You know I'm tellin' the truth. That makes you different. I don't mean bad different, now, so don't' go thinkin' that. Ain't I tellin' her the truth, Daniel?"

My gaze swung to Daniel, seated beside me. He nodded, his gaze averting mine.

Some little alarm went off inside me. Daniel was entirely too silent. Too detached. For the first time ever, my tears did not touch him. In fact, he seemed almost brooding.

"Do you think I'm wrong to love Ruth Bond?" I whispered, gazing at him. "To defend her?"

Still, his gaze did not meet mine; rather it stared out the window, simmering with some mystical, goaded stimulus.

"I didn't mean it's *wrong*," Doretha's soft clarification drifted past me. I was too focused on Daniel to even register it.

"Daniel?" I persisted, needing to *know*.

Slowly, his head turned, until his gaze locked with mine. My heart sank right to my toes. Turquoise glittered like sunlight flung over the ocean. And I knew he didn't really see *me.* He saw ghosts from his childhood — phantoms of *that kind* of woman.

And even as I railed inwardly at the unfairness of it all, I understood Daniel.

I sucked in my breath, held it, and let it out on a tired gust. "Never mind." I arose and strode out the front door, slamming it behind me, ignoring Doretha's concerned "Sunny? Honey, I didn't mean..." I set off down the street like my skirt tail was on fire, with no idea where I'd go.

Aunt Tina's anger permeated my house, rose from it like wavy sheets of heat. *Was* it my house now? *"Don't ever come back!"* Suddenly, it did not seem so. I started to detour to Emaline's, but her soon-to-be-stepmother, Doris, flashed before me and kept my feet moving in another direction. Not that I didn't like Doris; it was simply that it was no longer Renie's house. Emaline still loved me and, though Doris liked me, she and I did not have the same history. No. I couldn't impose on them.

All things change. Daniel's words came back to me and I realized how true they were.

Next thing I knew, I was knocking on the pastor's door. Then I was in Lula's plump arms. "There, there, Sunny. Sit down and tell me all about it."

It all came pouring out. "So, I don't have a home anymore," I concluded on a teary, matter-of-fact note, feeling quite embarrassed and naked before her. "I suppose I could rent a hotel room even though it would eat into my savings."

"Or you could stay here. With us," said Lula in her ultra-understated way.

"Oh, I couldn't do that. You already have a house full, anyway," I sputtered, by now shamed to have dumped on her.

"Actually," droned Lula, "Rachel has a whole room to herself. She'd be tickled to share it with you. Wouldn't you, honey-bunch?"

Rachel dashed across the room and threw herself at me, startling me. "Pleath, pleath, *pleathhh*, Thunny?" she pled like a perishing kitten to a milkman, lisping sweetly through slightly protruding teeth, a result of continued thumb-sucking. "You can thleep with *me, dontcha know?*" Her chocolate-brown eyes sparkled with excitement and I burst into laughter and hugged her hugely, overwhelmed that this family opened their arms to me while Aunt Tina callously threw me out.

"Well, heck," I gazed into the sweet little face, "I can't turn that down, now, can I?"

~~~~~

"Please, Sunny," Sheila wrung her hands as I stuffed clothes into my battered old suitcase. "Please don't leave."

I paused in my packing and looked at her, hurting for her, for me, for everything. "I don't want to, Sheila, but I can't abide the prejudice and hatred here. Plus, I can't stay here when I'm not wanted."

"But-but Timmy and I want you," her voice shimmied up to shrill and I stopped to hug her long and hard.

"I know you do, honey." I turned her loose and recommenced folding and stacking underclothes in the large paper grocery bag I'd switched to after filling the suitcase.

"*Please*, Sunny," Sheila wailed. "Stay." Tears trailed down cheeks.

I turned my face away, hardening my heart. "I *can't* Sheila. I — can't. You just don't understand."

I folded down the bag's opening and moved to the dresser for my comb and brush, almost missing Sheila's exiting, tearful reply, "Neither do you."

~~~~~

The Acklins were more permissive than Nana with Daniel and me. "Lord have mercy," Lula droned, "you're getting' *married* in a few weeks. If we're ever gonna trust you it'll be now." So, they let us date any time we wanted to.

Only thing was, we both worked like tomorrow held another Depression, putting away every penny we could spare into our little bank account, so there was little time to date. But it was nice knowing we could if we wanted to.

It was kinda difficult listening to Daniel extol Mr. Melton's virtues. Made me feel like gagging, remembering his age-spotted old hands groping all over me. But he was, after all, Daniel's boss. And Emaline's grandpa.

Lula began inviting Daniel over for dinner several times a week because Wayne liked to talk to him. "He's a good fellow," said Wayne, "interesting."

Daniel was. And closed-mouth that he was, he couldn't resist opening up when Wayne gently probed beneath the tough veneer. Soon, the pastor knew all about Daniel's troubled childhood and his mother's abandonment. And he astutely picked up on Daniel's fury.

One night, as we sat around talking after the children were in bed, he said, "Daniel,don't you think its about time to settle all this and get on with your life?"

I felt Daniel stiffen on the sofa beside me as his hand painfully squeezed mine. "What do you mean?"

"Go to your mama and resolve all this anger and resentment."

"I don't know where she is," came his tight, gruff reply.

"Then find her. Until you do, you'll always be her prisoner."

Wayne had said the right words. Daniel didn't like the idea of being imprisoned by Mona.

Daniel took a deep, deciding breath and blew it out. "Me 'n Sunny's getting married in six weeks. How would I start searching? And when?"

Wayne grinned and reached to shake Daniel's hand. "How about tomorrow?"

~~~~~

Daniel left two days later after kissing me dizzy, leaving me light-headed and weak-kneed as he took off in the car he'd bought from Walter when his foster-brother got a new one. Actually, Walter had all but given it to Daniel. Said the trade-in was so low on it he'd rather Daniel have it. Anyway, with Daniel in a good car, I wouldn't worry as much.

Mr. Melton gave Daniel an open-ended leave-of-absence after Daniel explained the situation to him. While Daniel celebrated his boss's goodness, I was thinking how the old man's generosity spawned from guilt over how he'd violated me.

Walter, Berthie, Doretha, and I waved him off from the Stone's curb. Tom was nowhere to be seen. "Okay, little brother, you take care o'yourself, now, y'hear?" Doretha kissed him on the cheek and gave him a snuggly, sisterly hug.

"Hey!" Walter howled, palms up in supplication. "How 'bout *me*? I'm your brother, too."

Without missing a beat, Doretha said, "you don't count." I broke into laughter at her standard, flat rebuff.

Berthie gave Daniel a warm hug and said, "Now, where is it you're a'goin'?"

Daniel had already told her three times in the past hour but he patiently explained it to her again, his eyes looking misted. She shook her head and smiled sweetly, clearly still not understanding.

Not one to entertain solemnity, Walter grabbed Daniel for a rowdy bear hug, nearly picking him up off the sidewalk before releasing him. Poking his finger into Daniel's chest, he said gravely, "Take care o' that car now. Y'hear?"

Daniel burst into laughter and playfully poked him in the ribs, turning it into a mock skirmish that ended with another rocking bear hug. I marveled that such closeness had developed between the two. But Walter had been good to Daniel; better, said Daniel, than any other male in his life. I think that was the crux of it — Daniel hadn't had any other males in his life in recent years, save ol' man Taylor.

My turn. When Daniel's arms closed around me, I couldn't help it, tears puddled in my eyes. Then ran over as my face burrowed into the hollow of his neck. "I'm gonna miss you," I cried, feeling as cowardly as I'd ever felt in my life.

Daniel's cheek sought and found mine, then his lips claimed mine. Ignoring Walter and Doretha, who awkwardly shuffled nearby, we said our somber good-byes with more kisses and hungry, searching gazes that said *only a few short weeks and we'll be married and this parting will be just a memory.*

Had I had just an inkling of what lay ahead, I'd've held onto him and would've never, ever, *ever* let go.

<u>Chapter Seven</u>

"It so *purdy!*" exulted Daisy who, on her knees, turned up and pinned my wedding dress hem. "Not too fancy — jus' right, s'what I say."

"Anything fancier and I couldn't have managed it." Which was true. Taking into consideration my limited sewing experience, I'd chosen a simple, long, princess-waist dress, with three-quarter lace-trimmed sleeves, and scooped neckline.

"There," said Daisy importantly, "s'done. Jus' look at you."

I gazed in the long mirror we'd moved from storage and attached to the wall. I looked like — well, I looked like a swan. I didn't look emaciated anymore. Somewhere along the way, my skinny frame had filled out. Not like Francine's. Or Sheila's. But with enough curves to shape my clothes nicely.

"Lula said I could borrow her wedding veil," I said, relieved at the pastor's wife's generosity. "So I don't have to spend any more money, other than on food, for the reception."

"I be helpin' on that, now missy," Daisy climbed stiffly to her feet, chin stuck out. "Don' worry none 'bout that. Me'n Trixie and the others gon' see you got the nicest spread ever was."

I threw my arms around her neck and squeezed. "Ouch!" she shrieked. I sprang loose, wide-eyed. She reached to my bosom and gingerly extracted the culprit, a straight pin. We burst into laughter.

"Ahh, Daisy," I threw back my head and twirled in my lovely gown, feeling once again as light and exuberant as I had before Mama left. "I'm so *happy!*"

"S'a good thing," Daisy chortled. "Now, let's go see to getting supper finished 'fore the crowd comes in."

And a crowd it was. Seemed every stag male on the hill showed up.

"Baseball practice," Walter informed us as he joined a near-full table of men including sleaze-ball Buck Edmonds, whose only claim to fame was the fact that he could pitch a mean ball, Harly Kale, whose leering gaze I avoided, Clarence Bond (Ruth's uncle), Jack Melton, Emaline's dad, and his father, Mr. Melton. If the latter expected gratitude to thaw my frostiness toward him, he was disappointed.

Fact was, with the exception of Jack Melton and Walter, I was barely cordial to the lot of them.

Which did little to deter the sly leers. I grew more disgusted as ordering began.

"Hey, Sunny." Buck motioned to me as the other men joked about the evening's practice. I couldn't *not* acknowledge a diner so I moved to take his order. "What's the best thing on the menu? The most *tasty?*" he said quietly, licking his lips salaciously.

I stared over his head and said flatly, "The pinto beans and cornbread."

"Nono, Sunny," he stage-whispered, "I gotta have some juicy meat."

I gasped and glared at him. He grinned devilishly, knowing the commotion around us swallowed up the exchange. I shot Walter a helpless look but he was engaged in a heated exchange with Jack about game strategy. I rolled my eyes and addressed Buck again.

"Look. I don't care what you order. Just order."

"Now that's no way to talk to a good ol' boy," chimed Harly, who was seated to my other side. I jerked away from his touch, a supposedly accidental brush of fingers over my fanny. I slapped his hand as hard as I could, drawing chuckles from both him and Buck.

"Feisty." Harly's eyes glittered as they surveyed me. I swung my gaze across the table to Jack, whose interchange with Walter consumed him. Next to him, Old Mr. Melton's perusal of me, though hooded, was no less lascivious than Harly and Buck's.

I felt my heart turn cold. In that moment I hated the lot of them. They would not turn me into my mother. I opened my mouth to rail when a commotion in the foyer seized my attention.

Doretha rushed into the dining room. "Walter, your daddy's took sick. He's bad — him and Mama are on their way to Spartanburg General Hospital. Preacher Acklin's driving 'em."

Walter was on his feet and out the door in a flash. Despite his displeasure over his father's treatment of Daniel, he and old Tom seemed close. It was then that I noticed Doretha was trembling like a thin shrub in a gale.

I rushed to her and guided her to the lobby sofa. Daisy, hearing the commotion, now took the other men's orders. Thank God. I settled myself next to Doretha, who remained dry-eyed, despite the nerve spasms that shook her.

"What is it?" I asked softly, knowing this wasn't merely concern for ol' Tom, as she called him. No, something else bothered her. "Are you afraid?"

She looked me in the eye and I saw a deep torment in the hazel depths. "Yeh, Sunny," she said so softly I barely heard her. "I am."

"Why?" I asked, alarm spreading through me like wildfire. Why was she so terrified? "Tell, me, Doretha," I said, taking her cold, thin hand and squeezing it.

"I —" Her eyes seemed to unfocus on me and I saw them go somewhere else.

"Doretha? Are you afraid of being alone?"

She blinked and came back. "Yeh — that's it. Would you do me a favor?" she asked timidly.

"Of course."

"Would you come sleep at my house tonight?"

"Done." I squeezed her icy fingers one final time and went to tell Daisy.

"I'm going to stay with her tonight," I said over Daisy's shoulder as she delivered Buck's platter of fried chicken, pinto beans, and cornbread. "She's upset."

"'Course she is," Daisy said, grabbing the tea pitcher and refilling Harly's empty glass. "You'll take good care o'her, I know. Ya'll lock 'em doors, now, y'hear?"

"Yeh," Harly chimed in, "don' want no boogers getting y'all." He and Buck laughed uproariously at the quip, disgusting me as I left the dining room.

"Hey!" Jack Melton called to me. I paused, and turned. "Anything we can do?"

I glimpsed his father's surreptitious leer. "No, thanks. We're okay." I fled.

Doretha and I walked to the preacher's house to tell Lula I'd not be sleeping there tonight, sending Rachel into a tailspin of disappointment. After a few thumb-sized tears, she sent me off, mollified when I promised her a trip to the movies, with a lisped "I'm gonna mith you, Thunny."

"Me, too, sweety-pie." I waved from the sidewalk and blew her a kiss.

"We'll be praying for him," Lula called to Doretha from the porch, wiping her hands on her apron. I smelled the wonderful fried chicken and thought how Aunt Tina had bought extras like bacon and eggs for Alvin to devour while the rest of us ate our oatmeal. Thank God there'd been no such partiality at the pastor's house.

"Thank you," Doretha said quietly, more from politeness, I think, than conviction. I'd never known Doretha to go to church. Yet, she was the lovingest creature on God's earth. She seemed to occupy this little bubble of impenetrable space that kept her timeless and childlike. She seemed incapable of judgment. Yet her wisdom and perception, at times, astounded me.

The Stone house was silent when we entered. Doretha and I sat in the kitchen and drank hot chocolate for awhile and chatted. She wanted to know all about Francine's tuberculosis recuperation. I told her Francine had been declared clean and was revved up almost to her former pre-TB state.

"She won't be the same," said wise little Doretha. "Can't nobody go through somethin' like that and not change some."

"Yeh. You're right." I laughed. "I hope her change continues in the 'better' direction." Doretha, I noticed, seemed quite somber and preoccupied. I guessed it was because of ol' Tom's sudden illness. Though it seemed strange, given her downright aloofness with him.

But then, Doretha didn't react to life like most folks. Many times she loved when she should hate. If she hated, she didn't show it. Her heart was one of the most tender I'd ever encountered, at least with me. Walter alone brought out her truculence, one I attributed to the mysterious sibling pecking order. More of a comic-relief thing.

When we started to bed, Doretha suggested I occupy her downstairs room. "I don't sleep long at a time," she explained. " I'll go upstairs to Mama's room. That way, when I get restless, I won't keep you awake." She checked the doors to make sure they were locked and just as she turned to walk away, a soft rap on the door made her jump.

Cautiously, she put her ear to the door. "Who is it?"

"Preacher Acklin," came Cousin Wayne's familiar voice. Doretha opened the door and he stayed on the other side of the screen. "I won't come in. It's late." He paused and glanced around at the corner of the house, frowning, listening. "Thought I saw somebody —" He shrugged. " I just wanted to let you know that when I left the hospital a couple of hours ago, Tom was sleeping. It's his heart acting up, according to his doctor. Tomorrow's tests will tell if it's a heart attack or just a warning."

"Thank you, Preacher Acklin," said Doretha, sounding weary. She hugged me soundly and whispered, "I love you, Sunny," before turning to vanish up the stairs. I stared after her, surprised by the fervency of her words and wondering again at her nervousness. I yawned and attributed it to her being Doretha.

I turned out the lamp.

~~~~~

The bedroom was pitch dark as I snuggled up to the soft mattress and nestled my cheek into a downy pillow. I tucked the sheet up around my neck and inhaled its fresh outdoors/Rinso fragrance, exhausted but happy. *Seven weeks from now, I'll be a bride.* Excitement and anticipation threaded through me like a warm silken cord, plunging me into a sweet, warm state of desire. It was a good, *right* sensation, one that I now felt entitled to.

I smiled into the darkness and stretched luxuriously, sensually, with an overwhelming urge to purr. *I'm glad we waited. Our wedding night will be so special.* A long contented sigh floated past my lips and my eyes drifted shut.

Soon, waves of slumber set me adrift on a sea *that carries me into the arms of my betrothed, whose wonderful hands do magic things...fingers and lips caress and tantalize until I'm ready to swoon with pleasure. Then — pain.*

Swoosh. My eyeslids slit...*a twilight image looms in inky darkness, a faceless shadow above me. Still partly immersed in a world of enchantment and mystery, I wonder when did he come to my bed?*

A joyful "Daniel!" spills from me and everything grows still for a long moment. Confused, I blink into the night, increasingly aware of heavy weight anchoring me to the bed.

The feel, the scent of him is not right. And suddenly, I grasp that in this twilight world, all is not wonderful — terrible things happen. My eyes pop open. Realization rocks me. I'm not in my room. It's not him.... *Ohgodohgodohgod! It's not him!*

I sucked in a startled breath and the scream, bypassing my brain and sliding through my throat, was snuffed by something thick and flaccid and fabric thrust against my face. I panicked and tried to kick but strong, vise-like thighs pinned my own captive. I thrashed my head about to dislodge the mass from my face that threatened to smother the life from me, only to have it pressed more firmly in place.

Pure survival instinct kicked in. As I tried to buck the Velcro monster from me I painfully swiveled my head to the side until my nose and mouth hit an air pocket and I gulped in oxygen like a dying fish.

The searing, invasive member began to move again, revving up scalding pain that drew my mouth into a rictus of agony. Somehow, a scream exploded, a sound instantly absorbed by the blasted thing plastered to my face and I began to cry and moan, vulnerable as a mangled butterfly. Helplessness, a pit bull's fangs, seized me and completed the mutilation, turning me numb and icy.

Am I dead? No, I decided, because the torture continued for long, endless moments until the beast stiffened, shuddered for an eternity, then fell limp and even in my innocence, I knew. *The creep is spilling his seed in me. Noooooooooooo!*

Once more, I futilely resisted. *Too late, toolatetoolate.* Life drained from me and with it everything I'd fought so hard to keep.

I was barely aware of his sudden departure, this vicious lowlife who'd invaded, impaled, and violated me. Mild air washed over my limp body, one that could belong to another for all I felt. I hardly heard footsteps rapidly cross the floor, then a muted *click. Is that noise from a gun?* I knew I should be terrified but discovered I didn't care; would, in fact welcome a bullet through my brain. Nothing mattered anymore.

Unable to move, I was already wasteland, as good as dead. Footsteps rapidly paced to the open window. *Whoosh... plunk,* bulk hit the ground...swift footsteps retreated in a rustle of foliage. I peeled the thing from my face, now sodden with sweat and tears, and gulped in more air, peering at the thing that nearly killed me.

A pillow, a blasted pillow that minutes earlier had smelled clean and innocent. Like me.

No longer, no longer nolongernolonger wailed a dissonant dirge. I sunk deeper inside myself, pulling in the walls of my being, wrapping myself like a cocoon, wanting never to depart from it.

Wildflower-flavored air fluttered the curtains in the wake of the dark silhouette's nocturnal departure. Silence roared about me and the thick, slimy presence of evil lingered, goading me...*whore, whore, whore.*

And I ask, Where were you, God, when I needed you?

~~~~~

I heard faraway screams that went on and on and on until the room exploded with light and I saw Doretha, a pale gray specter, floating above me, gripping my shoulders.

"Sunny!" She gave me a few gentle shakes and my mouth closed. Only when silence fell did I realize it was me doing all the screaming. I peered blearily about me, further stunned, because I'd thought I was home.

Doretha's room. Disoriented, I reached down to feel the trickling wetness between my legs. It was sticky and hot. *Blood.*

"What, Sunny?" Doretha asked gently. Her voice quavered. She looked strange.

I gulped in air as spasms shook my body and shock's icy fingers tightened their grip. "He — he left through that window, I think," I whispered raggedly as my teeth began to clatter, pointing a violently trembling finger. Cool night air hit me as the white curtains rustled softly, languidly.

"Oh my *Lord.*" Doretha sat on the bed next to me, pulling back the sheet and lifting my gown, one she'd loaned me to sleep in. "You're bleedin', honey. Lay still. I'm gonna get a wash rag." Within moments she was back with a metal wash pan of warm water, sponging me off as I moaned with pain and humiliation. "Oh, honey," she whispered, "I'm so sorry. So sorry."

"Oh, Doretha," I sobbed, "Daniel's gonna die. Just *die*. We've been saving ourselves for each o-other —" My weeping crescendoed as Doretha wrapped her frail little arms around me, squeezing and cryin' with me.

"I-I'm like m-my Mama now," I wailed, "I want to d-die!" Doretha held me until my bawling wound down to glassy-eyed snuffling. "You're not like your mama or nobody else, now, y'hear?" she said hoarsely, swiping her hand across her wet face. "You're Sunny. Just — Sunny." She grew quiet for a long moment, then, "Did you get a look at 'im?"

I shook my head violently. "No." Then shuddered.

" Did he say anything?"

Another shudder. "N-no."

"Do you have any idea who he could be?"

"Not really." Then a mental replay of tonight's hotel diners flashed before me. "There's — Buck Edmonds. Or Harly Kale." I was suddenly gripped with chills. My teeth began to clatter. I couldn't bring myself to mention Bill Melton. Not even to Doretha. It was like stabbing Emaline in the back to reveal his indiscretion. "Th-they all heard me say I was coming home w-with you."

Doretha gazed at me, her eyes inordinately sad and bottomless. She gripped my hand. "I'm so sorry, Sunny," she said so quietly you'd've thought she was entering a prayer room. "Sorry I asked you to come here, tonight. You wouldn't'a been —"

"No." I squeezed her birdlike fingers. "It's not your fault. Actually —" my heart thudded even harder, "it coulda been *you*."

Her gaze lowered to our locked hands. She whispered. "I know. It shoulda been."

"*Doretha.*" How like her to accept the responsibility. Like she was the world's protector. "Please don't say that. Okay?"

She raised her eyes to mine, the sadness magnified, if possible. Finally, she murmured, "Okay." Then, "Do you want to call the police?"

"God, *no!*" Aunt Tina had had a phone installed but going there to use it was out of the question. In that instant, I knew beyond a doubt that I did not want anyone to know.

Doretha checked the window, where the screen had been ripped off and tossed to the ground outside. She lowered the window and locked it, then examined the front door, which remained latched. We kept watch there on her bed for the rest of the night, as though our vigilance would ward off further evil.

All night long, I kept asking *Where were you God?*

~~~~~

By morning, the shock began to dissipate a bit. Reality set in. Walter and Berthie came in from the all-night hospital vigil, looking pale and haggard.

"Don't leave me," Berthie murmured in a distant voice, "I don't want to be alone."

"Nobody's gonna leave you, Mama," Doretha soothed her as she steered her away. Berthie looked back over her shoulder at Walter, a stricken look on her face.

"It's okay, Berthie," Walter said gently, striding over to hug her before Doretha aimed her for the stairs. "Everything's okay. Nobody's gonna leave you."

Doretha tucked her mama in bed upstairs and came back down to join us in the kitchen. The eggs Doretha cooked were scorched but I couldn't have eaten them anyway.

"Daddy's holding his own," said Walter, rubbing a hand over his tired features. "They'll know more when they finish the tests today."

"How was Mama?" queried Doretha, setting cups out for coffee. Soon as she poured mine, I loaded it with cream and sugar, fighting the nausea that choked me.

Walter's huff of a laugh answered that. "Out of it, pretty much. But she slept most of the night on the hospital cot. I took the lumpy chair." His grin flashed, then dissolved, showing his strain. "They kept Daddy knocked out."

"Hey," he said gently to me, "heard from Daniel?"

Out of the blue, tears sprang to my eyes. I ducked my head to hide them. "No. Aunt Tina had a phone installed but that doesn't help me now, does it?"

"You really miss 'im, huh?" He took a long sip of hot liquid, studying me over the cup's rim.

"I really do," I managed to say without totally breaking down.

"I'm sorry, Sunny," he said quietly as Doretha banged down the coffeepot on the stove, "I didn't mean to make you sad."

"She knows that, Walter," Doretha said in that flat way she had of speaking to him. Any other time, I would've laughed. Not now. Not today.

Probably not ever again.

~~~~~

"Daniel called the other night," said Francine. She was still ebullient to be recently sprung from bed rest. Today, I hibernated in the hotel's mending room, a thing I'd recently begun, with the pretense of working on my wedding gown.

It was finished but nobody knew that except me. And perhaps Daisy.

Francine didn't seem to notice the change in me. I'd let out the folding cot and put clean sheets on it. It gave me a place to lie and think. At that precise moment, for Francine's benefit, I hunched over the machine, piddling with seams and pinning unnecessary adjustments. Not that Francine was aware of my silence. She was too involved in her own agenda. The activity simply gave me my needed distance.

"Daniel called?" My heart beat wildly, whether from fear or excitement at his name, I wasn't sure. I watched Francine mosey over to the little window that overlooked the street below, where men lined the rock wall like roosting crows, heads cocked for the sound of the three-thirty whistle. She eyed them hungrily.

"Yeh," Francine tossed back her tawny mane, her gesture of liberation. "Ol' battle axe Tina told 'im you didn't live there any more. He already knew that but he'd called the Acklins and Lula said you weren't there and he thought you might've dropped by the house. Anyway, Aunt Tina was just plain hateful. I wanted to slap her jaws good."

I felt like I *had* been slapped. I'd been staying at the hotel sewing room until late into the night, telling Wayne and Lula I was sewing on my wedding gown. We maids weren't allowed personal calls at the hotel so no one bothered me. I needed desperately to be alone.

How I yearned to hear Daniel's voice. But then — I felt like if he talked to me, he'd *know*. Daniel's sixth sense, where I was concerned, knew no bounds. I wasn't ready for that.

I avoided everybody these days. At school, I kept my nose poked in a textbook, keeping folks at bay. From there, I went straight to the hotel where I worked daily but spoke only when spoken to. Neither Buck Edmonds nor Harly

Kale had dined at the hotel since the night of the baseball practice. Nor had old Mr. Melton. I was relieved because I didn't think I could look either one of them in the eye.

Anger was my constant companion. I couldn't pray because I was angry with God for allowing this evil . Hadn't I been faithful to Him? I'd attended church regularly and tried to live a clean, exemplary life. I knew I was being unreasonable but I couldn't, at that precise time, help it. Hopelessness gnawed at me.

Today, Francine left just before the mill whistle blew, focused, no doubt, on drawing attention as she sashayed past Testosterone Corner. As I re-hung my gown, I heard the distant wolf-whistles. I usually would have grinned. Not today. The commotion merely fed my festering fury.

It was during the supper hour that Walter sauntered in and planted himself at one of my dining room tables. "Hey, Sunny," he greeted me warmly. I took a deep breath and made my way toward him, the effort taking every bit of energy I could muster. His gaze narrowed. "You okay?"

"Yeh," I all but snapped at him. "Why shouldn't I be?"

"You just look a little pale," he replied gently, picking up the day's handwritten menu and studying it.

"I'm sorry," I said, feeling nasty and mean. "I didn't mean to bite your head off. I'm just tired." I sighed, pencil poised for his order. "And I miss Daniel."

He looked up then and shot me his quick grin. "Figured as much. Bring me a bowl of blackeyed peas, a big hunk of cornbread, and fried potatoes." He slid the menu to me and leaned back in his straight chair, crossing sun-bronzed arms over his firm midriff and winked at me. " An' some of that fried streaked meat. I been cravin'it all day."

When I brought him his food, he touched my arm as I turned to leave. "Listen, Sunny. You don't need to grieve yourself over Daniel so much. He wouldn't like that. Y'know?"

I looked into his blue eyes. They were sincere. "Yeh," I smiled, "I know."

I turned to leave, the warmth of his concern lingering with me.

It's over. No need to worry anymore.

My smile widened as I approached the next diner.

When Daniel gets back, everything will return to normal — as though nothing ever happened.

Chapter Eight

Tom Stone died only days after being discharged from the hospital. Another heart attack. Walter took it pretty hard while Doretha showed no emotion whatsoever. I don't know that it ever dawned on poor Berthie what had happened.

No one knew how to get in touch with Daniel with the news. Seems he was traveling from town to town, staying with kinfolk along the way, his mama always two steps ahead of him. I didn't think Daniel would mind too much missing Tom's funeral. The man had never given him anything but grief. Daniel had lived with it. Bore it with grace.

I thought what a shame Tom Stone had let an opportunity to bless such a wonderful boy as Daniel slip through his fingers. Not only would kindness have nurtured and made a viable difference in Daniel's life but Tom himself would have reaped undying love and loyalty in return.

That was Daniel, as passionate in loving those faithful ones as he was in hating those who betrayed him. Like Mona, his mama.

Weeks passed and still Daniel did not return. I shoved back moments of panic and poured myself into wedding arrangements. When my nervous stomach began agitating in earnest, I had more trouble hiding it. Bouts of vomiting seized me, at first at all hours of the day, but especially after eating meals.

"Chile, what wrong with you?" Daisy planted herself between me and the rest room door, hands astride hips. Her chocolate-velvety gaze traveled the length of my crumpled body, near prostrate as I clung to the toilet seat, vomiting my guts up.

She waited until the heaving subsided before her strong hands pulled me to my wobbly feet. "How long you been doin' this?"

"A couple of weeks," I groaned, plopping limply onto the closed toilet lid. "Probably an ulcer. You know what a nervous stomach I've got." I jerked toilet tissue from a roll to wipe my mouth clean.

"Hmm." Daisy's astute gaze assessed my pale features for long moments. "Maybe." Another long silence. "You okay now?"

"Yeh." I forced myself to stand and splash cold water on my face. "I'll be okay in a minute. It always goes away."

As we made our way back to the dining area, I saw Walter come in. He stopped dead in his tracks when he spotted Daisy helping me to a chair. "Just give me a minute and I'll be okay," I whispered. She nodded, though obviously not at all convinced. Supper diners now spilled into the room so she had to get busy.

So did I. I rose unsteadily to my feet, tugged an order pad from my pocket, and approached Walter, who looked more astounded each step I took.

"What in God's name happened to you, Sunny?" His mouth hung open.

"Just an ulcer thing," I said, pen poised in dismissal of the subject. "Nothing to be concerned about."

His brows drew together. "Nothing? I don't call an ulcer *nothing*. Have you seen the doc yet?"

"No. I don't need —"

"Make 'er go, Walter," Daisy said over my shoulder, "She need to be see'd to." She moved on to take other orders before I could speak.

"You heard 'er, Sunny," Walter rose to his feet. "Get your things. I'm gonna call Doc Worley to meet us at his office."

I huffed and puffed like a daggum bullfrog but, with Daisy and Walter nipping at my heels, I soon found myself on Dr. Worley's examination table with my feet and legs in an iron stirrup contraption that pointed my knees at the ceiling in an exceedingly graceless way. I wondered, not for the first time, how he felt about my Mama's part in his interrupted retirement. He'd already probed and mashed on my abdomen until it ached and had churned up the terrible nausea again. Moments after my retching over the pail he stoically held for me, I found myself in this unsavory , undignified position.

A few minutes later, dressed and perched nervously on the edge of a straight chair, I awaited the old physician's reappearance. Walter thumbed through magazines in the outer waiting room. I thought again of the polar-differences between Walter and his late daddy. Walter's kind nature left ol' Tom looking like a demon.

I caught myself: it wasn't good to think ill o' the dead.

Dr. Worley entered the room. "Here's some medicine for your stomach, and a prescription for more if they help," he said, handing me some pills.

"Are ulcers hard to cure?" I asked, feeling my alarm grow.

"You don't have ulcers."

"I — don't?" The words sounded whispery, faraway.

"No, Sunny. You're pregnant."

I swooned. Yep. That's exactly what I did. Nearly went all the way out.

I barely heard the Doc say, "Does Daniel know?"

Daniel. Daniel. Oh my Go-o-od.

Then, everything *did* turn black.

~~~~~

"And after Dr. Worley asked me if Daniel knew, I passed out deader'n a quartered coon," I exhaled on a shaky breath, "When I came to, he didn't ask any more questions, thank God. Just told Walter to take me home."

"It's all my fault." Doretha, pale as a ghost herself, sat beside my limp bulk, now prostrate on her bed, as though posed for a wake viewing. I rolled my head to peer blearily at her. I'd just upchucked the hot dog Walter had insisted on buying me at the Super Grill — saying I'd not eaten a bite of supper. It was true. But the result was disgusting.

"Don't say that, Doretha." I patted her skinny little hand, unable to voice more at that precise moment.

"It's true, Sunny. If I'd not asked you to come here that night —"

"Please — Doretha, don't say that again." I shuffled my back against the pillows, raising myself a bit. "Ever. When you do, it's like you're saying it shoulda been you."

Her dark head slowly nodded, eyes downcast. "It shoulda."

"*Why?*" I asked, incredulous at her insistence.

" 'Cause," her gaze, soulfully sad, lifted to connect with mine, "you mean to make somethin' o' your life. Not like me — I don't matter that much."

"Doretha!" I sat up, took her by the shoulders and gazed into her bottomless gray eyes. "That's the craziest thing I've ever heard in my whole life. Your life does so matter! I don't know what I'd do without you being my friend. See who I came to tonight, don't you? Not my family, that's for sure. Nor Emaline. She's so — innocent. And I don't know how she'd take to my being pregnant and all...especially with her being engaged to a ministerial student."

Shame. I moaned as disbelief and shock blasted through me. "I don't know what Walter thought o' me groaning and takin' on like a fool all the way over here." I'd not told Walter anything except my ulcers were acting up. He watched me kinda funny but didn't say anything. Not even when I told him to bring me to Doretha.

The phone, newly installed, jangled from the living room. Doretha slipped quietly through the door, leaving it cracked as she left. "Hello," her small voice drifted back to me. "Daniel? My Lord. Where are you?"

Daniel? My pulse tripped into syncopation. I felt moisture gather on my brow. Cold sweat.

"Sunny? Come talk to Daniel," called Doretha. I arose on legs that felt jointless and stumbled my way to the living room. Everything looked dreamlike and hazy as I sank onto the brown couch.

"Daniel?" My voice quavered.

"Hey, Sunny," he murmured so sweetly I thought I'd die. I burst into tears, swamped with so many emotions they squiggled like a bucket of night crawlers.

"What's wrong, honey?" His concern hummed along the wires and into my skin.

"It's — it's just —" I struggled to gain control, swallowing back sobs for long moments.

"Sunny?"

"It's just that I'm so glad to hear your voice." I hiccuped then and we both laughed.

"Me, too," he said.

"Where are you? Did you find your mama?"

"In Memphis." A short, dry laugh. "Almost. Least I talked to a recent boyfriend. I found out all I needed to know. She'd already moved on."

"And?"

"And nothing's changed." A long silence, then. " I suppose once a whore, always a whore. I give up on 'er." The bitterness of his judgment smote me, turning me to ice. I heard no *forgiveness*. And I was in no position to counsel him. My numb fingers dropped the black receiver. Doretha grappled it from the linoleum floor and shoved it back into my hand, watching me closely, sliding her arm around me.

"I love you, Daniel," I whispered, grief squeezing tears and life from me. *No forgiveness. No forgiveness....*

All things change...all things change.

Everything had changed since I'd last heard his voice. Everything. Now, *I* was Mona, needing mercy and understanding.

"I'm coming home, Sunny," he said softly, "to my wonderful, sweet girl. You're like a breath of fresh air after being around Mona. I want to be there when you graduate. It's the beginning of our dream." The reverence in his voice shoved me over the edge. I burst into fresh tears.

Oh God! Oh God...

Fear has a coppery flavor. I can, after all these years, still recall its acrid taste on my cottony tongue. I tried to be brave. I truly did. But another fear latched onto me, digging in with wildcat claws — if anyone at school found out, I'd not be allowed to graduate. It was a written-in- blood law in

District Five. No person married or pregnant was eligible for a diploma.

"B-bye, Daniel." I dropped the phone into Doretha's outstretched fingers like it was a hot poker, then buried my face in my hands. "I want to die, Doretha. I just want to die. Daniel will never be able to let it go." She slid her arms around me and rested my head on her frail shoulder.

"Don't tell 'im." Doretha's quiet words connected , then jelled.

"What?" I raised my wet face and stared at her.

"You're right. He won't be able to let go of it. So, don't tell 'im. He don't have to know."

"We're getting married in a week."

She just looked at me, eyes faraway, yet — conveying a message I wanted to hear. One of hope.

My heart leaped. Could it be possible?

"Do you think —" I gazed at Doretha. Oh, dear *Lord*, how I wanted it.

Her little nod was all I needed. Daniel and I would still have our dream life.

Together. But first, I had to figure out *how*.

~~~~~

The solution came to me the next night. I would just let Mother Nature take her course with Daniel and me. I didn't exactly pray about it. Years later, as I look back, I realize I merely *told* God what I thought was the right way out.

"Me 'n Tack's getting' married next month," Francine announced at Nana's supper table. "I'm sure glad you'n Aunt Tina made up," she addressed me with a big ol' grin, so rare on her she looked like another person entirely. "Makes it a lot easier to plan things with you stayin' here."

I was glad, too. Aunt Tina had come by the hotel the night before and apologized for ordering me from the house. Not for saying mean things about Ruth Bond, mind you. Her benevolence didn't extend quite that far. But I was so tied in knots over what I was going to do about the mess I was in, I jumped at the peace offering like a starving dog to a pork chop. By bedtime, I'd packed up and moved back in.

So tonight was a celebration of sorts. Only the niggling apprehension riding shotgun in my bosom smothered the child's excitement inside me. Francine's display of joy was a milestone-thing. Seldom did she venture to include us in her exuberant moments.

Except for a tearful, thumb-sucking Rachel, the Acklins were glad to see me reconciled with my family

"You gonna have bridesmaids?" Sheila addressed Francine, her hope pathetically obvious. She was definitely going to be my attendant, along with Francine, and Emaline as my maid-of-honor. Daniel's best man would be Walter.

"Nah." Francine flipped her hair back and bit into her biscuit. "Except Sunny," she muffled around a mouthful.

Sheila's lids quickly lowered but not before I saw expectancy plunge and hurt flash in her eyes. "I didn't want to be one, anyway." She managed to sound flippant. "'Cept for bein' in Sunny's wedding." Her head lifted and her chin jutted out as she glared at Francine.

"Nothin' personal," Francine shot her a flat look. "Just don' want a big to-do."

My stomach knotted. *Why* couldn't they draw in the claws and simply be sisters? Why couldn't Francine *stretch* just a tad and include her baby sis in the thing? *Oh no.* That would flow too, too easily. Bile rose in my throat, burning. Nausea. I swallowed while pushing food around in my plate, trying to look like I was eating. I hated the way my sisters fought over everything and nothing.

Dang it! The food was a bit greasy for my weak stomach. Tasty, actually, by all mill hill standards. Nana's thickening milk gravy was the best in the world. But right now, I contended with the reality of its taste coming *up*. Not good. Bad, in fact. Very, very bad. Just that thought set my gag reflex into overdrive.

I arose and left the table as quietly as possible. "Be right back," I murmured over my shoulder so no one would follow. Being tonight's celebrity, I knew that would happen if I didn't put their minds at rest. "Gotta potty," I tacked on for good measure, just barely suppressing a gag.

Once inside the bathroom, the floodgates burst. I'd learned how to regurgitate quietly, flushing the commode all along to cover any splashing sounds. When the surge subsided, I brushed my teeth and washed my face before returning to the table, relieved to have my stomach emptied of the sickening mass called food. At that precise moment, I didn't see how I'd ever again consider edibles as anything but *nasty*.

I'd just taken my seat when I heard the front door slam shut. I sat with my back to the kitchen door but I saw the looks on Francine and Sheila's faces and I knew.

"Hey, Daniel!" Timmy called out, stumbling to his big adolescent feet. Now fifteen, he'd shot up in recent months, so help me Jehosophat, two inches. "Come on in, man." He scuttled about, grabbing an extra chair and popping it in beside me.

"Have some supper," Nana added, along with a chorus of assents. Even Aunt Tina loved Daniel. For some reason, this frissoned tremors through me like a loom's steel shuttle. Ominous emotions slithered through me. Unsteadily, I rose to my feet. Overriding fear was my desire to see, to *feel* Daniel, my Lion-Man.

Next thing I knew I was in his arms and *Lord, it felt so good* I thought I'd die. His lips brushed, then connected solidly with mine for a long moment before he finally loosened his grip on me, and after a slow drinking look into my eyes, greeted the others. That contact had my heart pitter-pattin' like that Tweedly-Dee Dee song.

Aunt Tina said, "Sheila, get him a plate and some tea."

Within moments, Daniel feasted on the same food that'd poisoned me. But my sickness subsided as I watched him, rapt with the brushing of our arms and inhaling the unique scent of him. God, how I loved him. No, I *worshipped him*, couldn't tear my gaze from his wonderful, gorgeous hands, sinewy arms, and intense countenance. His turquoise gaze bounded to mine time and time again. And I knew he, too, felt what I did.

I decided then and there, I couldn't lose him

~~~~~

Later, on our walk, streetlights cast planes and angles across Daniel's face, painting him mature and so handsome I felt like I would explode any minute. At the middle of Oak, a streetlight was out. Daniel stopped, took me in his arms and kissed me so thoroughly my joints dissolved

Then he took my arm and led me to a vacant house, whose back screened-in porch was unlatched. There, with the blind-wall two-thirds up, we finally had privacy. An old single-bed mattress leaned against the wall. Daniel flipped it over and we lowered ourselves onto it.

Tonight, I knew Daniel's need for restraint was not so intense. After all, our wedding was but a few heartbeats away. Graduation was tomorrow night, a fact over which, once done, I would heave a great sigh of relief. There was so much I couldn't share with him. So much. And I missed that aspect of our relationship so badly I wanted to weep and wail.

I felt a surge of guilt for what I was about to do, yet, at the same time, knew I had no choice. It was either deceive him or lose him. I could not willingly give Daniel up.

In the next breath, I couldn't've stopped the torrent had I tried. Daniel stretched his beautiful weight over me. It felt so right and when his pelvis settled, then undulated into mine, I met him grind for grind. The fire in me was deep, incited when Daniel raised himself above me and lowered his head and kissed me as heavy and carnal as I felt. I was mindless with a need for him to fill me, to somehow stamp out the awful violation that had taken place that nightmare night in Doretha's bed.

I pushed the thoughts aside as Daniel came into me, wonderful steel and silken heat — and at the same time reverential. For just a heartbeat, a flashback of the dark moment in Doretha's bed shook me. Then I realized this was Daniel. *My Lion-Man,* Daniel, the feel and taste of him sweetly familiar. *Right.* My intake of breath hissed...Daniel moaned softly, "I'm sorry, Sunny," and remained motionless for long moments. I was still tight and it dawned on me that he mistook my delighted gasp for pain.

Appalling regret swamped me and I sighed tiredly. Again, he misinterpreted the sigh. "Ahh, Sunny," he murmured hoarsely, "I can't wait —" He began to move in me, harder, deeper, creating a burn and soothing it at once.

The pleasure of it left me panting and gasping as his momentum built and raged like a wildfire that consumed us both, making us one. I exulted in it — the oneness. Gloried.

Daniel arched into me with a guttural, animal sound from deep within his chest and I felt him, penetrated as deeply in me as he could go, flood me with his seed.

His seed. Such precious seed. I clutched him to me, tears rushing to my eyes, spilling over.

His head raised. "Sunny? Are you crying?" His stunning turquoise eyes raked my features, as concerned as I'd ever seen them. "I'm so sorry, honey. I didn't —"

"Shh." I put my fingers over his lips to stop the words. They pierced like bullets. "I'm just so happy." That was partly true. Partly. I wrapped my arms around him, pulled him close, cradling his face in the crook of my neck, wanting to protect him so badly I trembled. How I loved him. And the only way to protect him was to keep the truth from him.

What Daniel doesn't know won't hurt him. In that instant in time, I was convinced it was true.

Minutes later, he made love to me again, this time more slowly, intent on giving me pleasure. The fire between us ignited to greater heights and I thought I'd pass away from ecstasy as he brought me to fulfillment — a purely artless, *instinctive* thing with my inexperienced Lion-Man. We muffled our cries against each other's necks, afraid some passerby might hear and come to explore. Afterward, Daniel held me as gently as he would a fragile china doll. I was so thankful that his image of me remained intact.

He doesn't know. Only other person who knows is Doretha, who won't ever tell a soul.

If only this had happened before Daniel's trip. But it had not. Now, I had to go with what I had to keep Daniel. I couldn't begin to face life without him. I didn't, in those moments, even entertain the word *deception* in my dealings with Daniel.

My mind simply deleted it.

Desperation painted my actions *protective* and *necessary*.

~~~~~

Daniel's face glowed from the audience as I walked across the school auditorium stage and received my diploma. My relief was enormous. Yet an even greater horizon loomed and a sense of foreboding followed me around like a black thundercloud. Our wedding was scheduled for Saturday and, on Thursday evening, I walked to the hotel to press my wedding gown. I planned to dress there for the ceremony, after which Francine and Tack would drive me to the church.

"Two days away," Daisy *tch-tched.*

I wasn't feeling very well. Supper had been fried fare. I swore I'd never look another pan of grease in the face again as long as I lived. "You lookin' mighty peak-ed," Daisy said, as though divining my desolation.

"Just overloaded," I muttered, pulling a hidden straight pin from a seam and checking for others.

Sheila strolled in, sexy as Monroe in white short-shorts and a snug white shirt. Against the white attire, her honey-tanned skin shimmered. "Mm *Mm,*" Daisy intoned, "jus' look at that purdy thang." Like Timmy, thirteen-year-old Sheila had shot up to statuesque svelteness in the past eighteen months, maturing much more rapidly than I had.

Sheila gave her a big, impulsive hug, effusive with the excitement of my approaching wedding. "Daisy," she trilled, "you jus' say the sweetest things."

"Don't give 'er the big head," Francine snorted as she ambled in, blatantly vying with Sheila for 'most sexy' in crimson short shorts and halter-top. My siblings shrewdly measured one another, each equally confident in her sensuality.

"I heard what you told Aunt Tina 'bout Tack." Francine swooped to confront Sheila, nearly toe-to-toe. "Still lyin', ain't you?"

"Wadn't no lie," Sheila said blandly, enjoying the rise from Francine, preening, in fact. "He tried to kiss me —"

"Didn't so," Francine's eyes slitted as she drew back to hit her.

"I dare you." Sheila stuck out her chin, hands planted on hips. "Wouldn't want to hit me for tellin' the truth, now would you, Frannie-wannie?"

To her credit, Francine didn't hit her, merely turned the air blue with her filthy mouth. I tuned her out and hung up my gown.

Timmy trailed in moments after Francine, looking distinctly misfitted in the small room. He now towered over his squabbling sisters, all legs and arms, bumping everything in his path to me. His affection for me remained childlike and constant. He bent to give me a big hug and a peck on my cheek. "Love ya, Sunny," he muttered, utterly unashamed, ignoring his sisters' ruckus.

"Love you, too, Timmy."

He smelled of Vitalis hair tonic. Suddenly, the wonderful smell turned deadly. I heaved violently, turned on my heel, and dashed blindly for the bathroom door. I didn't know Daisy had followed me until I came out the small cubicle to find her leaned against the doorjamb, arms akimbo, and a wise look on her face.

"You tol' Daniel about this yet?" One sooty eyebrow lifted.

"No." I wiped my face with toilet tissue. "No use botherin' him so close to the wedding. Ulcers aren't the worst things in the world, after all. I'm taking pills for them."

"Hummph." She pushed away from the wall, looking extremely cynical. "He ain't gonna like bein' kep' in the dark."

She walked away, going back to her kitchen post, where large white lima beans simmered in their own bacon-seasoned sauce, cornbread baked, and sliced potatoes sizzled with onions in big cast iron frying pans atop the wood stove. The smells that would have, only weeks ago, beguiled me, now tortured me.

I slammed the bathroom door shut behind me and fell upon the commode again, retching and heaving until my stomach emptied. I washed my face, rinsed out my mouth, and peered in the wall mirror.

"Ain't gonna like bein' kep' in the dark." Did Daisy suspect? *Lord help me.* Without thought I took off to the kitchen, finding her flipping golden crisp potatoes at the stove.

"Do you really think Daniel will be angry with me?"

I tried to hide my weakness and terror as she cast me a chastising look. "I reckon he will. Man don' like his fiancée keepin' things like ulcers from 'im, eh, Sunny?"

I dropped my gaze, relieved beyond measure. "No. I guess not." *Daisy probably knows,* I thought, *but she's pretending she doesn't. She won't say anything.* I went back to the sewing room to find Sheila and Francine near to blows.

"Hey, I can't help it if Tack finds me dee-sire-able," Sheila struck a sensual pose, with her shoulder-length hair falling over one eye. "And that's a fact."

"You li'l *hussy.*" Francine bore crimson talons as she lunged. "I'll scratch —"

"Stop!" I flung myself between them, getting violently jostled for the effort. "This is stupid! Sheila, why are you doing this?" I gazed at her, disappointment flailing about inside me.

She saw it. My disapproval. Her green eyes lost their sensual, incited glint, turning instantly defensive. "Just having a little fun is all, Sunny. Francine's always a'braggin' on how she's so much prettier'n me and sexier and all. Thinks she's better'n me."

"You're *sisters*, Lord have mercy! Francine, she's our baby sis —"

"*Half-sister*," Francine hissed, eyes like golden daggers slashing at Sheila. "Daddy don't even *claim you*, you lying bi —"

"*Stoppiiitt!*" I screeched, hardly recognizing my own voice. I glared at Francine. "I can't believe you said that."

Sheila spun on her heel but not before I saw the tears streaming down her pale cheeks. "Don't leave, Sheila," I called but she fled, disappearing from the foyer like a vapor.

Even Timmy glowered at Francine, shaking his dark head as he, too, departed, wide shoulders slouched as he sloughed awkwardly out the door.

"She had it a'comin'," Francine said, blissfully shameless in what she considered a coup. "Tack says she's making up every word of it. Hey, I know when Tack's a'lyin'. This time, he ain't. And does Sheila care who she hurts? Hell, *no.*" She tossed back her wild tresses and lit her Camel cigarette. I'd given up trying to shame her for smoking. The fact of TB-weakened lungs did nothing to faze her zeal for the vice. At the same time, the stench was deadly for me.

"Francine," I swallowed back bile, "that cigarette smoke makes me sick."

"Oh." She shrugged and ground it out in the metal hotel ashtray. "Sorry."

I went and put my arms around her. She returned my embrace. "Ahh, Francine, I know you've got a point about Sheila but that was hittin' awfully low, bringing that up."

"What's this I hear about you being sick?"

I spun around, heart in throat. Framed by the doorway, Daniel vibrated with ferocity. It was his face that impaled me, dark and fierce as any Roman gladiator's. Francine scuttled past him, pleased to escape more of my censure.

"Just ulcers, Daniel. Nothing to be —"

"Why didn't you tell me? I had to learn it from Daisy," he threw up his hands in exasperation, " who's very *worried* about you." It occurred to me that his fierceness was actually hurt. "Says you're throwing up all the time. *Dang it all,* Sunny. Why didn't you tell me?" Guilt waylaid me.

"Honey," I went to him, threw my arms around his resistant bulk, and pressed my face to his neck. "I'm sorry. I just didn't want to worry you now, what with the wedding and all."

The stiffness left him as his arms slid around me, clasping me to him. I hoped he couldn't feel my pulse running away like a terrified rabbit. Guilt was a tiger eating me alive. I hadn't realized it would be so difficult to keep up the pretense.

I closed my eyes, burrowing my face deeper into the warm crook of his neck and felt Daniel's arousal against my belly. Against another man's baby. *Stop it!* My eyes sprang open in alarm even as my body responded to his heat and passion. I groaned with longing when his lips sought and claimed mine and his exquisite hands cupped my bottom and molded me to him.

Oh Lord, please help — The prayer died right there. I was not fit to utter the Lord's name, much less petition Him for help. And I knew, in that terrible moment that I could not go through with it. I couldn't deceive Daniel. He deserved better.

I gazed up into the worshipful turquoise eyes and opened my mouth, "There's something I've got to tell you, Daniel."

"Miz Sunny," Daisy poked her head in the door. "That purdy sister o'your'n's outside, crying her lil' heart out."

Sheila. Heaven help me, amid all the mess in which I festered, I'd forgotten her. Daniel and I disentangled. "She didn't go home?" I'd figured her to do just that.

"If she did, she done come back. I s'pect she need you to soothe 'er, Sunny. Timmy be with her but — she need you."

I looked at Daniel. His eyes conveyed understanding and tenderness. How blessed I felt just then and a sense of peace filled me that I'd decided to tell him the truth.

"I'll tell you later." I squeezed his hand and rushed to the side screened-in veranda, where Daisy pointed me. It afforded a little more privacy than the front porch, which now rustled with early arrivals tarrying for the five o'clock supper hour.

Timmy forfeited his seat to me, beside Sheila in the porch swing whose chains fastened onto ceiling hooks. I watched him saunter back through the door to the lobby, which led to the front porch where he'd join Daniel in one of the big rocking chairs. As one, Sheila and I set the swing in motion.

Sheila snuffled. Her eyes were swollen nearly shut, her pretty features puffy and red. Slender hands lay in her lap, against tanned legs, where berry-tipped fingers danced their bizarre little dance of misery and desperation.

"Ahh, honey," I slid my arm around her shoulder and hugged her to me. "I'm so sorry you got hurt. I wish Francine hadn't said what she did. But you know how she is when she gets mad and what you said about Tack sent her over the edge."

"*Huh.*" Sheila crossed her bronzed arms and stuck out her chin, her foot sending the swing into a less sedate cadence. "She's said lots more than you know about, *before* I told on Tack."

"Did Tack really come on to you?" I asked softly.

"*Huh.*" She propelled the swing faster. "What do *you* think?"

"Did he?"

My foot halted the swing. Sheila grew still, her fingers resuming their dance. She watched them. "We-ell. He didn't exactly *come on* to me. More like teased."

"Sheila, it's wrong of you to tell Francine Tack did all those things when he didn't." *Who am I to talk?* I could've slithered through the floor cracks.

Her head swung around and our gazes connected. "Sunny, she's always a'tellin' me how ugly I am and how I've got funny feet and a big fanny. She tells me how stupid I am and what a big liar I am. But worst of all," her tormented green eyes probed mine, "is how she reminds me I'm not really full family. Just *half.*" She looked away, drooping with desolation.

"I hate 'er, Sunny. She's *mean* and spiteful and always talkin' 'bout how she's gonna be the one in the family to get rich. Ol' Tack's gonna be her meal ticket to paradise, to hear her tell it. The rest of us are gonna be settin' round barefooted, half-starved and on welfare. Thinks she's so much smarter. *Above* the rest of us." The swing started again.

"Let's get one thing straight, Sheila. You're as much family as any of us. Heck, with Mama's track record, who knows for certain who fathered *any* one of us?" That seemed to calm her some. "And honey, you're not ugly." I had to laugh at the absurdity of it.

"*Lord have mercy*, you're so beautiful you hurt my eyes. Everybody says so. And your feet are cute. Nobody's toes are perfect. They're like ears. Start lookin' at ears and you'll see what I mean. I think Francine's jealous of you, for some crazy reason. But you play right into her hands, Sheila, by saying outlandish things to get her attention and shock her. And when you brought Tack into it, well —"

"Tack *did* flirt with me." Her stubborn little chin projected itself again.

I opened my mouth to ask her to define flirting, as well as why she felt it necessary to tell Francine about it. Then I clamped it shut. Sheila, in her own way, obsessed as badly as Francine with being *out front.*

"Sure," I muttered, allowing her the last word, hoping it may compensate, in small measure, for Francine's cruel words, words I'd had no idea she used to hurt Sheila.

We continued to swing silently, my arm draped over her shoulder. I was thinking what a contradiction my little sis posed, with her razor-sharp tongue and waif-vulnerability, when I spotted Dr. Worley mounting the front steps, no doubt planning to take supper in the hotel dining room. For a moment, I smiled at the warmth his familiar face triggered.

Until I saw him veer over toward Daniel's rocking chair, hand outstretched in greeting. *Oh God! No. He thinks the baby is Daniel's.*

My heart stopped. My life stopped.

And as clear as day, I came face to face with the reality of something I'd heard all my days: *…you can be sure your sins will find you out.*

~~~~~

I waited for Daniel in the swing, dying a thousand deaths each time I inhaled. Sheila had gone home, trailed by Timmy. My heart raced like my sewing machine needle as I sat there, sweat soaking my arm pits and sheening my face. It was like standing on Hell's brink, knowing Lucifer would, any second, shove me over the edge. I stared into the flaming abyss, aware that I deserved every terror known to mankind.

When Daniel finally pushed open the veranda's screen door, his steps sloughed an entrance. At first, he didn't look at me. His features drooped with shock. *Oh god.* My swing stopped dead. I couldn't bear it.

"Daniel," I whispered. He slowly lifted his head until his eyes connected with mine. Behind them glimmered hurt, disbelief, then slowly, anger.

"Sit with me, Daniel. We need to talk." I couldn't believe my voice was as steady as it was, what with all the chaotic thoughts and emotions flailing about inside me. Shock. That's what it was. He didn't sit beside me, instead he deliberately plopped heavily into a rocker facing me, a safe four-feet away. That stung. Dreadfully. But I had to get through this, somehow. Make him see....

"Yeh," he muttered, shaking his head as if to dispel something slimy and clingy that'd attached itself to his ears. He looked off into the distance, at nothing, his gaze seemingly riveted to horrific atrocities. "Talk." His voice sounded flat. Dead. "We need to talk." Then his eyes met mine again. They suddenly blazed. "Okay, Sunny," he muttered though clenched teeth. "*Talk.*"

"What did Dr. Worley say to you?" A pitifully irrational part of me still, incredibly, hoped he hadn't divulged everything.

"You're pregnant." Disbelief washed over his face. He blinked it away. "How? Whose is it Sunny? It can't be mine. We didn't — not till this very week." He looked away, features again tight, near bursting. "I can't believe it." Hands flashed through dark hair. "Dear God. I *can't stand this.*" His head rolled back, features grimaced in agony.

I recoiled. "Daniel. I was *raped.*" *There.* I'd said it.

The turquoise gaze slashed to me. "Raped? God! This gets worse." He stalked away, pivoted, then returned, nearly nose to nose with me, hands planted on hips.

"When?"

"The night after you left."

"Why didn't tell me?" His voice was a lethal whisper.

"How could I?" My voice was a wimpy whisper. Sweet Jesus. It all sounded so contrived.

"I called."

"I — I tried. I just couldn't find the right time to —"

"The *right* time?" The eyes blazed again then turned deadly. "Right time." His lip curled up on one side, his eyes remained icy. "Who? Who was it?"

"I don't know. I — I was at Doretha's house, in her bed, the night Tom Stone was in the hospital with a heart attack. Somebody broke in, through the window." God, it took such effort to speak. "It happened through the night." I burst into tears, reliving the goshawfulness of it. Daniel didn't move an eyelash. I realized he was in shock as much as I. "I'm sorry," I whispered and wiped my face with my forearm. "I never saw him."

"Never saw him?" Daniel sounded skeptical. My heart began to break.

"No." Sobs gathered in my chest, throat. I took a deep breath, held it, and blew it out. " He covered my face with a pillow."

"You didn't hear his voice?" Again. Doubt.

"No, Daniel, I didn't hear his voice." My words came out sharper than I intended. I checked myself. After all, Daniel was hearing this for the first time while I'd learned to live with it to some degree.

He dropped heavily into the seat opposite me and hooked an ankle over his knee , belying the tension I sensed coiled in him like a livid cobra. "Don't you have any idea who it could be?" Suddenly, he seemed so laid-back it threw me. Then it dawned on me that he'd become analytical. Was that good or bad? My hands began to tremble in earnest. I clasped them tightly together.

"I've thought about it a lot," I said, trying in vain to keep the tremor from my voice. "I've suspected Harly Kale and —"

He was on his feet. "Why the hell Harly Kale?" His hands knotted into fists.

Gladys. Oh my god. "He's just —" I took a deep breath and exhaled slowly. My head still spun like whirly-bird wings and I grasped at the first thing that lit in my brain. "Gladys once told me to stay away from him because she didn't trust him. A-and Ruth Bond told me he'd raped her." I didn't want to say he'd actually come on to me that day when Gladys wasn't home. It was too inflammatory just then. I think in the very back of my addled mind was the strong motive to protect Gladys.

However, I had my own boat to row at that precise moment.

Mentioning Ruth's name earned me zero points. His features turned even more grim as he moved to stand gazing through the screen into dusk. "You said there was another possibility."

I hesitated, recoiling from further revelations. But heck, I'd already dumped tons of garbage on him. "I wouldn't put it past Buck Edmonds." I dropped my gaze to where my hands lay, icy and numb, against my lap.

His head snapped around. The glacier gaze pinned me. "Why?" Where was his compassion? His questions were so devoid of sympathy I despaired. My heart dropped lower.

"He's come on to me at times. I always pushed him away and —"

He spun around and advanced a few steps, stopping far enough away to establish *untouchable* distance. "*Always?* My god, Sunny, how many times *did* he *come on* to you? Why've I never heard any of this before? *Huh?*" He succinctly turned his back and strode away to the far screen to glare out.

"I didn't want you to be upset," I murmured, realizing how lame that sounded, even to my own ears. "Besides, there's nothing I can prove about either Harly or Buck." I opened my mouth to mention Mr. Melton then closed it. I couldn't, even under these circumstances, hurt Emaline. Anyway, I sensed that including him wouldn't strengthen my appeal to Daniel. Would, in fact, be detrimental. "You don't believe me, do you Daniel?" My words came out hoarse and whispery. This silent Daniel terrified me — this condemning person who wouldn't come within a three-foot distance of me.

He remained silent for so long I thought he didn't hear me. Then he turned and I felt his gaze on me. Dusk painted his face dim and his features nearly indistinguishable.

"When were you going to tell me, Sunny? Or were you just going to let me believe it was mine? Was that what that was all about last night when we —"

"No!" I sprang to my feet and rushed to him. He recoiled from my touch, shrank from my reach. I let my hands drop, turned and retraced my steps. I sank back into the swing and sighed heavily, feeling everything was surreal. I tried to dredge up anything hopeful in the situation. I couldn't. Yet — in one sense, it was a relief to have the truth out in the open.

I just hadn't counted on it being this way.

"Please, Daniel, sit down. It's hard to talk to your back and with you standing so far away. I don't want to talk so loud the world will hear. It's certainly not something I'm proud of."

Like some automated apparition, he returned and seated himself in the rocker.

"I owe you nothing less than the whole truth, Daniel," I said, finally meaning it. "I'll admit that I grew desperate enough to deceive you. I won't deny that. I didn't want to lose you. Can't you understand that?"

He didn't say anything. Just sat there, hands clasped across his torso, rocking slowly, watching me as though I were some daggum stranger.

"Anyway," I swallowed a lump and continued, "I realized I couldn't do that to you. I was gon' tell you tonight, whatever the outcome."

He remained silent, the turquoise gaze I'd found so exciting now scared me spitless. Minutes passed. He'd resumed staring into the gathering darkness while I sat there, heart-in-hand as he weighed my — *our* future. "Aren't you going to say anything?" I finally blurted, unable to endure the foreboding any longer.

Still long moments passed before he stood and paced to the veranda's far corner and back, where he halted before me. Nearer this time. My heart dared to hope. I gazed at him expectantly. *Please, God....*

"I wish I could believe you, Sunny. But I just can't. It's too much...the men you've — I won't say 'dallied' with but there you have it. And the fact that you let me make love to you while pregnant with another man's child blows me away. Just crushes me. If you'd just told me...." He ran his hands through his hair and then planted them on his hips as he rolled back his head.

"No, Daniel," I said, struggling to my feet. Awareness and nuance weighted and numbed me. "It wouldn't have made a bit of difference. You're just not a forgiving person." I shrugged, feeling as dead as his eyes when they lowered to meet mine. "Maybe you can't help it. I don't know. All I know is that I'll let you go if that's what you want. I do love you — more than ever, in fact. All this has made me realize how very much you mean to me."

I halted, swallowing back sobs. "I'd hoped we could go on together. I know that there's nothing that could make me turn my back on you because...." I began to cry quietly, I couldn't help it. My heart broke into a zillion little pieces as I stood there watching my life disintegrate before my eyes.

Daniel took a step forward, arms reaching...then he stopped, closed his eyes and clenched his fingers into fists before dropping them to his side. "Ahhh, Sunny. Why did it have to happen?" His eyes opened and I saw the tears. "I'll always love you. But I just can't live with this."

"Daniel?" I reached blindly for him but he elbowed past me, out the screen door.

Out of my life.

Chapter Nine

The next week still mists in my mind, all these years later. I do believe God protected me when Aunt Tina did the dirty work of announcing the wedding cancelled. The stated reason: Daniel got cold feet and ran off to join the Army. Which was, in a sense, true. Daniel did get cold feet. And he did run off to join the Army

Only thing, nobody else, except Doretha — who was sworn to secrecy — and Dr. Worley, knew about the baby. Without divulging anything more, I asked Dr. Worley not to tell anyone else about the baby. He gave me his word he would not.

Doretha tried to talk Daniel out of enlisting, insisting I was an innocent victim. But Daniel simply could not, at that precise moment in time, see me as *innocent* under any circumstances. He also couldn't reconcile to marrying a defiled, pregnant, lying Sunny. Period. End of discussion.

So be it.

Outwardly, I held my head up, drawing admiring remarks from those close to me. "Girl, you sure got guts. Not ever'body as brave when a feller runs like a skeered rabbit like that Daniel done," Daisy said time and again.

"Daisy, please don't say that again. *I am not brave.* I am one scared female." Then, to my humiliation, I choked up and fled to the sewing room, where my virginal white wedding gown still hung, deriding me with *what ifs*.

Oh yes, the shame of it was like flushing vinegar through an open shotgun wound. Yet, my secret overrode even Daniel's rejection and abandonment. Doretha was the only person to whom I could or would vent. She was always there, arms and heart open.

"What can I do, Doretha?" I sobbed on her shoulder. We sat in the living room while her mother napped upstairs. Doretha told me not to worry too much about Berthie overhearing us because her mama didn't remember enough these days to repeat gossip.

I'd burst in moments earlier after a violent bout of nausea. "Nana said 'was you a'vomitin', Sunny?' I lied, Doretha." I shook my head. "It never ends. I *hate* lying. But my folks couldn't handle it." I knew in my heart of hearts that those closest to me could not come to terms with this narrative in my life's story.

Doretha took my hands in hers, astonishing me again with her frail dignity. Her gray gaze met mine. "Thing is, Sunny, I don't think *you* could handle them *a'knowin'*. You'd nearly die knowing you was a disappointment to 'em, wouldn't you?"

How well she knew me. "Yeh. I would." I snuffled and blew my nose in the Kleenex she pressed into my hand. "So Daniel wouldn't even let you tell him about the rape?" I needed to hear it again.

"No." She gazed at me, her heart in her eyes. "I tried. I really did but he held up his hand like *'whoa'* as soon as I spoke your name. He lit outta here with his suitcase like his britches was on fire. Said tell you he was a'gonna join the Army." She shrugged sadly. "That's all he said, honey."

The back door slammed. Startled, I cast Doretha an imploring look. I didn't want anybody to see me with red, swollen eyes. I didn't want to do any explaining. It would mean more lies.

"S'probably just *Walter*," she rolled her eyes, making me giggle nervously. I could always count on gentle humor with the Walter-Doretha thing.

"Whaddaya mean *'just Walter?'*" His good-looking face poked through the door. As usual, a blond curl separated itself from the mane to dangle over his forehead. "I *heard* that, Doretha," he pointed a finger-gun at her, with deadly aim, "*POW*," then winked and flashed his quick grin at me.

His face sobered. "Hey, Sunny," he rushed over and hunkered down to take my other hand, "don't take things so hard. I could beat the stuffins' outta Daniel for takin' off like he did. Guy didn't know what he had."

"Don't blame Daniel," I said hoarsely, feeling slightly buoyed by Walter's words. "He didn't have much choice."

"Sunny don't want to talk about it, Walter." Doretha's bark was no more than a poodle's sigh but its timbre rang of protectiveness. "Why don't you just go on and let us girls be?"

"It's okay," I turned to her. She raised her eyebrow skeptically. "Really," I insisted.

She gazed at me for long moments, eyes unreadable. Then she stood. "In that case, I'll go upstairs and see about Mama. Call me if you need me, Sunny." Her gaze raked Walter for an insolent moment and she left.

I grinned. "She's really a cocklebur in the seat of your britches, ain't she?" Walter and I both burst into laughter. It was the first time I'd laughed since Daniel's exodus and I kept on till fresh tears riveleted down my cheeks. Walter grew sober as he gazed intently into my face.

"Whoa," he slipped onto the couch beside me and awkwardly put his arm around my shoulders. "Don't cry." His fingers squeezed my arm and then gently patted. "Please... don't cry, Sunny."

"I-I can't help it." I scrooched up my shoulders, then dropped them to a new low. "I just can't seem to get it all together these days, y'know?" Tears splashed on my hand holding the shredded Kleenex. "Here," he grabbed fresh ones and reached to ineptly blot my soppy cheeks.

"I'm a mess, Walter," I hiccuped, snatched the tissue from his hand, and blew my nose, wondering manically how so much liquid could come from one person's head.

"I've got an idea," he said, real upbeat-like. "Why don't we take in a movie tonight? Debbie Reynolds in *Susan Slept Here*?" He waggled his eyebrows comically, making me giggle like a silly teenager, which, I conceded, was exactly what I was.

"*Listen to me*," I gushed on a half-sob, half-snicker.

"Hey, I'm good medicine." He leaned and whispered in my ear, "'Cept with ol' Doretha." He did a Three-Stooges *whooo whooo whooo!*

Now that drew guffaws, weird shaky ones, but guffaws nevertheless. When I caught my breath, I said impulsively, "Yeh, let's go see Debbie."

We did. I begged Doretha to go with us but she declined., saying her mama needed her. So we went, just the two of us. And for the first time in over a week, I felt a bit of life begin to sluggishly stir within me again.

I'd gotten through another day.

~~~~~

Francine and Tack wed the next weekend. The church packed out. I suspect my cancelled wedding boosted the distinction of Francine's nuptials. And I'm sure the whole thing added a soap opera element of *"tune in tomorrow, same time, same station. Will Francine actually do it?"*

I wore a new red dress, Francine's choice for her maid-of-honor. I tried to repress *matron of honor* from my repertoire. It no longer applied.

"That hussy didn't even *show* for my wedding," Francine hissed under her breath in the hotel dining room, now set up for her reception. The food I'd bought for Daniel's and my reception now graced the tables, adorned by my decorations. No need to waste, Daisy had insisted and proceeded to prepare as though it were my wedding.

"Said she wasn't feeling well." I hadn't really believed Sheila until I saw her pale face and trembling hands. "Having a bad period." At least that's what she'd told me. There were times I couldn't read my little sister.

"On the rag, huh? That's her excuse? *Hummph,*" sneered Francine, then quicksilver-like pasted on her biggest smile to greet the Turners, Tack's family. Tack looked exceedingly happy. I suspected he couldn't believe he'd actually bagged the hottest gal on the hill. His aging parents seemed pleased enough with the match, as was Tack's older sister, Elaine Carly, whose husband Gene's drunken philandering was one-upped only by Harly Kale's.

Elaine hugged Francine and I noted her dress wasn't new, seemed a mite worn, actually. A pang of pity sliced through me. Her choice of husband had set her on a barren path, not only financially but emotionally as well, if gossip held truth. Impulsively, I stepped forward as soon as she'd greeted the newlyweds to give her a warm embrace. We'd seen each other in Tucapau Methodist Church. She always came alone. I gave Elaine an extra little squeeze, wanted to weep for her. She was such a contrast to her brother, Tack, and their parents, who all shined in designer clothes.

Preacher Wayne, as most folks called him, had performed the wedding ceremony. All the little Acklins were there, in top form. Now, Sarah tackled me at the hips, nearly knocking me off my feet. "Oh, Thunny," she lisped in her melodramatic way, "I mith you tho-o-o much."

I stooped and hugged her hugely. "I miss you, too, punkin'." We'd been to several matinees together, my little pal and I, with me trying, in vain, to keep her from knowing I cried all the way through the features. The wonderful smell of buttery popcorn evoked memories of Daniel's generous sharing with Timmy and Sheila, pulling the plug every time. Without warning, tears sprang to my eyes.

Those raisin eyes didn't miss a thing. Her chubby little hand lifted to my cheek. "What'th wrong, Thunny? You mith Daniel?"

I hugged her to me. "Yes," I whispered, "I miss Daniel." She knew her former hero had left me high and dry. Everybody did. Her innocent acceptance of Daniel's flaws warmed me. She still loved him, too.

Walter, dressed up in a pale blue suit and tie, managed to still be James Dean-loose and laid-back as he sauntered my way. He hunkered down beside me and teasingly pulled at Sarah's hand, whose thumb was imbedded in mouth. She grinned around the appendage-pacifier but her tongue kept right on lapping at it. "Aww come on," Walter coaxed, "let me taste it. You make it look so go-o-od."

Surprised, Sarah stopped sucking, stared at him for a long measuring moment, pulled the thumb out and generously stuck it up to Walter's mouth. Without blinking, he popped it into his mouth and did a reasonably accurate mimic of Sarah and had her giggling all over herself.

His gesture touched me for some reason. You'd have to love a child to partake of her saliva-slick finger. His tongue must have tickled because she went into spasms of giggles and quickly dislodged it, tucking it under her arm coyly, flirting with him. By now I was laughing too. It felt good.

Later, Walter walked me home. Fighting melancholy, I found myself asking him to visit awhile on the back stoop. "Sure," he said, lowering himself on the step beside me. His legs weren't as long as Daniel's. *Darn, there I go, comparing.* Daniel was gone. I simply *had* to get that through my thick head. He would be in Basic Training for at least six weeks, according to Doretha, and then only God knew where they'd send him.

"Has Daniel called?" Walter asked quietly, stunning me that he'd perceived where my thoughts drifted.

"No." I sighed and set my chin against emotions I had no right to. Not anymore. The churning in my stomach suddenly worsened and, without warning, I began to heave violently. I managed to spring to my feet and staggered to the grassy backyard perimeter before the messy part began. I felt Walter's hand on my back and the other at my elbow, steadying me. I tried to tell him not to expose himself to such a disgusting display but when I opened my mouth I merely heaved more heavily. Dear *Jesus*, why did the stomach insist upon giving up that last, deep vestige of food, that took such superhuman effort to dislodge?

Walter pulled out a white handkerchief, that'd been artfully folded into his suit pocket, and pressed it to my mouth and face, blotting away cold perspiration that beaded my forehead and upper lip. Sick as I was, I was impressed with his gentleness. His consideration. Tears sprang to my eyes.

"T-thank you, Walter," I managed to mumble. "I'm sorry you saw that."

"Hey," his arm slipped around my shoulders as he helped me back to the stoop, "no problem." He settled me on the step then lowered himself beside me. "Sunny — are you pregnant?" he asked gently.

For a moment, I was stunned by the suddenness of his question. Then, I felt myself sag with a strange relief. In a way, I wanted to vent. "Yes. I am." I laid my head back against the screened door and closed my eyes.

"Does Daniel know?"

I laughed. A dry humorless huff. "Oh, yes. He knows."

I felt Walter stiffen. "Then that's why he —"

"Uh huh." I sighed.

"Why that *bastard*," Walter muttered.

"No," I reached out to touch his rigid arm. "It's not Daniel's fault. You see, I was raped, Walter, while Daniel was away looking for Mona."

Walter gaped at me, an unfamiliar glitter in his blue eyes. Anger, I finally decided. "My god, Sunny. Who?"

I sagged even further and whispered, "I don't know."

We sat for long moments, he staring unseeing into the evening galaxy while I hugged my arms to me, suddenly chilled by memories. "What happened?" he asked quietly. Then he looked at me, intently, "is there any chance the baby is Daniel's?"

"No. He and I didn't — you know," I felt blood rush to my cheeks, "not until after I found out I was pregnant."

So I told him what had transpired that night. Walter was silent the entire time, staring ahead, listening intently. Then I went on to relate the conversations Daniel and I had had and how Daniel realized I'd started out to deceive him.

The whole truth. I felt incredible relief to finally unload it to another person I could trust.

Sometime during the discourse, Walter's arm had come around my shoulder and his strong fingers began to gently squeeze encouragement. That little gesture soothed me in ways I cannot begin to explicate. I was not aware that tears coursed down my cheeks until Walter's damp handkerchief reappeared to wipe them away. When I finished, my head lay on his shoulder.

We sat that way for a long time, silent and together. I felt drained but instead of being depleted, I felt a stirring of spirit — of hope for the future.

I lifted my head and looked at him. "Walter, I feel like I can finally pray again. For so long, I haven't been able to."

He gazed at me for long moments. Then he flashed me that quick grin of his. "I'm glad, Sunny. I know how much that means to you." When he saw my surprise, he said almost reverently, " Daniel once told me you're pretty religious."

I sighed and gazed into the star-studded June sky. "I guess I am." Crickets chirruped somewhere and I heard myself ask, "How about you?"

He threw back his head and laughed uproariously. "I'm many things, Sunny. But religious ain't one of 'em."

~~~~~

I spent increasingly more time with Walter and the more I did, the less I saw of Doretha. She disappeared with no more effort than a spooked Tinker Bell. It irked me because she'd been a mainstay during all my trials. So I naturally turned more and more to Walter for emotional support.

"What is it with Doretha?" I asked Walter one day when I'd dropped by and Doretha poofed into thin air. I sighed heavily. "Soon as I pop in she pops out. What gives? Has she decided I'm what Daniel says I am?" I was suddenly angry, oddly so. "I thought she was my friend." I choked up. "J-just look at me," I wailed. "I'm just a basket of hormones."

Walter swiftly moved to settle himself on the sofa beside me, by now comfortable with the supporting role. His arm slid around my shoulders. "At least you know why you're so near to cryin' most o' the time." His fingers gave a gentle little squeeze to my upper arm. Then he chuckled. "Don't you know by now what she's up to?"

I snuffled and gazed blearily at him. "Who? Doretha?"

He nodded, his eyes taking on a twinkle. "She's a'matchmakin'."

My eyes widened. "Us? You mean you and *me?*" I squeaked.

He drew himself up into the most formidable Sir Cedric Hardwicke snit I'd ever seen. "I beg yo' pah-don. Is that so *unthinkable*, might I ahsk?"

I snickered at his use of language, a tad advanced in places, for him. "You need a bit of work on that dialect."

"Made you laugh, didn't it?" He sank back into the sofa, propping his feet on the coffee table, a'grinnin' and looking exceedingly pleased with himself. "So I reckon it wudn' too bad."

"No," I agreed and burst into fresh laughter, lending myself to his humor. He didn't seem to possess an ounce of Daniel's darkness, his melancholy and —

There I go again. The laughter died and I pressed my fingers to my eyes.

"What is it, Sunny?" Walter's feet dropped to the floor and his arm came around me again and I found myself taking comfort from it being there.

"It's just — I keep thinking about Daniel." I looked at Walter, feeling as inept and helpless as a newborn. *Newborn.* Now *there* was another issue to face. "How could he have left me like this, Walter?" Indignation flared my nostrils. "Alone to face all the shame?"

Walter hung his head for a moment, then looked up at me. "That's just not so, Sunny."

"What? I won't face shame?" I gaped at him, gulping back more tears.

"You're not alone," he said quietly.

"Haaah!" I crossed my arms over my tender, swollen bosom — no longer resembling once-over-lightly eggs, more like two halves of a small hamburger bun — then grimaced and loosened them. " I can't talk to anybody — except you and Doretha — for fear somebody'll find out about the rape and the baby and broadcast it all over the hill. And now Doretha avoids me like I've got some daggum black *plague.* My family stares at me like I'm gonna go jump in the river any day now, putting another dark blot on them." I laid my arms across my thickening waist. "Like Mama didn't leave them with enough *nasty goop* to scrape at. Yeh, Walter, I'd say I'm pretty much alone in this thing."

He took me by the shoulders and turned me until I looked into his eyes. I'd never seen Walter angry before but, now, in comparison to his usual fun-loving self, he looked extremely irked. "You've got *me*, Sunny. Or hadn' you noticed?"

The fight went out of me. "That goes without saying, Walter. I'm sorry. It's just so — so *nerve-wracking*. Every day that passes, the baby inside me grows. Soon, I'll be showing and won't be able to pretend it's not there. The world will know."

Fresh tears puddled in my eyes. "Oh, Walter, how will I get *through* this? All I ever wanted was to be *good*. To marry Daniel and have a good life. A respectable life. To be a teacher and help others have good lives. And now…now, I've lost it all." I collapsed into his arms, buried my face on his shoulder and bawled my heart out.

Poor Walter, he patted me and kissed the top of my head and crooned *'It's gonna be okay, Sunny'* until I wore myself slap out and began to hiccup and snuffle my way back to composure.

Later, we ate supper at Nana's table. Everybody in the family liked Walter, not like Daniel, whom they'd adored, but I suspected they truly appreciated him looking after me following Daniel's shocking departure.

Fact was, they didn't know what to do with a fragile, weepy-mess Sunny. It made Nana overly jumpy and Francine do Road Runner escape pivots. Aunt Tina, still shell-shocked from Uncle Talley's betrayal, mostly didn't even seem to notice my mood swings from hound dog lackadaisical to Tasmanian Devil manic.

Emaline, well, I avoided Emaline. I wanted so much to pour my heart out to her but I was afraid her freshly dug-in spiritual stance — what with her being a future preacher's wife — might tap into a judgmental vein or at best make her a mite uncomfortable. I didn't think I could bear rejection from her. Too, seeing her and John together, planning their future, conjured up visions of Daniel and me just weeks earlier. It was too hurtful.

Only Sheila and Timmy remained constant in their tolerance and concern for my ever-changing ambiance. I promised myself they would forever remain my babies.

Tonight, Sheila watched Walter from beneath lowered eyelids, reminding me more of Mama every day. "Anybody ever tol' you you look like James Dean?" she asked Walter, bringing her tea glass slowly up to lush, full lips, watching him over the rim.

I stifled a nervous titter. The little *flirt.* She'd learned well in her fourteen years. At her age, I'd been skinny as a stick and pure as freshly Cloroxed sheets.

Walter looked amused. "Yeh," he muttered Dean-style, running his fingers through golden locks, disheveling and dislodging them. "Ever' once in awhile."

"'Cept for your blonde hair," Sheila added, fluttering long lashes at him.

"Looks more like Tim Holt to me," Timmy rumbled in his changing voice.

Sheila snorted. "That's cause boys don't really look at other guys past their hair color and muscles." Then remembering herself, she lifted her bosom subtly and angled Walter another come-hither look.

"Still up to your ol' tricks, I see." Francine posed seductively in the kitchen doorway, with Tack peering over her shoulder, sniffing out the food. Always in the past, Tack'd turned up his nose and refused to eat our meager fare. I suspected that now, only weeks into marriage with Francine, whose aversion to domesticity rivaled Doretha's, he wouldn't be quite so choosy.

"Have a seat," I said, "I'll get you plates."

"We done ate," Francine fluffed her hair. Tack looked pure pained.

"Come on, Tack. A growing boy needs more food," I coaxed as I made my way to the cabinet for plates, feeling a slight pang of pity for him. Only slight, mind you.

"Yeh, Tack," Aunt Tina chimed, coming out of her own fog momentarily to notice her surroundings. Uncle Talley's desertion had definitely altered her. She wasn't the same *I've-got-the-world-on-a-string* Aunt Tina of days gone by. "Have some supper."

Tack took the seat Timmy pulled out for him and filled his plate with generous portions of fried potatoes, chicken, and pinto beans as Aunt Tina cooed over him like a mother dove. Aunt Tina was from the old school that taught *fussin' over* equated *love*. When her Alvin took sick, she felt it her motherly duty to sit up all night, fretting over him. Anything less would *not* do.

Worry, the badge of love.

Sheila watched Francine with a predatory gleam in her slitted green eyes.

"Say Francine, how do you like that grand house o'yours?"

I wanted desperately to ward off warfare that would certainly result should my sisters be left to their own ploys. I poured Francine a glass of iced tea and placed it at one of the table's empty spaces. "Come. Sit." I tapped the chair incisively

Francine, not fooled for a second, locked rivalry gazes with Sheila for long tense moments before allowing me to divert her. "Since Tack made me some built-in cabinets and refinished the pine floors, I love it." She settled into the chair and I returned to my own seat. " 'Course, I need another bathroom. And I wouldn't mind havin' another bedroom." The village house was one of the larger, six-room versions.

"Don't want much, do you, Cleo?" Sheila lips V'd malevolently.

Francine's head snapped around. "Cleo?"

"Cle-o-pat-ra," Sheila enunciated as though to a moron.

Francine's gaze blazed and her nostrils flared.

"That's enough, Sheila." Nana's edict rang sharply in the air. Though she had no idea who the heck Cleopatra was, Nana knew maliciousness when she saw it. "Francine's a'visitin' and you'll treat her with respect."

Sheila's chair scooted back abruptly. "Then I'll be excusin' myself." She flounced from the kitchen with a definite new oscillation of hip movement.

My hand flew to my mouth as I stifled a laugh. Lordy, my desperate little sister would *still* do anything for attention. I looked at Walter, who watched me, his full lips twitching at the corners and I knew he shared my amusement. Without thinking, I reached for his hand beneath the table and gave it a gentle squeeze.

"Thank you," I mouthed silently.

His face sobered instantly. "You're welcome," he mouthed and I felt his strong fingers squeeze back.

Suddenly, I didn't feel as alone.

~~~~~

I'm not sure when the down-and-dirty panic began to invade me. Not the niggling kind. The *jar-from-sleep* kind that graduates to *won't-let-you-sleep-or-eat* and *walking-the-floor* kind. The kind that has the mind chasing its tail, playing the same horror-refrain over and over until it becomes a haunting litany, imbedded as in the groove of a record. The kind that takes appetite and rest and peace and reason from you, leaving you with only pain and torturous wide-awake, pacing nightmares.

Ones you can't escape.

Daniel's face was the last thing I saw at night and the first upon waking. Now I know how one can die from a broken heart.

I was careful to hide my distress from my family. Francine being gone helped. Her eagle eyes missed little. The Aunt Tina of old would have sniffed out pregnancy like a she-hound but now, with the finality of Talley's exodus a bald reality, I was merely a shadowy figure on the periphery of her dark melancholy. Nana's worried focus on Aunt Tina's angst diverted her attention from my ordeal. I kept plodding in a slow motion, horrendous quagmire.

Somehow, miraculously, I held it all together until one day when I went to visit Doretha, and Berthie answered the door wearing nothing but a white apron, her pendulous boobs bulging from each side of its bib. It was then that I really began to lose it.

"Can I help you?" she asked as though I were a perfect stranger and she the dignified lady of the manor. I gaped at her, thinking how even in this ridiculous state, she still maintained a measure of dignity.

The sadness of it tore at me. The absurdity of it pushed me over the edge.

My mouth went dry and my heart began pounding like a runaway bass drum. I feared my sanity was slipping away. No, I *knew* I was going insane.

I opened my mouth to speak. Nothing came out. Terror blasted through me like an icy arctic explosion. The spinning inside my brain crescendoed.

"Well?" Berthie raised her eyebrows imperiously "What do you want?"

"Oh God," I managed to moan, reaching out to steady myself. As my hand hit the screen, Berthie screamed, a loud, drum-splitting shriek that sent my adrenaline gushing like an unplugged fire hydrant.

"Git!" she hissed, swatting at me from behind the screen as though I were a horse fly determined to light on her roast.

Dear God, is the whole world going phobic or is it just me?

"Berthie," Walter appeared from nowhere, gently took his stepmother by the arm and coaxed her from the door, shooting me a pained *sorry, kid,* look.

"Doretha!" he bellowed.

I heard the back screen slam and Doretha's irritated little voice say, "What's on fire, Walter? I was trying to get the laundry off the — Oh, *my Lord*, Mama."

"I'm sorry, Sunny," Doretha murmured, not quite able to meet my gaze, thoroughly shamed.

Presently, she had her mother in tow and shuttled toward the stairs. Walter took my cold hand and pulled me inside, gazing at me with deep concern that grooved his brow. Uncertain, he said softly, "would you rather go for a walk, Sunny?"

I snuffled and gratefully took a Kleenex from him. "Yeh. I would." My teeth felt as though they would begin to clatter any moment. "No," I said, quickly changing directions. I didn't want to be seen like this, knowing how villagers gossip and embellish truth. I sighed raggedly. As I exhaled, my very life seemed to drain out on that breath. I sagged. Walter grabbed me before I slithered onto the floor.

Poor Walter dragged me to the sofa and stretched me out.

I closed my eyes and told myself to just relax and everything would be all right. But after a few moments, I felt silly just lying there, and tried to get up. I couldn't push myself up. It was as though I'd turned to concrete. "Walter!" I cried, panicked.

"It's okay, Sunny. Just relax and rest awhile." Walter pulled a straight chair over to sit beside me, holding my frigid hand. "I think I should take you to see Dr. Worley."

"No." I tried to sit up again but could not pry myself loose from the darned sofa. It was a magnet pulling me down, down, down…. "Oh, please help me, Walter," I whimpered, for once not shamed by my vulnerability.

"That's it." He arose, pulled me up and hoisted me into his strong arms. He carried me to his car and gently laid me out on the back seat.

Then he drove like a bat out of hell to Dr. Worley's office.

~~~~~

"Nervous exhaustion," decreed the village physician. "Young lady, you're gonna have to get some rest. I'm prescribing some pills to help you relax and sleep. And you're not eating enough for one. Much less two. That's gotta change. Now I know you're strung out over Daniel's poor behavior." He slowly shook his white head. "Wouldn't 'a figured him one to shirk responsibility. As I promised, all that shall remain between just the two of us. So don't worry about that. You get on with your life. Your stress is understandable. But you've got this child to think about now. Think you can manage that?" He was scribbling on his pad.

"Yes," I muttered, shamed and a bit annoyed that the doctor blamed Daniel for my pregnancy but relieved that he remembered his promise and would abide by it.

On the short ride back to the Stone's house, Walter's vigilance began to get on my nerves. "I'm okay, for goodness sake," I managed to say around a tongue too thick for my mouth.

"You need to take one of those pills for your nerves," Walter said.

"I said I'm *okay*," I snapped and immediately felt guilty. "Anyway, they're to make me sleep. I'm sorry, Walter. You've been so good to me and here I —"

"You don't need to apologize. I know I'm sorta hovering but it's hard not to, Sunny. I really do care about you."

I cut my eyes at him, trying and failing to make a comical face.

"As a friend," he added and shot me that quick grin. "'Course, with things the way they are, I could be more than that if you'd let me."

My breath hitched, scattering for a moment the fog, and my mouth dropped open. I'd never thought of Walter in that way. "Walter, you know how grateful I am for you being here so much for me lately." I shrugged listlessly. "Don't know what I'd 've done without you, in fact. It's just — I love Daniel. That's not changed." I gazed at him as my tears made his image go all fuzzy. "Probably won't ever. I miss him so…." I began to quietly cry. I couldn't help it. Just saying Daniel's name wrung powerful emotions from my soul.

Walter braked on the curb in front of his house. He slid over and put his arm around my shoulder. "I know, Sunny. I just — wish I could wipe out your pain. I would if you'd let me."

I took his offered handkerchief and blew my nose. "Yeh. Like…what can *anybody* do?"

"I could marry you," he stated simply.

Stunned, I turned to stare at him. "*What?*"

His quick grin flashed, then, "Hey. Am I *that* bad?" His expression sobered. "It *would* solve your problem. The longer you go, the less chance you'll have to make everybody think the baby is legit."

"Legit?" I blinked back more tears, fighting a conflux of distressful images and feelings. *Bastard.* That dreaded word emblazoned itself across a drive-in movie screen, flashing for the world to see.

Walter gazed into my eyes, as somber as I'd ever seen him. "I know what a nice girl you are, Sunny, and I know how you'd hate to lose such a good reputation. I think you and I could learn to love each other." He shrugged. "Heck, it's the best solution I can come up with. You got a better one?"

The question loomed in his blue, blue eyes. I'd never looked at him like this before, opening myself to attraction. His blonde handsomeness smote me in a pleasant way. Yet —

"I'm not attracted to you like that, Walter. I have to be absolutely honest with you. You've been too good to me for anything less. I still love Daniel so much it hurts and —"

"Where *is* Daniel?" he asked quietly, yet a subtle steel edged his words. "Is he concerned about you? Have you heard *anything* from him?"

I shook my head and closed my eyes, weary beyond words. "No. Not a word. And apparently, he's not concerned." Oh, that hurt. To say the words out loud was like putting a gun to my head and pulling the trigger. Only I didn't die. I was still alive with my bleeding heart stubbornly chugging away.

"Look, Sunny," Walter gently took me by the shoulders and turned me to face him. "If Daniel had come back, I'd 'a been the first to welcome 'im with a big ol' bear hug. But he didn't. And now, you've gotta face the music."

"But this baby isn't his," I moaned, aggravated that tears were cropping again, but feeling compelled to defend Daniel.

"You're entirely too understanding with Daniel, Sunny. If he'd 'a loved you like he shoulda, he'd 'a waded through the fires o' hell to protect you during all this. As it is, you got no way out 'cept to be stared at and low-rated to trash over somethin' you couldn't help."

His eyes misted, surprising me. When he spoke again, it was impassioned. "I want to help you, Sunny. Hell, so what if you don't love me? Main thing now is to get through having this kid and givin' it a name. See, I know how sorry you feel for Ruth Bond and her little girl. I do, too. And I hate to see you go through what she's had to." He gently shook my shoulders. "We could make it work, Sunny. I know we could."

I gazed at him through shimmery tears, feeling tossed about like a wildcat's trinket. Love cried *nooooo!* Fear shrieked *grab the buoy labeled 'respectability.'*

"What about it, Sunny?" Walter gazed deeply into my eyes and I felt something, like a shaft of dim light, connect us. That it did not shine brilliantly like the one between Daniel and me gave me a sense of unrest. At the same time, I deserted all hope that Daniel would rescue me. In the past three weeks I hadn't heard a word from him, had I? After all, the US Mail still ran and there were phones.

Plain and simple, he'd stopped loving me.

Our dream…gone. Dead. Only I hadn't yet buried it.

I took a deep, shuddering breath and exhaled. "Let me go to my room and think it over for a spell," I whispered.

"Decide now," Walter said gently. "I won't bother you again if you decide today not to marry me."

I crossed the street, climbed my stairs and spent the next hour in travail as I gazed across the rooftops to the river glistening under late afternoon sun. In the end, I had no choice.

An hour later, I returned to the Stone residence. Walter met me at the door, his expression guarded. I didn't say a word. Couldn't. I simply nodded.

Walter took me in his arms, almost reverently. "You won't be sorry, Sunny. I promise."

~~~~~

Preacher Wayne married us in the parsonage the next week. Walter had managed to rent the empty village house on whose screened-in back porch, ironically, Daniel and I had made love. I didn't tell Walter because I could see no sense in adding him to my list of casualties.

Nana, who'd remained strangely silent through it all, and Aunt Tina, who'd clung to the event as a life-line rescuing her from her stupor, together rallied to collect the newly-weds furniture from their own cache as well as relatives' and friends' castoffs.

I didn't feel free to use funds from Daniel's and my bank account. He had, after all, contributed the larger portion. Too, it was simply too painful to even think about things in terms of *ours.*

After the ceremony, I felt like a raw piece of liver. Actually, more like a zombie. Walter was exceedingly considerate, even offering to sleep on the old sofa of Mama's, that had been replaced in Nana's house — I'd begun calling my former home that: Nana's house — by Aunt Tina's newer, bolder patterned chintz settee. But I'd told him it wasn't right, him sleeping on the couch, that he was now my husband.

Husband. My insides recoiled at the very word, but I'd never, ever, let on to Walter. And when he turned to me and tentatively kissed me, I hid the fact that I felt nothing. Absolutely nothing. And as he explored my erogenous points, I tried to blank out Daniel's features and his touch, failing miserably. I ended up closing my eyes and pretending it was Daniel whose feathery, sensitive strokes aroused me to blazing heights of passion.

Later, in the following long, sleepless hours, I realized that it was *that*, plus raging hormones pitted to trigger a turbulent climax that had Walter hoarsely muttering an ebullient, "I knew it. I just *knew* we'd be good together."

So, my marriage to Walter started out in deception. And guilt.

I owed Walter. Big time.

~~~~~

A week later, we had supper at Nana's house. I'd begun to migrate there more and more in my off-work hours. I suspect it was more to escape memories of that back porch interlude with Daniel than to draw closer to Nana. Actually, Nana had been exceptionally warm and caring since my marriage. Tonight, I caught her watching me closely as we did dishes.

Walter had gone back to our place to watch *Death Valley Days* on our new black and white seventeen-inch television. Aunt Tina had recently bought a set but she occupied her screen watching *I Love Lucy* summer reruns.

"You okay?" Nana asked.

"Of course. Why wouldn't I be, Nana?"

"Walter good to you?"

"Yeh. Very." And though I meant it to sound enthusiastic, it fell flat.

"You sure?" Nana did something uncharacteristic. She took me by the shoulders and turned me to face her. I saw worry in her eyes and something I couldn't quite define.

"I'm certain." I forced a smile.

"When's the baby due?"

The floor nearly swept from beneath me. I had to grab hold of her arm to steady myself. "How did you know?" I whispered.

"Didn't birth two and deliver God only knows how many without knowing all the signs. I've knowed all along. That's why I can't understand Daniel —"

"It's not his fault, Nana."

Her faded blue gaze narrowed. "Don't know how you can defend him, Sunny, after he —"

"Please, Nana. I don't want to talk about it," I whispered, tears pooling. "I-I just can't." I knew Nana hated crying but I couldn't a'helped it if my next breath had depended on it.

The back screen slammed. Timmy came to a halt when he saw my face. "What's wrong, Sunny?" He immediately rushed to wrap his long arms around me, burying my face against his broad chest. "Is — are you and Walter — ?"

"No," I quickly squeezed him back and disentangled my arms to wipe my nose and cheeks. "Everything's okay."

"She's just havin' to get used to bein' married, is all," Nana said in her staid way, swiping the kitchen table with a damp dishrag. Timmy seemed to accept that. I was glad he'd lumbered in at that precise moment. I didn't want to lie to Nana.

After Timmy's departure, only thing she said was, "You're beholden to Walter, Sunny. Not many a'men would do what he done to spare you shame."

"I know, Nana," I said. "I know."

"Who knows?"

"Only Doretha and Walter."

"Nobody else don't have to know," she muttered, wringing out the dishrag before attacking the white cabinet leaf. "Ain't nobody's business."

In other words, don't tell a soul.

Didn't need Nana to tell me that. I'd already figured it out. But I was suddenly glad Nana knew. I opened my mouth to tell her the whole story, rape and all, but the words congealed inside my throat, lodging, unable to pass over my vocal chords and exit my lips. It was so enormous. Nana couldn't handle it. Somehow, I just knew.

Nana went into the bathroom, and I joined Aunt Tina in the den. She was engrossed watching Lucy getting splashed with water while trying to win a thousand dollars on a game show. When the phone rang, she was laughing and didn't make any move to answer it.

I picked up the receiver. "Hello?"

A long silence, then, "Sunny?"

My heart skipped three beats, no joke. "Daniel?"

"My god, I can't believe I caught you there. I've been calling for the past two weeks and —"

"You've been calling for two weeks?" I whispered as the world began to spin and topple.

"Your Nana wouldn't tell me how to contact you." He sighed heavily. "I don't blame her for being mad at me. I was a jerk. I even wrote. Did you get the letter?"

I swallowed a huge lump. "N-no. I didn't."

"Well, I want you to know how sorry I am that I ran out on you like I did. I've done a lot of thinking and realize I can't live without you, Sunny." Every word he spoke was a sword through my heart.

"Daniel —"

"No. Let me finish. My head was all messed up at first. Took me awhile before I realized that you're not Mona. You're good, honey. Nothing or nobody can't take that from you. Please — I want to take care of you…and the baby. I'll love it because it's part of you, Sunny," he said hoarsely. "All I know is I love you with everything that's in me." By now I was crying my heart out.

"Sunny?" Daniel's gentle voice ripped into my guts. "Could you — do you think you can forgive me?"

I snuffled. "I forgive you, Daniel," I said hoarsely, "I just hope you can forgive me."

"Thank God," he murmured, then chuckled with relief. "There's nothing to forgive you for, sweetheart."

"Y-yes there is, Daniel." I gulped and took a deep breath, then spoke the most difficult words of my life. "You see — I'm married."

The ensuing silence stretched out, groaned, then screamed at me. Aunt Tina, now caught up in my drama, had silenced the television. Nana hovered nearby, ashen-faced. But Daniel was my focus. I keened to hear him say how we could fix it.

"Who?" Daniel's voice was almost non-existent. "Who are you married to?"

"Walter," I whispered.

Another stretch of silence, then a moan, "Oh…my… God."

The line went dead. I dropped the receiver, buried my face in my hands, and bawled like a lost child.

I *was* a lost child.

I didn't care that Nana witnessed my terrible emotional abandonment. She'd turned Daniel away and sabotaged his letters to me. She'd destroyed my last hope.

In that moment, I hated her almost as much as I hated me. But I knew I would eventually forgive her because she'd acted out of love for me.

It was myself I'd never forgive.

~~~~~

On a lovely April day, Muffin squalled her way into the world. I named her Hope Elaine but Walter quickly nicknamed her Muffin. It fit. And stuck. I loved my little Muffin, who was my spitting image, as Walter happily pointed out. She became my whole world, which seemed okay with Walter because he was, from the moment I birthed her, just as smitten as I.

On one level, I was grateful for my lot in life. A beautiful daughter and a husband who was the most wonderful, attentive father imaginable. On another level, something inside me closed off, the part that feels deeply, and mourns. The part that rejoices and celebrates.

I knew something drastic had taken place. But it would be years before I knew what it was that had hulled up so deeply inside me, what became, overnight, untouchable.

Passion.

Part Two

"She opens her mouth with wisdom, and on her tongue is the law of kindness."
Proverbs 31:26

The Eighties to the present

Chapter Ten

"All things change."

Daniel's words rang in my head like a Tibetan Monk chant in years to come. With him gone, change rode the swords slashing at me from all sides. Nobody saw the altered me. I never let on. I simply kept shuffling one foot in front of the other, chin high, like an android, smiling, smiling, smiling my way through life's motions.

Trying not to think of Daniel. Trying not to see what was all around me, like a plague of mold, spreading so slowly one couldn't detect it at first, not until the green goop and stench of it smacked you in the face.

The smell of mold, to me, embodies departed life. It symbolizes death.

Nowhere in those next decades did change occur more dramatically than in the textile industry and its mill hills. Textile employment in Spartanburg County held steady at 19,500 jobs in the 1970's. But more than 5,000 jobs disappeared in the 1980's, and another 6,000 in the 1990's. Even as new, state-of-the-art mills were being built, and struggled to piece together a work force, some of the oldest mills began to go under.

Village life, solidarity as I knew it, slowly and unrelentingly disintegrated before my stunned eyes. It was especially heartbreaking for me. My sense of roots, as well as my fortitude-glue, was an outgrowth of the acceptance and nurturing of my mill hill family. At least it seemed so during those early days.

Seeing the handwriting on the wall, some villagers sought outside jobs and moved away, while others hung in there until the last minute, buying their houses at nominal fees, getting their mill walking papers, then stoically changing vocations.

My brother Timmy chose carpentry, a skill picked up in high school Shop. Actually, both he and Walter, being pretty good with the hammer and skill saw, initially went into business together until…well, I'm getting ahead of myself.

The majority of our mill hill folks remained intact, albeit imbedded in livelihoods ranging from auto mechanic to college-educated professionals. In the nineties, Walter Montgomery, Sr. died, leaving us true orphans. No one would paternally care for us villagers again as he had. Eventually we would be on our own, fighting for sewage service and streetlights, services once taken for granted.

But in the eighties, we who chose to remain mill hill villagers continued on as though things were as they had been. Especially me.

I clung to mill hill roots like an alert orangutan whose spike-nails dug in on the lookout tree from which it dangled. I gazed about me, vigilant, wary.

More and more, I pushed my button labeled 'denial.'

~~~~~

Tucapau Methodist Church buzzed with the excitement of change. This time, change meant *good*. I tethered myself to the pew. Outside, I was a calm lagoon. Inside, the child-*me* jiggled and twirled like whirly-birds loosed in a gale, an exceedingly rare occurrence in recent years.

My pizzazz of youth had not, yet, totally vanished. It just took more to lure it from that dark inner psyche in which it hibernated. Like this event.

I'd shamelessly haggled my family into coming today. Nana, now ancient and frail, Aunt Tina, joints twisted with arthritis, Francine, Timmy and Noreen, along with their teenage tornado, Gale, already occupied an entire pew. I perched on seat's edge behind them, saving seating space and watching for my other sister and my oldest daughter, Muffin.

My younger daughter Libby's advent had trailed Muffin's by two years. I missed my Libby but felt real peace about her life. She was everything Muffin was not.

I quickly pushed away the disturbing comparison.

I swiveled again, checking the door for Sheila, who'd promised to be there for the great return. At least it was great to me. Mostly, I could count on my siblings to support me at such momentous times. Not always *together*, Lord *no*! Caging Sheila and Francine in the same room, at precisely the same time, required steely, inspired cunning.

Over the years the rivalry between those two had escalated to untapped pinnacles, causing me untold grief until I'd one day decided to stop sweating unchangeable stuff.

Tack Turner, now suffering complications from advanced diabetes, seldom ventured outside his and Francine's roomy ranch-style brick home. Francine's lust for a fine house had not, years back, dimmed her familial zeal.

Yeh, despite her unflagging irreverence and, though her devotion was unorthodox and remarkably muddled at times, she *was* a family gal. In final negotiations she'd balked at being ripped from her roots, so Tack's dad had finagled a couple of acres from a friend on the village outskirts upon which to build.

Seemed Francine always got her wish, according to a dismayed, jealous Sheila, whose luck, had it not been lousy, would have been non-existent. Now divorced for the second time, my youngest sister was more beautiful than ever but, according to her, had never found a man who adored her as Tack did Francine.

And I wondered if there was enough adoration in the world to pacify Sheila. Truthfully, I didn't think so.

A flash of green tugged my gaze to the vestibule door, where Sheila hovered, extremely uncomfortable in spiritual ambiance. She was breathtaking in a kelly-green outfit, whose hem hit the top of her slender bronze knees while sun-streaked, wheat hair tumbled gloriously over shoulders peeking from beneath a sleeveless sweater top. I motioned for her to join me, knowing that sliding her into the row ahead of me would prove disastrous since Francine occupied the end seat. We hugged and settled down to wait.

Strange thing…no matter how bloody my female siblings' territorial skirmishes, each remained close and affectionate with me, considering me a composite of Mother Teresa, Joan of Arc, and Martha Stewart, with the beauty of a blonde, albeit *fluffy* Charlie's Angels' Jaclyn Smith. My-mymy. It did wonders for my self-esteem.

If only Muffin regarded me so.

Will Muffin come? I gazed down at the two little heads next to me, bowed over coloring books — a device to calm pre-Sunday School fidgets — and grieved again that my daughter didn't share my faith. Neither had her hero-father, Walter, who, true to his long ago warning, had put little stock in God-stuff. Not then anyway. Not for a long time.

I should have listened to my heart.

All water under the bridge. I sighed deeply. Instantly, seven-year-old Gracie's towhead snapped up to gauge my gesture. I smiled into the concerned little face, easing her puzzlement. A pang of longing shook me to my toes. *If only Muffin loved me like they do.* I'd cared for her babies from the cradle up, doing all the things a mother does for little ones, all the while praying that my daughter would one day magically snap into maturity and gush maternal love.

And daughterly affection.

Again, I thought of Libby, our little 'accident,' as Walter put it before his wit scattered like petals in the wind. Like Muffin, Libby had a mind of her own. Difference was, her spirit was predominantly compassionate. She was generous and giving. Oh, she went through a short period of adolescent emancipation when she mimed Muffin. But that soon got old and she began to scold Muffin for being mean to Mama.

Never mean to Daddy. Just to Mama. Somehow, I think Muffin's Mama-disparagement drew Libby closer to me, made her more protective. Now, however, Libby, her husband, Scott, and their daughter, Kara, lived over two hundred miles away in Summerville, outside Charleston.

It could have been a thousand miles as I rarely got to see her. Scott's successful land-development business kept him busy. Only on holidays would the little family migrate to Tucapau. How I looked forward to those times.

The girls' resemblance to each other was striking. Same coloring, build, and features. But somehow, Libby's was a softer demeanor, not as glamorous, yet just as pretty. I was the only one surprised at the similarities. At times I figured, in my altered, somewhat cynical frame of logic, that maybe God had felt He owed me and made the two girls like twins, to throw folks off the truth. In the end, I surmised it was simply a trick of Mother Nature to endow both girls with so much of my DNA. Libby's pool definitely drew my maternal genes.

I grieved anew that Muffin seemed to possess so little of them.

I sighed again and glanced at my watch. Nearly ten. It wasn't that Muffin didn't love the kids. I knew she did because there were moments when her heart and soul poured from those beautiful blue eyes, ones so clear that, in them, you glimpsed infinity. In a crisis she was fantastic. Day to day was another story.

Muffin's will was and is the strongest I've ever encountered. Her brilliance is inestimable, surpassed only by her stunning beauty. Her presence commands esteem. Her ice-queen aloofness inspires wonderment.

My flesh and blood, my daughter. After twenty-five years, I am still in awe of her. Until her twelfth year, along with Libby, she was my shadow, my greatest love, *myself.* She wallowed on my lap and snuggled beneath my covers, touching my face and eyelashes, wishing for the day she would be '*growed up*' and '*boo-ti-ful*' like Mama.

Then, in one moment, the light in her eyes, the one just for me, went out as succinctly as a cigarette lighter's closing *snap*. The change affected not only Muffin's feelings for me, but for others as well. It was as though, finding that turn-off button inside herself, she decided it was better to not feel anything soft. That way she wouldn't get hurt. I could understand, to a degree. My own mama had let me down. But I wasn't my mama. I hadn't intentionally let Muffin down.

Oh, it was so complicated because, in her eyes, I had ruined her life.

Yet, there were moments when the light would glimmer briefly and she would say, "Love ya, Mama," and my heart would sing like no tomorrow. It never lasted long, the sweetness. Just a word tumbling from my lips could set off that terrible rage gathered inside her like a hornets' swarm. But for those brief sweet moments, mother's and daughter's hearts touched, spawning fresh hope for better tomorrows. Still, against her remoteness, against her distancing, against her detachment from her children, I longed for restoration.

I prayed daily that she would come to love me — us — as she did her father.

Walter gleaned what nobody else in the world did; Muffin's affection. In her cerulean eyes, Mama could do no right. Daddy could do no wrong.

Even when, within his fogged psyche, she had no history as she did in mine.

Why, I pondered, did my life daily careen to the bizarre? *Is God punishing me?* I wondered again. *No! I did it all for her.* I closed my eyes and focused on Libby's phone call, earlier this morning. Libby — Muffin's antithesis. *"On my way out to church, Mama. Just wanted to tell you I love you."* I lived for those calls. They validated me. At times, they kept me sane.

I stirred restlessly, glancing again at my watch. Ten o'clock.

Footsteps in the vestibule sent butterflies a'flapping and flailing in me. The sense of pleasure was so rare as to feel almost spooky. Like it knocked my chemistry off-balance. But today, I brushed the disturbing impressions aside.

Emaline's come home! After all these years apart, my buddy and I would be together again. Cousin Wayne had long ago departed this pastorate, reassigned to a foothills church.

When a heart attack felled the last pastor at Tucapau Methodist, forcing an early retirement, the Upper South Carolina Methodist Conference assigned Emaline's husband, John Davidson — now a twenty-year veteran of the cloth — to Tucapau Methodist Church. Chances were that they could stay with us indefinitely, seeing as how the conference pastor-supply was so sparse.

Today I'd come early to my roost, loath to miss a moment of the new parish couple's arrival. They were to finish moving into the village parsonage within the week. Of their two grown children, one son, David, now attended Clemson University. The other, Johnny, owned a real estate company in Myrtle Beach.

The approaching footsteps belonged to Doretha and Alvin.

Dear Lord! I felt as honored as royalty. Doretha had not, in all the years I'd known her, darkened a church door. Even when marrying Alvin she'd opted to wed in her living room, joined by Rev. Pate, the Baptist pastor.

I still had to blink twice, seeing them together after twenty years of marriage. Alvin, short and stocky like his dad, reminded me of a blonde, aging Mickey Rooney. Miracle-worker Doretha had taken Aunt Tina's spoiled brat and pivoted him 180 degrees. Mystically, her understated, muscled-will overrode Alvin's s passive self-absorption.

He remained devoted to Doretha, even when, in her soft-spoken way, she laid down the law about sharing the cooking and cleaning. She still hated domesticity. Alvin patiently picked up the slack. And he was an attentive, giving father to their adolescent daughter, Tammy. Would wonders never cease? When I'd invited them to this special service, I had no idea they would show.

On their heels came Emaline and John.

Their entrance elicited an exuberant burst of applause. I rushed to hug Emaline, who seized me mightily. "Home, at last," she whispered in my ear, after which we erupted into brief tears of joy.

Muffin swooped in behind them, moving in that graceful, long-legged stride of hers, causing my mother's heart to leap even higher. She surprised me at times like this, smiling that big old white, white smile of hers and hugging me like she'd never let go, exuding some exotic, expensive fragrance. Sheila and the kids scooted over, making room for her to join us. "Wish Daddy could be here," she murmured as she slipped past me.

"Me, too. That summer cold has sapped his energy so I told him to sleep in. He'll be at Nana's to have lunch with us."

The service was sweet and melancholy and poignant as John spoke of meeting Emaline twenty-seven years ago on these very streets. During the rites, Emaline surprised everyone by singing *Amazing Grace* in a beautiful lyrical soprano timbre that sounded nothing like her lazy, slightly nasal speaking voice. She'd studied voice for years and I was so proud of her I could have burst into a million strands of confetti.

I was astounded to see Sheila quietly wipe tears from her eyes during the music, and wondered what transpired in that complex mind of hers.

I watched Ruth Bond Staggs accompany Emaline on the piano and my eyes misted. I recalled Pastor Wayne's 1957 efforts — to reconcile the church to Ruth's available talent — being rebuffed by stiff-necked, prejudicial deacons. Three years later, Joey Staggs, son of a mill executive, had flipped over Ruth after meeting her at the movies. Joey not only fell deeply for Ruth but also embraced little Sally as his own, eventually funding her way to Converse College and a teaching degree.

After Joey adopted her as his own, the *bastard* stigma flew away like cinders in a windstorm .

Like Walter had accepted Muffin. Those words I never spoke aloud. Who would I tell? Everybody, save Doretha and Nana believed Muffin spawned from Walter's loins.

Subsequently, Ruth Staggs became a pillar of village society and had, sometime later — because some are less swift to tolerance — unanimously been voted in as church pianist. Today, I smiled at poetic justice.

A fluke. The thought flashed through my mind, unexpected, shocking. My smile vanished. *Ruth's exoneration was, at that time and place in history, probably one in a million*. Uncertainty washed over me.

Would the villagers have shown me the same mercy? *I'll never know, will I?*

Times *had* changed, slowly, gradually. Emotions swirled in me, like dogs chasing their tails, regret leading the pack.

Why had I so quickly capitulated to fears? Only a few more days and Daniel and I could have —

Daniel. My heart still leaped at his very name. Through the years, on his rare visits to see Doretha — her mom, Berthie, died in a nursing home in 1970 — he'd carefully avoided me. And Walter. Still, a distant glimpse of his proud features sent a shock wave through me that could have emptied death row.

Fate hadn't finished with that. She tossed me another ten years later, when Walter left the house one day and never came back.

More poetic justice? Probably. *Oh well*, I drew myself up and squared my chin. *That was another story entirely*. After the benediction, my eyes misted as John asked Emaline, dear Emaline, to join him in the church vestibule to greet each parishioner.

Thank you, God, I prayed, *for sending Emaline home.*

~~~~~

After the service, Nana insisted the pastoral couple join us for the noon meal. With Nana's frailty in mind, we'd all pitched in and contributed to food preparation. Nana's opening her home to them as well, the gesture bowled me over for long moments. I fought back tears and thought *Lordy, what a day.* What little emotions surfaced drained me dryer'n a gourd.

Nana had mellowed as she aged, like sweet, sweet pineapple mixed with ripe bananas. And though too frail to attend church regularly (even if she'd been inclined to do so), she had grown to love the former pastor's frequent visits in her home.

She'd tried, in her own way, to recompense for keeping Daniel and me apart all those years ago. I'd never enlightened her that Daniel was not Muffin's father. I know I should have told her. Problem was, there just never seemed to be the right time. And, as the clock ticked on, her health began to decline, making the revelation even more perilous.

Today, this act was another of her peace-offerings. Thing was, I'd long ago forgiven Nana. How could I not? She was, in truth, my mama and daddy all in one. She'd stuck with us, raised us, when my parents would not.

Anyway, any guilt to be dealt with was not Nana's; it was mine.

~~~~~

Emaline and I insisted on doing dishes, overriding protests and offers of help from the other females. We wanted the kitchen to ourselves to share and catch up. Pastor John — to his delight, we insisted upon calling him that — departed right after the meal to go home and study. "Actually," Emaline whispered conspiratorially to all lounging satiated and content around the table, "he's gonna take his Sunday nap. *Then* study."

We shooed everybody from the kitchen, soundly shut the door, and at last got down to some major catching-up. We bounded back and forth from silly girls to seasoned women. After gushing over what wonderful children we had, we laughed and elbowed each other at the hilarious aspects of motherhood and grandmotherhood.

Then Emaline grew sober, even looked a bit uncomfortable. " Sunny — what exactly happened to Walter in that construction accident? I mean," she shrugged tightly, "we never got to talk about it." I saw a flicker of hurt in her eyes.

Like all the other things we never talked about. I'd not returned Emaline's phone calls nor answered her letters. They'd eventually stopped. I exhaled the guilt on a deep sigh.

"Look, if you don't want to talk about —"

"Nono. It's okay. First, let me check on Walter." I dashed to the front screen and satisfied myself that no one was close enough to eavesdrop through the kitchen door. I smiled to see Walter napping in a lounge chair on the shaded front porch. The July day was, for once, pleasantly warm, not the usual stifling hot temperatures. A soft breeze stirred. Next to him, in another webbed chaise, sprawled Tack, open-mouthed in slumber. After church, Francine had picked him up at their house to visit for a spell.

I strolled to Nana's room, where in recent days she spent most of her time abed. Our clan-females lounged on the bed with her or in chairs dragged in from the kitchen, to gossip and cheer up the matriarch, whose health continued downhill with alarming swiftness. When I peeked in, Muffin held avid court, drawing laughter with a bawdy story, a side she never shared with me.

I quietly retreated and returned to the kitchen. Emaline gave me her big benediction smile, bringing some mystical balance to my spirit.

She handed me another dripping pot and said, "Only thing's changed about this kitchen in all these years is modern appliances." We smiled as nostalgia peppered the air and piqued our awareness and memories and tugged us along from one panoramic recollection to the next. Our comfortable camaraderie, that allowed long silences to lapse, had survived the years.

I sensed strongly that she wanted me to finish the divulgence I'd started earlier. And she needed it given freely, without entreaty.

I owed her.

"That day... Walter went to work with Timmy as usual. They'd formed their own construction company, you see, since both had been laid off. The mill was slowly shutting down...." I blinked and vigorously dried the pot to hide my feelings, "I still can't believe so much changed so quickly." I stacked the utensil atop a mountain of others and let my mind drift back to that day....

Sunlight already filtered through the bedroom blinds when I awoke that morning. I groped to my right. My fingers traced the cold indention where Walter had slept. "Oh, no," I groaned and slung my legs over the side of the bed.

212 Emily Sue Harvey

"I'm gonna cook your breakfast," I called out, rather desperately. *Walter had gone to bed angry with me and, for once, did not respond to my excuses for not having sex. His joke that Libby was "our little accident" was not amiss because, due to our mating-infrequency, that was exactly what she was. That morning, I felt like the lousiest wife on planet earth.*

I'd wanted to see him off to his job at the construction site with a good hearty breakfast, to show him love and perk up his energy. *Liar, liar, pants on fire.* Okay, it was to assuage my stinging guilt, one that chewed me up and spit me out over hot coals to barbecue. Lately, he'd insisted toast with my homemade blueberry jam and hot coffee were all he needed in the early a.m.

That day, however, he puttered quietly in the kitchen, ignoring food, not responding to my cry.

"Lunch," I murmured, tidying up the few coffee grounds Walter so seldom dropped. He was the ideal husband, according to both Sheila and Francine — one of the few things they agreed upon. *"And — God A'mighty,"* swooned lustful Francine, *"he's such a ma-a-an,"* ending on a guttural groan.

I loved Walter but — *if only* I felt that passion for him. In that moment, the weight of his unhappiness crushed me. "I'll fix you a wonderful lunch and bring it out to the site."

He said not a word, just poured himself coffee in a styrofoam to-go cup, his handsome face closed. Other women drooled over him, yet — in his features, I saw not comeliness but a man who could be my brother, or cousin.

I gazed at him, eaten alive with remorse. "Walter, about last night —"

"No." His hand shot up. "Don't go there." He closed his blue eyes for long moments, then opened and focused them on me. For the first time ever they glittered with anger. He pivoted and headed down the hall for the front door.

"Please, Walter," I cried, dashing barefoot after him. Anger was so foreign to our connection that, in it, I sniffed some obscure portent. I grabbed hold of his arm as he wrenched open the door. He stopped and glared at me, then at my hand on his arm, further setting my emotions to tail spinning. I loosed my fingers to release him, forcing myself to lighten up. "We need to talk. Tonight?"

And I knew in that moment from whence sprang my fear. Though not embraced as my lover, Walter had become my best and dearest friend. Now, I saw that crumbling to dust. How would I fend without his alliance?

His blue eyes narrowed coldly. "Oh! The lady wants to talk, does she? *Talk.* That's all you ever want to do!" His voice rose to a roar. "Well, I'm through talkin', y'hear, Sunny? I don't wanna talk. I want a daggum wife who don't treat me like I've got the *mange* every time I try to touch her."

"I'm sorry, Walter," I whispered, appalled that I'd let it come to this, but knowing deep, deep inside, that I'd had no choice. "I can't help it —"

Suddenly, he stepped so close I could see minute flecks of gold in his blue irises. "Well, I can't help it either, *ma'am.* I'm through wiping your nose and hind end. Get somebody else to tend to you. I want a *wife.*" The door slammed loudly behind him. My hands flew to my mouth as I smothered emotions I was not able to even begin to decipher. The sarcastic *"ma'am'* pierced depths he'd honored in the past, the part of me who still hungered to be a teacher. *With that scathing word he'd stomped my dream into mud. I wept openly, forehead pressed to the cool doorjamb.*

Today, I gazed at Emaline through tears. "I lost my scholarship. *My dream.* It hurt. Yet — I couldn't fault Walter. He'd been good to me. And an exemplary father. He even insisted I enroll at Clemson and I did go for the next year, only to be interrupted by another pregnancy. " I rolled my watery eyes. "To be truthful, it was an unwanted one." I added quickly, " but I wouldn't trade Libby for all the degrees on the planet." I snuffled loudly before continuing.

"I'll always owe Walter, no matter what happens. But I couldn't give him the one thing he wanted, Emaline. My heart." I blew my nose into a fresh tissue she'd pressed into my hand. " Outwardly, I was a model wife. Only Walter and I knew of the moments when, during sex, I would freeze up like *rigor mortis.*"

"Aaww, honey," Emaline took me into her arms and warmed me as she'd done years ago, when we were girls. Only then, Renie completed our snuggle circle. How I missed her. "You loved Daniel so much. It has to have been hard —"

"You just don't know how hard," I whispered in her ear, immeasurably relieved that Emaline understood and didn't condemn me to Hell. Maybe I was salvageable after all. Our tears mingled as we silently remembered those sweetheart days when we'd been so certain Daniel and I would marry and live happily forever after.

We released each other, dried our faces and re-tackled the dirty dishes.

She picked up a pan, plunged it into the hot soapy water and sighed, observing her fingers slowly scour the metal. "I've always wondered why Daniel spooked and ran. He was so crazy about you." The green gaze flicked up and met mine. "I've wondered, too, Sunny, why you married Walter so soon afterward. And why you feel you *owe* him. Looks to me like he's benefited as much from the arrangement as you." I gazed back at her, wanting to spew out the entire mess then and there and fall into her arms and squall like a starving newborn.

She stood waiting, soap pad clutched in hand, dripping, forgotten. I opened my mouth to speak but nothing came out. It was as though my brain opened a silo chute and dumped the whole grain load down my throat, closing and paralyzing everything in its path. Its import was too weighty to simply utter. Tears rushed to my eyes as I gazed helplessly at her.

We stood so for long moments until she blinked, looked away, and said, "It's okay, Sunny." She rinsed the pan and I grabbed it, thankful she'd let it go, knowing she sensed more beneath the surface. Emaline was no fool; had, in fact, one of the sharpest intellects I've ever known.

But…it was too, too much to go there.

Still, after all this time.

Tears spent, I recommenced drying and putting away the pans as Emaline scoured and rinsed. "Anyway, when I turned around from the door that day — after Walter left for work — Muffin stood there, glaring at me. She'd always known something was wrong but her daddy had just put it into words. And I'd as much as admitted it was true. Now she knew."

"What about Libby?"

"She was in the shower and didn't hear. Thank God. Initially, she was shocked at Muffin's rendition and was quiet for a long time. Eventually, she got past it. Libby's forgiving."

I put the last pan away as Emaline drained the water from the sink and wiped it clean. We settled ourselves at the table again. I clasped my hands tightly before me, studying them intently as I continued. I had to finish the story — for Emaline. It was long past due, this talk. I couldn't tell her the entire truth but I could tell her enough to help her understand.

"Had things not happened as they did — Muffin might have gotten past it. But — later that afternoon, I got the call. Walter had fallen from a three-storied structure and was transported to Spartanburg General Hospital, in critical condition. It was touch and go for days, then weeks; a surgery crisis at every turn.

"But he was strong. He made it. Physically. Mentally — he didn't. Brain damage. His memory was gone. To him, the girls and I were total strangers. He didn't want me around him for a long time. He warmed up to Muffin right away. Bonded almost instantly. Of course, she charmed the socks off him. When Muffin sets her mind to win someone over, there's no stopping her." I smiled ruefully. "His acceptance of Libby — and of course, me — came slower but when it did, it *took*."

"Strange. At first, we hoped his memory would return but after that first year, then two, the doctors said it was permanent. Of course, seeing Walter today, you know that wasn't the only change. His personality did a flip-flop. Gone was the take-charge, witty man, to be replaced by one so placid and child-like it breaks my heart."

I gazed into Emaline's eyes, still the color of lagoon blue-gray. In their depths, compassion pooled, swam, overflowed. "Muffin has hated me from that day. Says I stole her daddy from her. And — I guess in a way I did. Had he not been upset with me he wouldn't have been distracted and had the accident." I gazed at Emaline through fresh tears. "Call it poetic justice. I brought it all on myself because I wouldn't — *couldn't* bring myself to love Walter as I had Daniel."

"Ahh, honey," Emaline reached to take my hand and squeeze my icy fingers, "love such as that can't spring forth on command. Passion such as your's and Daniel's isn't always there. Don't you think you gave Walter all you were capable of giving, Sunny?"

I snuffled and swiped at my wet cheek. "Most of the time I believe I did. Libby's accepting attitude sort of convinces me I did okay. Other times I'm not so certain. I'm being as honest as I know how to be. I've prayed so much over that very thing...wishing and hoping that eventually the *feeling* would come." I shrugged limply. "It never did. And now it never will."

Emaline smiled gently, sadly. "At least Walter doesn't know how you —"

I nodded. "Yeh. Ignorance — in this instance — *is* bliss. So is his lack of sex drive." Fresh tears scalded my eyes. "I shouldn't have said that. Isn't that *appalling?*" I lifted my hands in supplication. "*I'm* appalling."

"You are *not* appalling, Sunny. You're human. Sometimes — don't misunderstand what I'm saying, now — God works in mysterious ways. When Walter lost his memory and sex drive, the situation became more bearable for you. Right?" She went on without waiting for me to answer. "All things work together...He simply allowed it. This way, nobody gets hurt." She came around the table, wrapped me in her arms and hugged me hugely, soothing me with her warm succor. "You're still Sunny. And I love you."

"Thanks, Emaline." She still was, to me, the wisest person on earth. "I just wish Muffin did."

"She will. In time."

In spite of my trust in Emaline's insight and faith, I wasn't so sure about that.

Chapter Eleven

Walter once asked me if it ever bothered me, not knowing for certain who Muffin's father was. I thought about it long moments and then said, "You're Muffin's father in every way that counts, Walter."

What I didn't tell him was that there were times during those years that I was nearly crazy wondering whose seed I had carried inside me for nine eternal months. The uncertainty haunted me. It was my own private cross to bear. I shared it with no one, not even Walter.

Anyway, that day after I said, "You're Muffin's father in every way that counts," Walter looked at me for a long time, saying nothing and then his eyes filled with tears. "Thank you," he rasped, uncharacteristically emotional. Before his accident, I could count on one hand the times he'd emoted anything akin to sentimental. Each time he had, it was Muffin-linked. Like the first time she'd said 'Dada', his face dissolved into mush.

But there were those times, late into the night, with Walter slumbering beside me, that I ran the faces past me, like a video: Harly Kale, who several years later dropped dead of a heart attack at age forty-five…Buck Edmonds, still living in Tucapau's Red Egypt section with his wife and three kids, carrying on his late mama's legacy of hovel-living….

And then there was Bill Melton, Emaline's grandpa, now in a nursing home with Alzheimer's. Each time I processed the equation, I always came up with the same solution: none. Had I pursued it as relentlessly as my adrenaline lusted after, I'd have driven myself crazy.

On one level, Muffin was *mine* and I wouldn't have traded her for all the silver and turquoise in Mexico. With Walter nurturing her, I couldn't ask for more. Yet — in my weaker times I fantasized that Daniel had fathered her, that when we made love that long ago night, a fluky thing occurred and his seed overrode the fiend's seed.

That was a dead-end.

On another level entirely, I secretly transmuted into a snarling, vicious predator, stealthily stalking the rapist who'd violated me all those years back. No one — absolutely no one but me knew the searing hatred I carried inside for that black-silhouetted, slimy, despicable monster.

It was a furor that shook me like a violent earthquake. It, and protecting Muffin's children, were the only passions left from my young years. And like the other, it was one I couldn't simply ignore. I wanted to. *Prayed* to. No matter how much I psyched myself that I was past it, no matter how much I denied its existence, it was there.

Like a rotten albatross around my neck, I still carried it, night and day, smelling its stench.

~~~~~

"Sunny?" called Sheila from my front screen-door. Through the wire mesh, even fuzzy and ethereal, even in her rumpled casual jeans attire, she took my breath. I rushed to unhook the latch. She stepped through and into my arms, trembling like January leaves in a whirlwind.

"What is it, honey?" I asked, holding her back to get a better look. Her eyes were puffy and red, her full lower lip trembling violently. "Come on, sit down and tell me about it." I guided her to my tan Naugahyde sofa and seated her, lowering myself beside her. "Spit it out."

"I'm a lousy mama, Sunny," she gasped between sobs. "I know I deserve what I'm getting but — when I lost the girls to Curtis, I didn't know things would turn out like th-this." I handed her tissues and she paused to blow her nose.

"Ginger won't even talk to me now she's married. Cassie's stopped going shopping with me on Friday nights — says she wants to do things with school friends. Michelle's mad at me for not showing up for her birthday party last month, even after I explained to her that I was out of town with Jerry, y'know, when I went along on his trip to Las Vegas?"

"How are things going with him?" I asked politely, hoping they were going nowhere. My sister instinctively picked losers, this time being no exception. Sheila's angst with her kids was commonplace by now.

"I don't understand Michelle, She's fourteen now. Old enough to *know* that I need a life of my own." She snuffled and took out her compact to repair the smudges under her eyes. I quietly watched her, wanting to say how she'd always put herself first. But more and more, I wondered *who am I to judge?*

"You know, Sheila, Michelle's a sweet girl and she loves you. I —"

She whirled about and glared at me. "I don't think you know her very well, Sunny. There's this other side to her when she gets ticked off about something."

I looked at her, slowly shaking my head. "Isn't that true of all of us? We all —"

"I wish just once, Sunny, that you'd really listen to me and understand." Her eyes glittered with rage, yet — strangely, not truly *seeing* me. It was as though, during these angst attacks, she was completely into herself, on a stage, alone, performing a script she'd written.

"I do listen to you, Sheila. I've always championed you, all the way back."

"Not always," she said, the anger leaving as quickly as it came. I watched her deflate like a stuck beach ball. "Remember when I begged you not to leave home that time Aunt Tina ordered you out? It just so happened that I was —" She stopped, eyes refilling with tears. She swallowed them back and went on, "I was being molested."

"But — who?" I asked with both reservation and dread.

"Alvin."

"My god." I let that sink in, shocked beyond words. "Did you tell Aunt Tina? Or Nana?"

"Are you kiddin'? After the way Nana reacted about Uncle Charlie? Would they have believed precious little Alvin could do such an evil thing? To them, I was always the wicked one. 'Little *hot tail, like her mama,*' Nana always said. She laughed bitterly and I saw her hands tremble as she took out a cigarette and lit it. She knew I didn't like smoking in my house but I decided she was too upset to be reprimanded this once.

She took a long drag off her Virginia Slim and blew it upward, thinking that in doing so, she spared me the second-hand smoke. "And another time. I know you never believed me when I told you Walter came on to me when I cleaned house for you each Friday, after you started to Clemson."

At Walter's name my insides knotted into a thousand tight little loops. "Let's don't go there, Sheila. That was a long time ago —"

"You barely let the words get outta my mouth," her lips curled at the corners, and her green eyes slitted, "before you called me a *liar*. Well, *sis-a-maroonie*, he did a lot more than come on to me. I was lettin' 'im off easy, actually." She leisurely stretched out her long tan legs, enjoying swiping at me for long ago grievances. Script-performance again. Sheila's vindictiveness was notorious and dreaded. Rarely was I its target.

Fact was, I still didn't believe her accusations against Walter. He'd denied them. And I knew him to be a man of character. A giving man. He'd given me back my honor when he could have simply walked away, like Daniel had done. It still hurt to think about Daniel's initial abandonment. It hurt even worse to think about his repentant return.

I wet my lips nervously, "Look, Sheila. There's no need to go back and drag —"

She stood abruptly, eyes glassy green flames, startling me into silence. "You took his word against mine, Sunny," she said quietly, lethally. "I don't know that I can ever forgive you for that."

I looked sadly at her, knowing she'd gone away into herself in that moment. What could I say? Then quite suddenly, she smiled. Sheila was back. Her eyes glimmered so like Mama's I nearly gasped. "But I love you, so I probably will someday. Outside that time with Walter, you've always been there for me. I mean, I can understand you leavin' when Aunt Tina threw you out."

Then I was on my feet and we were in each other's arms, cryin' like crazy that we'd hurt each other. "You're still my baby, Sheila. I love you."

"I know, Sunny," she smiled wistfully as tears trailed off her chin, her fingers gently touching my face. My poor Sheila…who'd had so little through the years. True, much of her misery was of her own making but in the final analysis, could she have altered her life's story plot?

During my two years at Clemson College, just before Walter's accident, I'd read something that now came to mind: "There are only two things which pierce the human heart," wrote Simone Weil, "One is beauty, the other is affliction." Sheila certainly possessed beauty. Ah, and the arrows struck her mercilessly, sometimes so thick in their rain as to block the sun. Other times, so subtly that only years later, like now, when the wounds festered, did Sheila even acknowledge they existed.

I watched her leave, chin up, but I saw the slight droop of lovely shoulders and like a comet, a memory from long ago soared in.

Francine and I took a taxi from the Greyhound bus station, silent in mutual concern for our younger sister. Sheila had run away, "…to find Mama," said the note Nana found on her pillow. She'd called from Atlanta the night before, " to keep ya'll from worrying," she said, but hung up when I'd asked where she was staying.

"I've gotta go find her before she gets to Mama." I began packing, afraid of what Sheila would discover if she found Mama. Instinctively, I knew it would hurt her worse than the initial abandonment.

I'd been surprised when Francine insisted on accompanying me when I set out. Nana offered to tend to Muffin, now a year-old, while Walter worked at the mill. He'd given his blessing to my mission: to find my sister and preserve what little self-image she had left. We'd finally, after all those years, discovered Mama's whereabouts. Leona, Mama's old pal, learned from Dr. Brock's sister, that the couple, now married, lived just outside Atlanta, in College Park.

"You nervous?" asked Francine, fondling her unlit cigarette, ready to pounce on it the moment we emerged to the outdoors of our destination.

"No," I answered truthfully. "I just — want to get it over with. Put it behind me. I have no illusions about Mama like Sheila does." In the ensuing silence, with only the motor's hum reminding me we were in transit, I thought how…somehow, life had taught me to flow. Sheila still fought the rapids

Finally, the cab stopped before a Georgian style, three-story brick mansion, whose immaculately groomed grounds alone intimidated. Beside them, our own straggly, patchy yards would seem afflicted with some rare, exotic plant-eating disease. Neither of us spoke as we disembarked, Francine to linger beside the taxi to light her cigarette, puffing away until her senses deadened, while I marched resolutely to climb brick steps, cross the mosaic porch, then punch a brass doorbell to the right of an enormous, elaborately carved mahogany door.

I rang the bell four, five times.

The door opened, revealing a black maid in uniform. "Nobody's home," she informed me politely, yet — something about the way she looked at me said she was lying. Before I could put voice to my suspicions, the door quietly shut.

I rang the bell again. And again. All the while my temper blazed. The nerve of this woman, who is my mother. It's not enough that she runs off and abandons us. Her maid slams the door in my face. I punched the bell again and again.

I yelled, "I don't want one cotton-picking thing from you! Do you hear me? I just need to talk to you briefly. And I'm going to ring this door till you speak to me. Sheila's run away and is trying to locate you. You can either answer the door or the neighbors will be disturbed because I will keep ringing." I punched again to demonstrate.

After another two rings, the door opened again. I recognized him instantly. The man who'd helped desecrate and destroy our home.

He stared at me coldly. "What do you want?"

I swallowed my indignation while composing my features. "I need to talk with my mother. Sheila's run away and she's in Atlanta, trying to find her mama. I'm trying to find Sheila. As I've said, I want nothing from you." The last words came out as cool as I felt. I didn't care.

His eyes raked me dismissively. "She doesn't want to speak with you." The door shut again, more firmly this time. And I knew it was final. Another thing I sensed: this man had kept our mama from us.

I was amazed that I didn't collapse in grief. I felt strangely detached as I walked back to the cab where Francine dropped her cigarette and crushed it to death with the toe of her snappy slings. "What did that lowlife say?" she snarled, ready for war.

I related our brief exchange, shrugging if off. I'd just started to climb back in the vehicle when another cab wheeled in behind ours and parked. Sheila bounded from it, a look of shock on her face. Even in worn jeans and some boy's football jersey pullover, she looked stunning. "What're you doing here?" she asked as I hugged her long and fierce. She squeezed me back so I knew she was glad to see me, had, in fact, wanted to be rescued.

"Looking for you," Francine spat. "This has got to be the stupidest thing you've ever done!" She lit another cigarette with trembling hands.

Sheila whirled on her, hands outstretched in supplication, "Look, I just want to see my Mama. Is that so stupid?"

Francine rolled her eyes and propped against the cab. She swung her arms wide, extending palms up. "Have a go at it, why dontcha? Good luck, kid." She took a long drag on her cigarette, exhaled through her nostrils, then glared into space.

When Sheila turned to peer at me, confusion marked her features. "What's she talkin' about, Sunny?"

I sighed, my pity for her rampant. "I've already been to the door, honey. She won't talk to any of us. Her husband came to the door and as much as ordered us away."

Before I divined what was coming, she tore off across that flawless lawn, aimed like a missile for the front door. Francine and I took off after her, wanting to spare her more pain and humiliation. But she was faster and began ringing the doorbell and banging on the door, screaming to the top of her lungs, "I want to see my Mama -aaa! Open this door! Now!" She kicked and shrieked nonstop for several minutes. Francine and I peered helplessly at each other and by mutual unspoken consent, stepped aside and let Sheila have her say. I couldn't help but gloat a mite, knowing the racket would mar the doctor's reputation.

When Sheila realized Mama wasn't coming to the door, the cursing began. Sheila's profanity made Francine sound like a nun. She screamed obscenities at our mother till she was hoarse and drenched with sweat, till she foamed at the mouth, till she collapsed on that blasted mosaic porch in a heap of grief, crying her heart out.

That was when Francine and I, together, scooped her into our arms and took her to our cab. We gently placed her between us on the back seat and left the damnable mansion and any good memories that had survived Ruby Acklin's initial abandonment. All the way to the bus station, Sheila, glassy-eyed and nearly incoherent, cursed 'Ruby.' For once, Francine wept with her.

And I thought, how tragic that it was something this terrible that provided them common ground.

~~~~~

We threw Nana an eighty-fifth birthday party at the Tucapau Methodist Church Fellowship Hall. With arthritis, she could hardly get around without assistance. Timmy's and Noreen's fifteen-year-old daughter, Gale, who was quite talented, sang the yodeling Western song, *I Want to Be a Cowboy's Sweetheart* and brought down the house. Singing was the one thing on which Gale — diagnosed at seven with ADD — focused long enough to follow through. Otherwise, she was a tornado in the making.

"Poor Noreen always looks like she's just two steps ahead of the undertaker," Francine muttered as we cut homemade chocolate cakes to serve. "That Gale makes me thank the good Lord I don't have any kids. I don't see how Timmy and Noreen stand it." She shuddered.

"Hey," I nudged her, grinning hugely, "she's *ours.*

"Don't remind me," she snapped and walked away to greet Doretha and Alvin. Their daughter, Tammy, rushed to join Gale, whose vigorous ambiance always attracted the fervent, heartier youth. Alvin's only evident genetic transference to Tammy was the blonde one. From Doretha came the sweetness. The origin of Tammy's exuberant spirit remained a mystery. She was the apple of her Gramma Tina's eye. However, her gentle kindness was not spoiled by Aunt Tina's obsessive adulation. Indeed, her reciprocal respect and affection for Aunt Tina encouraged me to take a second look at the woman who had, in days past, been unkind to me.

Nana huddled in a rocking chair, a pale, ancient little gnome who seemed to be in another time and place for the festivity's duration. Only when spoken to did so much as an eyelash flicker separate her from the dead. That she was hugged and kissed endlessly, fawned over, and pandered to seemed not to impress her. Only when Timmy sank to his haunches to ask if she wanted to go home did any life spark the dried-apple features.

Five minutes later, as I said good-bye to the guests, I was thankful Nana had left before the racket started. When a familiar strident voice began to rise in anger, overriding the dwindling conversational cacophony, I grew alarmed. Immediately a knot formed in my stomach and I turned to meet it head-on.

Across the social hall, Aunt Tina shook her long, arthritic finger in Sheila's face, fairly spitting out her diatribe. "You can't be happy unless you're tearing somebody down, can you? *You little slut!*"

Sheila's lips slowly curved into feline smugness and my breath grew labored. *Dear God. What now?* I rushed to where they stood planted in sparring stance. "What's going on?" I asked, noticing Doretha, pale as a specter, trembling, and Alvin, beside her, his flabby features a pasty green. Don't know who looked closest to fainting. My alarm shrilled.

My gaze swung to Sheila, "What?" I asked sharply.

"She's been tellin' lies on Alvin," Aunt Tina snarled under her breath, glaring at Sheila, "and I ain't gonna have it, I tell you. What're you grinning about, you *hussy*? I'll wipe that smirk off your —" She lunged, claws bared. I managed, just in time, to block her, getting my foot stepped on in the process.

"Please, you two," I implored, embarrassed beyond words, smarting from my aching toes. "Whatever you have to discuss, can't you at least do it in private?"

"Ever'body's gone." Aunt Tina still tried to push me aside but I held my ground. She wasn't as strong as she once was. "Tell that to *her*," she tossed Sheila a killing look. "*She's* the one who seems *hell-bent* on ruining good people's names."

Realization swept me. I looked at Sheila, who appeared elated at all the attention. "Sheila," I groaned, "you didn't?" I cast Alvin a glance and then gazed at her with dread.

The glitter in her eyes dimmed and she said, "It's the truth, Sunny. I told you it was."

"Sheila," I said quietly, "Why now? Why this way? You're hurting Doretha." I glanced over my shoulder at my friend and the husband she'd taken on and changed and my heart broke for her.

"She don't care a rat's-ass about who she hurts," Francine, bag slung over her shoulder, spoke over my shoulder. "At least she's lettin' *me* rest for the moment." She spun on her spike heels and made a hasty exit.

"Let's go home, honey," Alvin hesitantly ventured, taking Doretha's arm and leading her to the door and out into the night. She walked like a sleepwalker, rigid yet swaying. Her husband wasn't too steady either but he at least managed to steer her from bumping into anything.

"Dear God help us," I muttered, turning back to see Aunt Tina snatch her red handbag from underneath a folding chair and hook it over her skinny shoulder. She marched back to launch herself at Sheila for one parting shot. "I'd better not hear another word of this," she warned, rage quivering in her. "Else, I swear, I'll *kill you.*"

She exited on that grim note. I glanced around to see if anybody lagged behind and witnessed the ugly display. The place was deserted. The relief I felt was ridiculously at odds with the anxiety churning inside me.

"How did this happen?" I asked Sheila, whose eyes began to mist. Seemed when the audience left, so did her bravado.

She shrugged, shifting uneasily, loosing one periwinkle blue spaghetti strap of her silk mini dress. "I was just talking to Doretha and —" Tears spilled over. "She's so understanding a — and I found myself telling her about the men who'd abused me and before I thought, Alvin's name just — kinda *popped* outta my mouth, Sunny," she ended on a bellow and fell into my arms.

I understood all too well how it had happened...Doretha's empathy...Sheila finding in her a sympathetic ear... the spotlight, mouth running away. *Vintage Sheila.*

"Oh, honey," I whispered, sliding my arms around her. "What have you done?"

~~~~~

I dreamed about Daniel again that night. I awoke, moaning with longing. As Walter slept, I slipped from the bed and retreated to the den sofa with my pillow and a Catherine Cookson novel. But the words blurred.

I lay the book aside and let my mind drift back to the Christmas Daniel visited Doretha, when Muffin was six and Libby, four. He'd managed to avoid me till, on the last day of his visit, as I walked to the Company Store for bread and milk, we happened up on each other on the back alley. At first, I saw something like panic brush his face. Then, it was gone. It wasn't in Daniel to retreat from a threat. I knew that and used it. The need to hear his voice, to look into his eyes, pierced and overwhelmed me. I didn't swerve as he drew near and steadily met his unreadable gaze.

Suddenly, we were face to face. He didn't, as I'd feared, try to brush past me but stopped close enough that I could smell his Aqua Velva. His hands were jammed in his black overcoat pockets. The day was uncommonly cold and I wore a long, blue wool coat and matching gloves. My hair, still short but fuller, rustled in the arctic wind.

We gazed into each other's eyes for endless moments, until tears welled along my lower lids, then slowly spilled over and trickled my cheeks.

"One question, Sunny," Daniel said so softly I barely heard him.

I blinked and swiped the tears with my gloved hand. "What?" God, I still loved him so much it felt my heart was being ripped from my chest, that I was drowning in air and space.

"Are you happy?" His face softened and I nearly fainted from the impact of the concern that painted his chiseled features, more defined, more breathtakingly male than ever.

I peered at him, uncertain how to answer that. "I — I feel blessed to have two lovely daughters," I whispered, which was true.

He waited for more. Then, seeing none forthcoming, asked, "Is Walter good to you?"

I nodded. Not trusting myself to speak, for fear I'd fall upon his broad chest in turbulent tears of grief for our lost years.

Still not satisfied, he gazed even more deeply into my eyes, so near his minty breath warmed my face. "Do you love him, Sunny?"

I took a deep breath, feeling faint with emotion. "I love Walter, Daniel, for being so good to me and — and the girls. But I'm not in love with him." I finished on a whisper, feeling a twinge of guilt for voicing it. Only a twinge. "I never was."

Emotions played over Daniel's face, powerful ones, like a kaleidoscope of vivid mosaics flashing so swiftly they're not decipherable but stunningly majestic. Slowly, one hand slid from a pocket and lifted to my face, where an index finger caressed my cheek so gently I turned my face into his hand, capturing it against my shoulder, closing my eyes and savoring the love I felt pouring from his pores.

"It's hell," he murmured hoarsely. I nodded as fresh tears spilled onto his hand. I kissed the palm, now callus-free. He whispered, "Sunny, you know folks might see us together, don't you?" He inclined his midnight head to both sides of the well-trodden path, where windows gave access to our drama.

"I don't care," I groaned, meaning it for the first time in my life. "That's why I lost you, Daniel — caring what folks thought."

"You just think you don't care. But you do," he said gently, understanding. Knowing my very makeup.

I looked up at him then, still holding tightly to his hand. His eyes mirrored my own anguish. "Don't blame yourself, Sunny. It was my fault. I let you down in the worst way. I've died a thousand deaths in the past six years regretting —"

"Shh." I placed my fingers over his mouth. "It simply happened. Life stacked everything against us, Daniel. Even God didn't care."

He looked as though he was going to cry. He captured my hands in both his. "Sunny, I can't believe you said that. Don't ever give up your faith. That's one of the things that made you so special."

"Too late, Daniel." I gave him a rueful, lopsided smile. "I don't believe in dreams any longer."

"My God," he whispered, tears filling his eyes, "what have I done to you?"

"Daniel," I heard an edge creep into my voice, "stop that. I screwed up pretty well on my own, thank you."

He looked as though he'd take me in his arms. I keened for him to hold me. He swallowed and, with great effort, released my hands.

"Is — has there been anybody in your life since me, Daniel?" I asked, fearing yet needing to know. He hesitated, then nodded. My heart sank.

"I lived with someone for a couple of years. But we didn't have what you and I had." He gazed into my eyes. "Seeing you makes me tremble. Still, after all this time." His eyes blazed for a moment before he looked away. "She and I split a long time ago. In service, traveling helps keep me busy, unconnected with my feelings."

I raised my brows and laughed, startling him a bit, I think. "Feelings? *Feelings?* I haven't felt anything since you left, Daniel. My emotions are as dead as that tin can lying there."

I saw moisture gather in his eyes. "Sunny —"

"Until now," I whispered. "For the first time in six years, I feel. And y'know, I don't like it." I brushed past him and didn't look back.

Tonight, lying on the sofa, unable to sleep, I realized that, aside from those moments with Daniel, I'd not felt that stir of passion since the day he left me to join the Army.

~~~~~

"Lord, as I live and breathe," Gladys swept me into her arms and hugged me like no tomorrow. "Come on in, Sunny." She led me through her tiny, neat, four-room cottage and settled me in an easy chair that'd seen its best day, then seated herself opposite me in one just as worn, but clean.

"Oh, Gladys, I didn't think I'd ever find you. Nobody knew where you'd moved," I said, exultant that I'd finally tracked her down after all these years — only a few miles from the village. So near yet so far. Her lips, still supple, curved into a smile that spelled *at peace*. The brown eyes glimmered with love and acceptance — had they ever stopped?

I felt a pang of grief that I'd avoided her for so long. Age sat well upon her. Silver laced her black hair, now loosed from its Pentecostal bun and bobbed becomingly. The only mar to her slenderness was a little potbelly, but even that fit her well.

"You're beautiful," I said, meaning it from the bottom of my heart.

"So are you, Sunny."

We gazed at each other, our eyes moist, reliving years of affection and closeness that defied analysis or elucidation. Then I dropped my gaze to my protruding stomach. "I'm just a little bit more porky," I said and chortled.

"On you, it looks great, Sunny," Gladys said with utter conviction. "Skinny as you was, you could afford a little more meat."

"Try thirty pounds," I said and laughed as though it didn't bother me. Truthfully? At that point, it didn't matter that much. I'd not really computed its significance. That would come later.

"How have you been?" I asked, "What's been happening?"

"Well, you know Harly died, don't you?"

I nodded, dropping my gaze. "I'm sorry," I said, a half-lie. "It must have been hard for you afterward." The words sounded empty even to me.

"Not really," Gladys said in her forthright way, yet not unkindly. "You know I'm married again, don't you?"

I looked at her. "*Get outta here*! To who?"

"To Harly's brother, Vince. He's the good one in the family, the one I named my Vince after. Well, after Harly died, Vince — whose wife died five years back — he stepped in to help me all he could. He's totally opposite Harly." She smiled like a teenager and I found myself grinning all over myself. If anybody deserved a break in life, it was this woman.

"I always loved Vince's wife, Dorcas. He was good to her. I admired that in 'im. When she died, he took it hard, and I tried to help him. Well, after a time, we fell in love. I'd've never believed it." She chuckled and blushed becomingly. "And now, he treats me like a queen." She sighed, as though it was still hard for her to believe her good fortune. "I've asked myself over and over, how can two brothers be so different? But then, look at you and your sisters. Different as gold and asphalt."

I nodded, understanding. Coming from Gladys, it was not offensive, this reference to my sisters' less-than-wholesome reputations. Not knowing the secret I carried, she stacked them up alongside me and came up with staggering genetic contradictions.

Feeling suddenly restless, I changed the subject. "You still going to the Pentecostal Church?"

She updated me on church and offspring status, then fixed us a glass of iced tea in her minute kitchen. It all reminded me of a dollhouse but on Gladys, it looked right. She sat across from me when this huge grin broke over her face, in which I still glimpsed Ali MacGraw, and she said, "I'm sorry I don't have a banana pudding, Sunny. Remember when you used to come every Friday for your dish?"

"How could I ever forget?" I laughed. "And I remember, too, the time you taught me a lesson in manners by not offering me any one day."

Her brow drew together in puzzlement. "What? I don't remember that."

Still laughing, I went on to relate the incident to her and, when she still did not remember, I said, "That's okay.

Even if you weren't offended with me, I realized I'd taken advantage of your generosity by being a pig. I needed that lesson."

She reached across and took my hand, extremely solemn. "I'm sure that wudn' why I was unfriendly. It would've been connected to Harly, no doubt, honey. I'd never have denied you your helping of banana pudding."

With her absolution, warmth spilled over me, like cane syrup oozing over a warm pancake. I was still wallowing in it when the front door of her cottage opened and in walked what could have been the physical reincarnation of Harly Kale.

"Hey, honey," Gladys greeted him with an affection she'd never been able to heap on her late husband. She went to him and gave him a full hug and turned her face up for a quick kiss on the lips. Then she took his hand and said proudly, "Vince, I want you to meet a special person in my life, like my own daughter, actually. This is Sunny, who used to live up the street from me in Tucapau years ago."

I shook his hand and realized that, though his eyes were the same clear blue as Harly's had been, they didn't burn with that startling wildness. Still, the physical likeness gave me palpitations. So many nights when Walter slept beside me, I'd lain awake, convinced the black silhouette had been Harly, who had, after all, raped Ruth Bond and fathered Sally. I wondered at those times, *does Muffin's surliness echo Harly's? Is her mean-spiritedness genetic?*

I looked at my watch, exclaimed I was late for an appointment, quickly hugged Gladys, and made a quick getaway before she noticed my paleness and trembling hands. She knew me too well.

"Don't you wait so long to come back, now, y'hear?" she called from her tiny porch, waving till I was out of sight.

My hands were icy and sweaty as I clutched the steering wheel, breathing deep, slow breaths to steady my racing pulse.

The years had not, after all, diluted the memory.

Chapter Twelve

"Stop it, Muffin!" I threw myself between her and Gracie, whose terrified shrieks of pain had drawn me from the kitchen to her mama's room. I seized Muffin's hand before it contacted with Gracie's cheek again.

"Don't hit her in the face," I warned her. "You were never, *ever* treated this way and you're not going to do this to Gracie."

She shoved her finger in my face, hissing and spitting like a she-tiger hoarding her kill. "Gracie is *my child*. It's nobody's business how —"

"You will *not* hit her in the face," I insisted, not backing away. "You can't hit a child like this, Muffin. It's abuse."

She huffed at that. "I didn't hit her *that* hard, Mama," she said as though talking to a moron.

"Uh huh," I eyed her grimly. "You hit her hard enough to make her nose bleed."

"Aw, she's not hurt, are you, Gracie?" When Gracie buried her face in my apron, Muffin suddenly shrugged and turned away. "Gracie, you are so-o dramatic over the least little thing. You really get off on attention, don't you? Okay," she flicked her fingers hatefully at me over her retreating shoulder. "*You* raise her. See how much better you can do than me, huh?"

I drew Gracie to me and wiped tears from her pale cheeks. I blotted her bleeding nostril. Again, I sensed more behind my daughter's rages than mere temperament. What, I wasn't certain. Maybe drugs. She did love painkillers and had no problem getting them from doctors for a range of ailments from menstrual cramps to earaches to muscle strains. Whatever. Muffin lived on life's sharp edge, barely balancing her sanity at times.

Muffin knew no moderation. From food, cuisine only, to clothes, designer fashions a must. Her expensive tastes soaked up what little she earned with her sporadic real estate sales. After that, she came at me with her hand out.

Every time I decided to seek another job, I wrestled with the certainty that the children needed me. Walter was not dependable in a crisis. He was too emotionally fragile to deal with Muffin's erratic escapades and methods of discipline. Her life catapulted from one crisis to another, never quite leveling out in between.

Seemed little Gracie, now eight, drew Muffin's ire more than anything or anyone else, except me, of course. I could just look at Muffin and she was like "What? *What's wrong?* If you're ticked because I was late coming in last night, you can just *get over it!* I've got a right to a life besides sittin' here staring at these walls night after night."

I'd shake my head. "Muffin, Muffin — you're the only person in the world who starts a fight with your own self, then dances around the boxing ring alone. I have no quarrel with you." When possible, I walked away from her thunder. Fighting with no victories in sight was senseless and wore me out.

Gracie was different. She was helpless in the face of Muffin's rages. Once, during a grievance, Muffin pushed Gracie into her room and quickly latched the door behind them, locking me out so that I wouldn't interfere with the discipline.

Gracie's shrieks, "Mama, please don't...Oh, god! *Mama,*" had me banging and kicking the door screaming, "Don't you *dare hurt her! Open this door!*" Muffin ignored me.

I ended up sitting hunched over on the stairs, weeping. All had gone quiet in the locked room. Presently, Muffin appeared and loped down the steps, brushing past me nonchalantly. I rushed to Gracie, who lay sprawled on her back on the big bed, quiet, still. Only her eyes moved.

"What did she do to you?" I whispered, brushing a silky flaxen strand from her porcelain forehead.

Eyes wide, she demonstrated, speaking in a stage whisper, "She clamped her hand over my mouth when I yelled and pinched my nose at the same time. I couldn't breathe."

"You couldn't *scream,* either," Muffin drawled from the doorway, gazing smugly at me. "It worked, didn't it?" She sauntered away, unmoved by my concern for Gracie.

After that, I didn't trust her to deal fairly with the children.

Especially not with Gracie.

~~~~~

I don't know exactly when my metabolism did a somersault and ended up rolling in the opposite direction. The weight crept up on me so slowly, so gradually I was blindsided. Too, I'd been such a caricature *Bony Marony* in my younger years, that self-image stuck in my brain, even after my mirror began reflecting something else entirely.

I *do know,* however, when food became my source of comfort. It was right after Walter's accident and Muffin's emotional estrangement from me. I'd never had to watch what I ate so when I slid over that murky line, I hadn't a clue. That food equaled calories and calories, not burnt, tallied up fat had not, at that point in time, computed in my cranium.

So, blissfully unaware, I spent my time primarily in the kitchen, concocting tasty, rich desserts to reward, first, Walter's physical progress during his healing, then his great attitude in the face of literally starting life over, then for his being such a good person and loving Muffin through everything.

When I ran out of things to reward him for, I simply used food as a way of lovin', taking goodies to sick people, sharing delectables with Aunt Tina and Nana and neighbors — anybody as long as I kept some for myself.

At night, I rewarded *me* for getting through another day with hunks of chocolate cake or fudge brownies. Veiling my metamorphosis into unsightly obesity was my deepening affair with 'comfort' clothing; loose, smock-like blouses, elastic-waisted pants and skirts, and anything remotely resembling a mu-mu.

Denial raged, warring with everything in reality's path, especially the pea-brained fashion industry whose twelves were shrinking smaller and smaller and wearable clothes feeling more and more uncomfortable.

Too, my considerable height helped camouflage the bulk.

Early on, I'd steered Gracie and Jared into the kitchen, put aprons on them and taught them to cook. How they loved it! How I loved it. The sheer fun of it gave me endless opportunity to indulge in my obsession.

For a long, long time, no one commented on my thickening frame. When, finally, Francine did, she said, "Not many women can get away with carrying extra weight like you do, Sunny. Your face is still pretty as ever."

I was shocked. Yeh. I'd quit weighing years ago. Funny thing, it's like having a big old black mole right on the end of your nose and people act like they don't see it. Same way with fat. Its such a shameful thing, folks don't talk about it. They become enablers. They enabled me to deny its existence on and on.

After all, Walter adored me as was. Of course, Walter adored *everybody*. The man could make a party out of going to the grocery store. His sense of fun burgeoned after the accident. It was generous, never self-serving and I have to say, it went a long way in making life more tolerable and pleasant for me.

Almost as much as food.

~~~~~

"Muffin, have you thought any more about applying for welfare assistance for the children?" I asked. She stood at my bathroom mirror blowing her amazing tumble of wheat tresses into a chic straightened style. Amid divorce proceedings from Russ, she and the children had moved in with us.

She'd managed to max my credit card in short shrift, shrieking when I took it back. In the meantime, I owed money that I did not have. I'd had to quit my part time convenience store job. I could not, in good conscience, leave the children alone with Muffin.

We barely subsisted on Walter's disability checks. Nights found me sleepless, worrying incessantly while Walter slept as peacefully as an infant. But I couldn't turn Muffin out because she would, for spite, take the children from me. God only knew what would happen to them behind closed doors.

Too, deep, deep down I occasionally brushed souls with that little toddler who'd adored me above all others. Muffin was still my daughter and I would be there for her if it killed me. While analyzing this, I concluded that I did not have a martyr complex because martyrs love misery. I loathed it then and still do.

I stood in the doorway, admiring her careless beauty, one given freely from the Almighty with no strings attached. A beauty she took for granted, just as she did everything else good in her life.

Her perfect features settled into boredom. "You never talk to me unless it's about money. I wish you'd just shut the f__ up about it. I *know* I owe you thousands of dollars. I'm just sick of hearing about it."

Shock poured over me in waves, nearly drowning me. Don't know why her venom remained so hurtful but it did. "Muffin," I said quietly as my hands began to tremble, "I only want to help you. Jared's cold is worse and his ear hurts. He needs to see a doctor. You and the kids aren't covered with insurance any more since Russ lost his job. And Daddy and I can't afford—"

She shot me a look that stopped me mid-sentence. "Don't I know it, Mama. You tell me every chance you get. Don't you *get it? I don' have any money.*" The bored look returned and she went about primping as though I weren't there. *Classic Muffin*, swatting me away as succinctly as a pesky fly.

Hurt curled into a tight knot in my bosom, heavy and sick and horrible.

"Why, Muffin?" My voice rose, notch by notch, a thing I detested but could not seem to control. Perhaps it was genetic, a '*takes one to know one*' thing with her, the projection thing I studied in college psychology. Only thing, she read me completely off the chart, attributing to me cunning and brilliance I could never touch. "Why do you hate me?" I trembled violently from the hurt. I still could not, after all these years, believe the daughter I'd borne and loved so dearly loathed me so completely.

She didn't deny it. I didn't expect her to. Then, hurt turned to anger. The scenario always turned out this way, like the same movie reel, played over and over. Muffin's capacity to find my buttons was stunning.

"You're the only person in the world who treats me so despicably," I snarled, voice rising higher, like a tape reel sped up. I was horrified to hear myself.

"Yeh," she paused her toilette to smirk at me. "Everybody else just talks about you behind your back. About how you've let yourself go and how fat you are. What a control-freak you are."

She knew that would wound. Knew how I sought to help others feel good about themselves and how desperately I sought respect. "Why do you —"

"Would you just shut the f___ up? You go on and on *and on* about anything and everything, whining and —"

"Whining?" My tears stymied. "Talking to you is *bitching?*"I narrowed my watery gaze, suddenly furious. "How dare you?"

She rounded on me, eyes an icy blue blaze. "Just listen to you. Your voice *squeaks.*" She huffed, a reviling little dismissive sound.

I felt it solidifying inside me, the hopelessness, the sense of failure that always capped these scenes. Muffin checked her cool appearance one last time and, satisfied, turned on her heel to leave. I caught her by the arm.

"Muffin, does the fact that I gave you life not count at all?" I knew it did not but couldn't seem to stop from setting myself up. In the midst, in the heat of it all, I knew the whole thing with Muffin and me was sick. I just didn't know how to change it.

She pried her arm loose and coolly assessed me for a long moment. "Unfortunately, yeh. But don't forget Daddy; he had a big hand in it, too."

In that moment, not for the first time, I had to bite my tongue against the truth. "Yes, he did. He's a good man and —"

"Don't pretend you love him. Don't you *dare*, Mom," she hissed, "because I know better."

My mouth clamped shut. I refused to touch *that*. Didn't matter, however; Muffin still sniffed a little remaining flesh to scrape from my bones. "He'd still be *Daddy* if it wasn't for you."

"You'll never forgive me, will you, Muffin?" I whispered, feeling the last of the blood drain from my face.

"Probably not," she replied in as flippant a manner as she could manage. Her departure was swift and left me reeling amid a swirl of her expensive *Chanel No. 5* fragrance. *She always has money for her cigarettes and perfume.* I stood there for long moments, too stunned to cry.

"Mema!" bawled Jared, just waking from his nap. I rushed to him, finding him warm to the touch but not as hot as before I'd spooned over-the-counter allergy-cold medications to him. He cried, holding his ear. "It *hurts*." He gazed at me through tears, beseeching me to do something.

"Walter?" I called. He came sloughing from the den, where he'd pretended not to hear my tiff with Muffin. Even with his altered intellect, he adored her completely. Jealousy, hot and thick, stirred in me. I managed to toss it aside.

"We've got to do something about Jared. He's not eaten a thing today. I'm worried about him."

"Take 'im to see Dr. Jones, in Lyman," he said. "He'll give us time to pay 'im when we get the money." Like most other village services, our own doctor's office had, years ago, shut down.

Walter surprised me at times. In some ways, he was wiser now than before his accident. Life reduced itself to simplistic terms for him. His childlike observances shot right to the heart of matters. The cynical Walter of the past was gone. This Walter saw things through placid, trusting glasses. This Walter was peaceful and giving. This Walter even went to church with me and believed with a child's simplicity.

This Walter required no intimacy from me. God forgive me but I rejoiced that Walter's sex drive virtually vanished with his memory. I quickly pushed the *off* button on that line of thought.

Actually, this Walter was my best friend. In my world, at that particular time, its importance was right up there with oxygen. He watched Gracie while I drove Jared to the doctor.

I heaved a sigh of relief as I paid the druggist for the antibiotic. I could handle Muffin as long as I had access to the children, to care for and protect them.

Protect them. *God help me to do just that.*

~~~~~

Back at the house, Walter met me at the door. I could tell he was upset. "Russ called. Muffin's over at Russ's house, a'bangin' on his door, yelling at him that he's gotta pay her the child support. He's threatening to call the law on 'er.

You gotta go get 'er, Sunny." He was wringing his hands, virtually rocking on his heels.

"Calm down, Walter," I crooned, putting my arms around him, my heart breaking as it did every time he caved. "I'll drive over there and try to calm her down. Think you can watch the kids?"

He nodded, my touch soothing him. "You sure?" I peered into the robins egg-blue eyes that saw little of what they'd perceived all those young, carefree years back. Now they gazed at me with trust. "You can handle it?"

"Yeh," he winked suddenly and the crooked James Dean grin spread over his face. "I ain't *that* addled." I laughed, inexplicably delighted with the emergence of that little mannerism from yesteryear. Such appearances were rare and, each time it happened, it was like God tossed me a sweet morsel of gingerbread to keep me going. It eased the sting.

Oh yeh, I felt it, the guilt. Muffin, in that instance, had been right as rain. Her daddy would still be Daddy had it not been for me.

"You better get goin', Sunny," Walter reminded me, wringing his hands again, "else, she's gonna be in *jail*."

I cranked my temperamental 1978 white Ford sedan and rushed to Russ' dwelling in the Red Egypt section of the village, thus named because of the red dirt hills, though the yards were as neat as in any other village site.

"Honey," I put my hand on her arm, halting her. She rolled her eyes skyward, lips tight "Russ told Walter he was going to call the law if you didn't leave in the next ten minutes."

"I need that child support check and I'm not leavin' till I get it," she spat. Never have I seen anybody more splendid in anger than Muffin and Francine. Right now, Muffin ferociously outdid Francine. "He's not gettin' away with being late again."

"I know, I know, honey," I murmured, rubbing her arm to placate her. "It's not right."

I glimpsed tears in her eyes. "It's not easy being broke," I said.

From my own experience with poverty, I knew how desperate she was for the check and felt a flash of anger at Russ. Then, just as suddenly, I realized he had his own set of problems, lack of steady work being the foremost. "Russ told Daddy he didn't have the money yet. Maybe he'll have it by tonight."

"Yeh," she spewed, "right." She pulled her arm from my feeble ministrations and rubbed it as though to erase my touch.

Hurt swirled and sloshed, despite my determination to not think about *me*. "Muffin, Russ is threatening to call the law on you for trespassing."

"This is still my house, too. Our divorce isn't final," she insisted in her low, confident way. "I can't be accused of trespassing on my own property."

I thought again of her brilliance. Too much for her own good.

"But he could accuse you of disturbing the peace — or the neighbors could call, honey. I don't want you to be locked up. You need to call your lawyer and insist that Russ pay through the court system. That way you won't have to talk to him." *He won't have to put up with this humiliation, either.*

Russ wasn't a bad sort; he and Muffin simply tripped switches in each other that shouldn't oughta be disturbed and, in the heat of battle, he could give as good as he got. Muffin, the warrior, was no slouch, either. For each hole

Russ punched in their walls, Muffin had gotten in some solid, bloody claw marks on his face and arms.

How I prayed she would, for once, listen to me. I was increasingly appalled at their bickering, at the way their children's emotional well being slid right out the bottom on their priorities-totem pole

God must've heard me.

"Yeh." She lit a Virginia Slim and took a long pull on it. "Okay, you f__ *good-for-nothing*!" she yelled through the door. "I'd better see that check before night or I'm calling my lawyer and make you go pay through the court. They won't put up with this *late-crock*." She strolled nonchalantly to her 1980 red Porsche and sped away.

Thank you, I rolled my eyes heavenward, *for getting me through this one.*

~~~~~

"She hates me, Emaline," I said, swiping tears that pooled aggravatingly along my lower lids. I snuffled soundly, trying to regain a smidgen of control while my friend poured me a cup of hot coffee and placed it before me. The parsonage, one of the larger mill houses, sparkled of new paint and refinished pine and oak floors. Emaline's touch had transformed it into simple country elegance.

"Oh, come on, Sunny. She doesn't hate you," Emaline reached across her maple kitchen table to grapple and hold my other limp hand. "Your fingers are like ice," she said quietly, then took them between her hands and massaged warmth into them.

I closed my eyes, thinking how much love poured through this gesture. "Mmmm, that feels good."

"I know. Drink some coffee. It'll help warm you."

I looked at her. "Muffin might not hate me but she doesn't like me."

"Big difference."

"Not from my present perspective." I eased my fingers free and smiled, flexing them. I wrapped them around the hot cup, recalling that morning's scene. "Let's face it. Muffin will never forgive me for that day her daddy was injured."

Over the rim of her coffee cup, Emaline angled me a look of pure wisdom. "*Never* is a long time. I think she will. In time."

I slowly shook my head. "I don't know if I can make it through all this, Emaline."

Emaline's green eyes widened in mock horror. "Sunny not make it? Might as well say Stallone'll get creamed in his next flick." Then her sweet face relaxed into a look of pure love. "Sunny Stone, you're one of the strongest women I know. Don't ever let me hear you say that again, y'hear?" She chuckled then and slanted me a challenging look, "I mean, who'll take care of Gracie and Jared?"

That did it. I felt my spine straightening.

"Yeh. You're right." I gazed at her. "One reason I put up with Muffin's abuse is because I know that if Russ catches wind that *I* don't consider Muffin good mama-material — well, he might whisk the children away and file for full custody. He could move anywhere with them." Tears regathered. "I don't trust him to deal fairly with them either. He's prone to violence, as well.

"Remember my own father's relocation all those years back? Had he wanted to, he could have kept us in Chicago, away from Nana and Daniel."

Daniel. Fresh pain filled me as I pictured his face. I quickly pushed it away.

We were silent a long moment, a comfortable thing with us. Then Emaline cast me a searching gaze. "You need to try and get Muffin in church."

I gave a huff and shot her look of pure amazement. "Don't you know I've been trying that for years? Know what she said this morning when I brought it up?" I leaned forward without her response. "She said 'spare me your little motherly, spiritual lectures.' The venom I heard and felt from her still clings to me, Emaline. It's so — devastating."

"Yeh," Emaline conceded, a sad look in her eyes. "You don't deserve what she said to you last week, when you were so sick. I would have talked to her if you'd not stopped me."

"It would do no good, Emaline. Then she'd have her guard up with you and I don't want that to happen. You're too important to me and — really, I'd like to leave the door open between you two. She may someday need somebody to open up to." I smiled at her. "And you're the perfect one. Besides, I don't want her to know that I've talked to you. She's so paranoid, anyway. Makes a crisis out of the smallest things."

Like last week, when I was down with the flu. She'd begun banging things around in the kitchen when food didn't materialize in her hands. *"There's never any m__f__ing food in this place! I've starved for the past two days."*

"Why didn't you tell her to cook herself something?" Emaline had said when I shared it with her.

"Are you kidding? She thinks she's royalty, Emaline. Doesn't lift her finger."

Anyway, from the sofa where my aching body fought to survive the worst nausea and pain I'd felt in years, I'd groaned, *"Honey, there's food in there. You just have to heat it up. Remember, I cooked half a ham Sunday? And do you have to use that horrible language?"*

"Yuck. I don't want any more ham." Slam went the fridge door. "I'm sick of it. Why don't you cook anything interesting and —"

"I'm sick," I said hoarsely. "I'm not able to —"

"You never cook anything but what you like. I'm daggum sick of macaroni and cheese and okra and tomatoes!" She slammed her glass onto the counter and marched from the kitchen, mumbling all the way to her room.

I'd thought, up until that moment, that I couldn't feel any lower. I was wrong. The macaroni and cheese/okra and tomato thing cut to the bone because they were mainstay dishes I could afford and the kids liked them. Balancing my limited funds and tasty foods was my meanest trick and having it besmirched so callously struck below the belt.

I pulled myself from the sofa and, clutching the wall, struggled my way up the stairs to Muffin's room, where she lounged from morning to night — oblivious to her mess of dirty dishes and piles of discarded clothing — watching television or talking on the phone to friends; those nameless, faceless beings who miraculously regarded Muffin as sovereign.

I'd given up on trying to tidy her quarters, never mind asking her to do it. Her response was a blank look, like no speaka de English. I'd long ago conceded the battle. I was now convinced that she enjoyed the mess. Felt comfortable in it. Was, indeed, miserable without it.

"Why," I whispered from the doorway, plastered against the jam, gasping for breath, "did you have to create a scene now? When I'm so sick?"

She cut her cold gaze at me. "I've been sick with my nerves for days — worried silly by that sorry Russ."

I gazed at her through a haze of sorrow and anger and debilitation. "I don't understand you. I try to —"

"There you go — whining again. It's all you ever do."

Somehow, rage exploded through my weakness like a rocket blast. "This is sick, Muffin. I resent —"

She shot up off the bed, nearly nose to nose with me. "You got it." *This followed by some blistery name calling.*

The world turned red. Then purple. "You get out of my house." *Where did those words come from? It was from a different script.*

"You got it, bitch."

Today, I sighed and soaked up Emaline's caring like a sponge. "Muffin stayed gone until the next day, when she showed up laughing and charming as though the bad scene had never been."

"How did the kids take her leaving like that?" Emaline's perception was so keen, so real, that I had to examine depths I usually avoided like quicksand.

"They were relieved. It's difficult to get Gracie to even go in her mama's room very often, even when Muffin calls her to bring her food or fix her a glass of Coke or a thousand other things that keep her little legs running from morning till night. I have to force her to respond to her mama's summons. I tell her she'll have to face consequences if she angers her. That usually does the trick."

"Poor Gracie," Emaline murmured. "But we have to remember that *Muffin is troubled.*"

I snorted, not quite as sympathetic as my biblically sound friend. "So is Gracie, thanks to Muffin's haughty way of going at life. She's so self-absorbed that I sometimes wonder if she's got a case of clinical narcissism. She truly feels superior to me and rejects any and everything I say." I shrugged, feeling only a dead acceptance.

Emaline shook her head. "She doesn't know how lucky she is, having a mom like you. You're a lot like my mama was." We reached across the table and clasped hands, remembering Renie — sweet, kind Renie.

"Thanks, Emaline," I whispered. "That is the ultimate compliment."

~~~~~

I grabbed the phone from the kitchen counter. "Hello?"

"Mom? Did you return the movies?" Muffin tersely inquired.

"Yes, I did. They were a day late. Where are —?"

"Not now, Mom. Don't forget to pick up the kids at three. Gotta run." *Click.* Typical Muffin. Too impatient to hear me out. Her time was too, too important — exceedingly more so than mine. As was her money, earned by the few house sales she made for a realty company.

Muffin did just enough work to keep her job and buy luxuries. I'd paid the movie video's late fee, a fact she'd not even acknowledged.

It's not like I grow money on trees — I lopped off the uncharitable thought and banged the phone into its wall-cradle and switched on the counter top radio. From the Oldies station Tom Jones wailed that being loved was not unusual. I begged to differ with him. Shoot, I was ready to do battle over it. Love? At that precise moment, it was, as the old cliché goes, only a four-letter word.

Tom Jones made way for a one-hit wonder, *At This Moment?* It soulfully spoke of lost love and of wishing that he could just hold her once more. Unexpectedly, Daniel's face popped up before me, halting me in my tracks. The male voice became Daniel's.

As needy as a starving waif, I closed my eyes and, slithering down into a chair, allowed myself a moment of pure exultation in knowing I had once experienced genuine love with my marvelous Lion-Man. Ecstasy rolled over me, invaded me. I basked and marinated in it, *wallowed* in it until I felt giddy and loose and girlish again.

Then, with supreme effort, I pushed away Daniel's image with a raw pain that had never ceased in all those years. And I reminded myself *why* I'd not allowed myself this luxury. The plunge from ecstasy to agony was too, too harrowing.

Fact was, Walter and I were imbedded in deep-debt dung, mainly due to bailing Muffin's cute little tail out so many times since she and Russ had filed for divorce. Walter lost no sleep over it. But then, Walter lost no sleep over anything.

I fought down a surge of resentment, squeezed my eyes shut, counted to ten, then attacked the kitchen sink with a damp Ajax-crusted wash cloth. While on the phone with her, I'd been about to ask my daughter to dash over to Russ' small village house later in the day and locate some of the children's missing clothing. With them shuttled back and forth between the two dwellings, tracking their outfits proved difficult

Muffin's abrupt dismissal of me, of course, got her off the hook. I snorted. Muffin? *Responsibility?* She'd managed to avoid it like a slippery eel, through two births and all that followed. I dried off the counter and swallowed my anger, deciding to drive over to Russ' myself and round up their wardrobe, most of which would need to be laundered and ironed. In the next instant, I thought of my little Gracie and Jared. My anger dissolved.

I reminded myself that I did it for *them.*

Walter and I, ten years into our marriage, had moved into this two-story, six-room dwelling, the extra space a luxury. Now, the walls bulged with two extra warm, squiggling, moving bodies vibrating tons of energy that I'd'a sworn could blow them out. Of course, Muffin occupied her hallowed quarters. A second bathroom, upstairs, was under construction. That way, we'd run into each other less.

Perhaps peace would prevail.

I'd just run the mop over the worn, yellow linoleum-tiled floor when Timmy sauntered in, loaded with carpentry gear. He paused to give me my due hug and kiss. Even at five-foot-seven, I had to reach up to hug his strong neck. He'd made a handsome man, quite masculine, yet gentle. "Hey, Sis," he muttered in his soft, inimitable way. "How's it goin'? Enjoyin' a bit of quietness, huh?"

"Oh, yeh. Until three." I closed my eyes in bliss, ecstatic bliss after all these years of potty-training and refereeing and hauling little ones to church so they wouldn't grow up to be heathens. Finally, this year, with Gracie, eight, in third grade and Jared, five, in kindergarten, most of my day was calmer.

"Quiet but — *free?*" I shook my head and gave another snort. "That's a laugh. I'm not whining, mind you, just stating facts. It's like startin' all over with raising a family. I never run out of things to do." My hands rarely ceased labor until at least eleven at night, long after Walter lay snoring.

"Walter don't help?" asked Timmy, quietly, so Walter, watching The Price is Right in the next room, wouldn't hear.

"Oh, he'd help if I asked him to. I rarely do, honey. He's just —"

"Slow?" Tim whispered, kindly, understanding the situation.

I nodded. I could usually complete the task before Walter struggled past uncertainty and grasped the *how*. Walter's desire to please was childlike and extreme. Another reason I didn't rely more on him. To see him strive so hard to please just — well, it tore me up inside.

Then, I noticed Timmy seemed bothered by something. "Spit it out," I murmured, motioning for him to sit and taking a seat myself. "Tell big sister what's troubling you."

He plopped down in the kitchen chair facing me. "You're not gonna like it, Sis."

"So what else is new?" Despite my nonchalant shrug, I experienced a trickle of trepidation.

"Sheila's car's been parked at Francine's house a lot lately."

The alarm grew. "So?"

"While Francine's at work." He carefully monitored my reaction. "I pass there every day and, lately, it's always there."

I stared at him, a cold knot forming in my stomach. "What are you saying, Timmy? Do you think —?"

"I stopped by yesterday, just to see what was going on. The doors were all locked but I knocked till Sheila come to the door. Her hair was all messed up and her makeup smeared." He shook his head, gazing unbelieving at me. "Crazy thing was — she looked smug as a bug in a rug, y'know? Wudn't even embarrassed that I'd caught 'em together."

Sick to my soul, I asked. "What did you do?"

"Nothing. Tack come dragging outta the bedroom, all mussed up, too. He looked a mite scared, truth be told. But he bluffed it, saying as how Sheila'd been helping him clean out from under the bed. 'Spring cleaning' he said. Said he paid Sheila to come by and help out, since Francine don't ever do nothing to the house." He snorted. "Now, one thing Francine does do is pay Trixie Brown to keep 'er house clean. So Sheila ain't needed for that. But seein' as how Francine's always out doin' her own thing, well...." He let it drift off, leaving little to the imagination.

"Dear Lord," I muttered, "how did it come to this?" I'd been hearing rumors of Francine's trysts for years. Seems my sister was neither selective nor discreet. Tack had, apparently, just looked the other way, knowing she'd always come back home.

"So that's where Sheila's been getting money to buy all those new clothes," I murmured as shame, thick and slimy as ever, oozed through me.

"Sheila's been heading this way all her life," Timmy murmured, hurt and disappointment a'swirling in his big whiskey colored eyes. "And we always knew what Francine was. All the way back."

I nodded, recalling the time — when Sheila was fourteen and coming by to clean for me while I was in my first year at Clemson — that she told me *"Walter makes love to me while you're gone. He loves me. And I love him."*

"She's lying," Walter said when I confronted him, looking genuinely indignant. *"I've never laid a finger on her."*

"Why would she say you did those things to her? There must be something going on for —"

"Listen, she's always lied about everything," Walter implored in a reasoning tone. *"Who're you gonna believe — me or her?"*

I recalled the times she'd lied all through the years, getting each of us in trouble. "You," I'd said. "I believe you."

Sheila had stormed from the room, tears spilling down her cheeks, leaving me feeling rotten for days afterward.

"Actually," Tim's voice pulled me back from the past, "I don't think Tack can — you know." He blushed a little but his golden gaze remained unwavering. "If they haven't... well, sacked up together, it's not Sheila's fault."

"Francine said Tack is impotent," I corroborated his suspicions. "Has been for years, a result of diabetes. 'Course, that doesn't mean Sheila couldn't seduce Tack in other ways. She's probably flirting like crazy and he's slipping her money on the sly." Tack and Francine had invested money wisely — the one frontier upon which they'd united all through the years — amassing a sizeable retirement nest egg.

Timmy huffed a mirthless laugh, rising to his feet, "Francine'll kill 'er if she finds out."

I stood too, inhaling the deep sigh of distress. "Let's just hope she doesn't."

"Gotta get to work on that bathroom." Timmy aimed for the stairs, whistling softly, obviously lighter since sharing his burden with me. The heaviness now sat on me like a belly-busted 747. I'd rather not have known about Sheila's current rendezvous but would never hurt Timmy by saying so.

Lord help me. I pulled thawed hamburger from the fridge and began shaping patties for supper, seasoned, then sealed them in a Tupperware tray until later.

Going through normal motions, I felt myself relaxing and dark thoughts ebbed away. Through the years, I'd learned to turn most things off, like a remote control. It didn't work with Muffin. But, even there, I could "shelve" each problem until "later."

It didn't work with Daniel. I could just whiff *Aqua Velva* or banana pudding or fudge or buttery popcorn or any of dozens of flavors and memories of him would cork up like fizzly soda bubbles.

Sometimes, I simply closed my eyes and let them burst over and flood me. I'd marinate there until pleasure turned to pain. When they became too much, I would go sit down, take out paper and pen, and write little satire pieces about the kids and myself, or serious things, such as today's news about Sheila.

Moments later, the hammering began. The pounding was music to my ears. My little brother — would I ever consider him otherwise? — did quite well with his finished-carpentry business, one he'd begun when the mill began to curtail and lay off. Like Walter and myself, he'd bought his dwelling when Mr. Montgomery began selling them.

I felt peaceful with Timmy's lot in life. He had a good head on his shoulders and first-rate work ethics. He went to church with his family. Lord knew he didn't have the best role model in either father or mother but he passionately loved his wife, Noreen, a tall, lanky village girl, and his daughter, Gale. And he took good care of them.

I began singing along with James Taylor's *You've Got a Friend* as I rinsed the linoleum floor, shedding the sordidness of my sisters like a dead snakeskin.

~~~~~

More and more during the eighties, I thanked the good Lord I'd grown a tough skin along the way, a hide that arrows couldn't always penetrate. I convinced myself that I truly didn't need anyone to lean on. I really didn't want anyone close enough to me to get to know the Sunny with a past. I numbed out to anyone who reached out to me, pretending I didn't notice.

So, when Nana died in 1988, at the ripe old age of ninety-two, I grieved not. Oh, I missed her then and always will. But the deep anguish I've witnessed in others simply was not there. I felt gratitude, that she'd lived a long life, plagued only by chronic arthritis before her first stroke. Three more struck before the stubborn life and will inside her succumbed. In the end, I believe, she simply tired of fighting, went to sleep and didn't wake up.

Even so, she'd outlived Tack Turner by four years.

~~~~~

It was right after Timmy told me about Sheila hanging out at absentee Francine's house that Tack grew critically ill. In Francine's frequent absences, Sheila simply revved up her devotion to Tack. By now, I knew that Sheila did few good deeds without ulterior motive. Did Francine find out? Oh, yeh. She and Sheila had one helluva cat fight, which changed little of the situation except to stoke the fires of loathing. During that interim, my sisters avoided me like strep. They both, to some degree, loved fighting, got high on it, and knew I'd put a damper on it.

As for Francine, she had her own thing going. This time, with a married man, if gossip held truth. I can still hear Nana, lying in her sick bed, saying, "I don't see how that Francine can roll over on her back for every man sniffing around...."

~~~~~

Tack's death seemed anti-climactic, with all the shameful goings on. He died more nobly than he'd lived, with nary a whimper, from what Sheila relayed every chance she got to anybody who'd listen. Francine was furious but tried, for once, to hold her acerbic tongue. I think perhaps one reason being that if she spilled the beans about Sheila's transgressions, her little sister would, by her very nature, be compelled to return the deed a hundredfold.

On the day of the funeral Francine summoned Timmy and me into her bedroom and shut the door. "Listen," she said conspiratorially, "there's a second will somewhere. I just *know* it. It's just the way Sheila's acting. Like something's up. Y'all gotta help me find it 'fore Sheila gets her greedy little hands on it. That hussy's *shameless.*" She fought to hold her temper in check. Even Francine knew better than to throw a conniption during a family wake.

"I've got the keys to that Cadillac in the garage that Tack always kept locked up. The one he'd fixed up to resell? Toward the end, he didn't want me around it. I got this feeling about it, y'know? Tim, I want you to go out and check in the trunk and see if you turn up anything. Sheila's just left with that boyfriend of hers. I heard her say she's going home to change clothes. So its best you do it now, so she won't know. She's been plundering around like she's trying to find something. Probably lookin' for the car keys."

Tim hesitated. "I don't know —" He looked at me. I nodded. If he didn't do it, I feared Francine would and might truly freak out if she found something.

"Look," Francine grew as solemn as I'd ever seen her, "I've took care of Tack all these years. I done right by him till he got — well, till he couldn't be a husband no more. But I still took care of 'im, making sure he took his medicine and feeding him the right food and all. I know I've done things that I shouldn't but at least I took care of 'im. I feel I'm entitled to all we've worked together to have all these years. And I'm not gonna let somebody like that useless Sheila steal it away from me."

Timmy gazed at her for long moments, then took the keys from her and went outside. I watched her pace while waiting. Middle age rode and slightly drooped her features, yet passion buoyed them, painting them young and vital. I gazed at my own in the big mirror, seeing the same genetic sag in my jawline and beneath my eyes. Plus, I carried at least 30 extra pounds, maybe more, which bloated my features. Only difference was mine lacked the magic transformation of Francine's. I thought how I looked every day and minute of my forty-four years.

A few minutes later, Timmy returned with a large brown envelope. Francine locked the bedroom door, ripped into it and read, her features turning darker by the moment.

By the time she finished reading, she was livid.

She thrust the pages at me. I sat on the side of her Queen Anne high-poster bed. Tim lowered himself beside me and read over my shoulder. Tack had bequeathed one property, with a white comfortable cottage, to his sister, Elaine Carly. Elaine's husband Gene had died drunk the year before. Her son, Junior, now in his twenties, followed stealthily in Senior's tracks. Poor Elaine worked at waitressing, sometimes holding down two jobs simultaneously to pay rent on a rundown apartment in Spartanburg. The deed to this nice house would ease her burdens and make her comfortable for the remainder of her life.

"It's *mine!*" Francine hissed, as though reading my mind. A chill grazed my spine. Her eyes slitted. "He's not gonna give it to nobody else."

My heart sank. Francine had plenty without going against Tack's wishes to make life easier for his destitute sister. Actually, Tack had owned the house before he and Francine married. Technically, it was his to do with as he pleased.

264   Emily Sue Harvey

He hadn't figured Francine into the equation. He'd probably felt a sense of control when writing this new will and testament. It probably had made up, in a small way, for Francine's wild and loose ways through the years.

Too, Sheila had probably egged things on, not too difficult with an insecure, sick, dying man.

I read on. A twenty-thousand dollar life insurance policy was bequeathed to his aging mother, who was, at that time, as ancient as Nana and even more frail. I figured that was in the original will and that Francine would surely honor it. After all, the entire Turner family adored her. Francine had, miraculously, won all of them over from the get-go and somehow retained their affection and respect. How her wayward shenanigans averted their detection and censure was then and remains till this day beyond me.

I read on. The real stunner was the bequest to Sheila: another of their houses, a nicer one even, and a car — the Cadillac in the garage, in fact.

"That's why he put the blasted thing in the trunk of that car." Resting her fanny on the dresser table top, Francine lit up a cigarette, inhaled deeply, blew it out, and stared at the ceiling as though wanting to take it apart, piece by piece. "He thought Sheila would find it for sure. They plotted it. Only thing — he died before giving her the car key." She snorted. "Thought they could pull one over on me."

She pushed away from the dresser, walked over to me, snatched the pages from my hand and stalked to the bathroom. "I'll fix that."

Timmy and I turned to each other, mixed emotions flailing about in our gazes. Presently we smelled smoke. We rushed to the bathroom door and watched Francine holding the burning will and testament until it reached her fingers.

She gingerly tossed it into the commode and, with a flourish, flushed the evidence.

"Well, would you look at that?" She brushed her hands together. "It go *bye-bye*." She strode to retrieve her purse from the bed. "C'mon, folks. We've got a funeral to do."

Outside, as we pulled out in the gray family limousine, Francine, classy as gentry in her black ensemble, stared through the tinted window at Sheila, just arrived, who, pale-featured and vacant-eyed, hovered near the garage.

"Y'know," Francine addressed the other family members seated in the long sleek sedan, including Tack's sister and nephew, "Sheila said she didn't feel like going to the funeral. She offered to stay here and house-sit, you know, answer the phone and all. That was sure sweet o'her, wud'n it?" Everyone nodded and grunted assent. She smiled sweetly at me, as malevolent a smile as I've ever seen on a human face.

I knew she'd left the keys to the car on the kitchen table.

Then she leaned and whispered in my ear, "Lord'a *mercy*, I'd love to see her face when she gets in that trunk and can't find her *ticket to Easy Street*."

~~~~~

"Ain't that against the law?" Timmy muttered later, after the burial and during the family's reconvening at Francine's house.

"Yeh." I poured him a glass of iced tea to wash down his huge hunk of Emaline's chocolate cake. She and some church members brought it over to Francine's house after the funeral that evening, along with buckets of KFC and all the fixings. "I'm hoping nobody else knows about it besides Sheila."

"Knows about what?" Sheila appeared in the doorway, pale as yesterday's ashes. Her eyes burned, yet...seemed to not see Timmy and me, like Sheila was not behind them. *I've got to defuse this before it gets out of hand.* I thought fast, lowering my voice to say, "You know — about Francine's...." I let it trail off and shrugged sadly, allowing her to make of it what she wanted to.

"You mean her whorin'." Sheila's flat voice sounded like a trumpet blast.

"Shhh," I pressed a finger to my lips, frowning. "This's not the time to low-rate your sister. She's just lost her husband."

Sheila glowered for a long moment, then blinked, appearing behind her eyes. "You don't know all she's done, Sunny." She sighed and tears suddenly pooled along her lids. "You just don't know." Her voice was so desolate I felt something akin to pity. She'd been so close to her reward for seducing Tack. I could even follow a little of her warped reasoning, having been tuned in all through the years.

I went and wrapped her in my arms. Her head burrowed into my shoulder as she sobbed her heart out, leaving my good black Sunday dress sodden but that was okay. Timmy quietly left the room without saying a word. I knew he felt as torn as I, caught between these two sisters, who were equally matched opponents in life's wars.

Life had not been good to either of them; had, in fact, made them monsters.

We didn't always like 'em. In fact, rarely did. But they were blood.

And we loved them.

~~~~~

Don't know exactly when I started really distancing myself from Muffin. It probably came gradually, a reaction to her steadfast visceral rejection. How many ways can a daughter tell a mother, "Get the f__ out of my face"? Muffin used them all up and invented a few more select ones.

So I obliged her. I learned new dance steps that took me around, over, and under her rages and disparagement. I learned to simply tune her out when feasible. It wasn't always possible, when the children were involved, but I kept them close under my wing, like a hen does her dibbies during storms.

When Gracie started high school and Jared entered the sixth grade, their daddy, Russ Fant married a good woman, started to church and cleaned up his life. Even Muffin admitted he was a changed man and allowed him more access to the children. Russ' wife, Jennifer, supported her husband's new directions and threw away all the alcohol, drugs, Playboys, and best of all, insisted he adopt a brand new cleaned-up vocabulary.

"He's really, like, *changed*," Gracie gushed. My lovely granddaughter, a *sweet* version of Muffin, rarely impressed with anything, was blown away. Me? I was blown away, too. All the prayers I'd uttered through the years for Muffin… and now, turned out that Russ and Jennifer were the recipients. Go figure.

My life changed drastically after that. More and more, Russ took over the responsibility of Gracie and Jared. I'll have to say that Jennifer's sensitive spirit played a big role in blending our two families. She complemented Russ' new drive and sense of fair play. Never did they alienate the children from Walter and me. When either of the children grew homesick and sought me out, they were allowed that freedom. Likewise, when they missed their father and Jennifer, I turned loose and freely shared.

Muffin? She was still lost in that place where teens go between adolescence and adulthood. A place where growing up was indefinitely postponed

Only thing, Muffin was now thirty.

~~~~~

Doretha poured me tea. Just like she used to long ago when Emaline and I took treats over and basked in her presence. Today she looked much the same because her skinny frame and features didn't have enough spare to sag. She didn't even have a little potbelly like Gladys.

"I know you don't understand why I put Alvin out," she said in her Jackie Kennedy softness, with a Dolly Parton twang. "I didn't expect you to." She sat down opposite me, at Berthie's ancient but polished oak kitchen table. The shine was Alvin's handiwork.

Even though Doretha had 'run 'im off' after Sheila's disclosure of his incestuous behavior all those years ago, he and Doretha remained friends. He still came over every day and cleaned the house for her. Aunt Tina remained frustrated over the situation she couldn't control. Despite her pleading, cajoling, and outright bullying, Doretha remained unbending.

"I love Alvin," she said, daintily sipping her tea. "I just don't want to be married to 'im no more." There was little emotion in her voice. Only her eyes, those deep-set, gray pools, that looked eons old, revealed pain. "He sees Tammy all he wants to, can get 'er any time. I don't want to treat 'im bad. I hadn't told Tammy what Sheila said 'bout 'im. She don't need to know. He's 'er daddy."

"No," I agreed. "No use in hurting her, too." How well I knew that reasoning.

"I love you, Sunny," she said, startling me. It'd been so long since we'd sat together and talked like this. All those years in between melted and I smiled at her.

"I love you, too, Doretha. You've always been there for me. I'll never forget that."

Her eyes misted and something flickered in them before she lowered her gaze. "Not always. I wish I had." She looked at me then and a tear slid down her pale cheek. "Things mighta been different for you."

I frowned at her and reached for her hand. Her fingers were cold and thin as toothpicks, nearly non-existent. "You're not still taking the blame for — you know, that thing that happened all those years back, are you?" I couldn't put it into words, that would make it *real*. Not now, when I'd put it behind me.

A tear slid down her other cheek. She swiped it away with her free hand. "I reckon I am, Sunny. I won't never —"

"Don't." I shook my head. "It's gone. Past. Like it never happened." *Liar, Liar, pants....* "It makes me terribly sad for you to talk like this." That, at least, was the truth.

I saw her waver, inhale and let out a long jagged sigh. "Well, if you say so. I don't want to cause you no more grief."

I smiled at her, feeling better banishing the subject.

"Daniel's comin' home for a visit."

My heart skipped two beats then went into erratic cadence. "When?" I asked in a whispery thin voice.

"Christmas."

Three months away. "He hates me. I wish he didn't." After the time on the back alley when I'd turned my back and stomped off away from him, he'd avoided me like a plague. All these years. Three months and I'd see him again.

"He don't hate you, Sunny," came the gentle reply. "He wants to see you."

<u>Chapter Thirteen</u>

Bing Crosby's *White Christmas* blended peacefully with spicy baking aromas.

"Bye darlin'. You have a good time with Daddy and Jennifer, okay?" I hugged Jared and felt that little kick to my heart when he squeezed me back with all his might. He was growing up so fast. His shoulders were nearly level with mine now.

"You sure you won't feel lonesome, Mema?" he asked anxiously. And I wondered how much longer his love would be so free and spontaneous. How long before it would be "not cool" to love so transparently. *What a gift.*

I chuckled. "*Pshaw.* With Papa here with me? Nah." Then I whispered in his ear. "But I'll miss you like crazy. I can't wait to see all your presents."

He grinned and I knew I'd said the right thing. About that time, Gracie bounded down the stairs, loaded down with her hair and makeup paraphernalia, stuff she carried back and forth between her two 'homes'. I was as happy as they were with their sense of belonging with their daddy, as well as with their Papa and me.

Gracie hugged me and gave me a peck-kiss on the lips. "Bye, Mema. I'll call you tonight." She always did. No matter where she was, she always checked in with me. Not because I required it but because 'I just want to hear your voice, Mema.'

"Hey!" Walter bellowed good-naturedly, "How about me?" He arose stiffly from his La-Z-Boy and took only a half step before both grandkids tackled him, knocking him back into his chair, all three laughing like goonies. At times like this, I counted my blessings with Walter. He played as heartily as any kid, showering affection the same way.

Jared dashed to the front door, poked his head out and called to his dad who'd already gone to wait in the car. "Be there in a minute!" He ran back to plug in the tree we'd all decorated together. It was his thing, turning on the tree daily. "This is Christmas Eve," he said. "It's supposed to stay on all day today."

Francine dropped in for a minute, bringing our gifts. Family didn't get together, collectively, like we did when Nana was alive. We hugged and she said, "I've got one more stop before I'm finished. At Elaine's. She's gonna have cake and goodies and wants me to come by."

"How is she?" I asked, thinking again of the house Elaine should be living in, the one her brother, Tack, had bequeathed her. Instead, she lived in an old squalid apartment, still struggling to pay rent. Not only had Francine taken from Elaine, she'd gone to Tack's elderly, sick mother only days after Tack's funeral and asked her to sign a legal document. Trusting her, Mrs. Turner, nearly blind, had complied, never suspecting she was signing over her twenty thousand dollar life insurance policy bequest.

"Oh, Elaine's okay," Francine replied, snatching a piece of my homemade fudge from the counter on her way out. "Love ya, Sunny. Merry Christmas, y'all!" she called to everybody.

"Merry Christmas, Aunt Francine," cried my two, in unison, echoed by Walter's "and a happy New Year!"

"Let's go, kids!" called Russ from the doorway, winking at me. I really loved this new Russ, a much warmer version. But then, I thought uncharitably, anybody living with Muffin for long could suffer the loss of cheer.

"Don't forget to take your goodies," I reminded Gracie, who dashed back to the kitchen for the big gift bag containing holiday zip-lock bags, chocked full, that we'd packed for them to share with Russ and Jennifer. The three of us had worked the entire week before Christmas, cooking all our favorite cookies, candies, and cakes.

I would later write about my 'Crazy Christmas Cooking' in a newspaper column. But that's getting ahead of myself. Anyway, it was enough to feed an entire neighborhood. Walter had, with my help, even made an icebox fruit cake, of which he was unspeakably proud.

Another round of hugs and kisses and they were off for the next twenty-four hours. For just a moment, a pang of longing shook me. I gently pushed it aside and went to cut Walter and me a slice of my carrot cake. The recipe was from a Southern Homes Cookbook and was wickedly rich and wonderful.

I'd poured our coffee and turned on a Perry Como Christmas television special when Muffin and her current boyfriend, Joe, burst through the front door.

Joe was ashen-faced, frantic. " Muffin took a handful of prescription pills, saying she wants to die."

Before I could open my mouth to speak, she dashed up the stairs and bolted her bedroom door. My Christmas cheer died in that moment.

Walter began to moan and sob and wring his hands. I tried, unsuccessfully, to calm him. Desperate, I dialed

Doretha's number and explained the situation to her. She was at my door within five minutes.

"I've called EMS to come for Muffin," I explained. "I had to give Walter a heavy dose of his tranquilizer. He'll sleep through the night. I just need somebody here to —"

"I'll stay. Don't you worry none, Sunny." Doretha hugged me and then said, "Ever'thing'll be all right. You just take care o' your little girl."

My little girl. How long has it been since she felt like my little girl? I watched Doretha disappear into Walter's den, actually his bedroom nook with his own TV and old easy chairs for our frequent conversation times, when we shared cute and funny family stuff. Not much sad stuff. Walter didn't do sad well. His was exuberance or desolation, if aroused at all. Most of the time he was laid-back and pliable.

There was a knock at the front door. *The EMS.* I rushed to open it. He stood there, vapor trailing from his mouth, his features much the same, yet, different. More angular and lean and something else, something mysterious and elusive.

"Sunny." My name, sliding from his mouth, sounded like a benediction.

"*My God. Daniel,*" I whispered. My knees turned to mush.

Chapter Fourteen

I gripped the storm-door knob, opening it and gesturing. "Come in. My heavens, when did you get in? Doretha didn't tell —" Doretha, the incurable romantic, still, with everybody but herself. She'd wanted it to be a surprise.

Remarkably, my voice was steady. His gaze never left my face as he replied in a rich baritone (when had his voice deepened so)? "About an hour ago. What can I do to help?"

Help? I stared stupidly at him for a moment, then closed the door behind us. "About Muffin," he softly clarified.

I shook my head. "I'm not all here, Daniel," I said weakly, closing my eyes and pulling in a deep steadying breath.

"That's okay. I understand." I looked at him then and nearly gasped at the naked emotion on his face. The years melted away and I saw, *knew* that he felt my desolation and helplessness. My pain. It had always been so.

Another knock at the door. This time, it *was* the EMS team. I accompanied them upstairs, used a paper clip to unlock the bedroom door and stood back for them to collect a belligerent, near-incoherent Muffin and deposit her in the ambulance, where they proceeded to monitor her. Her boyfriend of the moment was leaving, saying he would call later to check on Muffin. I was glad he was gone. Things were complicated enough.

"Please…may I ride with her?" I asked, my heart flailing in my chest at the situation's gravity.

"No one but paramedics are allowed to ride with the patient," came the kind but firm reply. I still pushed my way into the unit to let Muffin know I was there. I gazed into her chalky features. She watched me as if from a great distance, eyes glassy, lids heavy. I leaned to kiss her, then nuzzled her cool cheek. "Why, baby?" I whispered.

Tears filled her eyes and her lips trembled. Her answer was breathy and so low only I heard her. "I don't want to live any more, Mama. You don't know how often I gaze at my ceiling for something to hang from. There's nothing there that would hold my weight."

"You'll have to leave, Mrs. Stone." The paramedic pulled on a stethoscope and pressed it to Muffin's chest.

I gave her one last kiss as the motor revved.

"We'll follow in my car." Daniel said, helping me from the unit.

I felt unnaturally grateful to have him there. "Thanks."

~~~~~

Muffin's face, half-buried in the ER pillow, was waxen. She curled on her side in fetal position. IVs and monitor chords snaked from her still, still form. The *beep…beep… beep* issuing from the screen splashed eerily over my senses, the heartbeat/pulse cadence a visceral blow to my own heart.

I'd never have dreamed today would end so.

Christmas Eve morn had started pseudo-normal, with the kids and I doing a wonderful brunch of pancakes, sausage, eggs, and orange juice. We'd just finished when Muffin, having slept near comatose for three days straight, descended the stairs. I was packing the dishwasher when we heard her uneven, muffled steps.

"Uh oh," whispered Gracie, raising her eyebrows at Jared. They quickly scuttled to their Papa's room, knowing Muffin rarely created a scene in his presence. I braced myself, hoping that this once she'd behave herself and allow me peace during what remained of the holidays.

"Mom?" she called sharply, more a summons to my ears. I nearly gasped at her ashen, puffy features. Her white, white fingers gripped the banister. She swayed and peered at me with glazed eyes.

"What is it, honey?" I went to wrap my arms around her but she pushed me away with amazing strength and staggered across the floor to a kitchen chair.

"Get outta my face," she muttered, sagging heavily into the chair I quickly pulled out for her. "Why'd you take my car?"

So she'd already seen the vacancy in our drive. Her venom had lost much of its sting over the years. I suppose I'd simply grown an armadillo shell, one that had thickened and crystallized with each horrific calamity. "You're in no condition to drive, Muffin."

"*Where is it?*" she hissed, managing a totally malevolent scowl. "It's *mine!*"

Her white Porsche was tucked away in Tim's garage but I'd not tell her until she was dried out.

"My name is on the title. I'm responsible if you get out here and hit someone while behind the wheel and —"

She stood, nearly knocking me over. "I-*want-my-car.*" She stumbled around the room and went on to call me quite a few choice names as I moved away and got my trembling hands busy at the sink. Some expletives were new. One in particular, blew me away. A four-letter word beginning with C.

I pivoted to stare at her. "That's a new low. Have you forgotten I'm your mother?"

"Have *you*? Taking my car is a new low, too." The face I peered into was as hostile as a stranger's whose home I'd broken into and trashed. She was no less indignant.

A spoiled brat.

As usual, Muffin had the last word. I walked away in disgust.

Now, in the ER, with her so close to death, I pondered how I could have handled the situation differently.

A young, blonde lab worker in cheerful colored scrubs pushed aside the curtain and rolled her heart-monitoring pulley into the small cubicle. She roused Muffin, made her uncomfortable. "I'm hungry," Muffin grumbled, groggily yet forceful. The technician promised to ask the desk nurse about food.

Her departure disturbed Muffin further. Her head lifted. I braced myself. Her glazed gaze searched, found mine. I watched her nostrils flare and, I swear, blue fire glimmer in those irises.

"Get me some food. *Now!*"

An RN entered. "I need a urine sample," she told Muffin. The thirtyish brunette nurse was pleasingly plump in her gay-pink scrubs as she stood at bedside, not nearly as hefty as me. For a split second, I wondered what Daniel thought of the heavier, matronly Sunny. For the first time in years, it mattered. "What'll it be, bedpan or catheter-tube?" asked the nurse politely.

"Bedpan," grouched my daughter, distinctly agitated at losing control. "Why can't I get out of bed and pee?" This spilled out finely tuned belligerence.

278 Emily Sue Harvey

"Because you're hooked up," I reminded her. My stomach knotted and roiled as I watched her momentum gain steam. A danged storm brewed as she settled her hips on the pink plastic urinal pan. My radar shrieked and careened off the nerve-screen. I felt a gush of pity for the poor, unsuspecting woman.

"Why do you need urine?" Muffin cut wary eyes at her.

"We need to see what drugs are in you," replied the nurse evenly. *Uh oh.*

"Guess what?" Muffin quipped airily, yanking the dry pan from beneath her, "I can't pee." With a flourish, she presented it to the nurse, who, by now, began to show signs of ruffling. Flushed, she wrote on her chart and headed for the door, glad, I was certain, to escape.

"You shouldn't wake me up," Muffin called after her. "I'm *ticked off* when I get woke up. Don't wake me up again, *you fat b-----!*"

I flinched, mortified, appalled, ashamed this female was *mine.*

Muffin's slitted gaze pinned me. I was numb. Dead. I felt pity for the medical staff and dread for what surely was to come. "Get me out of here. *Now!*"

I rushed to stop her from ripping the IVs and monitor needles from her arms, tasting disaster as my chest vibrated with palpitations. Muffin's strength, in the heat of anger, always astounds me but in that moment of struggle it shot to new summits.

"Please, Muffin. *Don't.* They're almost finished." I backed away, more than overwhelmed by the sheer force of her.

Her eyes rolled back in her head and she flopped back against her pillow. I thought for a moment she'd passed out. Then her lids popped open and she spat, "Get the papers.

I'll sign myself out." She jackknifed upright, startling me. Eyes blazing like an out of control forest fire. Muffin was again in charge.

"Get the f___ing Chief-of-Staff!" she yelled to the top of her lungs.

"Okay." I said quietly, to placate her. "I'll go see what I can do."

She relaxed just a tad and lay back on her pillow. I felt her gaze stalk me as I left.

Outside the door, the entire ER team clustered around the desk. The doctor said, "Don't they have a bed in the psyche section? We've got to do something." A nurse injected, "She's disturbing the other patients." Another added, "She's being *ugly.*"

"Security's on his way," added another.

I could have sunk into the floor unnoticed because they were so traumatized by my daughter, they were oblivious to my presence. No. That wasn't true. They simply lumped my daughter and me together, figuring that somehow, her nastiness was my fault.

I wouldn't even touch that. I'd spent thirty years trying to teach Muffin love and forgiveness and how to help others along life's way. I'd not done it by preaching but by example. No. I would not — *could not* take credit for her unkindness.

She was the most obnoxious person I'd ever known, bar none. And I was her mother.

Dear God. I passed the security man on my way to the ER waiting room, where Daniel absently watched a wall-mounted television playing a Boston Pops Orchestra Christmas concert. I took the seat beside him, startling him with my sudden appearance.

"How is she?" His deep voice vibrated with concern.

I chortled wearily. "Driving 'em all crazy. They've called security, Daniel. Even *they* don't know what to do with her. I'm at the end of my rope. I don't know what to do."

He took my hand and squeezed it. My heart did a flip-flop at his touch, then settled into *safety*. I felt a jolt of *déjà vu*, reliving the days when Daniel's presence always sent that cared-for feeling spiraling through me.

He stood. "You rest awhile. I'll go see what's going on." I started to protest, knew I should, but all I could manage was a grateful, tired smile and a nod. I knew I was wimping out but had taken about all I could for one day. So I sat there in that uncomfortable, hard navy-blue seat and listened to *Winter Wonderland* and a dozen other holiday favorites by the Boston Pops, feeling as sad as I'd ever felt in my life.

I couldn't even get a knot tied in the end of my rope. I'd asked the doctor, when I first arrived at the hospital, while Muffin was being pricked and prodded, "What should I do to have her committed? She needs help."

He shook his head. "You can't. Not without her being arrested first. She's definitely old enough to sign herself in and out of drug rehab."

So I felt my last hope slip away. Muffin didn't need an arrest-record on top of everything else. She'd never make anything of her life. Somewhere, deep in my mind, I reserved the certainty that someday Muffin would miraculously wake up, see the light, and turn her life around. That hope was like a spring bubbling perpetually in the depth of my soul. It was what I waited for, that kept me going.

Finally, Daniel reappeared. "She's calmed down. Sleeping mostly. I'd go back there with her if I were you. Regardless of all that junk pouring out of her mouth, she needs you, Sunny."

I stood and he put his arms around me, pulling me against his firm chest. My face burrowed for a moment as I inhaled Aqua Velva and Daniel's own clean scent. Then I grew aware of my bulk. I felt so ashamed.

"Daniel," I whispered, then looked up at him as his hands slid to my arms, then on down to lace with my fingers. "I'm so fat. I'm truly ashamed to have —"

"You're beautiful, Sunny." I gazed into the sea-mist eyes, trying to read his real sentiments. Then, he said it again, "The most beautiful girl I've ever known." His voice shimmered over my skin and raised the hair on my neck...my arms, all over.

Then I laughed, nervously. He looked a little puzzled. "I used to be so skinny, Daniel. Would you ever have believed I'd end up this f —"

"*Voluptuous,*" he insisted, looking as solemn as I'd ever seen him. "On you, it looks good."

I gazed at him, my grin slowly dissolving. "*Liar.* But, thank you," I managed to whisper. Then I cleared my throat and slipped from his touch, feeling instantly deprived, bereft. "I'll go rescue the staff from Muffin." I heard him chuckle as I spun away.

So I went back to sit with my daughter until the doctor came in with the blood test results. Muffin had already roused up to send me hunting more food. A nurse located small packs of soda crackers and peanut butter. Muffin attacked it, consuming it in moments. That girl could out-eat anybody I'd ever seen. I suspected it had to do with whatever drugs rampaged through her.

Dr. Hart handed Muffin the list of substances they'd found in her blood and urine samples. The list was long. Dr. Hart propped against the wall, clipboard tucked under his arm. "You're going to have to face up to your addiction problem," he said without preamble. "Coke is bad news. If you don't get help, Muffin, you'll end up dead. Someday you're going to mix drugs that have lethal consequences. I'm not going to lecture you. You're thirty years old and know what you have to do."

Muffin seemed unaffected by his words. Impatient even, for him to depart. My heart sank lower.

An hour later, Daniel drove us home.

~~~~~

Getting Muffin settled into her bed should have been a simple matter. Then, I remembered that nothing Muffin-connected was ever *simple*. Having Daniel there helped, for a short spell. Then, just when I thought all was well, when her eyes closed, I motioned for Daniel to follow me out, her lids popped open and her nice-girl persona shattered.

"I want my *car!*" she demanded. Her white-hot eyes blazed from ashen features. Her fury struck like a poison arrow, paralyzing me.

I wet my lips and looked at Daniel, whose assessing gaze anchored to Muffin's face. He was, I realized, coiled inside, ready to spring.

To defend me. That hadn't changed in all these years. The thought loosed me from the hypnotic fear that bound me before my daughter, like a bird before a stalking cat.

"Honey," I said soothingly, taking a step nearer, "you can't drive until you're feeling better. The doctor said —"

"*I don't care what the doctor said!. I want my car!*" she shrieked, springing to her feet so fast I nearly fell over from shock. "*Now! Do you hear?*" She advanced on me and I instinctively recoiled, fear gripping me — oh, yes, I feared Muffin. Violence seethed and bubbled in her, like the mysterious black liquid in a witch's brew. I gazed into her face, into her blue, blue eyes and saw only black. New shock coursed through me, causing my nape to rise — *someone else lurked behind them.*

A demon said a voice from somewhere.

Ice crept into my veins, chilling its way around my heart and through my brain and extremities. The hair on my nape rose up.

My fingers rolled into fists. "Come out of here! *Now!*" I hissed at the evil creature, knowing from my childhood sermons that there are forces of darkness that invade individuals at low points in their lives. I also knew demons were real. I'd felt them enough around Mama...and Francine... and at times, even around Sheila. All this came to me in that short moment, stunning me with revelation.

Muffin's eyes slitted and she retreated a step, knocked off-center by my unusual aggression.

"Leave her *alo-o-one!*" I shrieked again at the *thing* behind those blue eyes. Muffin tensed but the eyes did not change. I shuddered, revolted.

"Sunny," Daniel gripped my arm, yet gently. I gazed up at him, blinking, still reeling. "Come on. Let's let Muffin sleep."

"But it's inside her, Daniel," I insisted, my voice hoarse.

"She's *nuts,*" Muffin snarled and stalked to her bed. "Nuttier'n a *fruitcake.*" She flopped down, pulled the covers up and tossed herself over to face the wall. "Get out of my room!"

I don't know who was the happier to comply, Daniel or me.

~~~~~

Daniel and I drank coffee and ate slabs of carrot cake there in my little den, both tired beyond words. We didn't need to talk. Never had. It was as though we'd never been apart.

"But it's different," Daniel said quietly, startling me anew with his ability to read my thoughts and finish my sentences.

I would have laughed but the moment was too sacrosanct. Instead I sighed. "Yes. Things *are* different." We gazed at each other across the coffee table, over our propped sock and stocking feet. Our faces mirrored the other's lost dreams and regrets. "There's Walter," I whispered.

Daniel schooled his features and asked, "How is Walter these days?"

I smiled. "Walter's fine. Just fine, Daniel."

I saw pain flicker in his eyes. "I did both of you wrong, Sunny. I've regretted it every day of my life. Yet — I hated Walter for years. Envied him. Wished him dead."

"Daniel. You don't have to —"

"Yes, I do, Sunny. I wish I had your ability to forgive. I don't. But I want to."

I set my cake aside, appetite vanished. "You can, Daniel. Just…let it go. Y'know? We all, the three of us, did hurtful things but what is, is. Actually, Walter's the most untouched one of us." I chuckled. "Heck, he doesn't even remember his daddy. Or mama. After the accident, I was a total stranger to him. He would have gladly given me back to you had you asked."

I meant it as a joke but Daniel didn't laugh. Just gazed at me steadily until I grew uncomfortable. "What?" I asked.

"You," he said quietly. "Wish life could be so simple for me. You've always had a good heart, Sunny. You didn't deserve what life handed you. Not from your mama. Your daddy. Or me. But here you sit, able to laugh."

"Better to laugh than cry," I quipped, bit my lip to stem tears, then said. "You know Daddy died two years back, don't you?"

He looked shocked. "No. How — what killed him?"

"Cancer. We were all with him, except Sheila." I sighed heavily. "Felt she didn't belong there, in the family circle. Daddy hated things turned out like they did. He didn't plan to abandon us. We just had our lives here, with Nana. He acquired a new family and all...so that's the way it was." I shrugged.

"That's what I mean, Sunny. You don't let things get you down. You don't brood like I do." His wasn't whining. It was just fact, his dark side. We both knew it. We also knew that his dark side had separated us all those years ago.

"Remember that bank account?" I asked.

"Ours?" He asked, knowing good and well I'd avoided using 'ours' because it hurt too much. "Yeh. I hope you used it."

"Nope. It's still there. I've kept it all through the years. Most of it was yours, anyway."

"Use it when you need it." He didn't say anything more for long moments. Then he arose and pulled on his black leather bomber jacket, looking as trim and firm as eighteen-year-old Daniel. Yet — broader and more manly. I walked him to the door determined not to pay heed to the electric current connecting us, drawing me to him like steel to a magnet.

"Sunny, I'm leaving tomorrow. I'll be visiting all along but I've got business matters to take care of in Colorado in the next few months, before I retire from service. If there's ever anything I can do to help you and Walter, promise me you'll let me know. Anything."

I was in shock from hearing he was leaving so soon. My eyes misted. "I-I guess I figured you'd be here from now on." I huffed a little laugh, gazing at him through the blur. "Just wishin', is all. Take care now, y'hear?" I reached up to hug him and then his arms were around me for long moments, a time when he embraced me like he never wanted to let go, when my arms looped tighter around his neck. And I felt his lips press to my neck and his Aqua Velva mingle with my Avon *Wild Rose*, creating our own unique fragrance.

Suddenly, I was released and he stepped back, his eyes unusually bright, his rugged features solemn. "Remember what I said, Sunny. Anything. Just let me know."

I still reeled from the abrupt disconnection. "I'll be okay, Daniel. I —"

"I let you down once, Sunny," he whispered, his finger grazing my cheek, his lips a breath away. "I won't ever again."

In the next heartbeat, he was gone.

~~~~~

I turned from the door, wiping tears from my cheek. Then I saw her.

Muffin. Paused, halfway down the stairs. Eyes slitted, face cold. Of course, I was accustomed to her coldness but it was the stillness of her, an ungodly *awareness* that felt like she stripped me naked and skinned me alive. And I knew.

"You're jus' full of surprises, Mama," she said flippantly. Yet — her eyes, flat, glassy, spewing venom, said otherwise. "Now I know why you never loved Daddy. It was him. Daniel, wadn't it?"

I licked my lips, knowing she'd seen us embrace, heard Daniel's confession — all of it. *Dear God!*

"Muffin, it's not what you th —"

"*Stuff it,* Mama," she said flatly, descending, holding tightly to the banister rail. "I'm sure Daddy'll be interested to know about that touching little good-bye." She stumbled down the steps, and staggered toward Walter's room, knocking over a kitchen chair.

I stiffened. "Muffin! Don't you dare upset your Daddy over —" Seeing she ignored me, I rushed to block her. But considering her ER ordeal she was still remarkably strong, plowing past me as if I were no more than a floating feather.

Rammed by her, the door to Walter's darkened room burst open and she plodded through, bumping into furniture in her path. "*Daddy!*" she called as a glass on his little TV tray table went crashing to the floor, bringing Walter upright in his bed and, despite the earlier tranquilizer, quaking, his eyes wide with terror.

I could have killed her in that moment. Instead, I stood frozen in the doorway, hands pressed to mouth, dreading....

"Daddy," Muffin plopped down onto his bedside, right in his face, "there's somethin' you gotta know —"

"Muffin. *Don't.*" I rushed to Walter, on the opposite side of the bed. He turned frightened eyes to me and I took his hands in mine. "Don't listen to her, Walter."

Muffin snorted, slurring words, "I'll jus' *bet* you don' want 'im to hear this. I'm sick o' your lyin' and pretendin' to be so *good* when — hell, you're no better'n your *sisters.*"

All this time, Walter's head moved frantically to and fro, watching us each in turn, trying to decipher what horror poised to pounce. "What's she talkin' 'bout, Sunny?" His voice trembled. His eyes beseeched me, puddling.

Muffin roughly caught his chin and tugged, forcing him to look into her wild eyes, only a breath from his. "She's a *whore*, Daddy. I saw her carryin' on with Daniel, your *own brother.*"

I felt her words impact Walter, in the way his fingers squeezed mine till I felt pain in the way his gaze swung to lock with mine, stricken. "Wha — what's she sayin', Sunny?"

"Don't listen, Walter. She's only trying to hurt me. It's not true. I was only telling Daniel goodbye. He's leaving and won't be back for a long time."

"D-Daniel was *here?*" Walter sat up straighter, his senses visibly keening.

"Yeh," snorted Muffin, bobbing her head, "But you notice, he wadn' interested in *you*, Daddy. Only *Mama*. Don't that tell you somethin'?" Another snort. "That was *some* goodbye, all that huggin' and them saying how they're in love and —"

"That's enough, Muffin." I glared at her, horrified, wishing in that moment that she weren't my daughter. "This time, you've surpassed yourself. Even if you don't love *me*, why this cruelty to your father? He doesn't deserve this."

"Yeh, like you *love him.*" The bed shifted as she struggled to her feet and groped her way across the floor. She cursed when her bare foot connected with a shard of broken glass. I didn't care. Wished, in fact, that she'd feel just a little of the pain she so glibly inflicted on others. A zigzag trail of blood stains marked her wobbly departure.

Walter dropped my hands and peered at me as though he'd been shot between the eyes and just hadn't fallen yet. "You don't love me, Sunny?" he croaked, as innocently as Jason or Gracie.

My heart lurched. "Of course, I do, Walter." I gathered him into my arms and cuddled him, rocked him gently. "You can't believe Muffin. She's — her mind's sick and she says bad things to hurt people."

"Like mine?" he asked quietly, so naïve my heart splintered.

"What?" I asked, rearing back to gauge him. How pitiful he looked, the blue eyes tortured. Oh, how I wanted to t*hrottle* Muffin.

"Like my mind. *Sick.*" He seemed to cave in as his eyes drifted to stare into space.

"No! Your mind might be a little slow, Walter, but it's not sick. You're a good person who loves people. Muffin just — for some reason, can't stand to see others happy."

Walter stunned me by saying, "It's all that stuff she takes. Them pills an' all."

He sees, hears, and perceives more than I've accredited to him. "You're right, it is. Somewhere deep down inside her, there's that sweet little girl of ours, Walter, the one who loved like no tomorrow."

He looked at me then, puzzled. I smiled and brushed back that crazy curl that still, after all these years, sprang free to lay on his forehead. Only the yellow had evolved to white. "I keep forgetting. You don't remember, do you, honey? She was a real sweetie-pie. A real Daddy's-Girl…." I went on to talk about the baby, toddler, child *Muffin*. It was, to him, like a fairy-tale, his favorite one. As always, he began to grin and grin and watch me expectantly for the next funny or touching anecdote from those early years. I talked until his eyelids drooped. Then closed. Only then did I start to move away —

"Sunny?" He caught my hand as I shifted to stand. I lowered myself again, seeing the troubled look on his face.

"Hmmm?"

"You're not gon' leave me, are you? Muffin said you don't love me and — Daniel don't like me. Why don't Daniel like me, like Lee Roy does, Sunny? You're not gon' leave, are you?" His breathing grew labored as tears rushed to his eyes.

I leaned to quickly hug him. "Dear God, *no.* And I *do love you.* And Daniel likes you. How could he not? You're his *brother.*" I gently touched his cheek. "I love you very much." And I did, in a motherly, nurturing way. "You must believe that, Walter." I looked at him imploringly, hating that Muffin had done this to him, hating myself that I'd given her fodder by allowing myself to *feel* when Daniel —

"You do, don't you? Believe me?" *Please, Lord, don't let this wound be forever.* I held my breath for long moments, dying a thousand deaths.

Then suddenly, he smiled. "Yeh. I believe you, Sunny." Relief flooded me till I felt dizzy with it and I hugged him again. I had my best friend back and we grinned hugely at each other.

Then his smile faded. "Muffin's just — sick." He gazed into my eyes solemnly and I felt our souls connect in mutual sorrow. "But she'll get better, won't she?" His eyes beseeched me for reassurance.

I forced a smile. "Sure." He relaxed and his lids slid shut. My smile faded. *Will we ever have her back — our Muffin?* In that moment, I had serious doubts.

~~~~~

I called Doretha and asked to speak to Daniel. When I told him of Muffin's cruel revelation to Walter, he said, "Muffin's worse off than I thought." Not unkindly. Just acceptance.

"Daniel —" I hesitated, not knowing how to say it. Though I *knew* Muffin's emotional frailties, her calling me *whore* still stung. Badly. Shame oozed through me like slime. "We can't —" I couldn't go on.

"I know," Daniel said softly. "I know, Sunny. We can only be friends. If that's possible."

Silence crackled over the wires and my heart and soul felt like they slowly drained out my feet. I tried to take a deep breath and couldn't. I was drowning in space. "No — I meant...we can't see each other again, Daniel."

"I'd planned to move back soon in a few months."

A longer silence ensued. I felt gutted. My voice drifted from far away. "I can't afford to *feel*, Daniel. And seeing you, hearing you...makes me feel." The words were strangled. "I cannot feel and *survive*."

"Sunny —"

"Goodbye, Daniel." I dropped the receiver onto the cradle.

I was trembling like a dead leaf in a December squall.

But I wasn't crying.

Good. If I was lucky, I never would again.

Chapter Fifteen

The Tucapau Hotel's demise in the fifties was traumatic for me. And for Francine. The beautiful structure was the first of our village landmarks to go and, for once, Francine's sentimental attachment rivaled my own.

"*Dadgummit!* There ain't *nothin' sacred,*" she lamented, smoking as if it were her last cigarette before execution. We stood frozen to the sidewalk across the street, watching the wrecking crew smash the formidable edifice. Each section that toppled and exploded into fragments of wood and dust ripped through my heart like a jackhammer.

"They don't need it no more," monotoned common-sense Nana, back at the house, where Francine and I continued to wallow in our angst. "Everybody's got cars now and can live anywheres. They can drive to work here. No need fer a hotel."

I knew it and so did Francine. But that didn't ease our sense of loss. Nana's forbearance did not, for a long time, seep in and aid in our acceptance. But I still had a trace of youthful optimism at that time. Overcoming was much easier then.

And, after all, the remainder of our little village remained intact.

~~~~~

Four weeks after Tack's death, Francine's paramour, Martin Black, moved in with her. "I ain't marrying no more," declared Francine. "If I do, I'll lose Tack's military pension and social security benefits." That was, then, and remained thereafter, the bottom line for Francine: money.

I reminded myself to shut my gaping mouth as my sister, still lovely in her middle years, padded barefoot across her creamy white carpeted floor and settled on the snow-white sofa as gracefully as a leopard. And just as regal. She gazed at me with a trace of defiance.

"Not marry?" I peered at her, bewildered. "I mean, it's too early with Tack just being buried and all — but what will folks say, Francine?" I finished on a plaintive note, knowing deep in my heart that I groped in vain for anything *solid* in Francine to which I could appeal.

"Y'know, Sunny," she purred, examining her Cherry Red toenails, "what folks think of me stopped mattering a long time ago."

"Did it ever?" The words were out before I knew them to *be*. But I was angry at how carelessly she tossed caution and character to the four winds.

"Not really." She stretched her long bronze legs, sheathed in red stretch capris and regarded me dispassionately. "Life's too short to worry 'bout things like that, Sunny. Martin's been with me a long time and I love 'im. He loves me. We want to be together. People live together now without getting married. What's so terrible about that?"

"It's not right; that's what's so terrible about it." I gazed long and hard at her, trying my best to glimpse something — *anything* to make her realize the import of character and integrity.

"Get over it, Sunny." She slid to her feet, strode languidly to the kitchen, and peered in the refrigerator. "Want

a Coke?" Her way of saying the conversation was over. I experienced the same desolate acceptance as I did with Muffin. Those two sure shared some genes.

"No. I'm off. Walter's got a doctor's appointment. His
annual checkup. He's not been feeling well for months now
and I'll feel better when he's run through some tests." Un-
ruffled by my disapproval, Francine hugged me goodbye
and I left with a terrible, sick feeling in my gut. Disappointment flailed away inside me and I thought how with Tack,
at least Francine had been *married*. To cohabit like this, was
like throwing muck in respectable villagers' faces.

In my face.

Will I ever live all this down?

And even while doubt badgered me, a tiny, tiny glimmer
of hope remained alive.

~~~~~

In those coming years, Francine surprised us all by remaining, by all standards, faithful to Martin Black. She even
named him the sole beneficiary in her will. At first I resented her total commitment to a man who'd abandoned his
own family to unlawfully join himself to her.

When I'd initially reprimanded Francine for being a
home-wrecker, she raised those perfect eyebrows at me and
drawled, "Why, Sunny, you can't break up somethin' that's
glued together real tight, now can you?"

Francine remained shameless.

And I remained dismayed. Yet…time has a way of mut-
ing such things, softening the rough edges. And through
the years, I came to accept, as much as possible, the union. I
realized that, in the end, I had no say-so anyway so why let
it bother me?

Sheila? After marriage number three ended in a bitter divorce she emulated Francine by moving in with a "rich dude from Jacksonville, Florida."

"He ain't no Burt Reynolds but, *honey-chile*, all that money makes up the difference." Her beauty, like Muffin's, was slowly fading. A harsh lifestyle quickly jaded the dewy skin and dulled the clear eyes to faded October grass.

None of family, including Sheila's three daughters, glimpsed her for several years.

~~~~~

"Walter's been a bit unsteady on his feet at times," I told Emaline over coffee in her cozy little parsonage kitchen.

Over the past ten years, the church had upgraded all the appliances and laid new shiny white, vinyl tile flooring. Most of the fresh coconut cake she'd made the previous weekend had disappeared, what with the two of us dashing back and forth between houses for our impromptu coffee klatches. *Whoever's* fresh cake of the moment served as refreshment till its demise. Emaline's appetite was hearty but she'd applied restraint all the way back and remained weight-cautious, eating only tiny slivers while my chunky portions rivaled that of any truck driver's.

"Reckon it's his sinus problem?" Emaline ventured.

"Don't know. It just seems to get worse over time. The doctor wants to do an MRI."

"Heard from Daniel at all?"

Her question, out of the blue, caused my pulse to quicken. "No." I pressed my fork into lingering crumbs, gathering them for one last bite, then found I didn't want it. My fork clattered to the dessert dish. "Why should I, Emaline? There's still nothing there for us. You know that. I wish he wasn't insisting on retiring here in Tucapau." I rolled my eyes in a hopeless gesture.

"Perhaps not what you want." Emaline gazed at me, her great heart in her eyes, a heart that, with every beat, throbbed *love*. "But, Sunny, you and Daniel *can* be friends. After all, weren't you close friends *before* the romance blossomed?"

She knew we had been. My sweet friend was just reminding me. Something warm and wonderful gushed through me at her words. And *warm and wonderful* was so alien to me by now that I nearly swooned as blood rushed to tinge my cheeks. "Yeh."

"There's no reason you can't go back there, Sunny. Not if you do it right, the way our Father orders it."

"Our Father?" I gave her a crooked, self-deprecating smile. "You breathe, eat, and sleep *Him* while I rarely give Him the time of day." I lowered my gaze in shame.

"He understands," insisted Emaline, not put off by my heathenish misgivings.

I looked at Emaline, hope flailing about in me. "I mean — could I really just feel — *platonic* toward Daniel?" Doubts swirled like crazy confetti in March winds, drawing my brows nearly together.

"All things are possible," she whispered, "when we get our priorities in order."

She reached across her kitchen table to take my hands in both hers and gave me her wonderful *blessing* smile, one that disarmed me of bad and negative thoughts. One that sometimes made me feel I could soar over mountains and hurdle wide rivers. "I mean — wouldn't the effort be worth it? After all, he *is* moving back home soon. You must remember that this is the only real home he's had."

He planned to move into the Stone's house, where Doretha still lived.

I smiled back, happy that, in Doretha, he'd found a sister. "I'll give it some thought."

~~~~~

"Mama, I love you and Daddy but this is the last straw." It was the day after Christmas that year. My Libby pulled on her gloves, then gazed at me with love gushing like a raging river from her cornflower blue eyes. "I don't want to hurt you. You've got enough on your plate as it is. But when Muffin not only didn't show up for our Christmas family get-together but *spent* her kids' Christmas money from you and Daddy, that hit rock bottom. I know how tight things are for y'all."

Libby's mouth slid into a grim line and the warmth left her eyes. She stared at the wall as though she wanted to pick it apart with a machete. "Mama, when she *'tried on'* Kara's new designer jeans outfit, then sashayed out the door, promising to come back *'in a few minutes'* then didn't come back *at all,* that broke Kara's heart."

She looked at me then, magnificently maternal. " Kara *adores* her Aunt Muffin and went all out buying her favorite expensive cologne — since nothing but the *best* pleases Muffin — with money saved from her little allowance...." She gazed soulfully at me, truly astounded. "Mama, *How could she!*" She swallowed her hurt and rage, hugged me tightly and whispered, "I'm sorry. You and Daddy are welcome in our home any time but we'll not be back here until I see a real change in Muffin."

The front door slammed in the wake of her abrupt departure, leaving me reeling like a child's wind-up top. My thoughts echoed Libby's. *How could she?*

Only joy I've had through the years is when Libby and her family come visit for holidays. Only time I feel even near 'normal' and validated and cherished by someone.

And Muffin blows it away as nonchalantly and succinctly as a danged sneeze.

Indignation roiled in me. Then protectiveness. I rushed to the phone and punched in Libby's cell phone number. "Hi honey," I said, "the minute Muffin walks in the door, I'll collect Kara's clothes and overnight them to you. Tell Kara not to worry."

"She's been trying to get Muffin on her cell phone. Muffin's not answering. Am I surprised? *No!* Am I disgusted? *Yeh!* You tell Kara, Mama."

The acidic tone didn't set well upon Libby, whose nature was usually sunny and warm and magnanimous. But, *oh*, how I empathized.

The rustle of phone changing hands, then, "Hello, Mema." Her voice was thick and wobbly from tears.

"Hello, Baby. Now, don't you worry, you'll get your clothes back. I'll overnight them as soon as Tara peels them off. Okay?"

A snub, then a snuffle. "Okay, Mema. I love you."

"Love you, too, sweety-pie. Bye."

Twenty-six hours later, Muffin appeared, eyes puffy, skin gray, long blonde hair in knotty disarray, the new jeans and layered shirts hanging soiled and wrinkled on her scarecrow frame like she'd slept in them. Which, no doubt, she had. She held up a hand before I could speak.

"I got Kara's and Libby's messages. Okay? *Christ Jesus, it's only jeans and shirts!* Just leave me alone. I'm exhausted."

This, she spoke over her shoulder as she literally dragged herself up the stairs, gripping the banister rail.

At that point, I had no desire to talk to her. I simply waited fifteen minutes, hoping she'd undress before she crashed into bed. When the bumping and thuds grew quiet, I tiptoed into her cluttered room, holding my breath, praying that she had shed them — and there they were, in a discarded heap on the stained carpet.

I snatched them up and quietly retreated. Downstairs, I checked the jean pockets for her kids' Christmas money, only salvaging a quarter, a nickel, and some pennies. My heart felt like ice, knowing how disappointed Gracie and Jared were. I couldn't replace our gift to them and it broke my heart.

My phone rang. I rushed to get it. It was Libby. "Mom, Scott said for you not to worry about the kids' Christmas gift from you and Dad. He's mailing you a check to cover it —"

"No," I said, tears puddling suddenly. "That's not —"

"It's done. It's in the mail. We *want* to do it, Mama. Gracie and Jared are precious, *good* kids and don't deserve this. I mean — their *Mama didn't even show up for Christmas with them.*" A long moment of quiet. "Over some *sleazy guy*, according to Kara. Did she ever show up?"

"Just an hour ago. I grabbed Kara's outfit and will launder it —"

"No. Just mail it. Kara said she'd launder it. And — thanks, Mama."

I sighed, thankful that I could do something, *anything* to ease my family's disappointment. Because I knew how heavily disappointment sat.

Seemed I'd lived with it forever.

~~~~~

Strange thing, when Muffin finally called Kara, she and her nineteen-year-old niece, who bore a striking resemblance to her Aunt Muffin — save her dark hair — wept together over the somewhat wasted holiday weekend.

"Libby won't talk to me," Muffin confided tearfully, surprising me with her contriteness. While I could bank on her reactions to *me*, I never knew what to expect when it came to other family members. "Kara did. I think she forgives me for wearing her clothes. I mean, I only *borrowed them! La de da!* You'd think I'd —"

"She wanted to wear them the next day for the holiday party the family is giving for friends, Muffin," I reminded her, cutting short her careening emotions. For once, she didn't leap down my throat. "They were her *Christmas present from her parents*, for goodness' sake!"

The starch melted from Muffin. She slumped dejectedly at our kitchen table, uncharacteristically penitent. "I *know*." Her haggard face reflected regret and my heart, still cool from its own sting, began to thaw.

"Give Libby time, honey. She's got a good heart."

"She's a *b----*," Muffin murmured, but without real force.

Why, Muffin's vulnerable. She actually needs family. A tiny, tiny glimmer of hope swam lazily upward.

I held it back.

Time will tell.

~~~~~

When Libby drove up from Summerville for Walter's MRI, she came straight to Spartanburg Regional Medical

Center. I'd had a moment's tension about how she'd react to Muffin, after the Christmas ordeal.

Muffin wasn't at the hospital but later, after the procedure, met us for lunch at Ryan's Buffet. Muffin strolled into the local restaurant's lobby, on the surface confident. Her blasé 'hey, sister *number two,*' didn't fool me for a moment. After a brief pause, Libby retorted, "Like *heck* you say! I'm *numero uno.*"

"Hey! I got a two-year, head start! *Nyahnyahnyahyah!*"

Then, they were in each other's arms. My eyes misted. A small corner of my microscopic world righted itself.

Thank you, my precious forgiving Libby.

~~~~~

"What all did the MRI report say?" asked Muffin later that afternoon back at home, genuinely worried. Walter now shuffled to his room to lie down. His limited energy had bottomed out.

I gazed at my oldest daughter. Time, drugs, and fast living had tarnished Muffin's stunning beauty. Having passed that great equator, forty, she was a shadow of her youthful, vibrant self. Stick-thin, she still moved in a predatory, feline gait. Her blue eyes, once clear as a mountain spring, were lackluster and more knowing and cynical than ever.

Oh, she could dress up and, with make-up artfully applied, still attract men. But the radiance was dulled. Libby had just departed to drive back home. She'd come to be with us for the MRI procedure.

"Nothing," I replied, taking off my toast-colored coat and gloves, soaking up the warmth of indoors. The December weather outside was brisk but not as arctic as the previous winter's Yule season. Now, rather than pine trees

302 Emily Sue Harvey

and spicy cider aromas reminding me of happy Christmases past, they triggered memories of the ER and a comatose Muffin.

Has it been really been nine years since Muffin's suicide attempt?

"Whadda you mean, *nothing?*" The old familiar edge crept back into her voice. Little had changed in the past years. Except that I'd distanced myself even more from my daughter.

I did it for survival. Muffin? Well, she still abdicated her role as my daughter.

Over the years Muffin had lived with first one man and then another. Nothing ever came of the relationships. She always ended up back home, with Walter and me. Muffin cocooned herself against anything that whiffed of depth and substance.

She still, I suspected, collected prescription drugs from any source possible, and continued to ingest them; because she had episodes of sleeping the days and nights away for no apparent reason, followed by days and nights of being away and doing God only knew *what*. Somehow, she'd managed to avoid a repeat of the long ago ER experience.

Miraculously, she kept some real estate deals funds trickling in. Oh yes, Muffin was — if not wise — *intelligent.* Having realized, years ago, that my coffer was perpetually bare, she'd set out to generate at least a modicum of an income.

Muffin, *inspired*, is still, to this day, brilliant. She is the most dazzling charmer and persuader on the face of this earth.

"Dr. Crow suspects its some balance problem, perhaps an inner-ear thing that goes off occasionally. Nothing that shows up on the x-ray. Gave him some anti-vert pills for when he has an episode. He doesn't want him driving at all. Too dangerous. " I walked away, busying myself, putting emotional space between myself and Muffin, a tactic she seemed happy with. We had, to an extent, managed to coexist under the same roof, virtually isolated from each other.

"Why doesn't she move out on her own?" asked Libby during the past Thanksgiving visit. "She's able-bodied enough. Besides, I hate to see you get stressed out with her shenanigans."

"It's okay, Libby," I reassured her. "We rarely speak anymore so there's little chance of clashing."

At times, I wondered why she didn't move out? I suspected that Muffin, strong as an imposing Goliath on one level, remained an insecure little girl on another. She simply refused to grow up. Walter's accident marked not only the disappearance of her daddy as she knew him but the death of her emotional development.

Me? Any dream of a magical mother-daughter closeness transformation died long ago. I moved about in a vacuum, sealing out anything troublesome.

It seemed an eternity since that day Daniel and I spent together at the hospital, followed by Muffin's vindictive revelation to her father. Thank *God* for Walter's childlike forgiveness and trust. An added blessing was that without much history, his brain and emotions had less to deal with.

With age, my senses flattened out more and more. My blonde hair slowly turned platinum. My emotions seemed dulled by Novocaine.

Secretly, I waited for death to come. Life's pleasures no longer lured me forward. Life had, in fact, stripped me of emotion. Even the animal-me was no more. I no longer felt anything remotely akin to sexuality.

Good.

Maybe Daniel and I can be simply friends, after all.

Part Three

"Strength and honor are her clothing; and she shall rejoice in time to come."
Proverbs 31:25

The present

Chapter Sixteen

In the nineties, the mill came down.

"Dear merciful God." I covered my face as the sprawling red brick structure, that stalwart symbol of life and culture as I knew it, crumpled impotently before my eyes. The sight challenged pictures I'd seen of World War II bombings. Most things I could ignore and shrug off. Even my Mama's forty-odd years absence dredged up no real emotion. Nor my Daddy's death. Not even Nana's drew sentiment.

But this did. Just as the riverbanks lay naked and exposed, so did I.

I could no longer pretend things were the same.

After the demolition and clean-up crews finished, an area spanning at least five acres lay stripped and defenseless along the riverbanks.

In coming days and years, I groped for meaning. For essence. For justification of *being.* For something to stamp out that dark blob on my life — one spawned in the sooty black of night in Doretha's bedroom. At first, with Muffin's birth, I'd felt a small sense of vindication. I'd brought forth a life, nurtured and loved my child. Then — another tragedy robbed me of even that.

If only Muffin had turned out like Libby…just half as good as Libby.

Heck, I'd have settled for just a *tenth.*

Always, when my thoughts drifted so, I would snuff them out. *Muffin* was not my problem. She'd not asked to be born. And it was wrong to compare her to Libby. Dead wrong.

Just as I'd not asked to be raped. She, too, was a victim, as surely as I. So, setting her out on her fanny, as so many folks told me I should do, was out of the question.

Because life had not dealt fairly with Muffin.

And, in causing her father's accident, neither had I.

~~~~~

The idea came unexpectedly. Writing had always been my friend. I'd kept journals all through the years, filled with my every thought and deed.

"You sure write purdy stories," declared Lee Roy De-Witt, our longtime neighbor. Lee Roy, whose age could've been anywhere from thirty to sixty, sported a bristly, coarse, mud-colored beard that never saw scissors. Likewise, his frizzled mud-toned hair, that, instead of growing down, migrated outward as in Bozo. His wiry, medium frame moved slowly, as did his words.

His mind, however, was another thing.

Years back, he'd one day simply moved in with the woman in the two-story house across the street and never left. A divorce marked his past. He shunned the responsibility of alimony payments like the plague. He simply stopped working at 'real' jobs. "Can't git blood outta a turnip," he was fond of saying.

When in the mood, Lee Roy earned spending money doing occasional odd chores. Seemed he could do most anything, according to many folks. Neither did Sally King's two adult children, who also resided there, work. Sally's wait-ress and house-cleaning jobs kept them all afloat.

Walter, who moseyed over to visit Lee Roy on occasion, described the scenario in the two-story as an on-going sleepover event. Lee Roy never really 'went to bed.' He simply snoozed in front of the TV, wherever he happened to be sprawled when slumber fell. No bed-down or get-up times existed in those walls. All occupants seemed programmed to time clocks set by a whimsical Mother Nature so no one could say for sure *if* or *when* Lee Roy and Sally cohabited.

I always gave them the benefit of a doubt. Muffin huffed and took little digs at them for sport. Walter? His mind never wandered in off-color directions. Like me, he simply enjoyed Lee Roy.

Lee Roy was Walter's best friend. He spent endless hours hanging out with Walter, talking about everything under the sun. When Walter didn't understand a complex TV plot or an evening news issue, I would hear Lee Roy patiently explaining it to him. His renderings often doubled me over with laughter. Course, I did that in private. Wouldn't hurt Lee Roy's feelings for the world.

Though I shared Walter's bed much of the time, I dubbed the entire bedroom enclosure 'his.' Even had a little sign over his door that read **WALTER'S ROOM**. He loved that. I'd bought him his own television with remote and easy chairs, so he could entertain his crony. Their TV menu consisted of westerns and detective plots, anything with a gun, while mine ventured toward Oprah and old romantic and musical films. So my TV docked in the den.

"You two already solved the world's problems for today?" I carried two dessert plates of apple cobbler and ice cream and set them on the coffee table in Walter's room.

"Nah," Lee Roy drawled. "Jus' the one 'bout the president's wife. Now, me'n Walter, we don't like to see Hillary stealin' the show like she does, do we Walter?"

Walter chuckled to avoid answering. Walter, for harmony, went along with most of Lee Roy's notions. And while the pre-accident Walter had glibly used wit to 'size-up' and 'dress down' folk, it was nigh impossible to prod the new Walter to bad-mouth anybody. Mostly Lee Roy entertained Walter with tall tales and colorful narrative.

Over the years I'd discovered Lee Roy's intellect to be surprisingly sharp. He'd asked to read some of my own little anecdotes about Gracie and Jared and had become a fan. Today, he surprised me with a suggestion.

"Say, since that feller with the Spartanburg Herald Journal either died or left — you know, the one that wrote that newspaper thang where he talked to people 'bout ever'thang under the sun?"

"The columnist who wrote 'The Stroller?' " I injected, curious as to where this was going. "Seymour Rosenberg was his name. Yeh?"

"Anyways," he stroked his mid-chest level beard, "I been a'thinkin'. You oughtta do a column fer 'em. Somethin' like his was."

"They've already found a replacement." I dispersed napkins with their coffee.

Lee Roy, not to be outdone, pondered for long moments as he nibbled his cobbler. Lee Roy subsisted mainly on cigarettes and coffee, the blacker and hotter, the better. Food, to him, seemed beside the point. But he always politely made a dent in my hospitality servings. "There's 'at Tyger River Times...y'know, the one comes out ever' week."

"The weekly paper," I murmured.

I ran it through my mind as I tidied up the bed and dusted the old dresser and chest of drawers. Writing *was* something that took me from the heaviness that daily weighted me down. Maybe there was room for another storyteller in a local weekly.

"Something like, 'Things Old and New'?" I ventured half-heartedly.

His mud-brown eyes rounded. "Yeh, at's it. You could let folk bend yer ear 'bout thangs a'goin' on they like or don't like. Then you could —"

"Do my nostalgia bit about things from the past. And satire about the present."

"Zack'ly." He nibbled his fruit dessert almost daintily, with a pleased look on his grizzled features. "You'd make a good'un."

"You *are* kidding. Right?"

"Naw. Ain't jokin' a'tall. Thank about it, Sunny. At's all I'm a'sayin'. Jus' thank about it."

I did. And the more I thought, the more I warmed to the idea. What else was I doing to make a difference? At one time, my aspirations to touch lives had shot right out the ceiling, spanned the skies, and spread into infinity.

At one time the little-girl-Sunny had known beyond doubt that she could leap up and touch the clouds. Even after Mama left, Sunny'd felt that she and Daniel, *together,* could conquer all the ghosts of their combined lifetimes. We could, I was convinced then, accomplish *anything* we set out to do

I never got that chance.

My spark of enthusiasm fizzled.

Too late.

~~~~~

Lee Roy was a danged *tick.*

"You thank 'bout doin' 'at newspaper thang?" Lee Roy asked the next day as he settled himself in his rust-gold easy chair angled in conversational favor toward Walter's matching one.

"Mmm." I muttered, non-commitally, hoping he'd let it go for now. I wasn't by any stretch of the imagination in the mood to make decisions.

"Well, you oughtta," he prodded, picking up his fresh hot coffee I'd deposited on the time-worn coffee table positioned halfway between their roosts. "Don't put thangs like 'at off, Sunny. You know you'd like it. Why, your story-tellin's the best I ever heard."

I scooped up one of Walter's comic books from the floor and put it back on top of the chest-of-drawers. After his brain injuries he'd relearned to read with my help and comics were his favorite because of the accompanying colorful pictures. I'd also taught him to drive again. He liked to drive on short treks, made him feel 'like everybody else,' he said, which meant 'normal.' I chauffeured longer ones, like the one to Summerville to visit Libby's family.

Lee Roy took a long, lusty slurp of steaming java, placed it back on its saucer, and returned it to the faded spot on the table. With dramatic deliberation, he angled his Bozo-head in a thoughtful stance to peer into space, stiff beard pointing straight ahead, meeting the stroke of grubby fingers. And though he wore the same old pants and shirts every waking hour, his 'woman,' Sally, found some way to get them off him and laundered at least often enough that he never gave off an offensive odor. If you didn't count the sharp smell of nicotine, that is.

I swept the floor with one eye on him, wary, edgy even on this particular afternoon, having earlier survived a small crisis with Muffin. Her high jinks left me overdosed on adrenaline, *on-your-mark*, poised for flight.

Lee Roy's arms dropped suddenly to the armrests and I tensed, knowing he wasn't through with me. "You need t'do it, Sunny. I'll bet ever-body in these here parts —"

"*Okay!*" I said sharply, palms out in supplication. Then softer, "Okay, Lee Roy. I'll check into it."

He grinned hugely, baring gapped, tobacco and coffee-stained teeth.

I sighed and handed Walter his remote. Presently, *William Tell's Overture* burst from the screen, punctuated by "*Hi yooo, Silver*" as I dust-panned collective dust bunnies from the doorway.

Yeh, I thought, I'll check into it.

~~~~~

My first column appeared the week before Christmas of the next year. It took that long to find a vacancy for a new column. I discovered in myself a penchant for satire:

Something mystical happens to me every year from Thanksgiving till December 26. Christmas music sets it off, making long-ago memories pop to the surface like soda fizz. Each 'Rockin' Around the Christmas Tree' or 'I'll be Home For Christmas' transports me deeper and deeper into a rhapsodic trance that has Walter shaking his head, wondering 'why Sunny sorta loses it' every year at Yuletide. My biggest symptom is that I end up cooking enough goodies to feed all the starving pygmies in New Guinea. I glare at him and continue stirring my wonderful walnut fudge.

"Why do you want to spoil Christmas for me?" I grouch. He just doesn't GET it.

"I just hate to see you work yourself to death," says Walter, munching spoils from my fudge heap.

"Hey! I LOVE working myself to death," I retort, while something deep inside me concedes that I DO actually go a little mad. It's like this hypnotic flailing inside me won't let up until I do thirty pounds of walnut fudge, fifteen pounds of mound candy, five gallons of Rice Crispy/Snickers balls, ten dozen peanut butter balls, twenty pounds butterscotch fudge, and though I SWEAR each year I'll not do them again, I cannot resist doing several batches of yummy chocolate-toffee bars.

"But why so much?" asks party-pooper Walter, as he snatches a couple chocolate-toffee bars and crams his mouth full.

I roll my eyes at his duplicity.

"Tradition," I say. And, dear Lord, on one level it is. I've done it since I was a teen practicing high school home ec recipes. The ritual evokes childhood memories of Grandma & Grandpa Acklin's fragrance filled house during holidays, tables sprouting delectable treats. On another level, I remind Walter again, it was Grandma Acklin's GIFT to me. I never felt more loved than there, in her home, knowing in my child's mind that she'd prepared all this in honor of ME. She celebrated ME with all those goodies.

"Now, it's my turn to celebrate my loved ones," I tack on. I must mention here that once my bake-off pantry is filled, Walter is first in line to package up 'love gifts' for special ones. Too, whenever moved, we bless those outside our family circle.

So, here I am, five weeks later, ten pounds heavier, crash-landed back to sanity.

I'm also exhausted.

"Y'know," I tell Walter, swollen feet propped on coffee table, "I'm getting older. And...maybe I AM a little excessive. I think next year, I'll just kick back and not do the cooking thing."

"That's a good idea, hon." He winks at me. And I know he's patronizing me.

He doesn't believe me.

But I'll remain staunch in this decision. Immovable.

Until next Thanksgiving, when I hear the first strains... "I'll Be Hooome For Chriiiistmas... You can Cooount ooon Meeee... "

After the Middle Tyger Times came out, calls, letters, and e-mails (doing the column required my purchase of a computer) bombarded me, folks joking that they wanted to be some of those 'outside the family' to be treated with my compulsive goodies.

My next column evolved from a letter-to-the-editor in the Spartanburg Herald. A local man wrote a letter placing mill hill folks in an extremely unflattering, redneck genre. The response was livid and proud. One e-mail I printed said:

In response to Mr. Greene's Mill Hill Mentality letter: I thought it was very rude and classless. If Spartanburg County is not cultured and classy enough for him, I'm sure Greenville would welcome him with open arms.

Let me remind him that Spartanburg was the heart and soul of textiles for many generations. Change is very difficult. Thank God for the huge corporations like BMW and others for locating here. They've helped replace many lost textile jobs.

We are at a crossroads about which direction the city and county should go. But don't make fun of many generations of fine people who grew up on mill hills. I grew up in Arkwright and had a great childhood. I'm very proud of where I come from.

Mr. Greene suggested people are afflicted with "MHM" (Mill Hill Mentality). That's one illness I'm glad I have.

Another read: *After reading Mr. Greene's letter on MHM, I just brushed the cotton lint out of my hair and tried to understand why he is so bitter. The man needs a sense of humor. As I was reading his letter about converting the Marriott into a "wrassling" center and fish camp, I 'bout choked on my snuff....'*

This topic went on for several weeks before another, a ban on public smoking, took its place. Villagers crawled out of the woodwork commiserating or celebrating each moment's controversy.

In the cacophony of opinions, I found myself distracted from my own home-front dissonance. Discovered myself stimulated and entertained. The anecdotes, sandwiched in along the way, drew raves from every stratum of readers, from elementary students to literary folks. Walter was delighted to be my comic foil in the spoofs, guffawing as Lee Roy read them aloud while they lounged in their easy chairs on late afternoons.

My busyness with writing proved to be a blessing. It regenerated my brain.

It helped me not think of Daniel.

Another thing happened: my addiction to food began to wane.

~~~~~

When Sheila, who had spent much of life devising ways to get attention, began to complain of dizzy spells, I didn't get too disturbed. "It's probably nerves," I told her more than once, since her emotions still skyrocketed at things both great and trivial

My laid-back response seemed to reassure her, at first anyway. "I hope so, Sunny," she said, then her lips began to tremble. I hurtled from my kitchen chair and around the table to gather her in my arms.

"Honey," I murmured, "don't worry so. Things like this are usually nothing to get all worked up over."

Her head began to move from side to side. "No — it's not that. It's my girls...Sunny," she convulsed into sobs, "I-I've...lost...my...g-girls."

"Oh, Sheila," I tried to soothe her, alarmed.

"T-They wouldn't come to my house for E-Easter. Said I'd not b-been a Mama to 'em and they didn't want to h-have anything else to do w-with me." The crying intensified and her body, noticeably thinner than ever before, quaked as though she rode an off-balance, gyrating washing machine.

I led her into the den and lowered her to the sofa and slid in beside her. "Sheila, honey," I said gently, "it can't be all that bad. Why wouldn't the girls come to your house for Easter?" Dread oozed through me as kaleidoscopic images flashed a lifetime of the girls being farmed out to their individual dads.

She snuffled, exhausted and gaunt-eyed. "Ginger and Cassie are angry at Michelle for working in a strip joint."

Shock splintered through me. "Michelle? Is she bartending?"

"No, Sunny. She's *stripping.*" Frightened, haunted eyes peered at me. "My *baby's stripping* and is *proud* of it." Tears puddled again. "She won't listen to me, Sunny. The other girls don't want to take their kids around her."

I sucked in a deep, quaking breath and exhaled slowly, seeing dots before my eyes. I shook my head slightly to clear it, then arose and paced to the window to even-out my reaction.

Will this lewd stuff never stop? Are these the sins spoken of in scripture that are passed from generation to generation? The sheer plausibility of it slapped me like the wrist-flip of a wet towel. It stung.

Sheila's face contorted with agony. "Ohhh...Suuunny! I've lost 'em...I've lost my girls. They won't even talk to me on the phone. I told 'em the doctor thinks something serious is wrong with me and they *still* wouldn't come...." I rushed to comfort her, knowing there was more to the story than my baby sis reported.

"Ohhh God," she moaned, beginning to rock back and forth, with my arm draped around her sagging shoulder. I thought *Sheila, the shocker is now the shocked.*

She startled me when suddenly, she snapped upright and gazed at a point in space. Anger glazed her eyes. "It's not right, Sunny," she singsonged and a chill rippled up my spine. "It's Curtis' fault, too. He's as much to blame as me. I know he was doing things...things with both men and women." Curtis was the last husband, who'd. 'claimed' all the girls as 'his.' He was the most decent of Sheila's exes. He and I still stayed in touch and he remained concerned about the welfare of each of the girls and grandchildren.

"Sheila, that's not true," I said, not wanting to hear all the outrageous venom that poured like volcano ash from her pretty mouth.

She sliced me a *get-with-it* glare, not really *there* behind those green eyes. Suddenly they narrowed to mere slits. "I remember how he'd go up to men and think I wud'n lookin' and he'd be so *touchy-feely* it was disgusting."

"Sheila, Curtis is by nature an affectionate, *touchy-feely* person. That doesn't make him —" My words shut off. She was no longer with me as her mouth tightened into a cynical smile and her eyes shimmered hatred.

I didn't for a moment believe my sister's charges. Sheila's memory was quite selective in such cases. I remembered the times she'd embellished facts concerning me till even *I* nearly lost sight of truth.

Francine's observation was more to the point. "That l'il *hussy* could almost make a person believe that day is night, and dark is light. She's *dangerous, I tell you.*"

Sheila had that ability to sway folks. She simply re-hashed her version of happenings, over and over, till, to her, they became reality. It was her *conviction* that snared the listener, that drove home her tale's seeming veracity.

"I took 'em all out of my will," she whispered, startling me with her *return.* "I've got that big settlement coming any day now — remember that sexual harassment suit I filed against Mr. James who owned Steel-Tex? Well, I'm being awarded enough that I'll never have to worry 'bout money again." Then she dissolved into tears again, plastered herself to my shoulder, and moaned, "my girls…my girls. Why, Sunny?"

My mind spiraled…*poor Mr. James.* Just how much of Sheila's charges against her ex-employer were true? *Poor girls…poor Sheila.*

All of them are the losers.

I held her in my arms till she snuffled and hiccuped. "I can't believe my baby's doing those things, Sunny." She gazed beseechingly at me, like she did when she was a child, like I could do something to make things right.

This time I couldn't.

~~~~~

I called Cassie, wanting to get to the bottom of Sheila's overwhelming torment.

"Hi, honey," I said. "Just talked with your mom and she's pretty upset that you girls wouldn't celebrate Easter with her. What's happening, Cass?" I had a good rapport with all Sheila's girls. Had tried to always understand their perspectives of my sister. I'd tried, in my own way, to fill in, to take up some of Sheila's slack through the years: making sure they had birthday cakes and Christmas gifts, and cards when they accomplished the honor roll or won some school office. I loaded them down with goodies every chance I got and loved every minute of it.

They nestled deep in my heart.

A long tired sigh. "Aunt Sunny, Mama's never really 'been there' for us and now she's wanting us to flock to her like dibbies and we can't do that. She always talks bad about our dads and wants us to *agree* with her that they're sorry jerks." Her laugh was forced and sharp. "I mean, if Daddy hadn't been there for us, what would've happened to us? And this thing with Michelle — she's a *stripper*, for God's sake. Not only that but she's training her daughter, Tracy, to strip, too. I'm no big religious person, like you, Aunt Sunny, but I know what decency is and what it's *not.*"

"...*religious person, like you, Aunt Sunny.*" If only I were....

I felt sick at heart. Sheila had really done a number on her kids. But she did, in her own crazy way, love them. "Couldn't you two just try to compartmentalize things, Cassie, and treat holidays as sovereign times of family —"

"If it were only that, I could. But when I tried to talk to Mama about it, she went into one of her snits and said things to me — in front of my children — things like she accused me of *selling drugs...and prostituting. Lies.*" She choked up and grew quiet for long moments while my stomach churned over Sheila's indiscriminately, razor-sharp tongue. "She's not changed, Aunt Sunny. I can't have my kids hearing such trash about me. I've worked hard to gain their trust and finally felt I had it. Mama had them so confused —" She broke off on a sob.

"It's okay, honey," I murmured. "I understand."

And I did. Too well. Sheila *had* lost her children. Her sins were just now finding her out.

I understood, too, her grief.

It was the same sorrow I felt over Muffin.

~~~~~

"Way I look at it, the feller was dealin' in drugs. The shootin' ain't racial a'tall," declared Lee Roy as I swept under his feet. "That 'ar feller was tryin' to run 'is car over them *po*-lice officers, was what he was a'doin'." He took a long slurp of coffee and resettled it in its coffee-table groove. "*They'd'a been stone crazy* to not shoot at 'im."

Walter nodded blandly, one eye on the TV Twinkie commercial. Lee Roy's scrutiny of the moment was the subject of last week's column, dealing with a black drug dealer's shooting death at the hands of two white police officers who'd claimed the suspect was running them down with his car. Afterward, some folks called it a hate crime, racially motivated. I'd simply printed opposing opinions.

It stirred up lots of discussion from all quarters, Lee Roy's corner being the most verbose. "Anyways," Lee Roy recommenced, "when a car comes at ye, you ain't gonna take time to note the color o' the driver's skin 'fore ye commence shootin', *by crackie*. Ain't that right, Walter?"

"Yeh," Walter muttered, flipping the channels, stopping at an old rerun of *Hunter*. He loved Stephanie, Hunter's pretty sidekick. 'But she ain't as purdy as you, Sunny," he always claimed, grinning. I teased him that she was his 'sweetheart' but I knew her main attraction was that she could handle a .38 as well as any man.

I collected dessert plates and headed to the kitchen. Walter's held only crumbs while Lee Roy's brownie lay half-consumed. His teeth's half-mooned bite left it grinning derisively at me. It reminded me that I'd not eaten a one of the batch Gracie and Jason had helped me bake last night. They still, on their visits, wanted to do our cooking thing together.

Nowadays, I bagged and sent most of it home with them, or immediately shipped it out via Lee Roy, who stopped along the way home to disperse treats. He loved the benevolent Santa Claus persona the gesture gave him. I loved making him feel good.

Everybody was happy. Especially me when I looked in my big round old-fashioned-dresser mirror and saw my clothes hanging like burlap bags on my thinning frame. My weight loss wasn't a conscious one. It simply happened as months passed and my newspaper column kept me hopping and thinking about something beyond my own hearth.

It was time.

Chapter Seventeen

The event caught me off guard. I suppose I'd thought it would never happen, that I wouldn't have to eventually deal with my feelings. Not a word of warning foreshadowed his arrival. Early in May, Daniel moved in with Doretha. Her brother's homecoming bowled Doretha over. Actually, Doretha's ~~'bowled over' was not your usual kind. She simply walked~~ around with this little Mona Lisa smile on her small, thin face, one she rarely wore. Actually, all her rare smiles were mystical. Alvin, now bald and round like his father, remained estranged from Doretha. He lived with his mama but daily spent time at Doretha's catching up the housework.

"Dangdest thing I ever saw," was Lee Roy's only commentary, careful not to malign my good friend, Doretha, nor Alvin, my kin. Unspoken law on the mill hill was and remains that the vilifying of one's kin is taboo *unless* a same-clan kin starts the maligning. In such event, even the most courageous, seasoned gossip must proceed with trepidation, not daring to cross over a certain invisible boundary. Since nobody knew exactly where the unseen line lay, they were prone to play it safe and use generic statements, such as Lee Roy's cagey "Dangdest thing I ever saw."

I remained silent, giving Lee Roy no encouragement to further pursue the topic, even though I, too, considered

Doretha and Alvin's arrangement most bizarre. But, I figured it seemed to work okay for them.

The first weeks of Daniel's homecoming found me inordinately occupied with column deadlines so I had little trouble avoiding him. I stayed busier'n a one-legged tap dancer so as not to think about him being close-by.

Until the birthday party.

Gracie's nineteenth birthday party was June's big mill hill event. Started out, Walter and I were throwing it, then Emaline wanted to help, joined by an insistent Francine, followed by Aunt Tina, Doretha, and finally, Sheila, never far from the limelight, jumped aboard.

Financially, as the old saying goes, between us all we didn't have a pot to piss in. What we did have was the kind of love that combined all our resources and energy to cook mouth-watering food and festive cakes and gather a riot of colorful wild flowers from meadows surrounding the village. Emaline pulled out her best crystal punch bowl, and filled it with an ice-cold sweet concoction of Seven-Up and fruit juices.

We foraged small crystal flower vases from the church's storage and filled them with clustered wildflowers to center each white-clothed table.

Lee Roy hauled in two coolers brimming with ice. Everybody stopped what they were doing to check him out in his heretofore unheard of *cleaned-up* status. He'd decked out in one of Walter's outgrown plaid shirts and razor-sharp creased khaki slacks, his hair moussed and tucked determinedly behind each ear. 'Course, that tamed effect only lasted for about thirty minutes, till the June day's humidity sprang it loose in wildly frizzed, Bozo-disarray.

We'd reserved the Methodist Fellowship Hall for the event. Emaline would have had a conniption had we done otherwise. Now, as a rule, no age-lines exist in mill hill celebrations like those found in suburban upper-middle class partying. Virtually everybody we knew, young and old alike, got an invite, if not personally by phone or over-the-fence, then via the village grapevine.

Our *dressing up* consisted of sharp casual slacks and accessories, topped by styles ranging from teen girls' bared midriffs to matronly frilly blouses. I wore a classic peach slacks and sweater ensemble that hugged my newly slimmed shape, a topic of much discussion throughout the evening.

"You look *wonderful*," Emaline took in my new look as we unveiled domed casseroles and Tupperware containers, "like *sexy*." I shot her a wary look and she flashed a rare wicked little grin, relaxing me immeasurably to find that all these years as a preacher's wife had not turned her into a prude. I already knew that but the reminder unleashed spurts of jubilation that trickled warmly through me.

Emaline's little gesture finished turning my world right side up again.

At least for the moment

~~~~~

Francine and I were flapping open another white cloth to spread on the last table when Emaline nudged me and whispered in my ear, "Don't look now but I think you're gonna have to work on that *friendship thang*."

Even before I turned, I knew. Seemed every hair on my body rose up.

A tall familiar figure swept through the doorway, then paused. His black hair glistened and the turquoise eyes swept the gathering until they found me. My breath hitched as they drilled into me like laser beams. He wore simple black slacks and a white button-down collar, open-necked shirt. As always, simple clothes, on Daniel's rugged frame, managed to look fabulous. His stillness pulsed with energy, like a cougar readying to pounce.

I watched his mouth form my name.

A thrill shot through me as mine silently formed his. *Daniel.*

His eyes never leaving mine, he wove his way to me. I'd forgotten the confident way he moved. I'd forgotten how lean he was and how angular his features and how incredibly virile he looked all over.

Of all the scenarios I'd imagined for this reunion, I'd never fathomed this. I recognized the glint in those fierce eyes and the thrust of that strong, cleft chin. Little flecks of silver lightened the midnight black temples. His face remained unlined. He seemed as young as the night he'd left to join the Army.

He stopped no more than a foot from me. Our gazes locked and I felt the impact all the way through me. The power of him sizzled and vibrated over my senses, shook me to my core. He had to know the sensual power he still wielded over me.

But I knew right off that he was dealing with me honestly, no attempt to dazzle or pressure me as only he could do.

When he spoke, his deep voice rumbled across his broad chest. "I know how you feel, Sunny." His gaze slid down, slowly, caressingly, over each feature of my face, then returned to lock with my own. "I promise…I won't embarrass you or cause you more dishonor."

"Daniel," I licked my lips, saw fire flash in his eyes before they hooded. "I — I don't know what to say." I shrugged weakly, quaking with hidden emotions. "I can't —"

"Don't turn me away this time, Sunny." Then I knew the look on his face to be vintage Daniel. Lion-Man, Daniel. "Friends. That's all." The defiance there was stubborn, *fierce*. And then, I glimpsed the little boy, Daniel. The vulnerable Daniel. It was only a heartbeat glimpse, but it shot straight to my soul.

We stood like that for long moments, he, resolute in reconciliation, I determined to keep my shield firmly in place. Then I saw it. A tear forming along his lower left lid. The haunting features seemed frozen, yet — the tear gathered… then swelled until it spilled over and trailed down that strong, chiseled cheek… a crystal bullet, revealing a chink in the Lion-Man's armor. He didn't wipe it away. Brutally ignored it. Like the bleeding blister on his thumb.

My heart split. I took a deep shuddering breath and slowly let it out. I literally saw dots for a moment. Then I remembered Emaline's words…*there's no reason you can't go back there, Sunny. Not if you do it the way our Father orders…*

Please…I prayed, *give me a right heart.* Suddenly, in a flash, I knew I could do it.

I smiled and stuck out my hand. "Friends."

He blinked. Like the quick stroke of a paintbrush, surprise shaded his features, then evaporated. He smiled then, the big, wide one that made his eyes glimmer like emeralds, making my knees go weak. His big hand clasped mine and I felt its warmth all the way to my toes. "Friends."

~~~~~

No one seemed to take notice of our little episode. Emaline and Francine had sensitively moved away to other tasks, allowing us privacy. The older folks, who knew something of our past, had mostly died off. The others had forgotten much of it. This time, I was glad Muffin remained consistent in her late appearances. I didn't want a repeat of her tirade the last time she saw Daniel and me together all those years ago.

I hope she makes it. Poor Gracie still hadn't given up on her mama. Occasionally, I still felt the stirring of hope, when Muffin would slip up and smile at me. I say 'slip up' because her disdain had been so deliberate and focused through the years that anything beyond that meant self-treason to her. The slip-ups only reinforced her justification for hating me. Oh, I could read her like a Nora Roberts novel. Sadly.

Long ago, I'd let go of Muffin. Like I'd let go of deep emotions. The Serenity Prayer daily challenged me to recognize things I *can* change and those I *cannot*...I especially prayed for *the wisdom to know the difference.*

I'd thought that now, I did. But — seeing Daniel again I wasn't so certain.

Please...make me strong.

I tried to avoid Daniel for the rest of the afternoon but each time I turned around, there he was, helping in a dozen ways, carrying heavy trays from the kitchen, emptying garbage, making fresh coffee in the huge coffee makers, heaping food on plates and carrying them to elderly, slow-moving folks.

"That 'ar Daniel, he's a nice feller," Lee Roy informed me as he deposited his half-eaten food into a nearby canister and helped himself to more black coffee. "Says he used to live here."

Lee Roy had moved in with Sally not long after Daniel's infamous exodus. He wasn't privy to the situation. "Yes, he did."

"What did he leave for?" Lee Roy took a long swig of steaming coffee then waited expectantly for revelations to spill from my lips.

"Why don't you ask him?" I replied none too gently. His eyes rounded. Then I said more kindly, "I've gotta go check on the tea refills," leaving him peering after me, eyebrows cocked curiously.

Muffin came in bearing a present just as folks lined up for dessert.

"Hi, Mama," she gave me a quick, perfunctory hug, her blue eyes casing the gathering, no doubt gauging its likelihood for excitement. Muffin's most-used expression was *"I'm bored."*

"Wish I had *time* to get bored," remained my favorite rejoinder.

I saw her locate Gracie, embrace her and present her the gaily-wrapped gift. My heart warmed as Gracie tore into and tossed aside colorful tissue and ribbon, then squealed with delight over the expensive Gucci gold earrings and matching bracelet her mama had ordered online. Muffin attentively fastened them on for her to model, drawing lots of *oohs* and *ahhs* in the process. Then, arm in arm, they moved outside to stroll and have a mother and daughter talk. It happened more frequently now, this maternal leaning.

Relief and pleasure surged inside me. At least, for Gracie, hope hovered. For Muffin's and my healing, I held no such delusions. Just acknowledging the rift between us brought that dead, heavy weight of defeat crashing back into my chest.

I veered my thoughts elsewhere, laughing to see Lee Roy holding court with my other *Things Old and New Column* fans. He was the infamous *good friend and neighbor* of the celebrated Stones, Sunny and Walter. Lee Roy was the best PR man on the face of planet earth.

I tried to stay away from Daniel but found it difficult to avoid a six-foot-two, hundred and eighty-five pound male who remained underfoot practically all evening.

Actually, it worked out for the best because, by degrees, I found myself relaxing and reclaiming the easy affability we'd shared as adolescents. I slid more and more into my old comfort zone. *More like brother and sister,* I told myself. Then, *nah, maybe cousins…distant cousins. More like neighbors?*

I was able to laugh by now and see how absurd it all was.

It's all in my head, I finally concluded Just notions.

I could turn that off.

After all, that's what I've done for all these years.

Yep. That'll work.

~~~~~

"Law, Gladys!" I shrieked when she arrived on the arm of her teenage grandson, Chris, who left his Granny with me and quickly migrated to the girls. "How did you find out about the party?" We hugged long and hard.

"At church. One of the members here in Tucapau visited our church for a revival last week and told me 'bout the party. He knew we was friends from way back. I've bent his ear talking 'bout you so much. You're still purdy as everything."

"So are you, Gladys." She was. Her hair now was completely gray and she wore it in soft curls, clipped back on each side. I tried to ignore the way one of her eyes behaved.

It seemed off-center somehow. Strange. Almost eerie.

Finally, she erupted into a rolling, full-belly, *Gladys* laugh. "You're a'wondering about my eye, ain't you?" She always *knew*. Ignoring my red face, she divulged, "I lost it and they've put this danged glass eye in. They give it to me. Free, it was. Its just that — it won't stay in place all the time. Just ignore it if you can."

I tried not to show my shock. My pretty, vibrant Gladys...*lost an eye*.

"What happened? To your eye, I mean." Seeing how she didn't seem too concerned about the change in her appearance, I relaxed some.

"Glaucoma. Had headaches like you wouldn't *believe*. Nothin' couldn't help the pressure behind this eye. Pain dang-near *killed* me, Sunny. Finally, I told my doctor to take it out. Against his better judgment, he did and my headaches went away. Never had another'n."

"Mymymy, Gladys. What a life you've had." I hugged her again and she laughed as though losing an eye was of no import. "Where's Vince? Your husband."

"He died last year, honey. Same way's Harly did — dropped dead of a heart attack. Runs in the family, I s'pose."

"I'm sorry, Gladys. You seemed really happy with him."

She smiled and said softly, "I was." And I thought *how strong she is. Turns loose and lets go when it's time.*

"Oh!" I grabbed her hand. "Got somebody I want you to see." I pulled her along, searching the crowd till I spotted him toting stacked used paper plates and cups to the corner garbage can. He'd just dumped them when I called to him.

"Daniel," I grabbed his hand and tugged him around. "Look who's here!"

His face lit up like the Fourth of July, Christmas, and Easter. "Gladys!"

Gladys peered at him from her one good eye, puzzled. "Who're you?"

"*Daniel!*" we both cried together.

Her mouth flew open and she squealed "Lord'a mercy! *My good-looking feller!*"

They flung themselves into each other's arms and laughed and rocked forever, till tears ran from their eyes. Finally, Gladys pushed him back to take a better look. "You ain't changed a lick. Still handsome as ever. No. *More* good-looking, ain't he, Sunny?"

"Yep," I managed to say without getting too weak-kneed. The trick was to not look too closely at Daniel. And to not *think*. "He just moved back in with Doretha."

"Come home, huh?" Gladys said, shaking her head thoughtfully. "You always was a good boy, Daniel. Like my own young-un."

Red began to creep up Daniel's neck but he lifted his chin and said solemnly. "You're like the mama I never had, Gladys. And I mean that."

By now, Gladys' good eye began to roam back and forth between Daniel and me and I knew memories of the past stirred, as did her curiosity about our present feelings for each other. "How's Walter," she asked, never the subtle one. Always the moral, *upright* one.

"He's fine, Gladys," I said, smiling, feeling gloriously innocent. "Ornery as ever. Nah, just kiddin'. Come on, let's go find him."

Daniel stayed behind. I felt his gaze trailing me.

~~~~~

At dusk, some of the youngsters ventured outside to gallivant on the lawn.

"Look at them," Emaline nudged me. I glanced out the window and saw my niece, Gale, doing a cartwheel, followed by Doretha's daughter, Tammy, who sprawled on her fanny, drawing howls and hoots from her cousins. She scrambled up, mouth grimly determined, and hurled herself into an equally doomed spiral of limbs. I saw Gladys outside watching them, as captivated by gymnastics as ever.

The years dropped away and I was a young girl again, hurtling myself fearlessly through the air....

In a heartbeat, I was through the door and outside. I helped Tammy to her feet. "Here, watch me, honey," I said. "I'll show you how it's done."

In the next instant my flat palms struck grassy sod and my feet flew up, up, up directly above me. In that heartbeat, suspended upside down, blood flooding my cranium, I felt every bone in my body shift — *Oh God! I'm not a young girl anymore* — till gravity eased and my feet completed the orbit and struck earth once more.

I concealed my trauma behind a wide, wide smile, dusted my hands together and blinked back a plague of black blotches. Fact was, I felt every *second* of my advancing age. The jolt of it felt lethal.

I glimpsed Daniel, hands in pockets, ankles crossed, propped against a distant wall, shadowed so I couldn't make out his features. My heart, just beginning to stabilize, did another drum roll. Then he stepped forward into the glow of a nightlight and I saw the big old grin that stretched from ear to ear, the *I know* one

Applause erupted. "Yooo, Nana!" hollered Jason, chest puffed-up like a rooster at sunrise.

"Walter," Lee Roy crowed, "did ye see that? The ol' girl's still got it, ain't she?"

Walter grinned proudly and surprised me with a jaunty thumbs-up. I glimpsed the handsome, long ago Walter and my eyes misted. He'd been slowing down too much lately to suit my peace of mind. I figured that, like with me, advancing age was the culprit.

I laughed and gave him a thumbs-up, too.

I owed him so much.

~~~~~

Sheila never showed up for Gracie's party.

"I'm still havin' dizzy spells, Sunny," her voice slurred a bit when I called her the next day. "Headaches, too."

Unease slithered through me. "I'm sorry, honey. We missed you. Is there anything I can do for you?"

"Nah. You've got your hands full with that newspaper column and taking care o' Walter and all. Dr. Hanna's prescribed me painkillers and a bunch of other stuff to try and stop all this crap. If it don't, he's gonna order an MRI." She gave a silly little laugh. "I'll be okay."

Alarm shot through me. My gut said something was dreadfully wrong.

"Promise me you'll let me know if you need anything," I insisted, heart thumping against my chest like a crazy drum.

"Oh, I will." Silence. No dramatics or weird spacing-out. No ranting or bitterness against her girls.

"Is Johnny there with you?"

"Oh, yeh," she said sweetly, " Johnny really loves me, Sunny. He won't leave me."

Silence. No *"like my girls did."*

"Bye, baby. Love you." I choked back tears.

"Love you, too, Sunny. Bye."

I stared at the receiver, fear gripping me.

What now?

~~~~~

Emaline and I had established a weekly Thursday evening ritual of dining together at my house. I would haul
out all my leftovers, adding hers and maybe a fresh serving
of chicken or ham or *whatever* to complete our 'sister' meal.

Still girls at heart, we'd long ago adopted each other
as sisters. Only thing missing from the rites was blood
mingling.

Walter didn't mind at all. Usually, he and Lee Roy ate
their meal on TV trays while watching their favorite pro-
grams so we girls had the kitchen to ourselves.

"Let's ask Francine and Sheila to join us," Emaline suggested one Thursday night as we finished the last of the
fried chicken and potato salad. "I'd love to claim them as
sisters, too."

"Sure," I shrugged. "Why not?"

Francine was tickled for the invitation and joined our
sisterhood circle the very next week. "Did either of you ask
Sheila to join us?" Emaline refilled our glasses with iced tea.

"I did," I replied. "She's not too enthused, I guess you'd
say."

Emaline peered at me, puzzled. "Why?"

I gazed at her sweet, trusting features. She didn't have a
clue. "I think she's sorta...territorial," I said and shrugged
apologetically "She apparently doesn't want to share me
with you."

"I'm sorry she feels that way." Emaline grew quiet and
thoughtful.

Francine snorted. "She don't worry 'bout sharing *me* none. I hardly ever see 'er anyhow." She took a hefty bite of carrot cake. "Mmm, this is *sinful*, Sunny."

I grinned. "Better you get the calories than me."

"You sure look good now," Francine's shrewd eyes gauged my new thinness. "Don't get t' looking *too good*, now, y'hear?"

"Oh shut up, the both of you." Emaline's little nose flew up in the air. "You skinny hussies make me *sick*."

Francine did a Mae West fluff of platinum-white hair and said huskily, "Eat your heart out, honey."

Emaline threw the last half of her biscuit at Francine, who whooped and threw one back.

Twenty minutes later, we were still laughing and snortin' like hogs and cleaning up the mess.

~~~~~

Sheila's malady turned out to be a brain tumor. Malignant and inoperable. At first, she was inconsolable. Terrified. True to his word, boyfriend Johnny Mack stayed with her.

I hurtled into denial, pulling out all stops.

Outwardly, I was staunch and supportive. Inside, horror of the disease festered. Cancer had already claimed Daddy. Now, it had designs on Sheila. Just how genetic was it? I read as much as possible on the subject, searched the web for the latest breakthroughs and encouraged Sheila with any morsel of hope I found. It must have helped because eventually she calmed and pulled up something deep inside that helped her grasp the good moments.

"Walter," I said one morning in early December as I thumbed through a Toney Bus Tours guide, "I'd like to get Sheila's mind off her illness. She needs something *fun*. Let's book for this bus tour to Disney World. If I can get so many folks to sign up, we can get ours free." A card-carrying homebody, Walter was, if not animated, surprisingly comfortable with the plans. His energy reservoir drained out easily but I reasoned that, at Disney World, we could slow our pace to accommodate that.

That week, I put a couple of sentences in my column about the trip and *whoa!* The response was this rip-roaring stampede. Seemed everybody in the Middle Tyger River area wanted to go to Disney World with the Stones. The bus seating was limited, so we ended up restricting those signing up to *family* and close friends. I booked the trip for the first week in January. That would get us through Christmas first.

"How long is it gonna be?" asked Walter. In the question I sensed apprehension dawning.

"Oh," I quickly reassured him, "only for a long weekend. From Friday morning till Sunday evening. Not long at all."

He visibly relaxed and resumed watching *Perry Mason*.

Early in the a.m., three weeks later on a frigid January morning, we huddled together, the lot of us, expiring excited puffs of vapor as we waited for the bus to arrive in the deserted BiLo parking lot. Our group included Walter and me, Lee Roy, Francine, Aunt Tina, Timmy's family, Emaline and Pastor John, Muffin, Jason, and Gracie, Gladys Kale, Ruth Bond Staggs, her daughter Sally (now married and a school administrator), and Joey Staggs.

I'd nearly bowled over when Doretha, Alvin, and their daughter, Tammy, signed up and now, here they were, ready to go. Sheila and Johnny Mack arrived. She was gaunt but as joyful as I'd ever seen her. Her blonde wig, a sexy one, actually, kept the jokes afloat for awhile, then another car careened into the lot with late arrivals. Sheila's girls, all three, spilled out and dashed to bear hug their mama, who promptly burst into sobs of happiness.

I choked up on that one. *Thank you, God. You do still hear me.*

Just as the bus appeared and bags were being hoisted into the luggage compartment, another eleventh-hour traveler screeched into a parking space and the driver emerged, winded and determined to get aboard.

Daniel.

My heart nearly burst with joy at the sight of him. Was it wrong? Still? To secretly celebrate him in my heart? I honestly didn't know.

He swept aboard, his hand squeezing my shoulder as he brushed past, making his way to a seat in the coach's mid-section. I'd given Walter the window-seat to keep him content, not easy when he was away from his fare of TV adventures. Lee Roy sat in the back, entertaining anybody who'd listen with his tales.

"Hey!" Daniel called out, "Not fair. All the window seats are taken!" I knew he was teasing. That was his way of livening things up.

"Come on, handsome," called Gladys. "You sit with this good lookin' ol' woman here and she'll give you the window seat. Deal?"

"Deal." He promptly claimed the promised seat and in a burst of exhaust fumes and anticipation, we embarked on our dream trip.

It was fodder for the next week's column:

JOURNAL OF A MAD TRAVELER

The day is here! My family clan of fifteen and horde of friends board the Toney Tour Bus this frigid January dawn, cheerfully mindful that Orlando, our destination, is ALWAYS balmy. We fight for window seats and settle down for the journey that will transport us to the chimera world that is Disney. We depart Spartanburg on a tide of anticipation. In Georgia, conversations ebb as magazines pop up and seats tilt back in snooze position. At lunchtime, despite endless goody-snacks, we pile into Cracker Barrel like ravenous waifs. Seated first, Walter and I are served LAST and as I hurriedly gulp down a vitamin gel capsule with my food, it lodges in my throat.

The silent drama commences: I gasp and peer desperately at Walter, who is stricken because he's seen this before. Not fun. He whirls me around and whacks me between the shoulder blades. My breath grows shallower. I'm on my knees now, face to the floor, eyes watering. The restaurant is so quiet you could hear a gnat burp. Walter yanks me up to my feet, back to him, and balls his fist under my ribcage Uh oh! He's never done a Heimlich before.

Unghhh! Ribs crack. Poor Walter. Poor me. I am blue. Help! With shaking hands I seize the water glass for one last gulp. The capsule slides down. I survive. No time to eat.

Dash through icy drizzle to bus. Can't WAIT to get to sunny, WARM Orlando!

Take Advil for aching ribcage. Pass around leftover Christmas candies. Everybody finicky, brought their own, thank you very much.

Destination at last! Bedtime. Morning too soon...motel TV news says record cold weather for the next two days. Add light jacket to apparel. Clan already aboard bus, yelling, "hurry!" as I jog through freezing wind, wincing at my ribs' clamoring protest.

Disney at last! Monorail broke down. Backtrack through endless lines to different site, ANOTHER endless file to a ferryboat that transports us to theme park. Day cold. Brrr! Ribcage smarting. Clan buys gloves, hats, and sweaters to knock off chill, all DISNEY emblazoned and costly. Hands freezing. Find warm place. Magic Kingdom. Parade...I'm momentarily thawed after lunch in warm Colonial Restaurant.

Soon, feet like ice. Food lays heavy in stomach. Would trade my kingdom for a warm jacket. Stores all out. Sundown. Temperatures sink like Titanic. Ribs thrumming like bass guitar. Stomach now churning. When does hypothermia set in? Catch monorail to find warm bus.

Bus not in parking lot. OH GOD! No place to thaw.

Walter's resolution: 'We'll ride the monorail till the bus comes. At least it's warm here."

Two, three trips. Door springs open. "You two. Get off!" roars a Disney marine-sergeant female. "Make room for others who need it more."

Walter flashes a feral grin. "No way." He presses his back to his corner. "We're riding back to the bus lot."

Walter's my hero.

We disembark at parking lot. Bus is there, thank God! Warmth.

Nausea. Pain. Small bus bathroom...vomit all way to hotel. Virus.

Going to die.

Pass out in bed. Morning. Walter's face blurs overhead. "You going to Disney World today?" I groan, "No way." Alone. Float in and out of feverish oblivion until late evening. I survive. Weak and bored. Miss Walter. Bus rescues me. We eat late dinner.

GREAT TO BE ALIVE!

Next dawn: return trip begins. Window seats ignored. Blanket brigade exposes only snoring faces. Leftover Christmas goodies

treasures to kill for. Cracker Barrel trauma-
tizes so I opt for Hardees across highway.
Stop and load up with Florida oranges,
grapefruit, and Vidalia onions.

Cold! Keening for home and warmer temps.
Sunset. Reach parking lot...familiar cars. Ah-
hhh. At last. Disembark bus. Brrr! Freezing.
Walter jogs to van. Engine dead. "Cables,
anybody?" Lot nearly deserted now. Cables
appear. Crank up....

Thank God! Wave bye to friends, to sister
Francine, whose grin below red nose re-
vives visions of Santa and elves. "Let's do it
again!" she calls.

"Yeh!" I holler back. "When hell freezes over!"

That column drew more attention and kidding than any
of my others. Only thing was, Walter wasn't the hero who
did the Heimlich maneuver on me. It was Daniel who reacted promptly in the crisis. Neither did Walter jog to the
dead-engine car. Lee Roy charged the dead battery and got
the car going. But Walter was the only *hero* my readership,
by now, accepted.

"Hey!" Daniel shushed me when I tried to explain the
omission of his name the week the column appeared in the
Tyger River Times. He'd dropped by to see Walter. On the
trip, they'd formed some incredibly warm bonds.

The day I'd lain sick at the hotel, Daniel had taken Walter and Lee Roy under his wing and shown them a mar-
velously good time at the Disney Theme park. "You don't
owe me an apology, Sunny. I understand how folks think

about these things. You do satire and are entitled to take certain liberties with its creation." He grinned and tweaked my nose. "No problem."

I gazed at his straight back as he disappeared into Walter's room, juggling his cup of coffee, spouting men's humor and blending. I'd added another easy chair in recent days since Lee Roy was quite territorial of his perch. Small sacrifice, seeing as how the three men were virtual Three Musketeers.

Lee Roy had not, a month later, quit talking about the Magic Kingdom. "Them 'ar costumes was the purdiest thangs I ever saw," he told Daniel yet again.

"Weren't they, now?" Daniel responded warmly, spinning Lee Roy off into rhapsodic musings.

I smiled, warmed by it all. Muffin was slowly thawing toward Daniel since he'd been hanging out with her daddy. He and I remained spotless in our behavior so her shrewd vigilance had eased a bit. Sheila's girls continued to rally for their mama during her health crisis. In fact, the entire family was wonderfully *there* for Sheila.

I rolled my eyes upward. *Thank you for peace.*

Little did I know that it was the calm before the storm.

Chapter Eighteen

Over the next months I helplessly watched cancer ravage my little sister. It angered me. I prepared to fight dragons for her, to shield and coddle and do *whatever* to make her feel, for once in her miserable lifetime, *safe*.

And then she stunned me by cloaking herself in dignity and raw courage. I watched that beautiful, burning blaze of a woman slowly shed the luminosity that had always set her apart. I watched in horror the big C stealthily suck away her substance, leaving only an emaciated, skeletal shell.

We who loved her acted blind, like we didn't notice a thing.

She kept on a'smilin' because, even as she suffered pain and debilitation, Sheila was thrilled to have her girls back. And I think she could smile because — this is awful to say — the attention she had always so desperately craved was now hers. Provocation-free, the affection she'd thirsted after now gushed freely over her.

It was Emaline, sweet, sweet Emaline, who, without fail, daily visited the village house Sheila and Johnny now habitated. Johnny wasn't one of the money-guys Sheila had so hankered after but he made fair wages at the nearby BMW plant. And his obvious love for her made up for all Sheila's other formerly desired romantic-spoils.

Besides, she'd received that big settlement from the sexual harassment suit and didn't need Johnny's money. She could have bought a big ol' home anywhere but, in her final days, she wanted to nest here on the mill hill, her *home*, surrounded by those who loved her.

Tonight, Emaline served a wonderful dinner she'd prepared at home and hauled over to Sheila's house. She'd invited us all, family and friends, to the feast, knowing how it would buoy Sheila's spirit. "Where's your ol' lady, Lee Roy?" asked Francine while munching on Doritos and salsa appetizers.

Lee Roy took a careful sip of steaming coffee I'd perked especially for him, catering to his partiality to the stuff. "It's like this, Francine," he drawled, "Sal, she works all the time."

Francine's eyebrows shot up. "Why don't y'all all get off your lazy tails and go get jobs so Sal won't have to work herself to death?"

Nonplussed, Lee Roy took another noisier slurp and shrugged. "Heck, she *likes* t'work, dontcha know? And me? I owe so much back alimony that I won't never get it caught up. Won't pay me t'work full time."

"Why hadn't they put you in jail?" asked Aunt Tina, more than a little aggravated with Lee Roy's dispassion. She had it in for deadbeat dads and alimony dodgers because of Talley's no-account desertion, leaving her to raise their son, Alvin, alone. Oh, he'd been court-ordered to pay alimony and child support but he'd moved so far away, it would've taken the FBI to find him. Disgusted, Aunt Tina had simply let go and got on with her life.

"My ex done give up on me," Lee Roy drawled. Then he grinned, baring teeth, gaps and all. "Can't squeeze blood outta a turnip, dontcha know?"

Emaline uncovered a humongous baking dish that emitted a heavenly aroma. "*Law*, Emaline," Sheila shrieked, as energetic a gesture as I'd seen from her in recent days. "You cooked that Inflation Cornbread! Ohhh, it looks so good. Mmm."

Emaline's eyes lit up like candles. I could tell that seeing Sheila so excited over the layered meat, cheese, onion concoction, topped with crispy cornbread crust was reward in itself for the time and effort of preparation. Days earlier, Emaline had found the colorful picture and recipe in a magazine and showed it to Sheila.

And I thought what a clever way to whip a near-dead appetite back to life like that.

Daniel and Pastor John arrived with folding tables and chairs we'd borrowed from the church, followed by Alvin, Doretha, and their Tammy. Seating arrangements were snug and spilled over into other rooms but everybody was festive and *together.* Sheila's girls hovered about her, fetching food and drink for their Mama and it did my heart so good. Daniel was the last to be seated, managing to squeeze another chair in beside me.

I tried to ignore how my breath caught in my throat. Felt like I was gulping for air. To cover it, I raised my iced tea glass. "To Sheila!" I said and everyone followed suit. Her sunken eyes teared up. Then she smiled like a beauty queen and I loved her so my heart hurt and the pain mingled somehow with that of being so close to Daniel.

And yet so far away.

Like Muffin, who chose to sit at another table with Gracie, without so much as a 'howdy' to me. She ignored my salute to Sheila, a sly snub only I detected.

At least the moisture in my eyes was justified with no one the wiser because when I looked around, everybody else's eyes puddled, too.

"Thank you, Sunny," Sheila said, her voice hitching. "And thank you, Emaline, for making this possible. We're all *sisters* now, us Acklin girls and Emaline. We adopted Emaline, did you know that, Daniel?" I watched tears slide down her pale face. I also saw a new Sheila, one radiant with love and openness. Emaline went to her and hugged her long and gently, her own eyes red from weeping.

I heard Daniel's soft gulp and knew that he, too, was moved. "That's great, Sheila," he said hoarsely. "Just great. Nothing like family." He looked at Doretha.

Doretha, sitting across the table, gazed at him, a bit startled to hear him speak so of her. Then she smiled her Mona Lisa smile. And when Daniel's gaze swept to include Walter, well, everybody's eyes grew bright with new tears.

Me, after the first gush of pain, my emotions quickly withered and I was left with the same old flat, familiar sense of nothingness.

That I so easily slid back into nothingness struck me as weird.

On another level, I was glad.

~~~~~

It was Emaline who rallied when Sheila's condition, after that night, plunged. It was Emaline who caught her before she hit the jagged rocks of death's shoals and daily comforted her with her presence and words of wisdom and validation. Who cooked whatever Sheila felt she could ingest, then when my little sister could no longer tolerate solids, kept steaming bowls of chicken or beef broth on the bedside table. She who reminded Sheila to sip liquids through a straw and spoon into the reluctant, pale mouth just one more swallow of broth.

Emaline led my sister to find peace with her Maker and with life. It was a hard fought battle because Sheila had so lived and breathed strife that she'd been oblivious to the other side of life's coin. Emaline's love for Sheila demonstrated that other side and made it possible for me to truly get to know the real Sheila, the little girl inside her who had no angry agenda, no scores to settle, other than those with her girls, from whom she begged forgiveness.

"Mama," Cassie grasped Sheila's thin hand as my sister lay like a wounded bird upon her bed, as white as the sheets with no shades of color to indicate lips or nose, thin as a sapling and head shiny-bald. "We've already forgiven you." She gulped back a sob, then whispered. "I love you, Mama."

Sheila's pale lips moved ever so slightly, emitting a mere huff of sound. "Love... you... too." Her fingers squeezed Cass', white in intensity. The lips moved again. "E...maline?"

In a flash, Emaline settled on the edge of her bed, gently capturing the bony fingers. "I'm here, Sheila."

"Sing," rasped the weak voice. "You... know..."

Emaline smiled, her lips wobbled but with remarkable fortitude she reined in her galloping emotions and began to sing in a clear, sweet soprano, *"Amazing Graaace, how sweet the Sound..."*

Francine fled the room. I found her outside the bedroom, plastered to the wall, sobbing quietly. Dry-eyed, I hauled her into my arms. Francine pulled back for an instant, peered watery-eyed at me and groaned, "I've treated her just *awful*, Sunny." Tears splashed over and the head fell heavily upon my shoulder once more. "A-awful." Her body shook with remorse and despair.

"Go to her, then," I heard myself say. "Tell her you love her."

Francine pulled loose and went back in, where Emaline was finishing the 23rd Psalm. *"...and I shall dwell in the house of the Lord forever."*

Sheila squeezed Emaline's fingers and wheezed, "Thank...you."

Francine approached the bed, her gaze pinned to Sheila's still face, beautiful in repose, as death hovered, so close I felt its chilling presence, its tenacious intent, one that grew stronger by the moment.

I shivered and felt Doretha's frail arm slide around my waist. I gazed into her deep set, hazel, wise old woman's eyes and saw that she felt what I did, only she was meeting it head-on. I'd already, days ago, pushed that hidden *denial* button inside me. Suddenly, I wished for feeling. For grief. I closed my eyes and willed it to come. But nothing stirred that thick blankness inside me.

In that moment, I yearned desperately for something else. *Please God, let me feel your presence.* That too, eluded me. Alarm frissoned over me, then dissipated.

Francine dropped to her knees beside the bed, heaving with pain and regret and lay her head on Sheila's bosom. "I'm sorry, Sheila," she said hoarsely, gravely. "I love you so much, you know. Don't know why I never said that to you. Just stubborn, I guess." The white-blonde head raised and she stared into the face, willing the once spring-grass green eyes to open. They remained shut.

But the lips moved, just barely. "I... know. Love...you, too... Francine."

"Forgive me, Sheila, for all those times —"

"Shhh," The eyes slitted. "I ... jus' as mean. All...in... past. Don'... matter." A tiny, tiny smile. "We...sisters." The lids lowered again. But one bony arm slid around Francine's neck and my older sister lost it. She bawled like a baby, soaking the front of Sheila's gown but it didn't matter because it was right and overdue and healing for all of us of little faith.

The dark presence I'd felt earlier seemed to ebb and I moved to my sister's side, lowered myself on her bed, took her cold hand and whispered. "My baby. I love you."

The lips smiled just a tad but I knew. A tear appeared at the outer corner of one eye and slid down the waxen cheek. I watched it span the skinny neck and disappear into the pillow. "Sunny," came the wisp of sound. "Like… my… mama. Always… good … me. Loved… me…always." Her hand grew limp after those words and the chill returned. Her breathing grew more labored. A part of me wanted to breathe for her.

Another part had already let go.

I released her hand, arose and left the room and settled in a living room chair that gave me a distanced view of the bed. All three of her daughters surrounded her and softly crooned words of love to their Mama. "Please don't leave us, Mama," moaned one after the other, "We need you." And I thought how their pleas were but echoes of the ones uttered all through their lives.

Difference was, this time when Sheila left, she had no choice.

I watched in amazement as Emaline pulled them outside the door where I sat and told them. "Girls, your mama's tired. She's put up a brave battle. Now, she wants to go home to a better place, where she won't hurt like you've seen her doing recently. You need to give her permission to go, Cassie," she addressed the leader of the three.

"She's worried about Ginger, isn't she? She's afraid you two will give up on her." She gazed expectantly at them, a silent plea in her eyes. "You need to reassure her. Tell her to follow the bright light." Cass nodded and led the others back to the bedside.

On her knees, Cassie said, "Mama, just go to the bright light. There, you won't hurt anymore. It's okay. Me and Michelle, we're gonna take care of Ginger. Don't you worry about her." Sheila's breathing grew shallower as Cassie spoke. Tears now ran down the girls' faces, everyone's faces.

Except mine. I felt numb. Dead inside. *How I hungered to grieve.*

"Just follow that light, Mama." Cassie hand-swiped her damp face and leaned to kiss her mother's cold cheek. She looked shocked for a long moment. Then she peered around the room, searching for and finding Emaline's face. "She's gone." Her features, so like Sheila's at that age, crumpled in grief. "Mama's gone."

The girls' wails followed me as I arose and quietly walked out of the house. I sat on the front steps, gazing down over the housetops at the river, high from recent rains. It no longer held terror for me. The old dam, structured from earth's large gray boulders. still stood, proud and strong and invincible. One of the few remaining landmarks.

At least it's safe. The thought gave me a moment's comfort as I lounged amid death and devastation.

I stirred, pushing away the intrusion. A hand lightly touched my shoulder. Startled, I gazed up into Daniel's concerned, pale face. "You okay?" he asked and plopped tiredly down beside me, hands dangling between knees. Walter, tiring more easily in recent days, had hours ago left with Lee Roy, who would keep him company until I got home

Muffin had already come and gone, staying longer than I'd expected, actually, surprising me with the depth of her concern. She'd brought Cokes and a cold meat and cheese tray from Spartanburg's Beacon Drive-In and put them in the refrigerator before quietly sitting awhile with family.

I nodded firmly. "Yeh. I'm okay. She's better off, Daniel. She really suffered, you know." He gazed back at me, his turquoise eyes pained, heavy with sadness.

"I know," he said hoarsely, looked as though he'd reach for my hand, stopped mid-motion, then clasped his fingers tightly around his knees. "Still hard to accept. So young… beautiful. Such a loss…." I felt his gaze roam over my features but I didn't look at him. "Like so many other losses."

The words hit me like a mallet, penetrating my Novocaine-deadness, spreading over me like warm oil, driving away….

Abruptly, I stood and loped down the steps. "I've gotta go check on Walter," I called over my shoulder.

I didn't wait for his reply.

~~~~~

Sheila's death spiraled me downward, into a spinning, bottomless plunge, one devoid of light or hope. I couldn't even label it. Depression? It surpassed that. Anxiety? One had to *feel* to have anxiety. My thick cocoon blocked out sights, sounds, and sensations. Suspended, I waited. For what, I hadn't a clue. Death, maybe? At times, I thought I would welcome it. I was neither happy nor unhappy, neither angry nor joyful, anticipated nothing, feared nothing, loved nothing, hated nothing.

I was trapped in nothingness.

I was a danged automaton. Going through motions.

The headaches began. Walter's doctor prescribed me pain pills. Actually, I couldn't put my ailment into words. Except for the headaches. When they battered me, I tumbled into bed and slept them off. I refused to answer the phone or the door. I instructed Walter and Lee Roy, *God bless Lee Roy*, to say I was not feeling well. I knew Walter felt abandoned but I had nothing from which to draw to give back to him.

Nobody knew the source of my pathos. How could they? I didn't even know. I was good at camouflage. Had practiced it since Mama's disappearance. Anyway, everybody said I deserved time to recover from Sheila's death. Only I knew it wasn't grief. Not that kind, anyway.

Muffin even stopped complaining when frozen TV dinners replaced my cuisine.

Somehow I kept my newspaper column afloat.

I'm convinced that, in the end, that's what kept me sane.

~~~~~

"I got my new shoes soaked," Francine groused, slid the taupe suede slippers from her feet and plopped down, jean-clad legs pretzeled, on my bed where I nursed the beginning of yet another headache, this time escorted by nausea. "Durned storm! It's raining frogs."

"Hi, honey," I mumbled, slurring my words. "You're wearing a new cologne."

"Yeh," she perked up. "Like it?"

"Heavenly," I moaned, nearly gagging from the sultry smell. I rolled my feet to the floor, rushed to the bathroom and vomited.

Francine followed me, frowning worriedly. "What's wrong, Sunny?"

I shook my head, washed my face and went to stretch out again on the bed. "Tension, I think." I had to assuage Francine's curiosity and concern. But I so did *not* want to talk or analyze.

354 Emily Sue Harvey

She bent to hug me gently. "Missing Sheila, is all. You know," she resettled on the bed, facing me, "I miss her, too. Didn't ever think I'd feel this way 'bout her." She looked thoughtful, then sad for a few moments. "Too bad we don't learn this stuff till its too late."

"Mm hmm." My head began to throb in earnest as I fell victim to the heaviness of an iron anvil that squeezed till all circulation there ceased.

"You think she knows, Sunny? I mean — how I feel about her? How I *miss* her?" Her voice carried a desperation I'd never before heard in it.

"I know she does, Francine. You told her you loved her before —"

"I know. But do you believe in Heaven? Do you think she can hear us?" Her question was so child-like, I blinked away the mist and peered at her. Never a churchgoer, Francine had never given any indication of believing anything remotely connected to a hereafter. If only I were feeling less out-of-it. I hated to let the moment pass.

"I believe in Heaven," I said, " and I think God lets those who go there see the good things here on earth. Kinda like He pulls back a curtain when He wants them to see something."

"Like we're on a big ol' revolving stage here." Francine looked pleased.

"Yeh." I'd never stopped believing, I'd simply ceased feeling that comforting presence of my childhood days.

"What about that lil' dickens getting' all that money from that sex-harassment lawsuit?" She nudged my leg and chortled. "And she didn't even get to hang around to spend it." She fell instantly solemn, then choked up. I patted her leg as she cried.

When her tears subsided, I said, "I'm glad she changed her will and left her children their inheritance. Maybe it'll balance the scales some. They're set for years to come if they handle it wisely. So is Johnny."

Francine peered at me through red, swollen eyes. "You know he tried to give his part of the money to the girls but they're so grateful to 'im for making their mama happy, they wouldn't take it." She gazed into space, thoughtful, and I wondered if she was remembering destroying Tack's final will and cheating his benefactors out of their inheritance. I sighed and pushed away thoughts of things I could not change. The thrumming in my head accelerated.

Francine left a little while later and I was relieved to be alone. Pain's cadence, searing and persistent, was not unlike a muffled snare drum metering a funeral dirge. I shut my eyes and began to flow with Loritab euphoria. The tide swept me from harsh shores to float atop a tranquil, slow-lapping wave where pain could not exist.

From that oasis, I heard Muffin's faraway voice. "Mama?" She demanded my attention. "My car won't start. I need some medicine. I need you to take me to the pharmacy?" She shook my shoulder. "*Mom!*"

Already in twilight *bzzzzz* zone, I simply continued to drift. Limp. Boneless. When finally she gave up and left, I immediately sank into deep slumber, the coma kind. Escape.

~~~~~

"Sunny! You there?" Bambambam.

Loud pounding at the front door sliced through my stupor. "Wh —" I blinked at the wall clock. Five o'clock. Already dusk in November. I struggled to my feet as another series of raps exploded, jarring my eardrums. "Walter?"

I called weakly. Why wasn't he answering the door? He'd been complaining of tiredness. But what about Lee Roy? I peered into his room. Neither he nor Lee Roy was there.

"Sunny!" called a familiar male voice from my front porch. "Sunny! You there?"

On wobbly legs, I blinked back gray webs as I made my way across the room. I unlocked the door. "Fitzhugh," I croaked, "what're you yelling about?" I squinted at the tall, sandy-haired man in police uniform. Fitzhugh — pronounced Fitch-you — had kept us villagers safe all through the years. Was like a daddy to us all.

"Can I come in, Sunny?" he asked, fidgeting with his uniform cap.

Alarm slithered through me. A foreboding. "Sure. Come on in, Fitzhugh. Have a seat."

He entered but continued to stand. Through migraine haze, I squinted to read his solemn face. "What's wrong?" I whispered.

"There's been a wreck, Sunny."

"Wh — is it Muffin?" my voice cracked. She'd been trying to get me to drive her to the drug store for medicine. Drugs. My breath felt suddenly cut off. Oh God!

Fitzhugh's face gentled as he took my elbow and seated me on the sofa. "Muffin's got a mild concussion but she'll be okay. It's Walter."

The breath wheezed from my lungs. "Walter? But — he's here somewhere. With Lee Roy."

He squatted before me, taking my icy hands in his. "Muffin said Lee Roy left for home same time she and Walter did. Walter drove Muffin to Eckerds Drug Store because — well, she's been drinking. On the way back, the car hydroplaned and left the road, crashing into a tree. Walter's hurt bad, Sunny. I'll drive you to the hospital."

My hands flew to my mouth. "Walter's afraid to drive in bad weather...he panicked. Oh...my...God." I let Fitzhugh help me to my feet. "Just a minute, Fitzhugh," I said thickly, "gotta make a call."

Déjà vu. Walter's long ago accident flashed before me: the thing that stole my daughter from me. I wouldn't've thought it possible, but my body's numbness grew more pronounced. I glided across the room to the wall phone, jointless, an apparition. No floor beneath me.

"I'll call Doretha. And Daniel," I rasped. Is that my voice? It came from far, far away, echoing and bouncing around in my brain. I picked up the receiver and then everything turned black.

~~~~~

Daniel's face swam above me. Doretha's ashen, thin features joined his and something cool and wet stroked my face. A damp cloth in Doretha's gentle hand slowly scattered the darkness and, like a magnet, pulled up the physical me.

"You're back with us, ain't you?" Doretha's soft voice soothed me, made the fact of me stretched out on the hard floor okay. My confusion showed because she said, "You fainted. Fitzhugh called us to come over. Said you was about to call us before you passed out."

It all rushed back in on me, the accident, Muffin...she was all right, Fitzhugh said.

I struggled to rise. Daniel rushed to assist me onto my wobbly legs. "Walter?" I murmured, my voice so feeble it sounded like a sick bagpipe.

"Don't you worry none," Doretha crooned. "We'll get you there. Here, let me get you bundled. You're cold to the touch."

"Take it easy, " Daniel muttered, keeping a firm grip on me as Doretha got my coat from the closet and helped me into it. Then my scarf.

"I'm going to start the engine so the car will be warm," Daniel said and dashed outside. He returned within moments.

"It's uncommonly cold tonight," Doretha softly explained. And it was, for early November, as I discovered outside. The air was like ice and just as brittle. It caught and lifted my short tousled hair. Chill spasmed through me. Doretha and Daniel's breath exhaled snowy vapor trails while mine, shallow and rapid, emitted puny little gray puffs. My wandering attention latched onto them, desperate for diversion from what was to come.

Daniel drove us to Spartanburg Regional Medical Center in record time. The car was warm and I sat strapped in the front passenger seat, tilted back a little. Doretha worked steadily, trying to stabilize me; continuing to use the damp cloth on my face, neck, and wrists. Feeling slowly began to seep back into me.

"How's your headache?" Daniel cast me a concerned glance.

"Gone," I muttered, "thank God."

God. Where are you?

~~~~~

Once at the hospital, I made a beeline for Muffin in the ER. I had to see for myself that she was okay.

"Mama," she groaned and reached for me, hugging my neck as I leaned over her bed, kissed her cheek, and nuzzled her neck as I'd done when she was a baby. I inhaled her fragrance, a blend of nicotine, booze, hair spray, and some sexy Victoria's Secret formula.

In that heartbeat, I didn't care that she was flawed, didn't care that this affection came so rarely. I simply seized the moment and celebrated life with her.

Then, quite suddenly, she pushed me away to scan me. "How's Daddy?" she rasped, her cerulean eyes, like clear, endless mirrors, reflected worry.

"I'm going to check on him now," I soothed. "You just rest and maybe they'll let you go home tomorrow."

Not to be mollified, she grasped my arm, surprising me anew with her strength. "Daddy's hurt *bad*, Mama. And it's all my f-fault." Astonished, I watched the harsh planes of her face slide into tearful guilt.

This side of her only revealed itself during Daddy-related crisis. I battled the jealousy that flooded and shook me to the core. I'd forgotten Doretha was present till she brushed against my elbow to draw near to bedside. "You can't take the blame, Muffin," she said softly, sensibly. "Accidents happen to ever'body."

"But if I hadn't insisted he drive me to —"

"Doretha's right, honey," I took her rigid hand in mine. "If the weather hadn't been so lousy, the wreck wouldn't have happened." I gently massaged her fingers to relax them and smiled at her. "You're not responsible." Her grateful gaze pulled compassion from my soul that oozed through and filled me till it pushed out the ugly jealousy.

Doretha spoke. "Sunny, why don't you go see about Walter. I'll stay with Muffin."

I opened my mouth to tell Doretha that Walter was her brother and it was only fitting that, since he had serious injuries, she come with me. But something in her eyes made me stop, close my mouth and nod.

~~~~~

Daniel kept vigil at Walter's side while Dr. Wood, a surgeon, gave me the facts of my husband's injuries. "A ruptured spleen. He needs immediate surgery to stem the bleeding."

I nodded, signed some release forms and within minutes, followed as they wheeled Walter to the doors marked **Operating Room**. There, we stopped and said good-byes. He looked so pale and helpless as he peered beseechingly at me through pain-glazed eyes.

"You're gonna be okay, Walter," I reassured him as calmly as I could and leaned to kiss him lightly on the lips.

"That's right," Daniel said, capturing Walter's hand in his for a firm, reassuring squeeze. I choked a little at how close they'd become. Walter's gaze swept from my face to Daniel's and back and I saw a sweet peace relax his taut features.

"They gonna fix my spleen," he said happily, as though going out for a hot dog. The lump in my throat grew bigger. "When I come out, I'm gonna be good as new."

Daniel husked, "Got that right, buddy."

"Tell Lee Roy I'm gonna be okay, Sunny."

"You got it," I rasped, pasting on a smile.

A grin slid across his face as his lids lowered. It was still there when they whisked him through the OR door.

~~~~~

Muffin convinced Doretha to round up a wheelchair, deposit her in it and transport her to Walter's room. We waited together for news from the OR. Still in green scrubs, Dr. Wood appeared shortly after midnight.

"Mrs. Stone, your husband's spleen has been removed and the bleeding has stopped. That's the good news."

"Thank God!" Muffin gushed, closing her eyes in relief. Doretha rubbed her shoulders gently.

"The bad news is —" Dr. Wood turned grim, "we found a problem with his liver."

He gave that a moment to sink in as my knees nearly buckled and my hands flew to my mouth. "Oh God," I whispered.

"What?" Muffin demanded, rising from the wheelchair, despite Doretha's efforts to subdue her. "Did the wreck cause it?" Now sober, she advanced on the doctor, frantic.

"No, no," he quickly replied. "It's a condition that's been there for some time, by the looks of things."

"W-what is it?" my voice quavered.

"It's called Silent Cirrhosis because it gives little to no warning before its last stages." He patted my arm. "I'm sorry. I wish the news were better."

Muffin sank back down into her chair, her expression pale, stunned.

"He's been extremely tired lately," I murmured. "And he's complained of stomach aches. But on the other hand, he's grown two pants sizes so I figured...."

"Abdominal swelling," said Dr. Wood. "I suspect liver failure."

On her feet instantly, in two giant steps, Muffin was in his face. "Liver failure?" she shrieked, whirling to glower at me. "And you couldn't *tell he was sick?*" she accused. "I can't *believe* you!"

Dr. Wood, obviously as taken aback as I was from Muffin's abrupt attack, gathered his wits about him and continued. "After some more blood tests, I'll know more." He left quickly, relieved, I could tell, to escape the ugly family ambiance fermenting in Walter's room.

We all fell silent, standing as though figures frozen in a suspense video *pause.* Only Muffin remained animated. Anger sizzled and crackled the air as she stalked in circles about me, eying me up one side and down the other.

I met her gaze steadily, dreading what I would see there but compelled to connect, to get past it. After a long, contemptuous glare, she turned her gaze upon Daniel, who now leaned indolently against the far wall, watching her with measured detachment. He never blinked as she sighted and perused him for long moments.

When her attention returned to rest upon me again, there was a knowing look in her eyes. "Sooo," she drawled, "that's the way it is, huh? Of course," she added flippantly, "I already knew the score there, didn't I, Mommy dearest?"

"Stop it, Muffin!" Doretha stepped forward. "You shouldn't talk to your mama like that. She's a good woman." Doretha's rather bold chastisement left me speechless. Then, she softly backpedaled. "You're just upset and all and that concussion's not helping none, either." She reached out and took Muffin's arm. "Come on, let me take you back to your room. You need to rest, honey."

I was truly amazed when Muffin complied and settled docilely in the wheelchair. Then I noted her pallor and trembling. It hit me. *This is a replay of her daddy's first accident.* My heart lurched at the slumped shoulders as Doretha wheeled her from the room.

My knees buckled suddenly and in a heartbeat Daniel's hands caught me before I went down. "Come on, Sunny. Sit." He settled me in one of the comfortable chairs and gently chafed my cold hands in his, bringing me back to a semblance of balance.

"I'm fine now," I said, sliding my hands from his. The contact was too soothing.

Too painful.

Chapter Nineteen

Dr. Wood called me outside the room the next afternoon. Muffin, who'd been released that morning, trailed us to the hall. Without preamble, he said, "Your husband needs a liver transplant. Quickly. We need a donor and the waiting list will take too long. We need to look within the family for the best match. But if there's no one to volunteer there, we'll look elsewhere."

"Me," Muffin rushed forward. "I'll do it."

My heart gave a painful jerk then began palpitating. *Family...blood...Muffin's not blood. Oh my God!*

"I'll do it," I quickly insisted. "Test me." I shot Daniel a desperate look. Realization dawned and he stepped forward and took Muffin's hand, taking her by surprise

"Muffin, you're in a weakened state now. I'll go ahead and test, just in case, okay?" He spoke so gently and persuasively it took my breath. Apparently, it did Muffin's as well because she nodded assent then slumped submissively down in a nearby chair. Doretha sent me a troubled look over her head.

In those few moments, the atmosphere had so thickened that it would've taken a chainsaw to cut it. I felt suffocated. "I need a cup of coffee," I said, snatching up my purse and heading for the door. "Anybody else?"

"Decaf. Cream," Doretha opened and rummaged in her purse for change.

"I'm buying," I said over my shoulder. "Muffin?"

"Diet Coke."

"I'll go help," Daniel trailed me outside and fell into step beside me. I began trembling in earnest.

"What am I gonna do, Daniel? I can't let Muffin find out Walter's not her daddy."

"She won't."

"But if she tests…."

"Negative won't prove anything." I felt his hand cover my elbow and it released a soothing balm, spreading over and through me.

We paused in the deserted corridor and gazed out into the sunlit day. I looked up into his face and saw such caring my breath hitched. I swallowed a tiny, fluttery bird.

"Daniel, I need to talk to Emaline. She knows nothing of what happened all those years ago."

Astonishment creased his brow. "Nothing? You two were so close, Sunny…"

"I know." I closed my eyes and shook my head slowly. "I don't know why I didn't trust her with the truth." I looked at him then. "Might have saved myself some heartache had I gone to her then."

We gazed at each other, memories and emotions riding our features and swimming in our eyes, a wordless drama shared by us and us alone.

"One thing I do know, Daniel," I said as we approached the coffee shop. "I'll not hurt Muffin again."

~~~~~

Later that evening, I left the hospital, leaving Daniel with Walter. Lee Roy was visiting for a short spell as well. So I knew Walter was in good hands. He still looked like death and I felt guilty leaving him, but I was desperate to talk to Emaline.

Emaline answered the parsonage door. "Well, *Sunny!*" she hugged me, then stepped back, her brows drawing together. "Walter's not worse, is he?"

"No, thank God. He still looks terrible...but I really need to talk to you. There are some things I want to share, *need* to share with you. Things I should have told you years and years ago."

"*Whoa*. This sounds *heavy*,. Emaline cut her green eyes at me dramatically as we pulled out kitchen chairs and settled with our coffee.

"It all began while Daniel was gone to find his mama, the time I slept over at Doretha's. You know, the time her step-father, Ol' Tom was in the hospital."

~~~~~

"*My god*, Sunny." Emaline wiped her eyes and blew her nose two hours later. "Why in heaven's name didn't you come to me?" We'd drifted to her bedroom to lounge on the bed over an hour ago.

I shrugged limply and settled back against throw pillows stacked at the headboard. Emaline lay at the foot facing me, propped on one elbow. "I thought you'd judge me, Emaline. And at that time I couldn't handle that."

"*Judge you?*" She stared at me, tears puddling again. "Don't you know, Sunny, that you're my *sister*? My best friend in the world? God in Heaven, my *hero*. How could I *judge* you?" Fresh tears spilled over and ran down her cheeks. "I'm so sorry you didn't trust me to be there with you. Y'know, I could whine and wail about how hurt I feel but then — this isn't about me, is it? It's about you."

"Look." I scooted across the mattress and took her hand. "Don't take it personal, Emaline. I was as messed up as a wrecked rattletrap. I didn't even trust God. I quit praying." I met her sad eyes. "I still don't pray like I should. Seems I've shut down most all of me over the years."

"I'm sorry, Sunny," she rasped, snuffling, struggling upright to sit tailor-fashion. "Sorry for all you've been through. But this is a new day…a new beginning. And I, for one, am tired of you getting beat up on."

I smiled as she aggressively blew her nose. "Yeh. Me, too."

She smiled back, her nose as red as Rudolph's. "I want the old Sunny back."

My smile vanished. "I don't know about that, Emaline. Don't know as there's any of her left inside this aging shell."

"*Hah!* Aging shell, my eye!" she laughed then. A full, rolling one from the belly. "I saw that cart wheel you did at the party."

I burst into laughter. "Yeh. And y'know what? This old bod will *never* be the same." Just as suddenly as it came, the humor evaporated. "I pray that Muffin won't find out the truth."

She gazed at me for long moments before speaking. "Just remember that *whatever* happens will be for the best."

I thought on that. At one time, I'd staked my life on that biblical promise. Now, it wasn't in me to trust that implicitly. Didn't, in that moment in time, know that faith would ever again be the backbone of my existence.

"We'll see. If my life's been bad, Muffin's has been hell. She lost her daddy one time. I'll not take him from her again."

~~~~~

Neither Daniel nor I were donor matches. I tried to talk my daughter out of testing but, as usual, was no match for an impassioned Muffin.

"*Duh*! Mama! Look around you. Blood kin? *I'm it!*" thrusting out her hands, she angled me a condescending, scathing look. "Don't you get it?" She rounded on the doctor and insisted, "Test me, Dr. Wood."

Dr. Wood looked at me, half-apologetically, half-puzzled. "She's the logical candidate, Mrs. Stone."

Terror ravaged me as I pasted on a calm face. Dear *Lord! How can I divert this from happening?* My heart pounded in my ears and chest so loudly I could hardly hear the doctor's words. I cast Daniel a frantic look, then Doretha, who appeared dug-in with us for the long haul. Though she still distanced herself from Walter, she hung closely with me, offering endless support, from running errands to taming Sunny. She remained an enigma to me.

Help! shrieked my heart as I gazed helplessly at my friends.

Daniel said, "Muffin should test if she wants to. She wants to do something for her daddy." His gaze held mine, relaying a message: *humor her.*

Doretha's sad hazel eyes implored. "Daniel's right, Sunny."

I sighed deeply. "Okay," I muttered, still reluctant. "Of course you want to help Daddy, Muffin. Go ahead." *It won't prove anything if she doesn't match. Will it?* Years of duplicity warred against exposure. "I just hate for you to go through anything invasive or painful."

Muffin rolled her eyes. Dr. Wood grinned. "Spoken like a true mother. I'll assure you the tests won't be uncomfortable."

Except for me. As Muffin left with the doctor, a foreboding fell over me. One that threatened to smother the life from me. I gazed plaintively at Daniel and Doretha, my allies, my protectors, and groped for humor. "You two look like yesterday's leftovers."

Neither smiled. Doretha said, "Try not to worry, Sunny."

"Wouldn't help." I sank into a chair, propped my tired feet on the bed rail, closed my eyes and tried to relax. "As the old saying goes, its outta my hands."

~~~~~

I slept little that night on the hospital cot set up for me in Walter's room. Walter was restless, too. Aside from his lingering weakness, I think he sensed my desolation, though I tried hard to hide it.

"What's wrong, Sunny?" he finally croaked as I gave him water, worry in his blood-shot, sky-blue eyes.

"Nothing, honey." I leaned to hug him. Lordy, his skin felt hot. "Just tired. But there *will* be something wrong if you don't get some rest." I kissed his creased brow, readjusted his sheet and plumped his pillow. As I turned to go, he caught my arm.

"What is it?" I asked, troubled.

"Would you — you know, tell me about when Muffin was little?" he asked almost shyly. And my heart melted. It took so little to make Walter happy. And so I pulled a chair

up bedside and did just that. By the time I got to her tod-
dlerhood, he was fast asleep.

~~~~~

Walter's strength didn't come back as I'd hoped. X-rays
and MRIs filled the following days and hours. Each day
Walter seemed a little more limp and quiet. I asked the staff
about it but they remained evasive. "Ask Dr. Wood," they
always insisted. When I did, he said they were trying medications and to 'sit tight' and see how they would work. Said
Walter was too weakened for a liver transplant at present.

Grimly, Dr. Wood ordered further tests.

Emaline came a couple days later. "I'm gonna sit with
you," she said, grinning like a little Cheshire kitten and suddenly, the hospital room lost its tiresomeness, began to fizz
actually. For a few hours, the chamber became enchanted
as Emaline and I reminisced and giggled over growing-up
times.

Walter even rallied, perking up a little at some of our
outlandish recollections. "You didn't, did you, Sunny?" he'd
ask and Emaline would bobble her dark head up and down.
"Oh yes, she did, Walter. Trust me." And we would roar
with laughter at his disbelief until he, too, would begin to
chortle weakly.

Doretha joined us late morning, then Muffin near noon.
Daniel wasn't due till later in the day.

While Walter napped, we all traipsed downstairs to
the hospital cafeteria for a leisurely lunch. With friends to
buffer, Muffin was downright pleasant and I thought how
wonderful it was to simply enjoy being together. I indulged
in a rare mother/daughter fantasy, imagining that it would,
magically, always be so.

Then the foreboding I'd felt earlier descended again, like a black cloud, snuffing my joy. I grew quiet, watching the others interact, with Muffin being so animated and over-the-top entertaining...Emaline gushing good humor and fun...Doretha doing her quiet little *thang* with her gentle snicker-laugh and soft words.

Yet — I couldn't shake the portent hanging heavily in the air as we returned to check on Walter. When we rounded a corner in the corridor I nearly collided with Dr. Wood. I laughed shakily as he put his hand on my shoulder to steady me.

"I just left Mr. Stone's room," he said, his expression settling into gravity.

"Wh — is something wrong?" I asked. "Walter...?"

He avoided my gaze. "I'm going to order a couple more tests on him. But I do have some good news."

"What?" I was desperate for some good news. Anything to turn away the goshawful blackness hovering about me.

He looked at Muffin then. "You're a perfect donor-match for your dad." He smiled at me then, an *I-knew-it* one.

Muffin lit up, then slapped her hands over her mouth, too choked to speak. Tears filled her eyes, puddled, then splashed over.

Perfect donor match. Icy shock stealthily oozed through me as I watched the tears glide between her fingers. I looked at Doretha, who'd gone incredibly pale. Then at Emaline, who looked perplexed. Stunned. Woodenly, I walked over to Muffin and slid my arms around her. It was a knee-jerk, numb gesture but something deep inside me said she needed it.

Dr. Wood continued in his evasive way. "In the meantime, Mr. Stone's strength is going somewhere. He's too weakened for a liver transplant at present. I'll schedule a regimen of tests for tomorrow and we'll go from there."

That was when Daniel walked in. He took one look at us and knew that somehow, for whatever reason, the stink had hit the fan.

~~~~~

Muffin left the hospital to meet a friend for dinner. I was ridiculously relieved to drop all pretense. I could acknowledge that my world had been turned upside down and remained grotesquely tilted. Emaline left because of Wednesday evening prayer service at church. She hugged me at the door, remaining inordinately silent, watching me like a mother hen. I gave her a tight smile of reassurance, drawing it from God-only-knew *where*.

Only Doretha, Daniel, and I remained. The silence sizzling between us was of the uniquely stunned variety. Exhausted, Walter slept like the dead.

"Let's go get some supper." Daniel stood and reached for my hand. Reluctantly, I let him help me to my feet, astonished at how my legs vibrated beneath me. As one, we three silently made our way to the nearly deserted hospital cafeteria. Each in his own thoughts, we filled plates with food and took seats at a lone corner table. I took one bite of something and chewed. The wad grew bigger and bigger — I couldn't swallow it. I discreetly spat it into my napkin and slowly sipped coffee.

Daniel watched me with somber eyes. I avoided them. I wasn't ready for what lurked there.

Suddenly, Doretha sat forward, elbows on table, startling me with her atypically swift movement. "Sunny, we gotta talk."

I closed my eyes, felt my head begin to spin like a crazy off-balance top.

"I'm not ready for this." I pressed shaking fingers to my forehead and realized I didn't feel it. The numbness was back. The blankness. I welcomed it. I didn't want to know.

"You've gotta face it, Sunny," Daniel said huskily.

"No," I whispered, rebuffing reality. I shoved back my chair, then laid hold onto the table long moments for balance, during which I felt Daniel's hands gently but firmly steady me, then turn me until our gazes collided.

For long moments he just looked at me, emotions roiling in those turquoise depths. I felt nothing. Like a Lon Chaney zombie. Like I'd been baptized in Novocaine and gulped a gallon in the process. Something weird kept knocking around in my brain, something evil and horrifying that salivated to reveal itself.

I shook off Daniel's hands and retreated, staggering like a wino. Desperation kept me moving, racing from the footsteps trailing me.

"Sunny," Doretha stepped around me, blocking me, forcing me to stop. I averted my eyes and attempted to pass her, only to have Daniel's bulk abort my escape. "*Sunny,*" she spoke as sharply as I'd ever heard her speak. She took my chin between her gentle hands and forced me to look at her. "There's somethin' you gotta know."

For an instant I turned rigid as stone. My very soul was Normandy Beach. Doretha saw the panic. "You can handle it, Sunny," she softly reassured me but from the tremor in her voice, I'm not sure she really believed it herself.

"C'mon, Sunny," Daniel murmured hoarsely. "Let's brace up and get past this."

Let's brace up.... The fight in me fizzled and my knees turned to gelatin. Daniel had a good grip on my arm,

374 *Emily Sue Harvey*

though, and the two of them shepherded me down the hall to a deserted waiting room. There, Daniel settled me onto a settee and lowered himself beside me and I knew it was to buttress me in *whatever.*

Let's brace up. I lifted my chin, looked Doretha in the eye and said, "Okay. Let's have it."

Oh, I sounded so brave. Inside, I was scared spitless.

Doretha crossed her ankles, clasped her birdlike hands and sighed deeply. "Daniel told me that them blood tests and all prove that Walter is Muffin's daddy."

Daniel stirred. "Not proved, Doretha. *Indicated.*"

"Same thing." She didn't blink a deep-set eye. "Cause I know for a fact he is."

There was absolute silence. It roared in my ears and my delete button, for once, skipped town. "H-how do you know?" I rasped, my heart sprinting away like a crazy riderless race car. It went on for what seemed like eternity as Doretha sat there demurely, sickly pale, harnessing the courage to say what she had to say.

Doretha shot Daniel a steady, apologetic look. "I'm sorry, Daniel. I done you wrong, too, in keepin' quiet. I know this'll cause both o'you to hate me but I gotta set things straight. I don't blame you if you never have nothin' to do with me again."

"Heaven help us, Doretha!" Daniel exploded, as nervous as a bagged tomcat. "What do you know that we don't?" He shot a concerned glance at me.

Doretha licked her lips and looked down at her white, white hands, still folded in her lap. "That night you stayed at the house, Sunny, when you got — attacked," she paused and drew in another deep breath, exhaled, then looked at me. "Well, there was a reason I asked you to stay with me. I *was* scared, but not of somebody breaking in."

Her eyes sheened with tears. "See...Walter had been sneaking into my room all through the years, since I was thirteen, crawling into my bed and puttin' his filthy hands over my mouth to keep me from —" Tears spilled over her lids, trailing down her pale, thin face. She bit her lip for long moments, fighting for composure, her small teeth turning the skin white.

I sucked in air as if surfacing from unfathomable ocean depths. I felt as though somebody had socked me in the stomach and my breath refused to work. I'd thought, at first, that this might be one of Doretha's quirky little misconceptions of life.

Something far, far more sinister hurtled its way toward me, a flaming evil from which I could no longer hide

Daniel looked impaled on his chair, stunned. Suddenly, in one spastic motion, his torso thrust forward, his olive features corrugated with anger, puzzlement. "Why didn't I pick up on that, Doretha?" He held out his hands in supplication, regret. "I never had any idea —"

Doretha gave her little Mona Lisa smile, one that barely grazed her colorless lips. "He was too smart for that. He'd only come when he was sure you was asleep. Cause I threatened to holler out for you but he just laughed and slapped his hand over my mouth when I would start to scream. He was too strong for —" She had to pause again, eyes downcast, fingers clasped tightly, biting her lip.

"Anyway, Sunny," she forced herself to continue, eyes peering at the floor, and even through my fog of shock, I sensed how excruciating this was for her, "that night you stayed at the house with me, when his daddy was in the hospital, I asked you to stay cause I was afraid Walter would do exactly what he done." Her stricken gaze snapped up and latched onto mine. "I thought if he sneaked in and saw it was *you* in my bed, that he'd just tiptoe back out and disappear."

She gulped another rush of air and I saw her hands tremble violently as she latched her fingers together tighter. "When I dropped off to sleep up in Mama's room, I figured we was okay there at the house. He was at the hospital with Mama, anyway."

"Walter hadn't been to my room for a long time and I figured that maybe he wouldn't come no more. But when you screamed, I jumped off the bed and I knowed," she whispered. Her face crumpled as she shook her head slowly from side to side. Fresh tears cropped up. "I *knowed it was him.*"

For long moments, only her quiet sniffling broke the silence. I sat glued to my chair, heavy iron to a magnet, dark emotions roiling like a witch's brew. *The loud click I'd heard that night — Walter had re-locked the front door so as not to be detected, then leaped through the screen to make it look like a break-in.*

Then Doretha drew herself up, wiped her face, and looked at me again, determination slicing through her grief. "I know you won't ever be able to forgive me. Neither of you. Cause I stole your chance to be together." She slashed Daniel a look of utter contrition. "Cause I could've told you the truth. Only thing — I was afraid you'd do something foolish, Daniel. I didn't want to see you in prison or electrocuted over such a no-account as Walter."

Daniel, who'd been as silent and riveted as me suddenly sprang to his feet. "But — you let me *leave* Sunny," he scowled ferociously and ran an agitated hand through his midnight hair, now peppered with gray. With an animal-like groan, he paced to the window to stare out into the night, slamming hands into back jean pockets as though restraining them, as whipcord thin as when he was a youth.

"I tried to tell you, in my own way, but you wouldn't let me," Doretha fairly whispered, so emotionally spent was she.

He spun and glared at her. "Your *own way?* You only told me she'd been raped. How about the whole truth? Huh? That would've made a difference, you know. It just gave Walter a chance to move in on Sunny in her weakest hour." He took one step and halted, throwing his head back for a long moment, eyes closed tightly. "*God.* You just wanted to foist Walter off on Sunny, didn't you?" He looked at her then, eyes sparkling green fury. "To get 'im off your back. I remember how you avoided him. You could have told me. Or your Mama. Why didn't you?"

Doretha took Daniel's anger square on the chin. Only thing, she was white as a soda cracker, like one breath huff would topple her. Her voice was wispy as wind whispering through thick pines. "I did tell Mama. But it was too late for 'er to help me. She was already forgetting things or getting' 'em turned around. Ol' Tom didn't pay her no mind when she tried to tell 'im. I could tell he didn't want to know." She shrugged limply. "He sure as heck wouldn't have believed me."

"I would've believed you, Doretha," Daniel muttered darkly.

She swallowed hard and fought to speak. "I — I'm being honest now. And for once, I *will* tell the whole truth. The real truth is that you're right, Daniel. I did want to get rid of Walter. I would have died if he'd kept on —" She shuddered and closed her eyes tightly for long moments. When they opened they appeared dazed, desperate. "Else, I would'a killed 'im."

Her eyes begged understanding. "When he fell for you, Sunny, and was so good to you after Daniel left — didn't seem to care about you and your shame, I thought how it might be the best thing, you and Walter together. It would give your baby a name."

Daniel spun, strode to within inches of her and his eyes glimmered fury. "And it would free you from Walter." He slowly shook his head. " And I thought you were my sister."

Doretha visibly cringed but she stood and with great effort pulled her fragile cloak of dignity about her. Her eyes, focused at me, held such pain and regret it took my breath. My heart lurched at her ravaged, pale features. "I know I can't do nothing to make up to you for what I done, Sunny. But I want you to know that I love you. Both of you. If I could go back and do it different I'd do it. I'd give my life to give yours and Daniel's back to you." She pulled her purse strap up over her thin shoulder and shuffled dispiritedly out the door.

~~~~~

After Doretha left, Daniel watched me like a hawk, his brow creased with worry. I must have looked a sight because he appeared apprehensive, fearing I'd go off like dynamite any second. He didn't want to leave me later that evening, after visiting hours. But I insisted he go. Needed him to go. Assured him I was okay. Convinced him. Finally, reluctantly, he left when I promised to call if I needed him.

In my solitude, numbness wrapped and sealed me, insulating me from *it*.

I undressed, slid into my gown and robe and into bed.

Heavily sedated, Walter slept. I lay on the hospital cot in the semi-gloom of nightlights, watching him. Far down inside me, a rage quivered. It had been building ever since Doretha's earlier waiting-room revelations. With the memories, the numbness was beginning to dissipate beneath the quivering.

I closed my eyes. Not a hint of drowsiness slithered behind them. I opened them and, glaring at the ceiling, replayed Doretha's disclosures.

The night seemed eternal.

~~~~~

I must have dozed sometime in the early morning hours. When I came instantly and fully awake, dawn's silver light filtered through the hospital blinds. Inhaling hospitals' universal, ever-prevalent antiseptic smells, I arose then showered in the bathroom. Needling sprays of hot water brought my circulation into sluggish action again and when I looked at myself in the mirror, my ashen features peered back through steam-fogged glass. I wiped it down with a towel. From it, my eyes, large and slightly puffed from sleep, stared at me, no longer dull and dispassionate, but shimmering with rage.

Adrenaline bolstered and readied me for combat.

I quickly dressed, hoping the noise I made slamming things around had awakened Walter. But when I returned to the room, he'd not stirred. I refused to be deterred any longer. I dragged a chair up to the bed and stared into his sleeping face.

"How *could* you Walter?" I said in a chilling voice not at all like my own. "All those years and you *never let on.*" I crossed my arms and my jean-clad legs and jiggled my white Reebok foot. "Man, were you *good!* " I gave a nasty laugh, stopped jiggling my foot and shifted forward, closer to his ear, my hands white-knuckling the bed rail. His brow creased just a little. Good.

"Doretha told me about how you abused her all through the years. How she hated your guts. How she got me to sleep over that night because she was afraid you'd do just what you did."

My breath grew shallow. I struggled for air to speak. "S-she thought you'd sneak back in...find me in her bed and —" My breath hitched on a sob. "Thought you'd leave, not bother m-me." Tears now rolled down my cheeks as I ground out the words between clenched teeth. "But you *didn't, did you, Walter?* You *raped* me." I spit in his face and he flinched, eyes still tightly shut.

"Wake up, you miserable liar!" I sobbed. His eyes opened then, stunned, confused. I felt not an ounce of sympathy for him. I watched my spittle dribble down his cheek, onto the pillow as he peered at me, dazed.

"You stole my life, Walter," I snarled as the world around me turned red, then purple. " By God, it was *my* life! *My body! Mine! You-stole-it!*" I trembled so violently that the bed, gripped in my hands, rattled noisily. Walter's eyes white-rimmed with panic, but I was beyond caring. "What you did was *evil! Monstrous! And I hate you for it. Do you hear me? I hate you!*" I was on my feet in the next instant, fists raised in the air. I wanted to hit him so badly —

"*What are you doing!*"

I whirled at the shrill scream, arms still raised, tears streaming. I blinked at her, looming in the doorway, the jolt of her appearance stemming my sobs. Her face was pale as burnt-out ashes, eyes glassy and wild. I slowly lowered my arms, felt myself spinning, spinning downward, like a free-falling 747, knowing I was going to crash painfully.

"Muffin." Her name wrested from my mouth on a thin wheeze of air.

She descended on me, claws and fangs bared. "What're you *doing to* my daddy?" she wailed angrily, *protectively*. "What do you mean telling 'im he's *evil?*" She burst into tears. "That you hate 'im? A-and him so *sick....*" She rushed to him then and gathered him into her arms, weeping. "S-he didn't mean it, Daddy." She shot me a scornful look. "She's nuttier'n a fruitcake."

Even in my own fury, I knew how it all looked to her.

Walter began to cry then, the bawling, little boy kind. I watched in horror as he clutched Muffin to him, moaning, "She told me I done terrible things, Muffin." He cast me a desperate look. "What did I *do,* Sunny?" He swung his head from side to side, eyes pouring tears. "I didn't mean it. I wouldn't do nothing bad to you, S-Sunny!" He stretched out a trembling hand to me.

"Don't, Daddy," Muffin murmured, holding him closer, tears coursing down her wan cheeks.

Heart pounding like a sluggish bass drum, I peered at the two of them, feeling spiked walls closing in on me. *Tell her the truth.* I opened my mouth to speak, inhaled sharply, and nothing came out. The air hissed from my lungs. I snapped my mouth shut. I couldn't do this to Muffin. *Not if it killed me.* In that moment, I wasn't sure it wouldn't.

Woodenly, I moved over to the bed and took Walter's hand. Muffin scurried away as if I were a walking contaminant. Walter burst into fresh sobs and gazed at me, blue eyes pleading. "Sunny," he rasped, "please don' hate me."

I sucked in a deep breath, blew it out. "I don't hate you, Walter," I lied. I didn't want to look at him but beneath Muffin's x-ray scrutiny I forced myself to focus on his top pajama button and give him a wobbly smile. "I'm sorry."

He visibly slumped in relief, clutching my hand so tightly I nearly groaned from pain. And suddenly I felt like the Wicked Witch of the West. What had I been thinking of, ranting at him like that? In Walter's child-like mind, it *had never happened.*

My mind was another matter entirely. My memory was clear as fresh-caught rain. Even after all those years the horrors of that night cropped up like garbage at the county landfill. My flesh smelled the rot and felt the slime oozing through me. I shuddered.

I looked at Muffin's ramrod back. She'd gone to stare out the window. *Walter IS her father. At least I don't have to hurt her in that way.* I called the nurse to give Walter a sedative to settle him. Muffin ignored me as the shot took effect, refused to even look at me. Me? I felt like a piece of dead wood waiting for the ax to fall. After Walter drifted off, I picked up my purse.

"Where you going?" asked Muffin from across the room, distanced from me, her face inscrutable.

"Coffee."

She followed me out. I was under no delusion that I was off the hook.

I wasn't wrong.

"I've been trying to figure out why you treated Daddy like that." Her voice was quiet. Eerily quiet yet pulsing with nuclear energy. "I didn't hear all the conversation, just where you called him 'evil and monstrous'. I really don't understand. Why don't you explain?"

I couldn't tell her that she'd been conceived when her daddy raped me. I just couldn't. Not even to save myself. It wouldn't help my case, anyway. She'd feel even more justified to hate me. Even more convinced I didn't truly love and value her. How could I, when she'd resulted not from love but from rape? No, she couldn't handle the truth.

God help me, neither could I.

I had no time to formulate a credible justification for lashing out at my sick, defenseless husband. *Husband.* I nearly gagged on the term. Recoiled from it. I knew that, to Muffin, I was despicable. So I threw myself at her mercy, knowing full well it wasn't there. "I just lost it, Muffin," I fabricated lamely and shrugged. "I'm burnt out. I just got tired of his demands and I just — lost it."

We walked on several steps as she processed that and as my pulse switched tempos several times, each more erratic.

"Well, just for the record," she paused at the exit door and cast me a withering look. "I hope you die and rot in Hell. I'll never forgive you. *Never.*"

Sick at heart, I watched my beautiful daughter, skirt swishing around long, brisk legs, disappear through swinging glass doors.

<u>Chapter Twenty</u>

Fortunately, in coming days, I didn't have to squirm beneath Muffin's accusing light-washed eyes. She currently lived with a man she'd met at a nightclub.

They all sounded alike to me, the men, faces, and backgrounds kaleidoscopic images, ever changing. In retrospect they all merged into a multicolored, nondescript blob. Between liaisons, she always came home, to her old cluttered room.

Through the years, her housekeeping had not altered a whit. I've never known anybody to court mess like Muffin. She gloried in, *rolled* in it. Piled ankle-deep were clothes, shoes, spilled pills, discarded candy and goody wrappers, dirty dishes, make-up bag, hair carry-all (gypsy-hearted, she stayed on *ready*, to move out at a moment's whim), luggage still half-packed. You name it, it was there, strewn from wall to wall, spanning under-the-bed, trailing across nightstand, dresser, and chest-of-drawers. She remained blissfully unencumbered by it all.

I'd considered the possibility that one of three things propelled her in that direction: (1) rebellion against my penchant for cleanliness, (2) slothfulness, or (3) she had a mental problem. Perhaps a lethal combination of all three was my final surmise.

Whatever triggered Muffin's mystical love affair with clutter, I never found its antidote. One development overshadowed the crisis following Doretha's divulgences.

Dr. Wood faced me three days after I learned of Walter's deception, somber as I'd ever seen him. "Mr. Stone has cancer. It's spread to the lungs and lymph nodes. I'm so sorry. We'll make him as comfortable as possible during the little time he has left. Needless to say, a liver transplant is out of the question. He'd never live through it."

He watched me closely, concerned, waiting for a response. Something. "What about chemo?" I asked, thinking what *irony*, that all Muffin's donor-match status accomplished was to expose Walter's evil.

"We could go that route but I'll have to be honest with you. It would only give him, at most, four to six months."

I felt certain the good doctor attributed my lack of response to shock. The news rolled off me as though oiled canvas sheathed me. I was, predictably, numb again, encased in an invisible crystal bubble, one bullet and arrow-proof. One that kept feelings at bay.

I'd done a lot of thinking in the past week, since Doretha's divulgences, and all of it reaffirmed what I'd known all along: something inside me was wrong. Flawed. I drew scandal and shame like a lightning rod during a summer thunderstorm. Seemed, too, that everybody around me got struck, to some degree.

So, I reasoned that the best thing for me to do was to let go of them all.

That way, nobody'd get hurt.

~~~~~

Muffin vetoed the chemo regimen after one treatment left Walter violently ill. She refused to allow any more. Walter's health plunged dramatically from one month to the next. I took him home for his final days. Already weakened by the automobile accident, he never regained any of his former resilience. I prayed he did not detect my revulsion every time I had to touch him. I tried to hide it and felt I succeeded.

"Here," Lee Roy took the wash cloth from my hand. "Let me do that." Grateful beyond words, I arose from my stiff, aching knees and Lee Roy knelt beside the bathtub to help Walter finish his bath.

Walter smiled weakly at his old buddy. "How's it goin', Lee Roy?"

Lee Roy grinned like a possum. "If I was any better, I'd be flyin'."

"Y'seen Daniel lately?" Walter asked, his voice gossamer thin, but I detected in it a thread of anxiety. At moments like this, Walter's insecurity bled through.

"Naw. Daniel's kep' hisself scarce these days."

"Muffin hasn't been around much, either." Walter's words were flute-like and dismal.

Muffin did drop by daily to check on her daddy but her visit was more a fly's lighting than a butterfly's linger. She completely froze me out so I pretty much kept out of her way. Her curtailed times made Walter more vulnerable and lonely. To cover my own distancing, I called on Lee Roy more and more.

Walter missed Daniel. With no memory of the past, he couldn't connect the dots for the whole picture. So, he simply yearned to see people he loved. At times, my mind did battle over the complexities of the situation. I always opted to push my denial button. That way, I could ignore the emotional ramifications of an up-close insight.

It was too much to handle. So I didn't.

Daniel and I talked little after that night at the hospital. He called and tried to break through my wall of resistance. I sensed his own anger at Walter's betrayal, but he wisely banked it down. He would later tell me that his tight-mouthed reticence sprang from knowing that just a word in that direction could push me over the edge. In that case, many people would be hurt, the chief one being Muffin.

No, Daniel simply encouraged me to talk to him about my feelings, hoping it would relieve the terrible anxiety he sensed gathered in me like a hive of bees, whose low-buzz activity could, in one provoked moment, implode into a vicious frenzied attack. But for me, to talk about it was to experience it. So I remained implacable. I had to. I'd attracted too much heartache, so much so that it had splashed over on those I loved.

Days of joy, light, and hope were a thing of a long ago forgotten youth. *Did I ever really experience those happy times?* I briefly wondered, my wet hands pausing, my head spinning. I slid dirty glasses into the dishwater. Nowadays, my path always seemed to lead into deep woods, shrouded with low-hanging fog and gray shadows.

"I got 'im back in bed," Lee Roy said from the bedroom doorway. He ambled over to me at the sink. "I'm kinely worried 'bout 'im, Sunny," he said quietly, placing his and Walter's dishes on the counter. "He seems real down today. It's not like 'im to not talk. Like he's givin' up, dontcha know?" He shrugged listlessly, grief pulling at his grizzled features. "I hate to leave 'im but I gotta go work on them new neighbors' lawn mower." He waved over his shoulder as he shuffled out.

Suddenly, I felt a rush of guilt. Walter was in his last days.

You don't owe him anything.

Maybe not but — I began scraping and washing lunch dishes, busying myself so as not to think. It didn't work. My loyalties were jerked about so in recent days that my *numb* and *denial* buttons did double-time. I noted that Walter had barely touched his green bean casserole, one of his favorites. Pity hovered.

No, in one sense I don't owe him. At least not in the sense that I once thought I did. But at the same time, I thought of how he was no longer the Walter who'd violated me. And I thought how his time was running out. Least I could do was make the days as pleasant and comfortable as possible.

I'd do as much for a stray dog.

Pity crashed over me in tidal waves. The hard shell around my heart cracked loudly, split.

I gazed through the window at the sun-washed day. Across the back alley, kids bounced acrobatically on a trampoline. A new family. More and more of the old families were moving away to the suburbs. An invisible conveyer belt soon deposited strangers into those empty spaces. They came from all sides.

Sadness washed over me.

Then, an idea struck me. Walter's birthday loomed on a near horizon. I would do something to cheer him up.

I sighed. Maybe in the long run a little of the cheer would splatter over on me.

~~~~~

Lee Roy was beside himself helping plan Walter's party. Daily, Libby called from Summerville, she and Kara both determined to be in the family loop of preparations. In the end, we decided against keeping it a secret. It was the right decision.

Walter visibly rallied in those days as we gathered colorful decorations, laying them out for his approval, planned refreshments, and prepared an invitation list. I let him listen as I called practically everybody in the village, reaping near-unanimous participation.

Again, we opted for the Church Fellowship Hall. "What if he's not able to sit for the entire evening, Emaline?" I whispered so Walter wouldn't overhear. He and Lee Roy watched an old rerun of *Murder She Wrote* on TV, Walter dozing off-and-on in bed, Lee Roy roosting in his chair, now pulled close to the new hospital bed Libby and Scott purchased and had delivered.

"Then we'll just transport his hospital bed there to prop him in," she said so logically I had to laugh. "Good idea, huh?"

"You always come up with good'uns, Emaline."

"What good'uns?" piped Lee Roy from the other room, craning his long neck to see us, cocking his ear toward the open door.

"Nothing, *nosey*," I yelled back and heard his gleeful chortle, one echoed drowsily by Walter's.

Emaline slid me her benevolence-smile and whispered, "You're doing me proud, Sunny."

My responding smile was tight, but a smile nevertheless. Then she casually said, "You're going to invite Doretha, aren't you?" Her emerald eyes were big and round and innocent.

I stared at her for a long moment, then snarled, "Don't push it."

~~~~~

"I wish I didn't have to stay in bed," Walter rasped, his breath mildly labored. Number four on the scale of one to ten.

"Well, you do," I said gently, straightening his collar and tucking the sheet corners again. He wore pajama bottoms with the new blue shirt, a compromise for comfort. "This way, you won't tire and have to leave your own party, doncha know?" I was surprised that, sometime during those planning days, the disgust I'd felt for Walter stole away into the darkness of a moonless night.

At some point something deep inside me had compartmentalized the old and new Walter. For the moment, the former evil man lay tucked away somewhere unknown to me.

"Yeh," he groaned dispiritedly.

"Look, Walter, there's Muffin!" I distracted him from his angst. He perked dramatically as she rushed to him. I quickly moved to other duties, dodging Muffin's contempt. Truth be known, I needed this party as much as Walter and wasn't willing to relinquish my good cheer to her whims, justified or not.

The Fellowship Hall shimmered with immense bouquets of riotous colored balloons and festive streamers. Walter's bed centered the great hall. Rolled up a ways, he could see everything that went on. While Gracie, Jared and Kara pampered their Papa, Emaline, Libby, and Francine hustled about mixing punch and arranging plates, napkins, and cutlery. A huge three-tiered birthday cake, compliments of Muffin, hovered next to the serving table. Carrot cake layers oozed thick, frothy cream-cheese icing, Walter's favorite.

Not too beholden to timetables, village folks started trickling in as much as an hour early. That was okay. We'd announced the time with that in mind so everything was in place. Nearly every long-time, able-bodied villager moseyed in during the evening. Daniel arrived with Doretha. I was a little taken back and it must have shown because Emaline was at my elbow in a heartbeat.

"Close your sweet mouth," she whispered in my ear. "To everything, there is a season."

I turned to glare at her. "You invited them."

"This is the season to forgive, Sunny," she added quietly. "Daniel forgave Doretha." She shrugged, "If you're honest, you'll admit you would've felt terrible leaving them out when the whole village was invited. It's for the best."

I dragged air into my lungs, held it, then slowly blew it out. "I don't know if I'm ready."

She just smiled at me, touched my arm briefly and was gone, leaving me feeling as if I were in somebody else's skin, strange and edgy.

Sheila's three exuberant daughters spilled through the door, dressed in new, expensive avant-garde fashions. They each hugged me hugely then went to spoil their Uncle Walter.

I wandered to a quiet corner to rest a moment and watch Walter's interaction with his guests. From a distance he looked incredibly old and feeble, barely responding as he tired. But in a symphony of love, everybody seemed to know exactly what notes were needed for harmony; a hug, a handclasp, a big ol' face-splitting grin, or soft spoken words of affection. Walter smiled often, reaching out as much as his illness allowed him.

Good.

My lips struggled into a smile and I noted how big the effort, how draining all this was for me. I didn't know anyone had approached until the seat next to me, against the wall, filled. "Gladys isn't here."

I looked into Daniel's eyes. They were sad, so terribly sad that I felt a twinge of response. A tiny flicker, then it was gone. Feelings were no longer an option for me.

"She's in a nursing home now," I said, glancing away, seeing Lee Roy dab at Walter's mouth with a napkin. I looked closer, hoping he'd not gotten sick —

No. A bit of the broth he sipped had dribbled was all. I relaxed.

"I'm sorry to hear that, Sunny." We sat there for long moments in silence, his gaze on me. I didn't look at him. "Where've you gone off to?" Daniel asked. "Where's that girl whose smile used to light up Tucapau like a million spotlights?"

I shrugged. "I don't know, Daniel." I looked at him. "I just know she's no longer around." I looked away.

"That's too bad," he said gently. "I miss 'er."

He arose and I watched him saunter away, a little disappointed and at the same time relieved to be alone.

I fixed Walter a tall glass of iced ginger ale to sip in hopes it would settle his queasy stomach, knowing that he wouldn't be able to ingest the sandwiches, nachos, dips, potato salad, and all the other party fare. Lee Roy tried to get some more chicken broth down him later, as folks piled plates high and settled at tables to feast and celebrate.

Muffin pulled a chair up to Walter's bedside, alongside Libby, to eat and chat with him. I quietly retreated. I admired her devotion to him. I expired a little huff of a laugh. Rolled my gaze to the ceiling. *Surprise! I'm not jealous.*

I nibbled cold ham and cheese, my stomach balking after a few bites. I kept to myself, observing, thinking about what I'd write in my column that next week. The party, of course. It would be upbeat, no mention of Walter's illness. That would come soon enough.

"Can I sit down, Sunny?"

I looked up. Doretha stood there, uncertain, as forlorn as any Dickens' street urchin. From years of affection, my heart responded. "Sure. Take a load off."

"Thank you," she said softly and lowered her thin self into the chair next to me. "I appreciate you lettin' me come," she said. I heard her swallow. "I've missed you. You don't have to say nothin'. I just appreciate bein' here with y'all. I won't bother you none. That's all I wanted to tell you." She arose, eyes downcast, hands clasped before her. "Oh," she looked at me then, "I let Alvin come home."

My eyebrows shot up to my hairline. "Yeh?" She was a bag of surprises.

"Yeh. I figured that if you could forgive Walter and Daniel could forgive me, I could forgive Alvin." She cast her gaze down again. "Anyways, what I done to you and Daniel was as bad as anything Alvin coulda done." Eyes locked with mine again, those age-old, wizened gray eyes. "S'funny how you can forgive when you need forgiveness yourself, you know?"

I nodded slowly. "Yeh. I do know, Doretha." *It's called mercy.* I stood, gathered her skinny person into my arms. and hugged her tightly. Tears puddled in her eyes.

"Come on," I said, grabbing her hand and pulling her along. "Let's go sing to Walter."

We sang *Happy Birthday* as Daniel and Lee Roy wheeled the cart carrying the titanic birthday cake to Walter's bedside. "Look at how old you are, Walter," Lee Roy crowed.

"Them candles could light up a whole danged block." Then he valiantly blew out the candles for Walter, whose breath had grown shallower with evening's passage.

Muffin fed her daddy a bite of cake, after which he refused more. She crooned to him and washed his face with a damp washcloth. A knot formed in my throat. I looked away. He was her whole world. Envy, I realized, had given way to dread.

Dread for when he would no longer be there for her.

After which I would lose her for good.

~~~~~

The party left Walter in a comatose exhaustion. At least I thought it was exhaustion, till he remained that way for the better part of the next week. I called Dr. Wood and described his symptoms.

"Do you want to bring him back to the hospital, Mrs. Stone? We could make him as comfortable as possible. Or do you think he'd do better at home, surrounded by family and friends?"

"So — you're saying...."

"I'm sorry, Mrs. Stone. There's nothing else that can be done except keep him as comfortable as we can."

It was a no-brainer. "Home. I'd like him to be home."

So, in the end, that's where he passed away, peacefully, in his sleep, only two weeks later. I called Muffin as soon as I found him early that morning. I'd awakened suddenly at 4 a.m. and felt strange. Something was amiss. Walter had had a good day and drifted off to sleep with a contented look on his features.

But — that morning, something in the atmosphere didn't set quite right.

I dashed to his room. He hadn't moved. I leaned over and whispered, "Walter?" I touched his hand. I jerked back my fingers, scalded by his skin's iciness. I whiffed feces and I knew.

"*Oh, my God,*" I moaned, rushing to the phone to call Muffin. Before the words could all spill from my mouth, her phone had clattered to the floor. I called Libby in Summerville and wept with her. She and her family would be in by late that night. Muffin burst through my door within minutes, as shattered and fragile as a battered little bird, weeping and wailing and rocking, holding her daddy, oblivious to death's fetid odor.

I called Fitzhugh Powers, our now retired village policeman, friend, and guardian all through the years. He'd come by regularly to check on Walter and lift his spirits. His sweet wife, Pauline, would lift mine. "Don't you worry, Sunny," he said today, hugging me. "I'm here if you need anything."

Doretha and Emaline, whom I'd called after my daughters, stood by quietly and unobtrusively, oblivious to the import of their very presence. Daniel propped against a kitchen counter, arms and ankles crossed, eye and ear tuned to need. My, how they all buttressed me.

Dr. Fleming had pronounced Walter dead an hour earlier, having been summoned by Daniel, who'd taken over and, along with Emaline, was seeing to calling Wood Mortuary and all the other things death entails.

Lee Roy huddled in his easy chair next to the bed, face in hands, weeping inconsolably. Daniel moved to place soothing hands on his quaking shoulders.

A lump the size of Africa throbbed in my throat and chest. I tried to console Muffin but she brushed me away as she would a mosquito. So I moved to the window and stared helplessly past the roof lines to the river flowing beyond and thought how much I'd lost on these, her hilly shores, wishing my sweet Libby were already here. Having her around always made whatever load of the moment a little lighter.

When Emaline rushed to comfort Muffin, my daughter fell into her arms and surrendered her trust. An arrow pierced my heart. I was glad Emaline was there for Muffin. Still, the arrow gouged and burned.

Today's loss transcended all others. After all Walter had been my best friend for many years. But his death triggered another loss that rendered me without hope.

I gazed over the hills of my village, clinging to them, tearless and desolate and resigned because I *knew.*

Muffin was gone. It was just a matter of time.

~~~~~

Muffin took to her old room to grieve. I'd long ago purged it, propelled by sheer revulsion. Knowing she'd be gone for awhile, the reward of knowing it would remain sparkling clean for a spell was well worth all the backbreaking/sweaty exertion. I peeked in on her, sprawled face down on her bed, clothes already strewn hither and yon. She didn't move when I said quietly, "Muffin, do you need anything?"

"Yeh," she said flatly, her voice as rough as dried corn husks. "My daddy."

I softly shut the door and immediately heard something solid and hard hit with a loud *thud* from the other side. I flinched. A shoe, no doubt. Doretha, lingering outside the door, jumped, startled. "What was that?"

I shrugged, not bothering to answer. I'd handled worse. For now, Muffin was reclaiming her comfort zone. It helped her cope. And when she coped, I could handle everything else.

"You okay, Mama?" Having witnessed the little scene, Libby was at my side in an instant, her arm around my shoulders. She and Kara had driven up early, leaving Scott to wrap up loose business ends before he trekked to upstate for the funeral the next day.

I nodded, reassuring her, then moved to the kitchen where neighbors already appeared. Somber-faced, aproned genies loaded tables and counters with food and drink, answered phones, received visitors, and saw to the bereaved with military precision.

The Southern way. Bereaved folks do one thing: *grieve*. This rite intensifies on the mill hill where bonding is near-visceral, where grief's MO ranges from mindless weeping, such as Muffin's in the wee hours, Lee Roy's sporadic, quiet sobs, my white-faced, tearless desperation, to the good ol' boys' quiet humorous reminiscences and ribbing of each other, to the outside smokers brigade of total denial. It all fit. All deemed appropriate.

I acceded to Muffin and Libby's wishes for the funeral. It was the one time Muffin did confer with me, albeit formal and distant. Emaline's husband, Pastor John, conducted the simple service at the Methodist Church, where Walter had, in later years, attended with me. In his own childlike way, he'd accepted every sermon as gospel.

Muffin wept at Pastor John's recollections. She'd strategically placed herself between Gracie and Jared, with me to Gracie's left and Libby next. That was okay. Gracie was so *there* for her mama. So was Jared. I marveled at the beautiful adults they'd become.

I smiled to myself. *See Muffin? I'm not a total washout.* Gracie's hand squeezed mine in that moment, as though she read my mind. We gazed at each other and smiled, sharing a timeless blood-related connection. Emaline stood and sang a benediction song, *Amazing Grace*, Muffin's choice. The distance between my daughter and me seemed infinite but warmth filled me that she'd loved her father so.

After the funeral, family and friends returned to the house, where more food burgeoned from the table and fridge. Church ladies moved silently about, seeing to every need, unobtrusive and gracious and kind. While cousins visited all over the house, Libby, Emaline. and Pastor John mingled, filling in conversation and greetings, enabling me to collapse in a chair and move not a hair nor utter one sound for the duration of the meal.

"Mama," Libby knelt to hug me good-bye," I hate to leave you but Kara's got classes tomorrow and —"

"You go on now, y'hear? I don't want you driving late into the night. I'll be okay."

I touched her hair and her cheek, soaking up the love flowing freely from her generous heart. Her eyes misted and she hugged me again. "I love you so, Mama," she whispered in my ear.

"I love you, too, darlin' daughter. Be careful driving." After Kara's warm embrace and kiss, they departed, leaving a Grand Canyon void.

Francine pulled up a chair beside me and sat down, rousing me from the stupor that gripped me. I blinked back misty webs of lethargy and peered into her red, puffy eyes. Oh yes, she grieved full-throttle for Walter, the perfect *sexy* man of her younger heyday. Even now I didn't have it in me to disillusion her with the whole truth.

"I got somethin' to tell you." She reached to take my numb hand, surprising me. She gazed at our linked fingers, long and slender appendages so alike I now marveled at the heritage from our long-gone mother.

"I done something I shoulda done long time ago. You know that house Tack wanted his sister to have, that he put in his last will? Well, I decided to sign it over to Elaine last week and —" Her face crumpled and she bit her lip. Francine hated mushy emoting, denigrated anybody who did it. But I watched in amazement as she did just that. I squeezed her fingers.

She snuffled stoically, stuck out her chin, still a fairly tight, pretty one even on an older woman. "Anyway, I told her after the funeral I wanted her to have the house and she was so grateful and happy she said she wanted to dance a jig." She snorted. "'Course she didn't. It's not in 'er. She's still too whacked-up by that deadbeat, Gene." She rolled her eyes upward, "God rest his sorry soul." She gazed at me again, eyes ablaze with anger. "'Course Junior took up the slack his daddy left and robs 'er blind. The house is somethin' he can't take."

I felt a trickle of warmth and embraced her for long moments. "I'm real proud of you, honey. You did the right thing. At least Elaine won't have to worry about rent now. She'll have a nice, warm place of her own. Was it all right with Martin?"

"Oh," she waved a hand, "my darlin' husband does what I want, doncha know, Sunny?" She winked slyly at me.

"You're lucky, Francine," I said, meaning it. Not many men would delight in Francine's quirks and love her to high heaven, unconditionally. Hers did.

Most everybody'd left by now. After Francine departed, the last of the church ladies packed away leftovers, wiped and swept up every last stray crumb in the kitchen, then vanished. I sat there in that easy chair for a long time, eyes closed, mind shut down except for the lingering good feeling about Francine's turn of heart.

At first, the sound didn't register. From upstairs the female voices could have been a too-loud television volume. Then I realized it wasn't coming from a TV. I got up and made my way up the carpeted stairs, dreading a possible clash with Muffin but feeling compelled to check out the racket.

As I drew near her closed door, I recognized Doretha's voice. Something in it halted me mid-stride, hand on doorknob. Muffin wept and moaned.

I opened the door. They both looked at me with red, swollen eyes. Muffin appeared dazed, out of it. I stepped inside, in one sweep of eyes taking in the slowly encroaching clutter, empty closets, and bulging suitcases readied to vacate.

I'd been expecting it but had hoped she'd stay at least a few days to acclimate to her loss. "You don't have to go, you know, Muffin," I said quietly. "You can —"

Abruptly, she stood. "Oh, but I do." She lazily slid her purse over her shoulder. "I can't stomach another hour in this house. With Daddy gone, I'm outta here for good." I'd thought myself toughened to Muffin's gibes. But now, facing an endless estrangement, her words slashed me to threads.

"You can't do this," Doretha stepped forward and gripped Muffin's arm. "Muffin, you don't know ev —"

"Doretha!" I spoke so sharply even Muffin looked startled.

Doretha peered imploringly at me. "But she needs to —"

"Don't you *dare*," I literally snarled.

"Don't dare *what?*" Muffin demanded, eyes darting from one to the other, baffled and curious. "What don't you want me to know, Mama?" Her eyes narrowed. "What've you done now?"

"It's not what *she's* done," Doretha snapped, defying my challenge.

"Doretha, if you say one more word, " I fairly hissed, "I'll never speak another word to you as long as I live. And you can carry that to the bank."

Muffin caught my arm and spun me nose to nose with her. "What're you hiding from me? What horrible thing are you keeping from me now? Huh?" Her mouth flattened into a tight slash of cynicism. "Spit it out, Mama. Nothing can top the evil I've seen in you."

A sad smile slid over my lips. *Ah, honey, you just don't know.*

"That's probably true," I said quietly, shot Doretha a warning look and left the room. I'd cleared three stair steps when it happened.

It was so sudden I had no time to react. One moment, Muffin grabbed my shoulder, shrieking, "Don't you *dare* walk away — *keeping secrets* from me!" The next moment the world became a blur of head-over-heels, tumbled, grotesque images as muffled *whumps* pummeled my moving body parts.

From faraway, screams pierced the air.

Then a vast cold surface halted my catapulting somersaults, slithering me into instant, agitating, prostrate stillness. Inside, my head still orbited, albeit slower and slower as moments stretched on. "Sunny?" A man's deep voice tugged at me from a distance. "Sunny!" it grew closer, louder. I cracked my eyelids.

"Daniel?" I rasped, squinting at the head above me that moved like an ocean wave. I flexed a finger on the hand wedged beneath my hip and identified the hardwood floor.

"Hey," he patted my cheek, peering into my eyes. "You okay? Say something, Sunny. For God's sake, *say something!*" He slapped my cheek a little harder.

"Stop!" I croaked, turning my head away. "You don't have to *hit* me."

I slowly rolled over, pushed myself up, and tentatively moved extremities until satisfied nothing was broken. Only one foot shot pains when flexed. Then I noticed all of them watching me, features tight with apprehension, Doretha, Daniel, and Emaline. Muffin was paler than usual but she did not rush to aid or comfort me. It no longer held any shock value.

"Lordy mercy," I shrilled, "what yall looking at? Haven't you ever seen a person fall down steps?" I struggled to stand, grasping Daniel's arm as he pulled me with the other. When I took a hesitant step, I heard an audible release of breath all around me.

"Take more'n that to do me in," I muttered with dark humor, favoring the throbbing right foot. It worked. A nervous chorus of titters revealed a collective relief that I'd not done serious damage to myself. Then I remembered.

I turned loose of Daniel's arm and slowly turned, gazing about till I located Muffin. "Why?" I whispered.

"What?" she scowled, wary.

"Why did you push me?"

Chapter Twenty-One

Muffin's bags disappeared out the front door within minutes, after she used some choice blue terms to inform me that she had *not* pushed me down the stairs.

"It's true, Sunny," Emaline assured me after Muffin's Jaguar roared from the outside curb. "I came to the foot of the stairs when I heard the commotion. I'm pretty sure your foot missed the step — that's why you fell." Set amid pasty white features, green eyes grew bright with tears. "You scared the daylights outta me, girl."

"Sorry," I muttered unrepentantly, wishing I'd not been so implacable in accusing Muffin of deliberately throwing me down the stairs. "But, truth is, she wanted to kick my tail down those stairs. I know that and so do y'all."

I stretched out on the sofa, groaning as soreness encroached upon my bones and joints, knowing I'd not get off scot-free after such a tumble.

Emaline pressed ibuprofen tablets into my palm. "Here," she lifted a glass of water, aiming the flexible straw at my mouth, "take these." I complied, growing aggravated at Daniel and Doretha sitting across the room, watching me like I was some daggum bug under a microscope.

"I'm *okay, y'all*," I snapped. "Stop that."

"Sunny, you shoulda let me tell Muffin about —"

"I meant what I said, Doretha. I'll die before letting her know what her daddy did." I peered at her for long moments, daring her to defy me, blinking to obliterate the wavy movement that had evened out to an occasional ripple. She dropped her gaze to her clasped hands in her lap. I rolled my head to stare at the ceiling, feeling mean and obstinate but I had no choice.

I would not sacrifice my daughter. Not ever again.

~~~~~

"Sunny," Lee Roy peered unbelieving at me, "I can't believe you'd put cuss words in your column."

I burst into laughter. That week's column was entitled, *I Hate that Dam Hole!*

Lee Roy perched on the edge of his easy chair, which I'd moved into the den since Walter's death. He clutched the Middle Tyger River Times, watching me warily as my laughter wound down. "It ain't like you, Sunny," he waved a hand at the paper's column, shaking his grizzled head woefully. "What're folks a'gonna say?"

I sniffed back more tears of mirth and peered warmly at him. "Lee Roy, what I'm talking about there is that big ol' hole in the river dam that the foreign fellow knocked in it, the one who bought up all the land around the river area."

Lee Roy thought on that for long moments, till realization dawned, lighting his blue eyes. "Awww, so that's what you mean. That dam hole…" He grinned suddenly, all gaps and stubs. "Tha's purdy good, Sunny."

I fell solemn, throwing Lee Roy off pretty much. His grin dissolved. "You still sore 'bout it?" he asked guardedly.

"Yeh," I sighed, "I am, Lee Roy. I probably always will be."

Only days before Walter's death, unsuspecting, I drove through the village, down the hill, and started across the newer river bridge, one erected in 1980. I first spotted the machines on her bank and the rocky shoals below.

Then I saw it.

In the very center of the ancient rock dam gaped a huge *ugly* hole. I pulled over and climbed from my car, stunned. *It can't be!* It had to be a nightmare. I squeezed my eyes shut. Surely I'd wake up and discover it the same as always.

I drew in a deep shuddering breath, held it, and released it, feeling oxygen shoot out my fingers and toes. I opened my eyes and looked again.

It was still there. Ohgod*ohgodohgod....*

This one last landmark, *our landmark*, gouged and smashed like an old castaway skid row fence. Pain slammed my chest, choked me, misted my eyes.

How majestic she'd stood, our dam, strong and invincible. Or so I'd thought.

One by one our landmarks had toppled. The hotel gave way to parking. Bad enough. But when, in 1972, the Community Center, that hub of village life for longer than any of us could remember, crumbled into a brooding heap of brick, concrete, and three-inch beams, it took with it a little bit of everyone who'd ever had his hair cut at the downstairs barber shop, or cheered Hopalong Cassidy in the upstairs movie theater or sipped Cokes at Abb's Corner Café in back.

The *Spartanburg Herald Journal* headlines read:

An Era Ends in a Pile of Brick, Wood, and Plaster

I hovered there on the river bridge with this fast-forward video flashing through my head, showing one scene after another... the mill itself succumbing, pain chopping away at me. Later, the elementary school that housed four generations of my family, shut down. At each transgression, my heart screamed *Nononono! Please don't take away my roots.*

Then recent headlines in my own weekly newspaper blasted:

THE WALLS CAME DOWN
Tucapau Mill Fades Into History

My spirit strained against the truth of it. At the same time, the same spirit read the accompanying story, glorying in the indomitability of ancient village folks, who remembered working at the mill in the forties for fifty-cents an hour 'to learn' and were later raised to seventy-five-cents an hour. They recalled paying one dollar a month for rent and, later, buying their house for $500.

Ola Trumane recalled being so short at fourteen she had to stand on a box to work, making $7 to $8 a week. "The dust was so thick," she said, "you couldn't see twenty-feet in front of you."

Years later, they'd cleared the dust and added air-conditioning. Each one interviewed felt gratitude to have worked inside her walls. And I thought how those wrinkled and stooped mill hill villagers now perched on death's cusp and would soon be gone. I swallowed a painful lump and read the history account.

In 1893 a group of Spartanburg businessmen set sail on the Middle Tyger River to cast their fishing lines. When they rounded the river's bend and saw beautiful Penney

Shoals, the idea of a textile mill on her banks was born. A village consisting of workers' houses soon sprouted from the red clay hills, anchored later by a hotel, school, stores, churches, and shops.

"Tucapau" (pronounced *Tuck'-uh-pa*) was an Indian name for "strong cloth" and fit the mill and community like suede gloves. Predictably, some villagers slaughtered the beautiful name with deliberate mispronunciations and mill hill denigration, such as *Turkey-Paw* and *Turkey Scratch*. To some, the humorous misnomers simply hid an obstinate proclivity against 'citified' articulation. It provided others a venue of total disrespect for convention. 1936, Spartan Mills assumed the operation and later changed the name to "Startex." Some folks, including me, till this day use *Tucapau* interchangeably with *Startex*.

All us mill hill folk had thought, at one time, that the mill would be here till the end of time. If Mr. Montgomery, Sr. had lived, it might have been. That ninety-percent of the disassembled mill structure would be reused did not cheer me up. Nor the fact that decking would be shipped to Mississippi, the heart pine flooring to Louisiana and the beams to England.

Even the bricks were cleaned and shipped overseas. Nothing wasted.

Whoop de doo. That was supposed to make me feel better.

In my next week's *Things Old and New* column, which I did on my laptop, tilted back in the lounger, injured foot elevated, I wrote:

> When, I now wonder, did I lay claim on everything VILLAGE as OURS? As MINE? Lord knows everything on earth is temporal. Yet, I DID lay claim and innocently embraced

this little mill hill as my heritage. And felt that despite minor cosmetic adjustments to her visage, she would weather gracefully along with me, her substance prevailing on and on. She was my legacy, to pass on to descendants for generations to come. Then, overnight, an outsider swooped in, bought up some river-bordered land, and felt compelled to demolish the river dam, stopping mid-way through, leaving a big hole. I spent two days on the phone with DHEC and the Army Corps of Engineers and discovered I cannot do diddly about it. The new owner is within his legal rights even if he did leave it looking like a Stephen King nightmare. Oh, I figure he had his reasons and had it not been him, it would have been someone else. Wouldn't it? I don't know. All I know is that after all the other familiar, dear landmarks falling, that dam hole was the final straw. I gaze at the jagged raw edges that reveal a muddy riverbed, and grieve. For what was... what will never again be.

"Sunny? You okay?"

I blinked at Lee Roy, whose slanted blue gaze said clearly he worried for my sanity. After the fall on the stairs that'd left me bruised and fractured, I'd been as sore and addled as a morning-after, beaten boxer.

By that nightfall, my right foot had throbbed so badly I couldn't set my weight on it. Overnight, it bulged to twice its size. I called Doretha.

"Don't you move, now, y'hear?" she said. "I'll be right there. Is the door unlocked?"

"No," I groaned, back pressed to the bed headboard. "Listen, you get here and I'll get the door unlocked."

By the time I crawled to the door and unlatched it, sweat drenched my gown and I was near to passing out. That's how Doretha and Daniel found me, curled into a fetal ball, moaning and nearly incoherent with pain. They threw on my housecoat and Daniel carried me as smooth as a gliding jet to the car and deposited me carefully on the backseat. There, Doretha slid downy soft pillows under my head and, from the front passenger seat, crooned to me as we rode to the hospital emergency room.

And I thought *this is getting to be a habit, them rescuing me like this.*

X-rays soon told the story: my foot was fractured. I would have to be off my feet for several weeks "Don't you worry, Sunny," Daniel said that night after he gently laid me in my bed. "I'm not leaving you till you're able to walk again."

"But you can't stay here!" I peered owl-eyed at him. "What would folks say?"

"I don't care crap what folks say, Sunny," Daniel said softly.

"I'm not leaving you." The painkillers given on the way home were taking their toll by now and I felt their buzz attack drive back the agony.

"Sunny?" Lee Roy, now on his feet, leaned forward from the waist, peering intently into my face. "You okay?"

I blinked, scattering again the deluge of memories. 'You mean aside from being widowed?"

He nodded uncertainly.

Are you okay? Lee Roy had asked. Well let's see, I thought: My oldest daughter is permanently estranged from me. My younger daughter lives nearly on another planet, with her own separate life that draws her farther and farther away. I sit on a black secret that could blow up several lives. Daniel's camping out here, giving neighbors lip-smacking fodder for gossip. I'm like a bad-luck voodoo charm to everybody around me. *Ichabod* may as well be emblazoned across my forehead because it seems God, along with everything and everybody meaningful has departed from me.

Was I okay? I managed a crooked smile, extinguishing my run-on thoughts of abandonment, yesteryear, and such.

"Yeh, Lee Roy," I lied, " I'm okay."

~~~~~

Daniel's ministrations to me were agony. The agony had less to do with bone-fracture than his touch. The more my flesh quickened, the more I shrank from him. Sometimes his very closeness set my flesh to sizzling. That was when I totally shut down and ignored him.

Daniel watched me, his expression unreadable. But sometimes when he thought I wasn't looking, I'd catch a flash of utter sadness before his shutters fell in place. One night, he said, "Let's go sit on the steps and look at the stars."

Surprised, I groped for a good reason not to. He wasn't fooled for a second. "C'mon, Sunny. You've been holed up in these four walls for days on end. A little fresh air'll do you good."

He supported me with his arm around my waist, shoulder beneath armpit, hoisting my weight till I felt light and buoyant as I hobbled alongside him, my good foot barely brushing the floor. He leaned to lower me down onto the back door stoop and, in a blink, his grasp slipped and I went off-balance. My weight knocked him backward onto the porch. We tumbled in a heap, landing with me wedged between his sprawled legs, back joined to his torso. My touchy foot bumping the floor had me groaning. He rested beneath me, on elbows, tense for long moments.

"You okay?" he muttered, pushing upward till he fully supported me.

"Yeh," I said, then burst into hysterical laughter at the picture we made. The next second, I felt him shaking too, laughter spilling from him. I peered back over my shoulder into his face, gurgling like a silly girl.

Big mistake. His arms, strong and warm, slid around me and those eyes, those marvelous eyes glowed like silver in the moonlight, searching mine. One hand lifted to capture and tilt my chin. Before I could react, his lips swooped to find mine. The first touch nipped, the next delved into a mind-boggling exploration that dissolved my joints and set me aflame. That fast.

I tried to pull away. "I — can't breathe," I gasped.

"Me neither," he groaned, dipping again for my mouth, finding it, and kissing me thoroughly, till my head swam and my blood pounded in my ears. I reached and strained for him with all my might. Those beautiful fingers of his began a soft massage of my ribcage and next thing I knew, we lay prone, face to face, fractured foot be hanged. What was a little pain in the face of all this? I'd drifted so far from shore I was hardly aware of where we were. The pleasure of it was too much to bear…I wasn't ready for its impact.

"Wait," I finally managed to gasp between desperate kisses, pushing against Daniel's broad chest. "Please, Daniel, *stop.*" A note of desperation in my plea caught his attention.

He raised up to look at me, elbows planted on either side of my shoulders. "Okay. If that's what you want." His voice, deep and resonant, moved over my senses like skilled fingers over harp strings. I closed my eyes and willed the feelings away. "Is that what you want, Sunny?" he said softly. "Truly want?"

Oh God, what was happening inside me? All this sensation. Like a tidal wave it slapped and tossed me about, then deluged me. I was floating in *feeling*. I gulped back terror. I trembled from sheer sensuality.

That's all it is. Lust. I pushed with all my might, barely moving Daniel's weight. "Okay, Sunny," he said gently. "For now."

I blinked and struggled to rein in my pounding heart. "What happened to us being friends, Daniel?" The anxiety in my voice was pathetic. I couldn't help it. Here I am ready to go on out and meet my Maker any day now. Least that's how I'd been feeling for years now, like I was glued to a rocking chair with my eye on Heaven, waiting for the sky to split and receive me. Actually anticipating death.

These sensations I now felt had nothing to do with dying.

"You said we could be friends." A tiny note of petulance crept into my voice.

He gave me a boyish, lopsided smile. "I don't do friend too good with you, Sunny. Never could."

I pushed against him and this time, he complied and loosened his hold. He brushed a strand of errant hair from my face and his fingers lingered on my cheek.

"You're not helping one bit," I snapped, irritated out of my skull.

His smile spread then. "Naw. I guess not."

"Look, Daniel," I scooted from beneath him as he lifted his weight. "Let's just go inside and pretend this didn't happen, okay?"

He stood, reached down to hoist me up, wedge his strong shoulder under my arm, and brace me with his other arm around my waist. "Okay?" I persisted, desperation shrilling my voice.

"Sure, Sunny," he drawled unflappably. "Whatever you say."

Was it my imagination or did his fingers linger more on sensitive hot spots as he helped me into bed? But when I gazed up at him, his angular face was brisk and guileless.

"'G'night," I said as he reached to turn off my bedside lamp.

Next thing I knew, his hands captured my face and his lips claimed mine in a searing kiss that left me reeling when he finally let go. "'Night, Sunny. Sleep tight."

Dear God, where had those sensual urges come from? Until tonight, I'd been convinced they were dead.

I didn't sleep a wink that night.

~~~~~

The next day, Doretha appeared with crutches and informed me that she would take over seeing about me through the day. "I'll even sleep over here if you need me to," she said.

Stunned over Daniel's abdication, I muttered, "No, that's okay. I'll be fine by myself at night. I'll be able to maneuver with the crutches." For some reason, I was royally ticked. Lack of sleep, I decided.

She looked uncertain. "Well, if you change your mind, just give me a call."

"I will. And Doretha," she turned to look at me, her hand on the front door knob, "Thanks."

Her eyes grew bright for a long moment. "It's me oughtta be thanking you. You call me, now, y'hear?"

"I will."

After she left, I sat there, staring at the television screen, but today I didn't see or hear Regis and Kelly. Why all the *disappointment?* I'd told Daniel last night that I didn't want more than friendship, hadn't I? Had, in fact, pushed him away. Then why all this inner turmoil? *Just listen to me!* I shouldn't be too surprised at Daniel's flip-flop. After all, he'd vanished at another time, long ago. Just when I needed him most. A flash of last night's kisses triggered a warm abdominal tingling.

I crossed my arms in disgust. At myself for needing. At Daniel for bolting.

Why this time? Why, Daniel? A part of me felt cast-off. Another part relieved. Out of sight, out of mind. Partly, anyway. One thing was for sure; I couldn't afford another roller coaster ride.

Not in this lifetime.

~~~~~

In coming weeks, Doretha and Emaline alternated in daily care taking. I protested that I didn't need so much looking after.

"But we *want to* be here for you, Sunny," Emaline insisted. And I have to admit it *did* get me through some tough times. Not the physical. The emotions. Yeh, they kept poking up their ugly heads, in spite of my resolve not to *feel* them. There were times I'd have *died* for a glimpse of Daniel. But it seemed he'd decided to grant me my wish.

Alone. Again.

Lee Roy still visited but not as spontaneously as before. Reminded him too much that Walter was no longer there, I suppose. I continued taking refuge in my weekly column. Another thing happened; I began to think again. Yeh, that's what I said. *Think.*

One day, Emaline asked me point-blank, "Do you ever pray now, Sunny?" She turned from dusting my coffee table to wait for my answer, drawing my brows into agitation. My frown didn't put her off for a New York minute. "You're pathetic." Her dainty hand swept the air then pointed to me. "Just look at you."

I puffed up. "That's not fair. My foot's been —"

"I'm not talking about broken bones. I'm referring to you, Sunny. The total *you.*" Her eyes misted as she sank down onto the sofa, feather duster clutched in hand, facing my recliner, now raised to elevate my foot.

I peered at her through bleary, jaded eyes, dreading what she would say. I knew, on some level, that I had this coming. As Nana always said, "Everybody's got a reckoning day a'comin'." This was mine.

I wasn't ready. I closed my eyes, feigning tiredness.

"Please open your eyes, Sunny," Emaline said in a voice she rarely used, one used for petulant children. "What I have to say needs all your attention."

I opened them. The sweet face of my best friend radiated such love that something in my heart stirred, sluggish but persistent. My antennae raised and my head lifted to full attention.

"Sunny, you're a walking dead person," she said.

The impact of those words took my breath for a moment, then I chortled, "Look again, Emaline. I'm not *walking.*"

A twinkle lit her eyes but she remained resolute. "That aside. You've not been truly alive for years. Personally, I'm tired of you being so beaten down."

I scowled, defensive. "I'm not so beaten down."

"You are so, too," she insisted. I took a deep, angry breath and settled back because I knew she wouldn't hush till she'd said her piece.

"Oh Sunny," her voice broke. "I can remember when you called me the solid anchor in our relationship. Well, you were the *life and wind* of us. You were the one with real heart. How I admired the way you always got back up after getting knocked down."

I eyed her warily. "Where is this going?"

On a sigh, she exhaled heavily, like I'd punctured her with a saber. "I'm *not* patronizing you, Sunny. I respect you too much to do that." We sat in silence for long moments, allowing the assertions to sink in and process. The room was so quiet I could hear the birds singing outside.

She studied her hands and looked so sad my heart felt squeezed. When she looked up, her eyes were bright, and her mouth was working as she fought back tears. And I thought in that moment, *how much she loves me.*

Then a strange thing happened. My nose stung and my throat hurt and my eyes filled with tears. I'd not felt that in so long that it astonished me. Another emotion crept in. "I'm sorry, Emaline," I said. "That was mean and unnecessary." I snuffled and reached for a Kleenex on my little table. "I mean," I chortled hoarsely, "I don't see that many friends beating a path to my door." The tears pooled again, aggravating me. "Thanks."

She arose and came over to give me a big hug. "I'll go now."

"No," I gestured for her to sit back down. "Finish what you started. Apparently I need it. No, don't look like that. I'm serious. I *know* I need your input."

Emaline settled again, reclaimed her wit and dignity, then continued. "Sunny, it's really hard to tag what's happened to you. I've pondered a lot about what to say and I must confess the answer isn't a simple one. I don't dare be arbitrary in any counsel because I've not been exactly where you are. But I do know one thing: As a result of all that's happened to you, going all the way back to your Mama leaving, Sunny, you've lost heart."

"No joke," I muttered darkly.

She smiled. "Remember that song we used to sing, *You've Gotta Have Heart?*" I nodded. "Well, you always did. Until that awful thing happened to you." She finished on a whisper, as though saying it aloud would cause me to start foaming at the mouth.

"When I was raped," I said flatly. Then reminded myself to not toss her kindness back in her face. "Everything changed then, Emaline. Daniel left me and —"

This time when the tears came they gushed and sobs tore from my chest, shaking me all the way to my toes. Emaline dashed across the room and gathered me into her arms, weeping with me for all that was lost in my lifetime. Once I peered up at her through the blur, "I — I still miss Renie, Emaline. She was sooo like a mama to me and —"

A new torrent broke loose and we wept for not only mine, but her loss as well.

"Do you realize," I rasped later, as our tears ebbed, "that this is the first time I've cried in years? I haven't *wanted* to feel, Emaline! It h-*hurts too bad.*" Fresh tears came and I realized I didn't mind.

Later when Emaline was leaving, she took my hand and smiled. "Love isn't really love until you risk being hurt... or something like that." She hugged me bye. "This is the first step to recovery. It won't happen overnight, Sunny. But you'll find your way." She gave me a big thumbs-up. "You've still got it in you."

After she left, I sat for a long, long time in that chair, contemplating all we'd talked about. Lifetime's memories return to folks in different ways. Some folks remember when something nudges them, a picture or such. Others hear a song or see a movie or spot someone whose face reminds them of someone they once knew or loved. Or hated.

My memories come back wrapped in flavors. I smiled, thinking about the lemon-drop aura of Daniel's and my earliest sweetheart days. Where had all of life's sweetness and joy gone? Could I get it back? I picked up the Bible Emaline had unobtrusively placed on the little table earlier in the day.

It fell open and a passage from Psalms 42:1-2 leaped off the page at me.

> *As the deer pants for streams of water,*
> *So my soul pants for you, O God.*
> *My soul thirsts for God, for the Living God.*
> *When can I go and meet with God?*

Something wonderful and wild thrashed about in me. I recognized it from those sweetheart days, when I would dress up and wait for Daniel to arrive. The same anticipation now *ssszzzzzzed* in me. *When can I go and meet with my Creator?*

Something was happening to me. Something I'd never before experienced. A thought struck me and I felt as excited as a little girl doing cartwheels. A *trysting place*. I needed a place to tryst with my Love.

I could hardly wait!

~~~~~

"You want me to move that ol' chair o'mine back in here?" Lee Roy stood aside, admiring his handiwork. I noted that soft green paint still faintly outlined his fingernails when he picked a carpet string from new wooden blinds. He looked content and pleased.

"No," I said, hobbling with a cane across the floor. My foot was better but I still favored it and didn't yet venture outside. Emaline and Francine did my grocery shopping and Doretha stood by to do any other bidding. "The desk and chair look good in that corner, don't they?"

"Looks downright purdy," he said reverently. I'd told him the room was my new office. Not a lie exactly because I did do my weekly column in there. I just couldn't share its true purpose.

It was my own delicious secret.

~~~~~

My days began at 5 a.m. Some mornings, I arose even earlier, abuzz with expectancy. From a collection of CDs, a Christmas gift from Emaline, flowed rich joyful music.

Age ceased to be. I could have been an adolescent or a child or a young woman. I was in love! I forgot all about my tender injured foot. Buoyancy claimed me and I took up my tabret, a beautiful round, tambourine-shaped instrument with long tinseled strands, another of Emaline's gifts, and began to dance as I 'd never done before.

And I *felt* His delight in me. After the first time, I discovered that my foot didn't even twinge.

How I coveted and protected that time in my Tryst Room. Phone off hook, I'd retreat there for hours at a time, communing with and dancing for Him. Sometimes I lounged on the carpeted floor, simply being and listening.

No matter the weather, my mood, feeling bad, whatever, He was there.

For the first time ever, someone loved me unconditionally and would never leave me. It was a learning time. I celebrated each dawn, so glad to be alive and free and happy and *so in love!*

That wonderful presence touched the chords built within my breast, showing me that I am an instrument of music, dormant until touched… wafting sound and song from deep within, up, up, up till it splashes over like living waters over my feet and sets them to dancing.

Other mornings prose passages flowed through my fingers onto the computer screen: *Fresh from love of dance, Spirit free on the rise, How can this day mean more? As if sixteen I waltz in my dream for encounter with a voice like silk husk, calm as rain. Eyes turquoise. Handsome and quick, cool as can be. Stands tall and at ease. My name, Sunny, rolls unusually soft into close space…Deep is this man, calming his ways…Italian dark and Germanic pale sit like new Godiva sweet offerings…Loathe to break eye contact, touch of hands, smiles and sharings yet…. Childhood prayer surfaces mind: God is great, God is good, and I thank Him for this day. Child Sunny.*

Yes, the erotic me had, through Daniel, sprang to life once more.

And I was free to enjoy that part of me! It no longer shamed me.

I filled endless pages with things I learned in that room. One thing was how beautifully broad is the Maker's wonderful, terrible, fathomless, vast love for mankind.

How I learned so much so quickly is still a mystery. I learned that forgiveness is the most marvelous gift we can give anyone. So is unconditional love. So are our time and energies. And mercy and compassion....

There, I died to bitterness. How could I not? Because I know that each experience of my life took me on an odyssey that brought me right here to where I stand, whole.

Complete. My life's purpose is now crystal-clear. It's to love unconditionally. All else of value springs from it.

One morning, I forgot to lock my front door after I went outside to watch the sunrise. Back inside, in the midst of a rousing dance, a voice startled me. "Sunny, what you doing?"

From the doorway, Francine gaped at me, a look on her face I'd never seen before. A mixture of shock and awe. I began to laugh. It bubbled and spilled over and I ran to her and threw my arms around her.

"I'm doing battle," I informed her, twirling my golden tinseled Lion-of-Judah tabret around me. "In old Israel, the dancers and musicians led armies into battle, disarming the enemies."

Hands on hips, Francine declared baldly, "That's the purdiest thing I ever saw. I wanna do it."

And so, Francine joined me, her dancing vigorous and uninhibited while mine was graceful and joyful. I found that I didn't consider her an intrusion. There was room for both of us and plenty of love to go around.

She started going to church with me, one in an adjoining village that was a mite unorthodox and invited dancing in their worship. Emaline was okay with me going

422 *Emily Sue Harvey*

elsewhere as long as I popped in at the Methodist Church services often.

I ordered Francine a tabret and she was ecstatic.

~~~~~

Francine and I were scheduled to dance in an upcoming musical drama, *The Beauty of His Holiness*. I had a solo dance.

Rehearsals took place each Sunday morning before the eleven o'clock service.

"Sunny," Emaline asked me one day "If you could write an ending to the story of your relationship with your Mama, how would you write it?"

With no forethought, I said, "I'd find her." I felt tears spring forth. "I'd love her," I sobbed. "A-and I'd apologize for being so ashamed of her." My response surprised even me. And I realized how much I meant it.

~~~~~

I suppose it was a given that Emaline would eventually happen up on Francine and me in the Tryst Room. She did one sunny day when we were kicking up our heels and whooping with joy. Emaline dashed home and came back with her own tabret. If anybody'd heard us, they'd have sicced the law on us.

As it was, it was a prelude to a more complex, dark interim of my healing.

~~~~~

The novelty of the Tryst Room soon wound down for Francine. I figured she'd learned what she needed, was all. Then Emaline got busy with Bible school and other church functions. I don't know whether their gradual exodus contributed to what happened next or not. I doubt it. But one morning, I got up and the bottom fell out.

First, Lee Roy called early with the latest gossip before I laid the phone off the hook. "They done gone and sold that land up 'air where the Scout hut is," he divulged.

I closed my eyes. Pain, like a sword, slashed through me. *My beautiful oasis.*

"Who bought it?" I asked, my heart tripping into an erratic cadence. Outsiders had been buying up village properties. I shuddered to think what would spring forth from the changes.

"Dunno," he drawled. " I know'd you always liked that land, though."

"Yeh," I murmured, my heart breaking. "I did. *Do.*"

In the Tryst Room, I began to weep. And weep. And sob. A lifetime of losses paraded before me, reminding me of the times I'd not been able to grieve...Mama and Daddy's abandonment...the rape...the terrible shame...Daniel's desertion...Nana's death...Sheila's death...Walter's deception...Doretha's betrayal...Daniel's last rejection... my 'promised land' *sold.* I grieved for each in turn. For several days, I remained in the room, alone yet keenly aware of the astonishing presence.

The miracle was that I didn't reach for the denial button. Every time I started to, that presence said, "no." Just that. *No.* So I didn't. That same voice said, " Pain is love's companion. You must be willing to feel pain. Only then will you love completely and only then will you truly appreciate pleasure when you experience it."

Hey! It made sense. So I embraced it.

~~~~~

One blot hindered my total healing. *Muffin.* And it was the most agonizing pain of all. I wept for days on end, till my eyes felt permanently puffy and my chest grew sore from sobbing heaves. In the end, I discovered that the greatest lesson of all is trust.

"Emaline," I said one night as we shared coffee in my den, "in a situation such as mine and Muffin's, I simply have to trust that it will work out in the end."

Emaline looked troubled for a moment, then, "It's not right that she holds you accountable for your less-than-perfect marriage. After all, Walter tricked — Oh, well," she blinked away the darkness, sighed heavily, and continued. "All that's water under the bridge. Except — she needs to know you for who you really are. She's missing out on so much not letting herself love you like she should. She also needs the benefit of your love and wisdom."

I tucked my leg under me. "Y'know, if the Maker wants her to have a change of heart, He'll see to it. That much I know. In the meantime, I'm just gonna sit back and watch." I smiled, nearly purring, anticipation rising up in me again for the first time in days. "It's so exciting, Emaline. Through all these recent dark days of grief, I still felt this comforting feeling. I'm whole again." I shook my head in wonder as my lips slid into a wide smile, one I seemed to be wearing perpetually of late.

Not for the first time, I wished Mama could see her Sunny alive and full of happiness again. She always said she'd named me Sunny because of my big ol' smile, one from birth. Said my first smile appeared at three weeks, one that evolved into bubbling laughter that brought tears to her eyes. "I knew then you'd be my li'l ol' blessing in life," she'd said more than once.

Suddenly, Emaline giggled. A full, rolling belly laugh. From the old days. "I declare, Sunny. I do believe it's catching, what you've got. I feel like jumping up from here and doing a jig."

I leaped up and dashed to the CD player. "Just what I was waiting to hear!"

Chapter Twenty-Two

Downstairs in the little church, the cast of *The Beauty of His Holiness* milled quietly, reverently, adjusting costumes and saying little. I checked the sash of my dance costume, an ankle-length, modest white gown with a full, flowing skirt and simple ruffled neck and sleeves. When it flared, long white pantaloons assured modesty at all times. It was one of those simple designs that's more attractive worn than on the rack.

My platinum hair, short and lightly waved about my face, needed no confinement. Softly applied makeup brought out the color in my face. I held my tabret, meditating.

Emaline had promised she and John would be there for the performance. What a lifeline she'd been in recent days. As well as Francine, who paced nervously nearby and I knew she ached for a cigarette. She was trying to quit but stressful times, such as this performance, brought out her craving.

Martin had recently begun to attend church with her and was in the audience upstairs. I smiled, remembering her saying he was the only one whose presence tonight rattled her.

"Just focus on joy, Francine, like we do in the Tryst Room," I'd told her.

Suddenly, it was time. I climbed the stairs and stood at the back of the darkened auditorium, waiting for the scene to end and mine to begin. I didn't look at the people; I looked upward and began to commune. I moved to the platform, mounted it and stood barefoot center stage, in the spotlight.

When the music began, I felt the wonderful presence wrap and lift me to another plane, where my bare feet took wing and I spun and twirled and leaped, tabret sparkling and shimmering, and the little girl in me preened for a Father who wouldn't leave her. Near the song's end, I passed my tabret to a younger woman dancer who entered the scene, a symbolic gesture of passing our love and mantle on to those coming behind us on this road called life.

I exited the platform as she danced. I moved to the back of the auditorium and there, turned to watch the rest of the performance. My gaze swept the audience.

Libby and Kara sat on the front row, wiping their eyes. They'd left Scott behind in Summerville, as usual, to see to business. Next to them sat Emaline and John. And Martin. Then there were Gracie and Jared and their dates.

And Sheila's daughters. I smiled, feeling warmed and very loved. Further over sat Aunt Tina, Doretha, Alvin, Tammy and — I leaned to see who the man was.

My heart nearly leaped from my chest. *Daniel.*

Just then, the scene ended. Francine's spot came next. She was one of six female dancers. *Daniel, my God.* Once she was on stage, she harnessed her nervous energy and danced like she had it for breakfast every day of the week. I choked up, watching her, thinking how she'd changed so much in recent months. Thinking how none are beyond rescue.

In the grand finale, the call to all nations, I took my place with the others, amongst flags from many countries and colorful costumes denoting all races and nationalities. I glimpsed Daniel.

He watched me intently, features unreadable. I turned my face away, concentrating on the sign language we used along with the song's lyrics. To the music, we filed from the platform, down the aisles, and out the exit to the downstairs.

"How'd I do?" Francine's icy fingers gripped my hands.

"You did wonderful." We hugged hugely. " I know Martin is proud of you."

The rumble of feet above our heads announced the drama ended. Presently, the fellowship room, in which we stood, began to fill. Folks meandered to and through the refreshment line and filled their plates with catered food.

"Hungry?" asked Francine.

"No." I was too keyed up after sighting Daniel. *Daniel, Daniel, Daniel....*

Since the resurgence of my emotions, I had no more control over them than over a runaway freight train. *That's okay. It's okay. Whatever happens is supposed to happen.*

And then, I looked up and there he was, standing so close I could see the shimmer of his sea-mist eyes and the tiny white flecks of hair at his temples.

"Hey," he said softly.

"Hey," I said, and felt the corners of my lips curving up, wider and wider.

His hand slipped into mine. "C'mon." He tugged and I followed.

Outside, April air washed over me, deliciously fresh and mild. At his car, a new red BMW, I paused for him to open the passenger door. "Where we going?"

"Nuh uh. It's a secret." He pulled a scarf from the dash and said, "Turn around; I'm going to blindfold you."

"What?" But even as I spoke, I eagerly turned my head for him. I'd have laid my head on the guillotine, so complete was my trust in him. He gently but firmly tied the scarf in place, covering my eyes.

I giggled. Yeh. I really did. Letting go of the child in me was becoming second nature. Excitement had me going. The car purred away from the church and I relaxed. His hand found mine, strong fingers laced with mine

"Daniel, when did you get this new car? I mean — it's awfully expensive, isn't it?"

A rich laugh tumbled from him, one that rippled over me and left my skin tingling. "Sunny, this car is just the beginning. I've made some good investments in the past twenty years. Real good. It's time to start enjoying success."

"I-I'm glad for you, Daniel. I always told you success would find you." He was silent for long moments.

"Y'know what I was reminded of tonight, Sunny?" he said, emotion husking his voice. "I saw my Sunny up there dancing, the little girl I met and fell in love with. I've never been so proud of anybody in all my life."

My breath caught on a sob. Tears moistened the scarf and I snuffled, feeling his hand disconnect and then reconnect to press a handkerchief into my palm. "I'm sorry for being so weepy, Daniel, but I didn't cry for so long and then I prayed to find my emotions and tears again and —"

"Shh. Anything you do is okay with me, honey. Everything about you is beautiful."

The car slowed then, veering sharply left off the paved road. It rolled several yards, then stopped. Quietness hummed all about, crickets chirruped. Curiosity churned.

"Can I take it off now?" I asked.

He untied the knot and it fell from my eyes.

I blinked and peered at the shimmery sight. "*Oh my God, Daniel!*" The two-story house was lit up like a castle amid the trees and stone walks. For a moment, I didn't know where I was. Then I saw it — on the upper corner, silhouetted against the star-studded, navy velvet sky; the ancient Scout Hut. I put my hands to my cheeks and began to weep. "I can't believe what my eyes see," I rasped between sobs.

I craned my neck and looked again. It wasn't a dream. It was real.

"*You* bought the land! How did —?" I peered at him through a fog of tears.

"I did it these past weeks while you were laid up with your broken foot. I wanted it to be a surprise. I worked every waking hour to get it done. "

"Daniel, why —"

"I promised you," he whispered, lifting my chin with his fingertip. "Remember?"

I nodded slowly. Did I dare hope? "But — for me?"

"Yeh," he drawled in a deep way that was incredibly sexy. "But I had ulterior motives."

"Yeh?" I whispered.

"Yeh. I want to live here, too. Think that'll be okay?"

I burst into laughter. "Better than okay, you silly boy!"

Then he pulled a tiny box from his pocket and flipped it open. Inside sparkled a huge diamond ring…and then he was slipping it on my finger, murmuring, "This is another promise filled."

He leaned in and whispered in my ear, "That makes it official. We've gotta get married as soon as possible. We've lost a lot of time. Besides, we don't want folks talkin', do we?"

Then I was in his arms, lips tangling and meshing and I swear, I couldn't have cared less what folks thought.

~~~~~

The wedding was scheduled at the Methodist Church with John presiding. Libby was my matron of honor. I wanted to invite Muffin to flank my other side, but knowing her feelings for both Daniel and me, I refrained. My other attendants were Kara, Gracie, Francine and Emaline, who also sang our favorite love songs. One was *A Time for Us.*

Daniel's attendants were Lee Roy, who looked quite spiffy in his black tuxedo, brother-in-law Scott, Alvin, and Charlie Brown, a building contractor friend who'd helped fulfill Daniel's long-ago promise to me that I would have an *oasis* house of my own.

Just before I left home earlier, Lee Roy leaned stiffly to whisper in my ear, "I don't look *too* stupid with my hair in a pony-tail, do I?" He looked so distressed I gurgled with laughter, recalling how he'd balked at Daniel harnessing the Bozo bush with a rubber band at the scrawny nape.

"You look as handsome as Antonio Banderas, Lee Roy. You might just start a fad amongst these mill hill men." He blushed a little and moved on, obviously placated.

"I never told you how beautiful you were when you danced that night," Emaline said, adjusting my white veil, the one I'd planned to wear for my scheduled wedding years back. Cousin Wayne's wife had told me to keep it; she didn't plan on ever getting in a wedding gown again. Somehow, I'd kept it packed carefully all these years, along with the dress I'd made. With all the recent morning dancing, I'd thinned down to my girlish, firm size six. The dress fit perfectly.

"You looked like a little girl up there on that platform, dancing your heart out. But today, I must say, Sunny, you outshine even her." She hugged me and I couldn't stop smiling. My mouth just seemed to have a mind of its own and stretched from ear to ear.

A soft knock at the door reminded me that time drew near when my dream would happen. The door opened slowly and she stepped through it, looking uncertain.

"Muffin!" I started toward her, then stopped, beyond uncertain.

"Mama, I'd like to be your — bridesmaid. If you'll have me." Tears brightened her eyes as she stood there, shuffling her feet and squeezing her hands together.

I laughed and went to her and wrapped her in my arms. "Of course you can be my bridesmaid, Muffin. This is where you belong."

She slid her arms around me and squeezed, burying her face in the crook of my neck, weeping. "Oh, Mama, I'm so sorry for all the junk I've put you through. I know what happened to you — know how Daddy tricked you, the whole thing."

I stiffened — then pushed her back till I could see her face. "Who told you?"

She shook her head. "Don' matter, Mama. I know."

I angled her a fierce look. "Doretha?"

Another shake of her blonde head. "I'm not sayin'."

I glared at Emaline, whose face had gone inordinately composed and innocent. She said nothing. "Did you tell 'er?" I demanded, angry.

"Mama!" Muffin took me by the shoulders and forced me to look at her. "Read my lips. I — never — reveal — my — sources. The important thing is, I *know*. I'm still working through a lot of it. But I figured out one thing real fast: you got a rotten deal."

Her lips wobbled but she managed to continue. "And you managed to forgive Daddy." She swiped a cheek with her hand. "And I just hope you'll be able to forgive *me* for all those years of crap." She bit her lips and I saw her hands tremble as she gripped them together.

She snuffled and her voice dropped to a whisper. "I know I don't d-deserve it."

I gathered her in my arms, close. "It's called mercy," I whispered. "And it's free. You're forgiven."

She peered at me, eyes watery and red. "Jus' like that?"

I smiled. "Jus' like that."

Her smile was wobbly. "I'll make it up to you, Mama. I promise."

"You just did."

~~~~~

Seemed Muffin had confided in Libby about the whole situation. Libby, being Libby, had consoled her sister and handled the whole thing with courageous aplomb, and had insisted Muffin join the wedding party.

Me? I was ecstatic. It completed me. *Fini.*

By mutual agreement, we vowed to not discuss the Walter-subject outside our close circle who *knew.*

"The evil Walter was gone, The one who undoubtedly *did* carry on with Sheila. I'm just sorry I can't apologize to her for not believing her," I told Daniel later that evening, as we lounged in our new living room that smelled of sweet pine floors, new lumber and fresh paint.

Candles flickered all over, painting Daniel's features dangerous and dear. My head lay in his lap and his fingers worked slow, gentle magic on my neck, shoulders, and bosom, turning me boneless and lethargic and simmery. "The new Walter was a truly good man. The one I want to remember."

"Me, too," he murmured.

"Daniel," I licked my lips and the way his gaze settled there, I feared I wouldn't have time to say it, "you gave me back my life. You brought my senses into play again. For years, they've been dead. I thought my life was over. Virtually. That the sexual me was finished. You, and only you, resurrected that part of me."

His dangerous look intensified, thrilling me anew. "I think its time we take advantage of that resurrection, don't you," he said hoarsely.

Before you could say scat we were upstairs in bed. Funny thing…we spent long minutes simply looking at each other. When I tried to hide stretch marks spread like spider webs over my abdomen, Daniel pushed my hands aside and kissed them, his lips gentle as butterfly wings. "Everything about you is beautiful, Sunny," he said, the words like a solemn prayer.

"You, too," I whispered as he gathered me to him, flesh to flesh, heart to heart, soul to soul.

"A new beginning." His eyes plundered the depths of mine.

My smile faded. "A late start." I reached up to brush his lips with my fingertip. "Think we'll have enough time to catch up?"

He flashed me an endearing lop-sided grin that took me back thirty years. "I dunno, Sunny. But I'm sure gonna give it all I've got." His lips brushed mine. "How about you?"

I didn't have time to answer before his wonderful mouth claimed mine, but I didn't have to.

Daniel, my Lion-Man *knows*.

Epilogue

You don't know how to appreciate something till you've lost it. That's the way it was with joy. When it returned, I danced a celebration dance each day, honoring life and love and passion. I still do.

I also celebrate these hills upon which I was born and raised. Unto them, I give homage for safekeeping and nurturing and a sense of roots. They will also bury me. But maybe with divine providence, not for a long time.

Daniel can't do enough to make up for all those years we were apart. Neither can I. My faith has regenerated. It's not something I talk about often. But oh, it's there. When I see one of the village houses that time and wear has eroded, in my mind's eye, I see it as it should be, sparkling with a patina of newness, an honor to its past, present, and future. I pray for its complete restoration. Then I tuck the desire into my soul-niche that *believes.*

Without fail, Daniel will pick that sagging, peeling, dilapidated specimen as his next project. I don't have to utter a word. He just *knows.* With his degree in engineering, Daniel makes my dreams come true

Daniel, my Lion-Man, doesn't simply patch it up. Heck *no.* He aggressively guts the structure, leaving only bracing support-beams. He removes the big archaic, crumbling chimneys whose small grated fireplaces served well in decades past. Then he insulates walls and installs central heating and cooling, using extra emptied-spaces for needed closets and storage.

Daniel replaces old with new: wiring, plumbing, windows, doors, walls, ceiling, light fixtures, and roof. He exchanges sagging back porches for decks, and newly floored front verandas sparkle with thick shiny coats of battleship gray or maybe a softer dove gray.

My Daniel doesn't compromise the spirit of the mill hill village. Each of his artful restorations is a refuge, inviting folks to slow down in passing and gaze in wonder. The dwellings remind me of a Thomas Kinkade painting, where light spills from windows and you just know that inside you'll find family, love, warmth and joy.

Family. Has my relationship with Muffin done a dramatic turnaround? In some ways, yes. In others, changes come more gradually. After Walter's death, Daniel took Muffin under his wing and a sweet camaraderie blossomed there. He convinced her to go through drug rehab. Since completing that, Muffin *is* reaching out more to me, listening more.

At our urging, she recently went in for a complete medical checkup, one long overdue for a gal who's lived as hard as Muffin. She was diagnosed with Adult Attention Deficit Disorder. With daily doses of Adderall, she's more focused and her temperament has leveled somewhat. As a result, she's building her real estate business, and plans to move into her own condo very soon. Until then, she resides with us.

A healthy lifestyle is restoring her fabulous beauty. We get in the kitchen together and whip up nutritional, tasty meals. Most days, we enjoy long walks over our lush grounds.

Muffin will never be a Martha Stewart. But she does have spurts of neatness now, a great leap in a good direction. My heart soars when she gives me big hugs for no reason and calls often when she's away, just to say she loves me. Her maternal nature has kicked in even more and it's glorious. Ahhh, what more can I ask for?

Would I do anything differently if I could do it over?

Hard question. I would wait for Daniel, no matter the risk of scandal. But then, I wouldn't have my Libby, would I? So it all worked out for the best.

*Daniel…*Just this week, he stuck his head out the front door of our village-style house as I strolled the grounds inhaling late summer's floral bouquet. "Sunny, there's someone on the phone who wants to speak to you."

Curious at his tone of voice, a touch cryptic, I sprinted into the house (happiness does wonders for older folks) and took the receiver from Daniel. "Hello?"

A long silence ensued, then a quiet, "Sunny? Is that you?"

The woman's voice was rather frail. I frowned, puzzled. "Yes. Who is this?"

Another pause, then unsteadily, "Ruby. Your mama."

"Dear God!" Shock coursed through me. I nearly dropped the phone. Daniel helped me to the sofa to sit. "Where — why?" I finally gasped.

"Sunny, you gotta understand, honey, that I've been too ashamed to call y'all. I've thought about you so much and —" Presently, I heard soft weeping.

"Mama," I said gently, " don't. Please don't cry. I've wanted so many times lately to talk to you. To tell you I love you and to say I'm s-sorry." I, too, sobbed by now.

A loud snuffle sound drifted from the other end. "But, Sunny, why're *you* sorry? It was me —"

"I'm sorry I was so ashamed of you, Mama," I wailed and in a heartbeat, Daniel's arms held me while his hand gently rubbed my shoulder, arm, neck, anywhere he could touch skin.

My mother and I cried quietly for long moments.

"You had every right to be ashamed of me," she said hoarsely. "What I did was unforgivable. That's why I never called to ask you to forgive me. But…after Daniel called me, I began to have a little hope that just maybe, you might be able to. I know I don't deserve it but —"

"Oh Mama. You're forgiven." I laughed with joy. What a *glorious* feeling it is to forgive! "Where — I mean, is your husband still living?"

A terse laugh. "*Shoot,* he's livin' all right. With a woman younger'n our son. We've been divorced over twenty years. I'm alone, now. You just don't know how much I've missed y'all, how many times I reached for the phone, then lost my nerve."

I've even got another brother somewhere. So much to celebrate.

"Mama, we've got lots of catching up to do. When can you come for a visit?" *I want time to tell you that I now understand your passions since Daniel stoked my own back to life. In many ways I'm no different from you. Just in choices.*

My mother — myself.

In her eighties, Mama's had her share of health problems, but amazingly, none life-threatening. I knew a spark of the old adventurous Ruby remained when she agreed that we arrange for her to fly here. A reunion is set for next month, here at our house.

When I rang off, I gazed at Daniel. I licked my lips nervously. "I've got to say this. I want everything between us open and truthful. Remember how I hated Mama's ways and ran all my life in the other direction to get away from all that passion? Then here you come back into my life and wake that very thing up in me. Do you realize how ironic that is?" Gathering tears stung my eyes and nose.

He pulled me close and murmured in my ear. "You taught me to forgive, Sunny. Brought me down off my haughty high-horse, where I finally saw that I could love unconditionally, too."

"How did you know I would forgive her? And how did you find her, for goodness sake? And what about Mona, your own mama?"

"Emaline told me about your change of heart," he said softly. "I hired a private detective to locate her. Right now, he's searching for my mama. " His finger stroked my cheek. "I told you this was only the beginning, Sweetheart. So fasten your seat belt."

"Ah, Daniel, I miss those days when the mill hill was alive and bustling and didn't look so rundown."

He let loose a big ol' laugh and then a rebel yell. "This mill hill is gonna look like new."

"Like us," I whispered. "Kiss me, Daniel. I don't care if every daggum gossip around sees us."

Daniel did just that. Then grabbed my hand and we dashed out into the sunshine.

To the white arbor of the gazebo, to snuggle in a snow-white swing and to smell the yellow roses. And y'know, in that warm spring breeze, I caught the faintest whiff of *lemon-drops.*

Dear Reader,

Having celebrated with me the miraculous triumph of Sunny and Daniel, I hope you will join me for an equally inspiring odyssey in my next novel. Soon to be released *Cocoon* takes readers to the fictional Carolina foothills town of Paradise Springs, population 2,000.

When widowed, well-to-do Seana Howard meets Barth McGrath, a newcomer to their little town, she never dreams she'll fall in love again. Despite his somewhat quirky ways and near penury, she falls for the man. The only problem is that her married children hate the Yankee interloper.   When Barth proposes, her family is not happy. They do not trust the mysterious stranger. Who is he? Where exactly did he come from? What is his past? Barth is not forthcoming.

Against their wishes, Seana elopes with Barth and, despite the family schism, is happier than she's been in years. Then her happiness shatters when a mysterious illness suddenly befalls her, exiling her once brilliant mind to a dark nightmare from which she may never return. The eclipse is startling and complete. Will Barth, with such a short history with Seana, love her enough to endure the trials of caring for someone who has become a psychotic stranger? Can her family get past their suspicions of his dark past and trust his motives and love for their mother? Will Seana ever escape the dark cocoon and reclaim her brilliance and beauty? Her love and freedom? Her very purpose for living? Will life give her a second chance to spread her wings, like the beautiful butterfly?

Cocoon is a life-affirming story of one family's struggle to overcome seemingly insurmountable obstacles, one I hope you will embrace.

Hugs,
Emily Sue Harvey